The Patience of Rivers

ALSO BY JOSEPH FREDA

Suburban Guerrillas

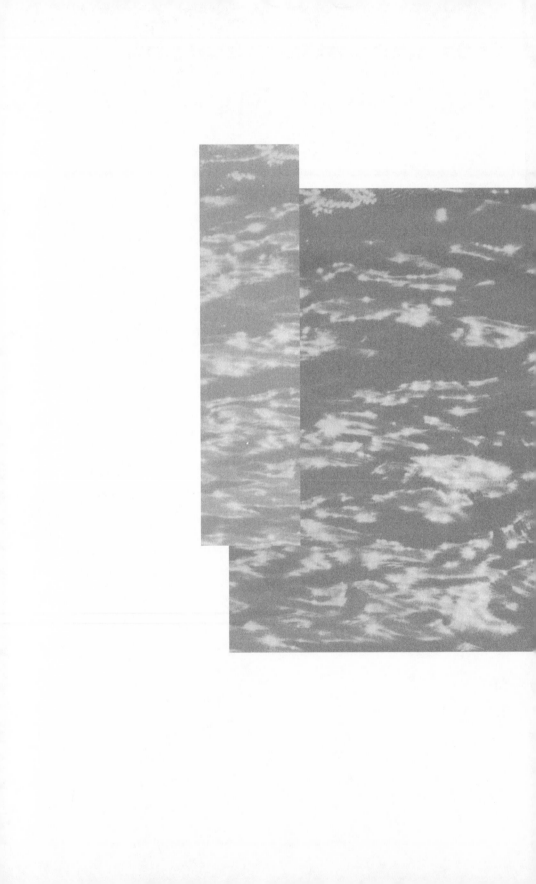

The Patience of Rivers

a novel

JOSEPH FREDA

 W. W. Norton & Company   New York   London

For information about permission to reproduce selections from this book,
write to Permissions, W. W. Norton & Company, Inc., 500 Fifth Avenue,
New York, NY 10110

Manufacturing by The Haddon Craftsmen, Inc.
Book design by Chris Welch
Production manager: Julia Druskin

LIBRARY OF CONGRESS CATALOGING-IN-PUBLICATION DATA

Freda, Joseph, date.
 The patience of rivers / by Joseph Freda.— 1st ed.
     p. cm.
 ISBN 0-393-05176-5
 1. Delaware River Valley (N.Y.-Del. and N.J.)—Fiction. 2. Family-owned business enterprises—Fiction. 3. Camp sites, facilities, etc.—Fiction. 4. Canoes and
canoeing—Fiction. 5. New York (State)—Fiction. 6. Young men—Fiction. I. Title.
 PS3556.R366 P38 2003
 813'.54—dc21

                                                                2002013330

W. W. Norton & Company, Inc., 500 Fifth Avenue, New York, N.Y. 10110
www.wwnorton.com

W. W. Norton & Company Ltd., Castle House, 75/76 Wells Street,
London W1T 3QT

1 2 3 4 5 6 7 8 9 0

For my Parents,
Betty Mae Robbins Freda
and
Matthew Joseph Freda

Contents

Acknowledgments

Thanks to my agent, Gail Hochman, and my wonderful editor, Carol Houck Smith, for their expert guidance in shaping this book.

I want also to acknowledge Sue Wheeler and Lisi Schoenbach for their early help to me on the path to publication. Their efforts on my behalf will always be deeply appreciated.

Finally, I am grateful for the love and sustenance of my wife, Elise, with whom every day is a creative act.

September 1969

THE BUSINESS WAS always there. It grew over their family like a big tree, casting its shadow on everything they did. It was there when Nick Lauria and his sisters needed jobs during the summer of 1969, the summer of Woodstock and the moon landing and too many boys dead in Vietnam. It was there when Nick's mother confronted her husband's business partner and changed their lives forever. And it was there even when it was no longer there, when it had finally slipped from their grasp and landed in the hands of someone outside the family.

Nick bucked another haybale down from the loft, and the radio news wafted up through the thick, dust-filled air: Ho Chi Minh was dead. Understanding came to him the same way the chaff and hayseeds choked his nose and eyes—slowly and inexorably. Ho was dead. Maybe now Vietnam was, too.

A truck rattled outside and his mother's boots thumped the barn floor. Nick opened the haymow door a crack. The fresh air felt good, so he opened the door farther and gazed out upon the Upper Delaware Valley stretching away to the north, the river itself on the right, shimmering between the mountain ranges—New York's Catskills and Pennsylvania's Poconos—drawing a sparkling line through layer after layer of green hills fading to deep aqua. In the middle distance a few horses grazed in the field, cream and dun and bay swatches that shifted as naturally as the grasses in the breeze. His parents' farmhouse shone white in the early-September sun. Directly below him, a battered stock hauler cut a red diagonal across the dusty driveway and intersected with his mother's yellow pickup.

The truck idled, the radio droned about Ho's death, and in the stall below, Stone Dust stamped his hoof and nickered, impatient at the interruption of his currycombing. Nick welcomed the breeze off the river, even with the diesel fume. Below, his mother faced off against two disheveled truckers. Nick swung down from the loft.

The truckers weren't the kind of people who showed up at the farm for trail rides or horseback lessons. The white lettering on their shit-spattered stock hauler said "KILEY'S AUCTION BARN, Bovina Center, New York." The sun glinted off the truck's windshield. A spidery crack ran from the windshield wiper to the rearview mirror.

Nick could tell from his mother's back and the driver's expression that something wasn't going well.

"Ten head, lady," the driver was saying. "That's what my shipping order says."

"I don't care what your shipping order says," Nick's mother said. "You're taking no horses off this farm."

The driver looked at her and chewed his teeth. His long sideburns flexed in and out. Kit stood stiffly, her ruddy ponytail businesslike on her denim shirt. She held her arms tight at her sides, as if to control them. Nick could see that her hands shook.

"You people placed this order," the driver said, "had us drive all the way down here. And now you say you don't want to sell your horses?"

"That order did not come from me, and these are my horses," Kit said. "Not one of them is leaving this farm."

She knew how these men happened to be here. She knew, or suspected she knew, the sequence of events that had led to this scene. Her eyes drilled into the driver, but she saw beyond him and his skinny sidekick, these mere props, to the hand that moved them.

At that moment a burgundy Buick LeSabre swung into the farm's long driveway, bouncing on its shocks. A cloud of red-shale dust rose against the mountainside. Appropriate, Nick thought. A dust-cloud always seemed to follow Ted Miles, and now it billowed down the lane towards them.

Over the dustcloud, way up on the mountain, a patch of orange leaves blazed out of the foliage. An early-turning maple, signifying the season to come.

Ted's Buick pulled in past the stock hauler, and the driver turned at the sound. So did Kit. A look passed over her face, a look of knowledge. Knowledge and acceptance.

Ted's presence gave the driver courage. He nodded at Kit, reached inside the cab of his truck, and came out with a shipping order on auction house letterhead.

"Says so right here, lady," he said. "Ten head to be sold at auction this Saturday night."

"And does it say who initiated the order?" Kit asked.

"Says it's per Ted Miles," the driver said, allowing himself a grin as Ted slipped out of the driver's seat. Ted wore a white shirt, sleeves rolled up, and khakis that cuffed squarely over his tasseled Weejuns.

"Oh, well, in that case . . ." Kit reached into her pickup and rustled in the glove compartment. She had started carrying a handgun the previous summer, after too many encounters with rabid foxes and raccoons had sent her to the hospital for the series of shots. Now, when she was out fixing fences or filling chuckholes, she kept her .38-caliber Smith & Wesson within close reach.

At the sight of the pistol, the driver smirked and glanced at his partner. Ted Miles, however, stopped short by the Buick's bumper.

"Now, Kit . . ." he said, and tried to work up his smile.

Kit regarded him. Of all the things Ted Miles had taken, or tried to take, from her and Francis—all in the guise of being "best for the business"—this was the last, the one thing she wouldn't allow. Her beloved horses—Stone Dust and Roxanne and Big Boy and Apache and all the others, twenty-four head in all, all hand-fed and -combed, tended with care and appreciation and love, as if they were children, and who always performed when asked, who always lined up in the corral and who didn't fight the bit or girth strap, or, if they did, like Frosty and Buckskin, put up only token resistance, a kind of joke on her, and who bore their city-bred, inexperienced riders with tolerance and docility around the well-worn trails of the farm and the surrounding hills, and by doing so kept filling the cashbox inside the first stall; who, like the big black gelding Midnight, took great pleasure in rolling in the pasture after being unsaddled, the day's work done, or who, like the Appaloosa Durango, waded into the river at dusk to drink nose-deep in the clear Delaware and then raise up, muzzle dripping, to gaze upstream with a calm that approached contemplation—now to be hauled away and auctioned off, subjected to who knew what abuse and ignorance and even the knacker's hammer?

"God damn you," Kit said, and Ted began working his face toward his next move.

Kit leveled the .38 at the shipping order and said to the driver, "You hold that good and steady for me, will you, while I sign it?"

The driver's grin froze and he whipped the paper out to arm's length, and Ted repeated in that placating tone, "Now, Kit . . ." and Kit fired with a shaking hand and opened one hole in the paper and another in the door of the stock hauler, putting an extra dot over the *i* in Bovina.

The driver dropped to his knees, and when he realized he hadn't been hit, scrabbled backwards. His partner eased toward the truck. The diesel idled. The radio broke into the Rolling Stones' "Honky Tonk Women."

"Get off my farm," Kit said.

The driver ground the gears finding reverse, and he tried rolling up his window while backing the truck, but the glass was shattered. He found a forward gear and roared out the driveway.

As the haze of red dust and diesel exhaust settled, Kit turned to Ted.

"You tried to sell my horses," she said. "You tried to sell this farm."

The gun shook in her hand, and then Ted did the one thing he shouldn't have done, the one thing he couldn't help doing. He smiled.

June 1969

1

NICK LAURIA TOOLED through town with a sense of already being late. His mother served dinner at six o'clock and expected everybody to be on time, tonight especially. But it was a beautiful evening, the MG's exhaust echoed off the buildings along Railroad Avenue, and low-angled sunrays glinted in the windows: Kut 'n Kurl Beauty Shoppe, Depot Bar & Grill, the Erie station. Pickups clustered in front of the bars. "In-A-Gadda-Da-Vida" thumped out of the open car, and a pair of tourists stopped their strolling and turned at the sound.

Nick felt good. The workday was over. The canoes were stacked for their morning runs. An evening of partying stretched out before him. He felt as content and warm as the setting sun.

In the passenger seat, Charlie Miles tried to read the paper against the breeze. They passed Van Vooren's Funeral Home and Charlie turned up the stereo's volume, as was his habit.

"Hey!" he said over the music. "Listen to this—"

But Nick downshifted, punched the accelerator, and snapped Charlie's neck back. He blasted the MG up the river road. He was about to drink a cold beer with his friends, maybe see Darlene. Then over to the farm for a quick birthday dinner. Party time, man.

"Listen to this, man—"

The fishing access came into view, and Nick cranked the music even higher. This was the town hangout: a big gravel parking lot with a boat ramp to the river, a few picnic tables under the trees, and a pair of outhouses on the far end. New York State Conservation Department signs said RESPECT PRIVATE PROPERTY and gave the limits for smallmouth bass, trout, and pickerel. Nick swung the MG into the fishing access with gravel spraying and Iron Butterfly hitting the drum solo. All the kids turned to look. Off to the left, the town longhairs—the freaks—had taken over the picnic area. They sat on the tables or draped themselves over their VWs and vans. The jocks hung out by the boat ramp, standing beside their Pontiac Tempests and Olds 442s, shoulder-punching each other and striking pumped-up poses. The greasers, to the right near the outhouses, lurked inside their jacked-up SS396 Chevelles and GTOs and Mustangs and passed beers through open windows.

Nick and Charlie headed for the freaks, and their arrival caused a general stirring among the tie-dye and fringe, a mass movement of hair and denim.

"Hail, the river rats!" shouted Ray Vann, toasting them with a bottle of Boone's Farm apple wine. Bear Brown jumped in front of the car and pounded on the hood.

"Hey, you birthday boys," called Cecie Van Vooren. "Over here!"

Nick switched off the ignition. Charlie pulled himself up by the windshield frame, perched on the seatback, and surveyed the crowd. With both hands he remade his ponytail, grabbed his sun-bleached curls, and brought them to order under an elastic band. The action did not seem effeminate to Nick or any of the freaks—as it might to the jocks or the greasers—but rather supremely self-confident, even sexy, since it flexed Charlie's tanned biceps and emphasized that he and Nick had just arrived from a fast, wind-blown ride in a sports car.

"Remember," Nick said, "a quick one. We're supposed to be over at the farm right now."

But the gang pulled them out of the car, stuck beers into their hands, sang "Happy Birthday." Shag Foley gave them brotherhood handshakes and Chris Beagle, a little grease-stained from his job in his father's garage, passed them a joint. Eliot Winklewitz strummed his guitar. Marisse Evans waved a stick of incense. The Van Vooren sisters—Eva, Cecie, and Darlene—proffered a bag of Hershey's Kisses. Nick and Charlie slapped fives and hugged the chicks, knocking back their beers and taking hits off the Boone's Farm bottle as it came around—the same with Eliot's hash pipe—digging the Butterfly's bass notes and the electric organ, which continued to pump out of the MG. Nick could see Charlie casting his eye about, and sure enough, as the general hubbub settled down, Charlie cut Chris Beagle out and took him off to conduct a little business. Charlie opened the fringed bag at his belt, Chris handed over a few bills, and the group was supplied with enough weed to get them through the evening.

Nick hung with the Van Vooren girls, the town heartthrobs. He got a kick out of watching them eat chocolate. They took it so seriously. Eva, the oldest sister, was considered the intellectual because of her poetry and guitar-playing and valedictory in high school, and now, having studied art for a year at Columbia and come back in granny glasses and long skirts with her wild, honey-blond hair grown out into a frizz, she seemed the closest thing Delaware Ford had to a worldly bohemian. Eva held a single Kiss delicately, with her fingers splayed. She studied the Kiss as if gauging the pleasure to come, and then chewed pensively, looking past the crowd with a dreamy, faraway gaze.

Cecie, the middle sister, dug into the bag and smiled coyly at Nick. "So, Nick . . ." she teased. "Want a Kiss?"

Cecie was the sexy sister. Darker hair, red clover in the honey, and still worn in a flip. Blue eye shadow. She was in Nick's class, a cheerleader, and when she took to the field during a football game, every hormone-bulged male eye in the bleachers locked onto her bouncing gold sweater or that satiny green vee beneath her twirling skirt. Cecie dated Terence Skinner, though, who had been captain of the football team and then gone to Syracuse on an ROTC scholarship. Cecie still wore his ring on a chain, and when Terence showed up at the fishing access she'd join him over by the jocks, but it was generally assumed that she'd ditch him when she went off to college in the fall. It was also widely known that despite her alleged devotion to Terence, Cecie had a crush on Charlie Miles. She flirted with him constantly.

"Hey, Charlie," she called, holding a candy to her lips. "Want a Kiss? Nick won't take one from me."

All the girls laughed, and Charlie told Cecie she was "playing with fire," and they rolled their eyes.

"Maybe Nick'll take one from *me.*"

Darlene, a sophomore, was the wild one. Two years earlier she had taken up the whole hippie thing, and now she wore her cornsilk-blond hair straight and to her waist. Sometimes she wove a little braid into it and tied it off with a bright thread or a strip of rawhide. She embedded wildflowers in the braid. She wore India-print halter tops and hiphugger bells that showed off her luscious midriff, and she wasn't shy about lounging around on the picnic tables. Darlene always carried a fringed leather purse for cosmetics and pot. She was quick to pass around a pastel-colored joint or to break out a small marble hash pipe. She didn't go out with any one guy, but lately she'd been showing attention to Nick.

With the Kiss on the palm of her hand, she gave Nick a glittering, covetous look. Jesus, he thought. Could she really like him? One of the high-toned Van Vooren girls going for a down-to-earth Lauria kid? It didn't seem likely, and he felt himself blush.

He brushed her wrist as he took the candy.

"Thanks." He tucked the Kiss into the pocket of his chambray workshirt. "I'll save it for later."

"Not too much later," Darlene said.

Eva leaned across her sisters to tug at Nick's shirt.

"Hey, aren't you late for dinner?" she asked, eyes big behind her granny glasses. "Your mom's been cooking like all afternoon."

Eva worked for Nick's mother in the summer, leading trail rides at the horse farm.

"We're on our way," Nick said. "Just wanted to say hi."

The music dipped and everyone turned to the MG, where Charlie had cut the volume. He held up the newspaper.

"Hey, everybody," he called. "Did you hear about this big concert?"

Concert? What concert? Far out.

"Down in Orange County," Charlie said, and shook open the Middletown *Times Herald-Record.* " 'Wallkill to get rock fête.' "

"Rock feet?" Bear Brown asked.

"A rock festival, man. Listen to this. 'Operators of a three-day rock and jazz festival expect to draw a crowd of twenty thousand in August in the town of Wallkill.' "

"Far out," Eliot Winklewitz said. "In Wallkill?"

"Yeah," Charlie said. "And check this. 'Woodstock Ventures has already signed contracts with Tim Hardin, Flora Nyro—' Right. Flora Nyro. Who do they hire to write these things? Okay, Laura Nyro . . . Richie Havens, Arlo Guthrie, the Incredible String Band . . .'"

"Joan Baez, Janis Joplin, Jefferson Airplane."

"The Airplane? The Airplane in Wallkill?"

"No shit. Jefferson fucking Airplane. Says it right here. They couldn't print it if it wasn't true." Charlie scanned the article. "Creedence, Moody Blues, Iron Butterfly—" He reached into the car and cranked the volume up, then down. By now Eva was reading over his shoulder. "Moody Blues," she said. "Blood, Sweat & Tears. Canned Heat."

"The Band. Crosby, Stills & Nash."

"Far out."

"Far fucking out, man."

It was the first time the kids of Delaware Ford had heard anything about Woodstock. In later years they would remember this moment— the evening sun slanting into the hair and faces of close friends, the good vibes from the beer and wine and dope, the heightened excitement of a big concert—as a turning point in the history of their county. But at that moment, all they envisioned was another good time. Nick heard the name Woodstock as he toked on a joint, and it made him think of a puff of smoke.

"Okay, cool!" Charlie said. "We're all going, right? We pile into my van and Bear's and Eliot's and we check this thing out."

"Yeah!" A general cheer went up, and they swirled among each other with exclamations about their favorite bands—"Canned Heat, man—goin' up the country!" and "I see a *good* moon, risin'!" Charlie

switched tapes, put on Creedence Clearwater, and cranked the stereo.
He and Nick waved at everybody, promised to meet them later at the
bar, and took off with "Susie Q" pumping into the sky. A quick blast
up Route 97 and across the bridge in Callicoon.

"So what did Chris spring for?" Nick asked.

"Nickel bag," Charlie said. He tapped the windshield pillar. "Hey,
it'll pay for our beers later."

2

WHEN THEY PULLED up to the farmhouse the first thing Nick heard
was his mother's voice, wailing like a police siren—". . . can't get here on
time, goddammit!" Oh, man. They shouldn't have stopped at the fishing
access. They should have stacked the canoes and driven straight over.

But Charlie grinned and said, "Happy birthday, man. Sounds like
Kit's on a tear," as Nick's father's voice came to them—"Wouldn't I
have liked to? Wouldn't I like to knock off . . ."—and then his mother:
"Pasta's all clammy, everybody waiting around all night . . ." The rest
was lost in a clatter of cooking pots.

"Wouldn't I like to knock off work at six every night and—"

"Tonight, Francis! Not every night. Not any night—"

Pot smoke and beer brack rose from the back of Nick's throat and
mingled with the river dank and the smells coming through the
screen door: garlic and warm tomatoes and the pungent zing of yeast.
And live cigarette smoke. Not good. His mother smoked when she
was angry or nervous.

"I had business—"

"Business, business! It's all we have now, is the business!"

"Kit—"

"You have the business, I have the business—" Close to the door
now, Nick could see into the kitchen: his father's back, his white-
haired grandparents on the right side of the table trying to distract his

sisters as his mother waved her cigarette: "Grandma and Grandpa have the business. Lisa Marie and Stacey have the business—"

Nick rattled the screen door and stepped into the kitchen.

"—Nick and Charlie have the business." His mother paused to appraise them and to drag on her cigarette. Her eyes smoldered with the anger she held for a world that did not run precisely on her schedule. The family had been celebrating the boys' birthdays together—they were only one day apart—since Nick and Charlie were little kids in cowboy boots and six-guns. Kit had done up her hair. Sweat beaded on her neck among her freckles. She had even put on lipstick.

"You drunk or sober?" she asked, and without waiting for an answer, addressed Nick's father. "The only person who doesn't have anything to do with the business these days is the one taking all the proceeds!"

"Kit, please."

She kissed Nick on the cheek, and he felt her heat, smelled her smoke and perspiration and resentment, which he knew was not directed at him and Charlie, not even, really, at his father. His mother smiled then and batted Charlie's ponytail and hugged him. "Happy birthday, you two deadbeats. Dinner was ready an hour ago."

She let the screen door slam behind her. The room held silent for a moment. Everyone was used to Kit's outbursts, which could break as suddenly as a summer shower and then be over as quickly.

"Happy birthday, you boys," Grandma said. "I'm afraid we had to start without you."

Fifteen-year-old Lisa Marie looked up from her curtain of hair, arched her eyebrows, and tossed her head: *Oh, man—another night with the Bickermores.* Twelve-year-old Stacey smiled, murmured, "Hi, Nick. Hi, Charlie," and went back to twirling her pasta around her fork.

Grandpa set a jug of his Guinea Red on the table. His Roman nose creased his face like a beak and balanced his thick, owl-like glasses.

"Happy eighteenth, boys," he announced. "The State of New York recognizes your legal right to drink and to vote."

"Not necessarily in that order," Nick's father said. "You get those last canoes picked up?"

"Four at Narrowsburg, sixteen at Skinner's Falls," Nick replied. "Two full racks."

"The people get back okay?"

"The Skinner's crowd had their own transportation. Camp Arrowhead. The Narrowsburg crew caught a lift with Shag when he passed through earlier."

"So we're all accounted for?" His father's hand paused on his wineglass. Nick noticed the liver spots and a vein running across the first knuckle.

"Yep. Racks are loaded for the morning. Ten to Hancock, five each to Long Eddy and Hankins. The rest are downriver trips." Nick had the same vein on his right hand, and he assumed that in thirty years he'd have the same spots.

His father wanted a nightly inventory of the canoe fleet, wanted to make sure no one was stranded on the riverbank, wet and anxious as darkness came on. He had to tie up the loose ends of business before the family could get on with the birthday celebration.

From what Nick could tell, the past year had not been the best of times for the campgrounds. Oh, the business was there. Despite a rainy spring, campers came every weekend, and many stayed during the week. They rented every canoe in the fleet on Saturdays and Sundays. His mother did well with the riding stables. But there always seemed to be a shortage of cash. When Nick needed to pick up some pop rivets and flashing to repair a damaged aluminum hull, his father had to approve the expenditure at the hardware store. When a shuttle van needed service at Beagle's Gulf, his father had to call the bank to check the balance. This seemed odd, even though Nick didn't know much about the financial end of the business. There seemed to be too much money coming in for these niggling little expenses to need such scrutiny.

"So?" His father turned to Lisa Marie. "The Gennaros pay their bill yet?"

Lisa Marie pushed a slice of panini around her plate and spoke without looking up. "They always pay when Paulie comes up from the city. They'll pay by the weekend."

"Let me know if they haven't paid by Sunday morning. I'll want to catch Paulie before he heads back down."

"Mrs. Keriotis pays us for her trail rides," Stacey piped up. "And she gave me a dollar tip."

Their father chuckled. "Did she now? Well, Cookie, you earned it." He glanced out the screen door, where Kit's cigarette smoke mingled with the insects coming up from the river. "The riding stable's in good hands, at least."

"Oh, sure it is," Grandma said. "The whole business is. You boys are doing wonderful things with the place. Everyone in town says so."

Nick's father was going gray quickly. When had that happened? The last time Nick had noticed, his father had some gray along his temples, but now, under the fluorescent light, he could see that the old man's hair had thinned to a steely gray all over.

His mother rattled the bugs off the screen and slipped back into the kitchen. She assessed the progress of the meal—everybody wading through the pasta nicely—and then made a plate for herself. Her face was calmer. She had not purged her anger, Nick knew, but at least she was not spitting and shooting off sparks now.

During the past year—Nick's senior year in school—his parents' arguments had flared up at dinner, in their bathroom in the mornings, through the walls of their bedroom at night. Nick hated it. So did his sisters. At the first slam of whatever happened to be in his mother's hand—a frying pan, the bathroom mirror, her hairbrush—or the grate of his father's tightened voice—"Now listen here, Kit . . ."—the need to move, to leave, to *go, just go* would stir within him. As the argument progressed—"Another six thousand dollars, Francis! He's bleeding us dry!"—he would feel the need for speed in his arms and legs, the urge to ram his right foot down on the gas and blast into forward motion, *Drive, man, just drive*, to feel the acceleration pulling at his face and pressing him back in the seat and to synch his arms through the shifter and the wheel and propel him down a stretch of imaginary blacktop until everything else—his sisters at the table, the morning grayness through his window, the canoe-racing trophies glowing on his dresser—was left behind and he was aware only of his parents' words and their powerful impetus to make him leave.

"He's got a point, Kit," his father might say. "Three more rental trailers'll generate fifteen hundred bucks a month. They'll pay for themselves in half a year. After that they're pure profit, and—"

"Pure profit? Pure profit? Show me a dime of all this pure profit we're always hearing about! Show me a nickel that that man—"

"Kit, we've got to spend some money to make money. It's—"

"Right! Right! When is the money going to start coming from *him?*"

"Plenty of it comes from him. He put in the lion's share in the beginning. He goes out and—"

"We put in the farm, Francis—your parents' farm! We put in the lion's share, don't you get that? Some campgrounds he'd have with that scrappy little woods of his!"

And on and on. During the school year, when Nick was still living at home, he would pull his pillow over his head at night, or turn up his radio in the morning. At the dinner table, when the argument flared, he would simply get up from his seat and go, no matter how little he had eaten, just set aside his fork and slide back and head out the kitchen door. He'd hoped his parents would take his point and try to control themselves over dinner, but they never did. Sometimes he'd drive to town and get a burger at the Depot or roast beef at the Wild Turkey, but most of the time he didn't feel like eating anyway, so he'd drive the roads. Or he might pull into the fishing access and smoke a joint and watch the river. Charlie was off at his private school, Felix Gustave was in Vietnam, and Nick hadn't been going out with any girl, so, as the need to move slowed and then stopped, a feeling of isolation, of loneliness, would settle over him like dust in the backwash. He would study the silent water or the wheeling stars or the wind whipping across the river grasses and he'd wonder where in all of this he was supposed to fit.

When he graduated in May, the first thing he did was move out. His grandparents had a little apartment on the backside of their house, and they were happy to have him nearby. He had said he wanted to be close to the campgrounds so he could respond to emergencies, but really he wanted to be away from his parents' arguments and he wanted to come and go without a lot of hassle. He'd be off to college in the fall and he didn't want to spoil this summer.

Charlie came home from school in May. Well, not exactly home. The Mileses lived in Basking Ridge, New Jersey, but their lodge on the property next to the Laurias was home for Charlie during the summer. And for Ted Miles, Charlie's father, whenever he was around. (Seldom for Charlie's mother. Margaret Miles could not abide the country.) After Charlie came back, he and Nick hung together most of the time—canoe practice in the early morning and working all day at the campgrounds and hitting the bars at night.

Lisa Marie had begun staying later and later at the campgrounds, meeting camper boys under the pavilion, listening to tunes on the jukebox. Stacey helped Kit in the barn, tending the horses and giving pony rides to other kids, and when she was doing that, she was fine. But away from the barn she had begun to fold within herself. At the table she would mound her food into complex fortifications and she would rock absently while working her way through the construction. Nick imagined sweeping both his sisters into his car and driving away. He was never sure where to, exactly, just pictured them driving off in his MG with the top down—Lisa Marie in the passenger seat and Stacey between them on the transmission tunnel—and they'd leave all the nastiness behind. But he knew what was really going to happen. They'd get through the summer by working and hanging out, and then in the fall he'd begin to leave his homelife behind.

The two birthday cakes—one chocolate, one angel's food—bristled with candles. Everyone sang "Happy Birthday," and during the last stanza, while Stacey was loudly and flatly changing the lyric to "You look like two donkeys, and you smell like them, too," Nick heard a car door slam. And as he and Charlie blew out the candles, the screen door rattled and Ted Miles stepped into the kitchen.

"Don't tell anybody your wishes," Ted said, smiling. "Or they won't come true."

In the bustle over Ted's arrival—Charlie shaking his hand and accepting a big bear hug in return, Grandpa saying something about the prodigal son and Grandma shushing him by handing Ted both a glass of wine and a slice of cake, and Ted basking in the attention— only Nick noticed his mother pick up her cigarettes and slip through the doorway to the mudroom.

"So where've you been, stranger?" Grandpa asked.

"Oh, here and there," Ted said. "Here and there. Staying one step ahead of the creditors."

Ted winked at Grandpa Nick, a promise to tell him more later. A big man, brawny going slack in the way of an ex-athlete, Ted had soft brown eyes and a stylish presence. Sideburns long enough to be considered cool in business circles. Gray-flecked sandy hair flopped over Kennedy-fashion, a wide-striped Gant shirt with a paisley tie, glen-plaid slacks. Nick knew, as they all did, that when Ted looked at you and smiled, it was as if he had thrown an arm around your shoulder, hugged you close, and called you buddy. That smile, Nick believed, had got Ted further in college, in the army, and in business than all his athleticism and brains. That smile would open doors, persuade men to follow, get contracts signed.

Of course, Kit had a more cynical view. "Watch your back, Francis," she'd warn. "That man could charm a snake out of its skin."

Presents appeared on the table. Envelopes with crisp twenty-dollar bills from Grandma and Grandpa. Mepps spinners and Daredevl lures from Francis and Kit. Lisa Marie gave Nick a copy of Jack Kerouac's *On the Road* and Charlie Walt Whitman's *Leaves of Grass*. Stacy gave them beaded rawhide bracelets. Ted took the boys outside to his Buick, pulled their presents from the trunk. He hadn't wrapped them, but the racing canoe paddles didn't need anything fancy. They were beautiful as they were: gleaming spruce shafts, steam-bent with blades of alternating strips of yellow spruce and red cedar. The paddles seemed light as pencils, and they balanced in Nick's and Charlie's hands like perfect tools.

"Those shafts are bent fourteen degrees for efficiency," Ted said. "You're going to see them replacing the big beavertails everybody's using."

Like the other canoe racing teams, Nick and Charlie had been using beavertails—twelve-inch-wide blades that really tore a hole in the river. But they had seen these narrower, bent-shaft paddles at this spring's races.

"They let your shoulders and chest do most of the work," Ted said. He demonstrated the stroke. His forearms flexed like straps.

"The blade's narrower, though," Charlie said.

"More efficient," Ted said. "You're not trying to push half the river, like with the beavertails. You're pushing just enough to move you forward. Less wasted effort."

Nick tried the stroke. The paddle felt crisp and alive.

"You guys are gonna tear 'em up in the regatta this year," Ted said, and slapped their backs. "Let's take a walk down by the river, see what they feel like in the water."

They walked down the yard, under the big beech trees that threw deep evening shadows onto the riverbank. Ted picked up a flat rock and skipped it across the surface. Nick did the same. Charlie waited. Ted squatted at the water's edge and dipped his hand and squinted upstream. Then he sprang onto a flat boulder three feet from shore, squatted again, and handled the deeper water on the far side.

"Nice and cool," he said. "Cool enough for trout. Don't usually get many trout below Callicoon, but the rain's keeping the temperature down."

Ted had made himself pretty scarce lately. Everyone was used to his comings and goings—that was his job, to be the wheeler-dealer, to go out and line up financing for a dozen camping trailers or a canoe operation downriver, and it wasn't unusual for him to be off visiting bankers in New York or investors in Connecticut—but when he disappeared more frequently and stayed away for weeks at a time, they all began to worry about him. Charlie would call his mother, and Margaret would be as clueless as everybody else. Then Ted would show up, cruise into the driveway and act as if nothing was different. Worry turned to suspicion and then to resentment. When the campgrounds filled to overflowing on Friday and Saturday nights, and everybody ran like crazy to keep up with the business, they imagined Ted sipping a highball in a nice restaurant. They couldn't help but be pissed off.

Ted had been a legend in the Miles and Lauria families ever since Nick could remember. Always doing the unexpected, always doing something wild. As a kid, the first stories Nick heard were about Ted the great outdoorsman, how he once paddled a canoe from Hancock all the way to Trenton, how he shot a ten-point buck off the cliff at High Rock from the rockshelter across the river, how he would hike into the hills in winter and sleep in a snow cave. He had been a collegiate athlete, a champion swimmer at Princeton, a terror in the single scull. He had served his country in Korea. He had gone out into the business world and been successful, had become a big-shot dealer of construction materials, and by the looks of the Mileses' Tudor house in Basking Ridge, he had done okay.

Margaret and Ted, who had met at Princeton, seemed modern in a way that Nick's parents did not. They let Charlie call them Ted and Margaret, as if they were friends. They had cocktails every afternoon before dinner, a ritual that seemed to Nick the essence of refinement.

Ted reached for Charlie's paddle, bent to one knee, and demonstrated the stroke. He rolled his shoulders and drove his upper arm forward—not up—to push the blade through the water. Even in his dressy clothes, Ted had a natural motion with the paddle.

"See? Your back and shoulders do all the work," he said. "Use your big muscles."

He stroked a few more times and then sprang back to shore. Wiped his hands on his slacks. His face turned serious.

"I didn't want to bring this up at the table," Ted said. "I didn't want to sound a sour note at the party. But turning eighteen means more than getting to drink and vote. It means you'll have to go register with the draft board."

Nick and Charlie nodded. They knew that. Nick felt the need to move, felt a phantom gearshift in his palm.

"You'll both be students in the fall, so you'll get deferments, but you need to register all the same."

Yep. They knew that, too. They'd talked about driving over to Monticello on their lunch hour.

"And whatever you do, stay in school." Ted said. "I'm not one to put any demands on you, Charlie, and I can't tell you what to do, Nick. Francis wants you to go to school for the education. The education is fine—you need it, you're going to have a harder life if you don't get it—but that's all beside the point as long as this thing in Vietnam is on. You guys go to school and stay in school, because it's a mess over there. Maybe by the time you graduate, we'll have come to our senses. I hope so."

This was a different speech, Nick knew, than they would have gotten from Francis. And he was surprised to hear it from Ted. He hadn't realized Ted gave a shit about what was happening in Vietnam or anywhere else—he mostly seemed interested in the business. New business ideas, new schemes to make them all rich. Baseball, sometimes. The Yankees. Canoeing, fishing. But never anything political or social.

A pair of swallows swooped down and made a low pass across the river, touched one spot in the center, and started a ripple that reflected the silvery evening sky. From the house came the clink of dishes. The back door slammed, and in the dusk he could see Grandma and Grandpa making their slow way to their car. Beyond them, down the lane, a rectangle of light shone in the doorway of the barn.

"You guys headed to town?" Ted asked. His tone was lighter. He'd done his duty as father, and now he was back to being their pal. "Maybe I'll catch up to you later."

He looked toward the barn. The lighted door threw a yellow trapezoid onto the packed-dirt ramp. Nick knew his mother was inside the first stall, her office, tallying the day's receipts or sprucing up the tack.

"I'm going down and say hello to Kit," Ted said. "See if she's still speaking to me."

Kit had an edge about Ted, and Nick wasn't sure why. Oh, Ted would come and go, and you could never pin him down. But he had always been fun, too. Where Francis's idea of a Saturday with the boys might include splitting wood and painting trim, Ted would show up with a rifle and some targets. Or he'd pile everybody into the car for a day at Yankee Stadium or the Bronx Zoo. He had taken them camping, taught them to pack a knapsack, to read a compass. He taught them with an easy manner and a sense of humor—"Load that heavy stuff in the top of your pack, and you're liable to go ass over teakettle down the trail." Ted had been as much of a mentor as Nick's father or grand-father, and since he wasn't a blood relation, he was like a *big friend*, someone who would stand by Nick and his sisters no matter what.

The boys lingered by the river, hefted their paddles, and imagined their practice run in the morning. They spoke quietly about going to the draft board, about Felix in Nam, about Denny Evans in his wheelchair. They watched the evening mist rise off the river. When they finally turned and walked across the lawn, a harsh noise from the barn turned their heads: The big double door screeched and slammed shut against the jamb and left a vibration ringing in the air. Then they saw Ted's broad-torsoed figure—a shadow in the gathering dusk—turn from the door, hesitate, and set upon a meandering course toward the house.

"Guess she's not talking to him," Nick said.

"Party's over, man," Charlie said. "Let's blow."

They passed the insect-clouded back door, and Nick smelled the dew rising off the grass, heard the drone of the tree-peepers. A bull-frog sent a foghorn moan across the river. From out on the water came a meaty splash, and Nick imagined a big bass torpedoing up from the depths to engulf a struggling insect, and then, breaking through the familiar membrane of water into the foreign night air, catching in its fish-eye the wholeness of the Upper Delaware Valley, and in its dim brain, a momentary perception of a bigger world.

3

IN THE SOLITUDE of the barn, she could feel almost . . . well, if not happy, then at least at peace. Fixing a bridle within the nimbus of her desk lamp, smelling the hay and the horses and the sweet feed, listen-ing to Big Boy shift quietly in his stall, she could be around the things that gave her comfort, the things she could control.

There were so many, these days, that she couldn't.

She punched the awl through the strap where Cherokee always

wore it to a fray, always tossed his head and resisted, always rubbed up against the paddock cornerpost until his bridle had become a patchwork of old shoe leather—different shades of brown and tan and even a patent-leather scrap from Stacey's cast-off Mary Janes—bound together with red or black stitching, so you'd think he was the poorest horse in the world, or maybe his owner was the poorest owner, and what the hell, maybe it wasn't far from the truth with the way the business was going. At the rate Cherokee wrecked bridles you'd go broke buying new ones, and there was nothing wrong with a good, clean patch. A good patch job meant that you took care with things, that you fixed them rather than threw them away.

A tread in the grit outside the barn door, a scraping at the wooden transom, and then Ted Miles stepped from the dusk into the lighted cavern of the barn. His appearance brought a familiar weight, a heaviness of knowledge, and caused her to jump and prick herself with the awl.

"Oh!" she exclaimed, and Ted, seeing what he'd done, quickly pulled out the tail of his shirt.

"Ah, jeez," he said. "I'm sorry. Here." But she shook her head and yanked open the desk drawer and plucked a tissue from the box.

"Another grand entrance," he said, smiling at her. "You okay? Here, let me have a look."

He reached for her hand but she pulled back and shook her head.

"It's okay."

"You sure? Here—"

"It's nothing." She wrapped the tissue around her thumb, tucked the end, and picked up the awl.

"Okay," he said. "Okay. I'm sorry. I didn't mean to startle you. I wanted to say thanks for giving the boys such a nice dinner."

Big soft eyes, big sincere look. But she knew better. Ted Miles was as practiced at appearing sincere as he was at looking concerned or delighted to be in your presence. He was a salesman. He got paid by convincing people he was sincere.

"The boys could care less about the dinner," she said. "They've got other things going on now."

"They're growing up," he agreed. "College in the fall."

Yes, well. A long way off yet. Plenty of time to think of that. Right now she was more concerned about getting through the weekend trail rides, about the split in Big Boy's hoof, about the rainy weather keeping the campers away. Right now she was concerned about Ted Miles standing in front of her with his shirt untucked and his tie askew, leaning on the doorjamb like he owned the place, which he probably assumed. She wanted to tell him to tuck in his shirt, to put himself in order. What if he walked away from the barn tucking himself in? What would Francis make of that? But she didn't want him to know he was bothering her, so she said nothing. Let him stand there.

"Well," he went on, "they're long past the days when they used to sleep in the same crib," and she caught a glimpse of the two babies nestled toe to head under a blue blanket. She warmed at the thought of them so young and vulnerable, but even though he smiled at her she wouldn't give it back, wouldn't go down some nostalgic path with him, if that's where he was headed, for whatever purpose. She punched the awl through the leather again, ran the thread in behind it, and pulled the stitch tight.

She had to keep one gait ahead of him. Whatever softening up Ted was trying, it would end with some new scheme that she and Francis were in no position to finance.

"How's Margaret these days?" she asked.

"The usual. Golf tournaments. Charity drives. Lunch with the ladies."

"Too bad she doesn't care to join us anymore."

"Hah!" Ted scoffed. "There's plenty Margaret doesn't care to join in anymore."

Margaret had always been too prissy for Delaware Ford. The town was too primitive. She didn't trust the water, wouldn't eat Grandpa Nick's apples. On the red-shale lane between the Mileses' lodge and the Little House, she had picked her way carefully, as if she feared stepping into quicksand or a nest of snakes. How had Ted wound up with her? Kit could remember when Margaret had turned his head: Margaret the stylish sorority girl, one in a string of pretty girlfriends,

Ted all tennis sweaters and roaring convertibles. Margaret had turned his head with her cashmere V-necks and her tinkling laugh, but she hadn't turned it completely.

Ted shrugged himself off the doorjamb and crossed his legs.

"You ever take a look inside one of these motor homes, Kit?" he asked.

Aha, she thought. Here we go.

"One of these Winnebagos, I mean, or anything like it?"

"Nope," she said. "Never had the urge."

"You ought to take a look sometime. Have the Wagners show you theirs some weekend. They're pretty amazing. All the conveniences of home, no hitching and unhitching, easy to back up."

"What's this got to do with me?"

"We're talking about them is all, might try renting a couple."

"Who's we?"

"Well, Francis and me, of course. I thought he'd have mentioned it."

But, of course, he'd know that Francis wouldn't have mentioned it. Francis kept everything to himself until he needed to talk, and even then he might not say anything. Not the chitchatty type, her Francis. Didn't spew out any damned idea that came into his head. Anything new would have to sit and marinate and stew until Francis had poked all sides of it, considered it fully, so that by the time he brought it up to her, he'd have already made a decision.

"Look, if it's more money you're after, you can forget about bothering us for it," she said. "We've got Nick's tuition coming up and it's been a slow season so far. You want to buy expensive toys, you'll have to look elsewhere."

"Kit, they're not toys." He straightened himself in the stall doorway. "They're business investments. The idea is to use them to make money, and there's enough potential in these motor homes to take care of all the tuition we've got. Mortgages, bills, the works."

She let him blather on while she stretched the new piece of leather along the old. She tuned out his sales pitch, let the worn phrases like "revenue potential" and "return on investment" fall away into the darkness of the barn, let her thoughts drift down the way to Big Boy, to his split hoof, which was beginning to heal. He'd be back in the rotation soon. She smoothed the leather of the bridle and the new stitches were bright and crisp under her desk lamp. Jesus. Margaret down there in New Jersey with her golf shorts and her gin and tonics, while *she* sat here in a dim barn punching holes in her thumb.

". . . and the market timing is right. We need to—"

"Ted." She raised her hand with the bandaged thumb and stopped him. "You're trying to sell expensive motor coaches to someone who's sitting here patching up an old bridle. Does that tell you anything?"

She held up the bridle. Tomorrow morning she'd slip it over Cherokee's head and he'd resist a little, but then he'd go out and carry his riders around the trail and earn his keep.

Ted snorted. "It tells me you ought to buy a new bridle."

"Well, that's the difference between you and me."

"Now, Kit . . ."

"No now Kits. Look, this motor home thing is between you and Francis. Keep it that way. I've got plenty to worry about right here."

"Well, we're all in this together, so we—"

"We're only in this together whenever you need something." He started to protest, looked hurt. "And speaking of being together, your kid would like to see you, I'm sure."

He looked at her with that scolded-pup expression.

"You haven't seen Charlie in weeks—go on up and sell him some of your Winnebargains. Go see your kid while he still thinks you're a big shot."

Ted shook his head, shifted in the doorway.

"Kit, I wish you could forgive and forget."

He turned toward the barn door. "Thanks again for the dinner."

He was draining the place, that she knew. Sure, he had put in the biggest chunk of money in the beginning. Sixty thousand dollars. She and Francis had put in half that, had pulled the college education money out of the bank and it had made her sick to do it. But they had talked it over with Francis's parents, and Grandpa Nick and Florence had agreed to put up the farm. Mix it all into one pot, turn up the heat, and work like hell. Then Ted would barge in and change the ingredients.

"Bastard," she muttered.

She set the bridle down, took the few steps to the barn door, and slid it shut with more force than she had meant. Maybe that was rash, maybe it was rude, but slamming the door behind Ted seemed the right thing to do.

She wouldn't allow herself to smoke in the barn, so she headed out back, out of the light, past the manure pile. She hiked herself onto the paddock rail, fired up a Lucky Strike, and drew the soothing smoke into her lungs. She exhaled into the deep blue dusk.

Out on the river, a fish jumped. Once, and then again.

Jump, you slimy bastard, she thought. Jump for your dinner.

4

IT WASN'T ALWAYS like this. She hadn't always lived with such anger, such a sense of uncertainty. She hadn't dreamed of living this way, with money problems, arguments. She could type, take dictation. Twenty years ago, she had sailed through her instruction at the Wilkes-Barre Secretarial School. She had a decent head for numbers, could handle somebody's books. She had always envisioned herself in a bustling office in Philly or D.C., getting as far as she could from her hardscrabble farming and coal-mining childhood, dressing smartly and bringing home her own paycheck, renting her own apartment and driving her own car—a Hudson or a DeSoto—so that when she'd visit the Scranton Valley on holidays they'd all say *My, but Kit's doing all right for herself.*

But then she had met Francis at a VFW dance in Honesdale, where she and her secretary friends had been invited one night, and she had liked his seriousness and his shy smile and the fact that he had to be coaxed into talking about the war. He didn't brag or tell wild stories as the other young men did, and it was only through his friends that she learned of his bravery, heard how he had saved his crewmembers after their destroyer was sunk in the Pacific. When they took a walk outside and the band played "In the Mood" and "Pennsylvania 6-5000," he did speak passionately about the flora and fauna of his native Upper Delaware Valley. He had come home from the war to serve as his county's agricultural agent. At the edge of the parking lot he pointed out a cluster of mayapple, raised the leaves to show her where the apple would form, and then he spoke about mountain laurel and how it covered the hillsides of his river valley, and how the shad blossoms always signified the fish's spawning run in the spring.

When he asked if he could take her to dinner the following weekend, she said yes, and then the dinners turned into long drives in the country and boat trips on the Delaware, and she found herself fascinated by his discourses on the pollination of pine trees and the hatches of flies that rose off the river surface. She had never had formal education in these things, could identify only the commonest plants around her father's dairy—Queen Anne's lace and goldenrod and stinging nettles, and the wild onions that made the cows' milk stink—so she paid attention, she looked where he pointed, and she followed his eyes as he rowed so that she began to see the warp and woof of the landscape as he did, the river and the hills and the sky running lengthwise and the infinite crosshatching of rhododendron and hemlock and fault-thrust bluestone, and soon she could answer yes when he asked if she knew what kind of tree with mottled bark grew in the creek valleys—"Yes! Sycamores!"—and yes when he asked when the eels began their run to the sea—"Yes, in the fall of the year," and she enjoyed answering yes to this young man, this Francis Lauria, who was so serious but who would swoop off the road to buy her an ice cream sundae, or who would suddenly turn the boat, row to shore, and pick her some black-eyed Susans. She offered him a silent yes when his hand moved from steering wheel or oar to her knee, when he kissed her shyly on the front seat or in the shallow water. Every ounce of her begged yes for a future together, for she felt safety under his hand, respect in his lips. This is a man, she thought, who would never hurt me.

And so, after his quiet passion for the land had taken root in her and begun to crowd out her vision of an office in the city, and she had met his parents, and he hers, she had said yes happily to his other, bigger question. The war was over. There were farms to kick into higher rates of production, forests to harvest for the building of new housing for a returning workforce, and Francis Lauria's agricultural advice was much in demand. There were families to start, schools to fill with children.

Life had been good. She used to love waking early in those days, when they still lived in the Little House next to Francis's parents, waking to the milk trucks rattling into the creamery. Early-morning sounds—the clatter of milk cans, the greetings of the men, the first birds—were muted by the thick river fog. Farmers' dogs jumped off the milk trucks and rushed through the greenery to mix it up with Siegfried, Grandpa Nick's German shepherd. She prepared breakfast, Francis's lunch. Got the kids washed and dressed. Through the early-morning bustle, she'd look forward to the resulting calm when Francis drove off and the kids walked down the lane, when she could throw a load of laundry into the machine and then head out to the garden to pull weeds or separate carrots.

Theirs was the last farm next to town. Not that there'd been what you'd call development in Delaware Ford, but she always loved that they could keep a couple of cows, some chickens, a garden big enough to feed everybody, and still walk to town for a pound of sugar or to pick up the mail. Stop at the end of the lane and say hello to Mrs. Gustave.

Later, when the sun had burned away the fog and the farmers had gone back to the fields, the way freight would rumble into the siding for the day's milk. The noon whistle would blow and she'd hear the town shift for lunch: The pickup trucks at the creamery would crunch down the lane, and laborers would drift toward the luncheon-ette and the gin mills instead of passing through or lingering around the railroad station's loading dock. In the afternoon, she might join Grandpa Nick in his apple orchard or garden. She'd mow the older folks' grass or help Florence with some chore: seal a mousehole with a tin-can lid, say, or wash the windows with white vinegar. Put away tomatoes and peaches for the winter. She'd help Grandpa Nick haul his eel rack or fix the sulky rake, or she'd putter in his "grotto" under the house, where the stone walls and floor were cool, and they'd sharpen tools or check the clippers in the bait tank.

The kids would come home from school and have snacks, and Francis would roll in and they'd have dinner, and then maybe the men would go fishing or they'd all walk over to the town field for a ball-game, or maybe just sit on the porch and listen to the birds settle in for the night.

Delaware Ford had always been a backwater of a town. A bennekill, Grandpa Nick would have said, a bennekill being a backwater of the river, a quiet place where the river seeped in behind a jutting penin-sula. The main current flowed by on the river side of the earthen strand and some of it leaked around the low end and backed into a channel gouged by the spring floods. The water backed in as far as it could and then it sat and waited. Bennekills supported still-water life: ferns, willows, suckers, bullheads. Every bennekill Kit had ever seen harbored at least one discarded tire.

Before the campgrounds came along, Delaware Ford had been a bennekill town. The main stream of American life seemed to flow on by, and what was left over seeped around to the townspeople, to dairy farmers and railroaders and construction workers. To boardinghouse operators and barkeeps and hunting guides. Physically, the town had-n't changed much since it was rebuilt after the fire of 1899. From the Van Vooren Funeral Home on the north end of town—a jumble of Victorian excess—through the two dozen wood-frame shops and bars along Railroad Avenue and Upper Main (all of them slightly off-kilter, slanty, peeling paint), and on down to the "industrial" south end, with Agway's bulk feed tanks, the coal company's bins, the creamery, and the crumbling old town icehouse, Delaware Ford looked pretty much the same, decade after decade. You could look at photos taken from the turn of the century forward, and in every shot you'd see the same buildings, the same street. Oh, the red shale got paved, electrical lines got put up, the lettering of the signs went through their gradual metamorphoses. Clapboards gave way to asbestos shingles and then to aluminum siding. Horses and wagons became square-cornered cars, which in turn became rounded for a while and then squared-off again.

Women's hemlines rose steadily. Men wore beards and then shaved them off, and then grew them back, and then shaved them off again.

But nestled into a spit of land between the western Catskill Mountains and the Delaware River, the town had nowhere to grow, and so once the stores and houses were established in the early half of the twentieth century, it never increased. Families came and went, businesses changed hands. Kick's Superette had been a Ford garage in the forties and fifties and a livery stable in the teens and twenties. The hardware store had been a notorious saloon and brothel, back in the heyday of the railroaders. The Delaware Inn had always been the Delaware Inn and the Opera House had always been the Opera House, even though it hadn't heard music in a long time.

The campgrounds had a big impact on the town. It brought back the tourist trade. The boardinghouse business had died off in the fifties and early sixties. City people no longer took the train out to the country for their vacations—they could fly off somewhere, or drive on good roads, or even stay put. They had moved out of Brooklyn and Queens to the new suburbs of Long Island or Westchester—they believed they were already in the country! Businesses in the Catskills felt the difference. The boardinghouses began to close down all over Sullivan County, and the same with the big hotels and resorts and bungalow colonies in Monticello and Liberty and Fallsburg.

In the middle sixties, though, river dwellers noticed a change. Canoe traffic picked up. Scout troops at first, and then two- and three-canoe groups of young men outfitted with camping gear and fishing rods. Then young couples and retirees. People pulled into the river towns with canoes on their cars, looking for places to camp, but the campgrounds were few and far between. Bob Lander had a rustic place at Ten Mile River, and the Egherts let people camp on their cow pasture in Cushetunk. Grandpa Nick was happy to oblige anyone who hiked up to the house to ask permission to camp on his lower flats, as long as they stayed out of his cornfield and took their trash with them. Sometimes he even surprised them with a tractor load of firewood or a gunny sack of sweet corn.

In the evenings, when Ted was around and Francis had finished dinner, they'd stroll across the upper field to look down on the cluster of tents by the river: sagging little canvas pup tents or, when Scout troops were there, high-walled army tents secured with thickets of ropes. Other canoes would pull in, and the canoeists would confer with the campers already settled, and most of the time they'd unpack their gear. Sometimes they even walked up the hill to speak with Ted and Francis.

"A damn shame," Ted would say as the voices of the campers rose to the upper field. "Grandpa Nick's not charging them a cent. He could be pulling in five bucks a head, making fifty or sixty bucks a weekend without lifting a finger."

Francis wouldn't say much in return, would purse his lips and keep his hands in his pockets, and sometimes nod a little.

Kit knew that the idea for the campgrounds got its start on these evening jaunts. It began as a glimmer of hope, a tentative first conversation. She wasn't sure in whose mind that first glimpse appeared, but she liked to think that it arose out of a conversation between her husband and Ted—maybe as they fished in a quiet eddy on the river, maybe over a couple of beers on Grandpa's porch—and she liked to think that the idea was forged mutually, that it came together only as both men spoke of their dreams and desires and ambitions. Francis was ready to retire from the county, and Ted was always looking for another scheme. Kit never knew exactly how it started, but in 1965 Francis began talking about the idea and by the following year they all had decided to pool the family properties and develop a campgrounds.

She would hear them on the back porch, planning it. Ted would describe a shining vision on the banks of the Delaware, campsites brimming over with bright tents and trailers, happy customers bustling about, and a cash register that never stopped ringing.

"Hell, Francis, we're only two hours from New York!" Ted would exclaim. "We'll promote it in the *Times* and the *Daily News*. We'll draw 'em out of the city like flies to fresh horseshit!"

They'd be on the porch of the Little House overlooking the upper cornfield and the lower meadow, the barn and the sycamore and willow groves down by the river, the Mileses' woods to the north. It was exciting, she had to give it that. It would mean something important for their families. It would mean something for the whole town.

"Everybody's set up now," Ted would say. "The World War II crowd came home, got on with their lives, and now they want to enjoy life. Spend a little of what they've been working for. We can help 'em do that!"

Francis would smile at Ted's enthusiastic outbursts, or maybe not even that, although sometimes he'd kick in a practical comment on the seasonal nature of such a business—winters being what they are in the Upper Delaware Valley—or on the need for getting the right permits from the county and the state. Francis would not be taken in by Ted's sales pitch. He was one of the World War II guys who had gotten on with his life—Ted, younger, had built airstrips in Korea—and he would sip his beer seriously as he pondered such practical matters as how to run thousands of feet of water pipe under the stony earth of his family's fields, how to snake electrical cable through the Mileses' thick hemlock and maple forest.

Ted always had an answer for these things, of course. He sold construction materials for a living, after all. Knew the best contractors, could get the best prices on supplies.

"Nothing to worry about, Francis. This job's a piece of cake."

Ted had been right about that, or seemed to be, when the first big yellow trucks with Jersey plates pulled into town, when they began offloading bulldozers and road graders and backhoes with the block lettering IANNACONE on the sides. The men who drove these rigs were all sunburns and workboots and business. They set about their jobs without horsing around. The townspeople watched these caravans trundle along Railroad Avenue and they'd speak to each other at the post office or in the coffee shop.

"Big doings down there at the Laurias' and Mileses'," they'd say. "Big camping grounds they're putting in."

"Believe it when you see some big city money coming in."

"Hell, it's already coming in. All that equipment needs fuel, and Mort Beagle says he's pumping a lot of it."

"Those men need fuel, too. Getting hard to find a seat at the lunch counter, noontimes."

Ted used his contacts in the construction industry to get the sitework done, to get good prices on gravel and water pipe and septic tanks.

"We're getting it all wholesale, Francis," he'd say, as the bulldozers gouged roads out of Grandpa Nick's deer meadow. "Below wholesale, even. I'm calling in all my favors on this one."

Ted would stand with his hands on his hips, his legs spread, overseeing the logging and stump-pulling as campsites were cut into his family's hunting land. He stood with the assurance of a man who knows he's the boss. Who believes he's the big shot. Francis stood silently by—smaller, trimmer—blueprints under his arm, notebook in hand. He'd jot notes to himself, consult with Ted on the site of a new well or with the construction foreman on the path of a road. He was the doer, Ted the deal-maker. Where Ted would be gone for days lining up construction crews and materials, talking with the public-relations people, taking travel writers to lunch, Francis stayed at home and kept his feet on the ground, made sure everything got done according to plan.

And things more or less did. The Iannacone construction men bulldozed and graded the roads and then rolled them with crusher run. They carved campsites out of woods and meadows, seeded them with fescue and rye and bluegrass. They trenched in water lines, hung electric wires through the trees. They built log buildings: the office, the store, the roofed pavilion for square dances and rainy days. Shower buildings and outhouses popped up throughout the grounds. That first year, the focus was on infrastructure. Over the winter, Ted promoted the coming season by manning a small booth at the Sportsmen's Show at the New York Coliseum and the Outdoor Recreation Show at Madison Square Garden. He passed out brochures, gave people coupons for a free night to come up and try the place. In the spring, he ran ads in the New York and Long Island papers.

People started coming. Tent campers at first, and then pickup campers. That first summer, it was mostly family working the place:

Francis running the grounds, Nick and Charlie showing people to their sites and selling a little firewood. Kit tended the store; Lisa Marie helped her. Stacey was too little, so she stayed with Florence. Ted was always off doing his thing, and then he'd show up unexpectedly. By the second summer, the travel-trailer and motor-home crowd arrived, dragging or driving their motel rooms with plush carpeting and stereo systems and air conditioning. By 1969, Francis and Ted had pretty much achieved their initial vision: The campgrounds was a green and groomed garden spot on the Delaware, the campers were happy and plentiful, and the city money was pouring over the counter. On the big weekends—Memorial Day, Fourth of July, Labor Day—the line of campers waiting to register backed out of the driveway and into town. A canoe livery and trailer rentals had been added. Francis and Kit had bought the horse farm across the river so the campers could go trail riding, and they moved the family over there.

It had been good to move out of the Little House, to their own spread. Grandpa Nick and Florence always shared their place openly, but still, it was good to be on their own land. Good to be working around big animals. Kit had spruced up the place—painted the house and barn, restrung all the fences, trimmed out the gardens—and now it looked presentable to the horseback riders who drove down the lane every day. It had felt good to exchange a trail ride or private lesson for cash that went straight into the strongbox and from there to the bank. Felt good to know that she was helping pay down the mortgage that was in her and Francis's names—and, she could never quite forget, Ted's, as cosignatory of the note, since they used the campgrounds as collateral and as part of the business they'd get a better write-down on taxes and operating expenses. If she kept the place looking good and the horses in fine fettle, she could keep the money coming in. She could keep digging them up out of the hole.

She just wasn't sure how deep the hole was now. It had been thirty thousand cash to start the campgrounds, and a mortgage of thirty-five for the horse farm, and there had been Ted's requests for a thousand here, a couple thousand there. For an inventory of Coleman equipment, for rental trailers. Somehow they had found the money. But Kit was always skeptical. She didn't trust Ted when he assured them, "Once we show 'em we've got the seed money to get rolling, Kit, we'll get the investors interested. We'll use their money, Francis, not ours."

"Giving our money to that man is like tossing it into the river," Kit told Francis. "It'll wash right away."

"Now, Kit . . ." Francis didn't like to hear harsh words about his friend.

"Francis, he's Jesse James without a gun."

And Francis didn't know the half of it. Francis thought he knew Ted. Ah Francis, she thought. Stay content in your loyalty. Forgive me my trespasses, my impetuousness. Her husband was a mild, forgiving man. A good father. He had been her rock, her cornerpost, for twenty years. Thank God for Francis, she often thought.

5

NICK PICKED UP the garbage as Charlie eased the truck from site to site. Most of the campers were still asleep, their canvas doors zipped shut, so Nick removed the garbage-can lids gently, coaxed the full bags out, spun them to twist shut the necks, and then tossed them onto the back of the truck.

It was nice, working along the river, with the sun burning away the fog and glinting off the riffles. The hushed voices of people waking inside Winnebagos and Airstreams, the running of water, the smell of frying bacon. A good day opening up. Nick and Charlie liked to service the riverbank sites and those on the Knoll before the canoe rentals started. Across the lane was the area called the Meadow, a low-lying flats that held sixty campsites; those sites, as well as the thirty trailer sites on the Upper Field and the forty sites in the rough, wooded North Area, would have their garbage hauled later.

They were finishing the river sites when Ted's Buick came jouncing down the lane. Nick assumed Ted would stop, since he hadn't shown at the Wild Turkey last night, hadn't taken any time to catch up with Charlie. But Ted didn't slow down, didn't wave or even nod when Charlie beeped the horn and Nick raised his hand. The Buick swept along in its own dustcloud and then swung into Phil Sweeney's site in the Meadow.

"Jesus, man," Charlie said. "What gives?"

"Must need to see Phil worse than us. You see him at home?"

"Huh," Charlie said. "I didn't *get* home."

"You're kidding me. What?"

Charlie laughed and a sly grin spread across his face. "That chick at the bar? Camping up in the North Area with her friends?"

"Get out. She was with all those fraternity jerks."

"Was," Charlie said. "Emphasis on the past tense."

The Wild Turkey had been hopping when they'd arrived last night, not only the local kids but a big party of campers. Suburban kids— Long Island, they looked like—in all week for some canoeing and partying. One girl with long dark hair and a Fordham sweatshirt had locked onto Charlie and hadn't let go. Charlie played it cool, drifted between his barstool and the pool table, so as not to incur the ire of the loud-mouthed frat boys in her party, but Nick had noticed him talking to her several times. Her eyes had been rapt and unwavering. Eventually some of her crowd had drifted out, and when Nick left at one o'clock Charlie was sitting alone with her.

"They're all a bunch of friends from high school," Charlie said. "She wasn't really with anybody."

"So where'd you go?"

"Took the bus up to High Rock," Charlie said. "She dug the view."

Nick laughed because he knew Charlie wanted him to, but he also knew what was coming.

"She dug the view, dug the bus, dug my ass with her fingernails."

Of course. Another conquest for Charlie. It was yet another version of the story he'd heard too many times: Charlie meets girl, Charlie charms girl, Charlie beds girl.

"So anyway," Charlie said. "I didn't see Ted at home."

Okay, Nick thought. So Charlie didn't make it home last night, and maybe Ted did. He couldn't always figure out the Mileses. Sometimes they'd be close and buddy-buddy, other times distant and removed.

"Let's go have a little father-and-son reunion," Charlie said. Nick jumped onto the running board and clung to the outside mirror.

Ted was getting out of the Buick when they bucked to a halt by Phil Sweeney's site. He was dressed more casually today: khakis and a blue polo shirt. Deck shoes, no socks. Hanging out for a couple of days, maybe.

Charlie greeted his father from the driver's seat.

"Morning," Ted said and looked at Charlie expectantly.

"Just saying hi," Charlie said.

Nick knew that Charlie wanted Ted to say something normal, to greet him as his son, to shoot the shit for a few minutes. Ted studied Charlie and then glanced at the trailer. The door was shut.

"Fine morning," Charlie said. "Great morning for picking up garbage."

Ted glanced at the trailer again.

"We've got some fine half-eaten hot dogs back there, some gnawed-on chicken bones. Dregs of beer, shitty diapers, SpaghettiOs the maggots haven't gotten to—"

"Charlie," Ted interrupted. "Where were you last night?"

"Crashed at Nick's. We partied pretty hearty so Nick hauled me to his place."

Nick was surprised at how easily Charlie lied to his father, but he found himself nodding along to verify the story.

Ted finally broke out his grin. "Well," he said. "You don't seem much worse for the wear."

"It's in the genes," Charlie said. "Where were you the last two weeks?"

Charlie spoke directly, almost in challenge. Nick would never have addressed his father that way, but Charlie and Ted had a different relationship.

"Business, Charlie," Ted said. "Taking care of business."

"Been to see Margaret?"

The trailer door rattled, the screen kicked open, and out of it jumped Phil Sweeney. Phil was a fidgety, jittery, tight-wired little man. He bounced off the single step, pulling on his Mets cap as he came, swiped a beer can off the picnic table, dunked it into the trashcan, plucked another up out of the grass, and tossed it from hand to hand, shaking the dregs into the air.

"Jesus," he said, blinking under the brim of his Mets cap. "Some wake-up call you offer here." He said it *offa he-ah*. "A stinkin' garbage truck, coupla hippies, and a visitor from the distant past." *Gaw-bidge, visituh*.

"Phil," Ted said, offering his hand.

"Ted." Phil shook Ted's hand, but he didn't smile. "You come to personally pick up my garbage, Ted? How thoughtful. What personal service."

Nobody ever talked to Ted this way, except maybe Charlie. Francis might object to one of Ted's proposals, but he did so in a straightforward manner. The campers always treated Ted with respect; he owned the place and they wanted to stay in his good graces.

But Phil was different. He was a quick-eyed drywall contractor from Newark—or so he claimed—and he took inordinate interest in the campgrounds. He was always hanging around the store or the canoe shed, taking in everything and snooping about the business. He asked Lisa Marie how many sites were reserved for the weekend, he pulled Nick aside and wondered about the profitability of canoe rentals, he nabbed Charlie and grilled him on Ted's plans for the place. One night after Nick had closed the office and was sitting on the bench to relax, Phil had stepped out from under the pavilion. "Look around, Nick. This'll all be yours someday." Yeah, right, Phil. Every last headache. Every last Phil Sweeney. "You'll be a millionaire someday, kid." He was always buttering up Francis, and usually tried to curry favor with Ted. Nick and Charlie wrote him off as a kook, but Francis shook his head. "More there than meets the eye," he said.

Whenever Ted was around he stopped to talk to Phil, sometimes had a drink with him. Ted seemed to want to see Phil now.

"Well, I won't keep you guys from the garbage," he said.

"Right," Charlie said, and goosed the accelerator. Then he picked up the paper and rattled it. "Hey Phil, you see the paper this morning? Yankees won last night. Mets got their butts kicked."

"Yeah, well, they won their last eleven games," Phil said. "Lotta season left. Just pick up my garbage, and let me visit with Mr. Personal Service here in peace."

Charlie gunned the motor. "We'll catch you later, Phil—got to finish the river sites first. Boss's orders."

Phil gave Charlie a dirty look and Charlie carved a big rumbling circle around Phil's site. Nick hung tight to the outside mirror.

"So what was that all about?" he asked through the window.

"Hell if I know," Charlie said.

"Phil seemed a little pissed at Ted."

"Phil's pissed at everybody." Charlie ran his hand through his hair, blew some air. "And everybody's pissed at Ted these days. Let's finish up this fucking garbage and get on with it."

During the week, the campgrounds needed a million little tweaks and tucks to shape it up for the weekend. There was grass to mow, roads to repair, rental tents and trailers to move. Nick and Charlie would get the garbage going early, and then Nick would oversee the canoe runs while Charlie handled the construction projects. Charlie had always been good with his hands, had always built something— bookshelves for Ted or kitchen cabinets for Margaret—and he always had the finest woodworking projects in his school: Chinese boxes with dovetailed drawers, an elegant chair with an inlaid seat. After the big construction was finished at the campgrounds, Charlie got the ongoing carpentry jobs: building tent platforms, new steps for a shower building, a dock for the boat launch. Even as a teenager, his work was as good as the commercial guys'.

"Oh, Ni-ick! Ovah he-ah, please!" Mabel Cusack called from her permanent campsite in a little sumac grove on the riverbank. She waddled out of her twenty-four-foot Aristocrat with a bag of garbage. "Buff must of died again—you didn't come around yesterday."

The big red garbage truck was famous for its infidelity. The Big Ugly Finicky Fucker had been christened by Chris Beagle's brother Clifford, who had been a B-52 mechanic on Okinawa. When he left the Air Force and came back to work in his father's garage, Clifford wound up under the International Harvester's hood once a week. He said the truck was as big and ugly as the BUFs, but harder to keep running, so he added the extra letter and gave the truck its name.

Nick took Mabel's garbage and gave her a new bag. The trailer door slammed and Mabel's husband, Ralph, stomped out in his cowboy boots.

"Lotta noise up in the North Area last night, Nick," he said, shaking his Stetson hat. "Could hear them coons wailing till midnight."

Ralph and Mabel were cops in the city. Redneck as they came. Ralph worked traffic and Mabel had a desk job in the precinct. They'd wear the NYPD blues all week, and then on Friday squeeze into cowboy boots and Stetsons and bulging western shirts, and sock into their campsite with Merle Haggard on the eight-track and scotch and sodas close at hand. They bitched all weekend long about how the campgrounds was letting in too many longhairs, too many blacks, too many this and too many that, and it was ruining their stay. "We're looking around for next year, Nick," they'd say. "We told your fawthuh." But they came back every summer, tottering along the rocky lanes in their pointy boots, eyeing each new arrival as if they had some jurisdiction up in the Catskills.

"I'll check it out, Ralph," Nick said. "Butch is supposed to quiet everybody down after ten."

"Butchie? Whaddya talkin'?" Ralph said. "He was right down here drinking with us, your night watchman. How the hell could he be keeping order?"

They finished picking up the river sites, and then crossed over to the Meadow to get a couple of the regular campers before the canoe runs. Nick and Charlie always treated the regular campers special, as these people parked their trailers on campsites all summer and provided steady business. Some, like Ralph and Mabel, were pains in the butt. Others, like Celeste Gennaro, were terrific. Nick approached Celeste's compound quietly, but as soon as he lifted the lid off her can, Celeste pulled back the curtain inside her tiny Serro Scotty and called out: "Good morning, Nicholas!"

"Morning, Celeste. Pretty quiet down here."

"They was all up late last night, Nicholas. They're exhausted."

Celeste was a mother, grandmother, auntie, and day-care center all rolled into one. Her husband, skinny little Paulie, worked as an electrician in the city, and Celeste would set up housekeeping on Memorial Day and not budge until September. Paulie came up on weekends. During the week, Celeste's daughters and their kids would stay with her, plus the kids' friends, so there was always a swarm on their site. Celeste was a large woman, all flowing hair and tent dresses, and she grew tomatoes and peppers outside her trailer. She had a screen house and tents set up for her relatives and kids, and somehow they all contained themselves in their flimsy summer digs.

"Come in for a second before you go, Nicholas." Celeste swatted the door open from where she sat and shoved a box of Spaulding Krullers across the table. "Take a couple of doughnuts for you and Charlie. Keep your energy up."

"Thanks, Celeste," Nick said. "How'd you guess I haven't had breakfast yet?"

"Oh, you guys is always on the move. You don't stop. Come down for lunch and I'll make you a nice sandwich. Always room for one more."

That was the great thing about the garbage run: People gave them stuff. Coffee, doughnuts, sandwiches. The campers thought it was a lousy job, and they were always grateful. On the afternoon run, the straights gave the boys beers. The freaks gave them joints. The garbage run was easy work, and Nick and Charlie usually got a buzz on.

The Summer of the Perpetual Buzz, Nick called it. Everybody was on something. Wine, beer, pot, hash, speed, ludes, peyote, psilocybin, acid. It seemed like the right thing to do, crank up the reality a bit. Enhance it with the Stones or the Beatles or the Airplane. What the hell. Their work didn't require a great deal of precision. They weren't exactly air-traffic controllers or heart surgeons. They ran canoes up and down the river, set up people's tents, delivered propane bottles. They cleaned outhouses and oiled the roads and gave fishing lessons. They mowed the grass with a brush hog that could whang a rock right through the side of a Winnebago.

After work Nick and Charlie usually hit the bars. They'd run into their maintenance man, Miller, at the Wild Turkey and he'd be toasted, regaling the bar with the latest misadventure at the campgrounds. The guys from the railroad would settle in at the Depot, and they were usually good for a game of pool or some quiet bullshitting. The Jewish camp counselors would drink in the Delaware Inn—beautiful, exotic girls with almond eyes and shiny dark skin and wild hair that went on forever—and Nick and Charlie would try to get friendly with them, though they usually kept to themselves. The crazy bunch of freaks from up in the Beechwoods—Lucas Bliss and his lady of the moment and his twin sister Juicy Lucy and the rest of them, who lived in teepees when they weren't running around the country in their school bus—they'd blow into the Wild Turkey or Doc's with their wild colors and their dogs and usually a flute or a conga drum, and it was party time until the wee hours. The bars stayed open until three, and the Wild Turkey's bartender, Jake Skinner, could always be counted on to shut off the neon and declare it a private party that would rave on till sunup.

It was a wild time, the Summer of the Perpetual Buzz. It felt like the rules had been suspended, like you could party and dig each other and run free, and it was okay, there were no penalties. No. That wasn't quite it. The penalties were so big, you had to live as if they didn't exist. The rules hadn't been suspended; the kids just ignored them. They had been aware of bad things in the world from an early age. Nick grew up with a dread of nuclear fallout, a kind of poisonous snow that could kill you even if the Russian bombs didn't. He and his friends had learned as first-graders to duck and cover, to hide under their desks or in windowless hallways when the missiles came. And now, with the war in Vietnam and assassinations of their leaders and riots in the streets, who could blame them if they drank or stoned or tripped themselves into happy mindlessness?

It was his last summer at home. In the fall he'd go to college, and if not there, to Vietnam. He figured the least he could do was have a good time.

6

LIKE A DISTANT forest fire, the war in Vietnam burned somewhere beyond Nick's horizon. He'd get whiffs of it on the evening news or in the paper, and several local boys had felt it up close: Greg Streeter came back forged harder than he had been in high school; Denny Evans came back in a wheelchair. Felix Gustave was over there now. Felix would write to Nick and to Eva Van Vooren, his old girlfriend, and at first his letters were full of bravado: *Here I am in the Nam, old buddy. It's raining like a bastard. I'm hanging here in the hooch. We're in a safe area now, but word is we're moving out to Injun territory this week.* He'd mention facts about the life over there: . . . *village a klick down the road and you can buy whatever you want: beer, grass, boom-boom. . . . Mama-san sold me a pineapple yesterday, and Sarge gave me hell it could of been a booby trap.*

And like a fire, Vietnam held a terrible attraction. If you faced up to it squarely, went into it with the right equipment and attitude and luck, you might find out what you were made of. He knew that Greg Streeter and Denny Evans had learned something about what kind of men they were. Felix was learning that now. World War II had done the same for his father, as World War I had for his grandfather. But Vietnam was different. Nick couldn't tell, exactly, what the dispute was in Vietnam. Oh, plenty of people claimed the war was necessary in order to stop Communism, but the dominos didn't seem destined to topple all the way to Delaware Ford. Life in this little corner of New York State—in all of America—was too far away and too established to be affected by a political dispute in an Asian jungle. When he got down to it, Nick didn't have anything against the Vietnamese people, certainly nothing worth strapping on a gun for.

Felix had had his own reasons for going. Old Man Gustave for one. Eva for two. Getting out of Delaware Ford. Felix was a bright guy, and even if he hadn't been headed for college, neither was he stuck in town. "Maybe I'll take the Chevy and hit the road, man," he'd said to Nick in the spring of his senior year. "Bomb from place to place for a while, listen to the radio. Wash some dishes when I need money, spin a wrench in some garage. I'd like to meet a cowgirl, man, out West someplace, or a California girl. I want to see some country. Big mountains. Big rivers. Big life, man. Ain't gonna get that on some SUNY campus."

Nick always pictured Felix behind the wheel of his white Impala, his wiry red hair bristling, his wide, freckled face grinning amidst the chrome and the cherry rolled-and-pleated interior. Felix had done all the work on his car, added touches like fender skirts and twin chrome antennae. He used to thunder up and down Route 97, roar across the bridges into Pennsylvania. He and his football buddies would go ramming around, or he and Eva, she perched beside him on the bench seat, her scarf tied to his rearview mirror. From Grandpa's orchard, Nick could always hear Felix's dual exhausts blaring across the creek viaduct and up Cemetery Road.

Felix had surprised everybody when he enlisted. He was never a gung-ho military type like some of the kids whose fathers had been grunts in World War II. But Felix always surprised everybody. He was a bundle of anomalies: He could work algebra problems in his head but he'd step right into a fight if some greaser started on him. He knew local history as well as Nick's grandmother but he was once caught dismantling the old weathervane from the top of the Opera House. He was known as a fierce competitor on the football field but he was kind to the Lauria kids.

"Every generation has its war, Nicko," Felix said the day he enlisted. "My old man and yours had World War II. Our grandpas had World War I." He paused and nodded through the trees to the Mileses' lodge. "Ted had Korea. Vietnam's mine. It ain't much of a war, but it's the only one I got."

Whenever Nick pictured himself going to Vietnam, he thought of rabbit hunting one morning. Five years ago it had to be, because the campgrounds wasn't there yet, and he had been walking down Grandpa's tractor lane to the river, cradling the .22 rifle his father had given him on his thirteenth birthday. He was determined to bring home a rabbit or squirrel. Not because his family needed the meat, but because hunting game was something the men in his family did when they reached a certain age. It was a misty morning by the river, with early sun filtering through the trees, and it felt good to be walking with the gun in the crook of his arm. As he rounded the bend where the lane dropped to the river, there they were: two rabbits feeding on the grass between the wheel ruts. He drew a bead on the larger of the two, and as he did, he noticed the calm in the black eye that looked back at him, noticed the twitching nose and the grass blades disappearing into the nibbling mouth. As he squeezed the trigger, waiting for the firing pin to crack down, Nick understood that he was about to kill the male of this pair, the husband, that the rabbit and his rabbit-wife were out getting their breakfast as they did every morning, and the last thing they expected was this gun-toting intruder who would disrupt their lapine cycle of feeding and sleeping and procreating, and he almost paused, thought about easing the pressure on the blue-steel mechanism so intimately connected to his right index finger and his brain circuitry, but even as he thought this and considered backing off, the slight change in the surface tension of his skin was enough: The gun fired. The male rabbit went down and kicked himself around in a circle while the female skittered this way, that way, panicked and unsure what to do until she stopped by the side of the lane—ears cocked, nose quivering, sides heaving—and saw that her mate wasn't rising. When Nick took a step forward, she sprang into the underbrush.

He thought he would feel some elation at bringing home his first kill, but instead he felt only a strange disruption of the morning's energy and a sadness over having taken a life, regardless of how small and insignificant it was. And when his grandfather saw the rabbit and said, "Okay, boy, now you've got to clean it," he set at the little corpse with a sharp knife, but the stickiness of the blood and the tufts of fur and the stench of the fat and guts caused him such revulsion that he couldn't complete the task. He would never be able to eat such a mess. He threw the half-butchered rabbit onto the dump pile in back of Grandpa's barn and wiped the knife on his bootsole.

He knew that if he had completed the process, had steeled himself enough to go out and do it again, he would get used to killing and even to eating what he had killed, but something in him resisted this blunting of emotion. From that day on, he had not hunted for sport. He had, when asked, gone out and shot the occasional woodchuck in his grandmother's garden, or blasted away with a shotgun at the crows in his grandfather's corn patch, but he had not gone out to kill without purpose.

When he thought of going to Vietnam, he remembered killing the rabbit for no reason other than that it was expected of him. He would not do that to a human being.

There were men in town—his father among them—who would think him a coward for feeling this way. And the thought of being so labeled was enough to make Nick consider joining the army. Maybe it wouldn't be so bad. Maybe he'd get assigned to Europe. Right, like Felix did. "If you volunteer, man, if you volunteer? You get your pick of assignments. That's what the recruiter said." Felix had grinned at him like he'd wanted to believe it. "So I'm going to Europe, man. Going to learn radio operations. Twiddle some dials, yak on the headset, drink vino with French girls."

Felix didn't get to Europe, but he did become a radio operator. *Since I'm the FNG, I get to hump the radio. It weighs about thirty pounds, and on top of all your other crap it's a ball-buster.* Nick pictured his old friend laboring under a heavy pack, pictured him slogging through a rice paddy or along a muddy jungle trail, and he remembered how he and Felix and Charlie used to hike up into the woods and camp out, how Felix, a little older, always led the way and taught them his woodsman's skills: how to build a fire, how to cache their food for the night. Now he was doing it for real, and Nick knew that Felix's time in the woods around Delaware Ford would serve him well in Vietnam, but he also knew Felix was on no camping trip.

It could happen to any of them. He and Charlie would get college deferments, most likely, but Shag or Bear or Chris could get their draft notices any time.

VIETNAM WASN'T THE only aspect of the bigger world that nudged at the border of the river valley. Every day the paper carried articles about big-time rock and roll, as plans for the Woodstock concert continued. Charlie eased the garbage truck from campsite to campsite and called out the latest headlines: " 'Wallkill faction girds to block folk festival.' " And " 'Cool rock, hot tempers . . . Ruckus erupts as rock fête rocks Wallkill.' "

Nick sent a garbage bag of corncobs and wine bottles through the air. Fermenting corncobs always smelled bad, even through the plastic. The bag hit Buff's steel bed and the wine bottles smashed in a satisfying way.

"Oh, man," Charlie said. "They're blowing it. The townspeople down there are trying to kill off this concert. Listen to this: 'Wallkill proposes anti-festival ordinance. The Wallkill Town Board is considering amending the zoning with a local law that will outlaw mass gatherings such as rock festivals. The proposal comes in response to plans by Woodstock Ventures to host a massive concert in the town.' Blah, blah. Oh man, those fuckers are killing it off."

"Bummer. They better not. It's too cool. All those bands an hour away?"

Buff started coughing before they could get off the Meadow, and then crapped out entirely by Phil Sweeney's site. Ted's car was gone. The boys tried to sneak away, but they didn't get ten feet when Phil hollered from his window.

"Criminy, Nick! Charlie! You're not leaving that thing here."

Nothing was ever right enough for Phil. The roads were too muddy when it rained, too dusty when it didn't. The grass was too long, the mowers too loud. The garbage didn't get picked up enough, or, like now, Buff was disturbing his space.

"Hey, Phil," Nick called. "You know how Buff runs. When he's ready to move, he'll move."

"I'm not paying to smell garbage, Nick. I don't come up here to smell garbage. Business is so good you can afford to drive away paying customers?"

"I'll tell Miller, Phil," Nick said and kept walking.

Miller McDonald's Studebaker sat in front of the main shower building, next to the campgrounds store.

"Jesus Aitch Kee-rist!" Nick heard from the men's bathroom, and then the clatter of wrench on concrete floor. "Sons a bitches!"

Miller never cared who was around and didn't curb his language for man, woman, or child. He barged out of the bathroom and slammed tools against the trunk of his Studebaker. In his middle fifties, florid and rounded from too much beer, Miller had two speeds: thrashing on self-righteous outrage as he was now, or cruising on an alcohol-inspired jest with the world. When he was not repairing leaky propane stoves or unplugging clogged chemical toilets or straightening the sickle bar on the tractor, he'd likely be drinking a beer with one of the campers or sitting on a stool in one of the local roadhouses—with devilment in his eyes and a quip for the ladies. One of the pervasive, middle-of-the-night sounds was the roar of Miller's Studebaker—his Rutabaga, the kids called it—as its unmuffled exhaust announced his way home after last call.

He looked up from the Rutabaga's trunk and jerked a cigar stub from between his teeth.

"Goddamn kids from town!" he exclaimed. "I can't find a goddamn thing!"

Miller had a wonderful paranoia about the kids from town. They were the cause of all his troubles. When he drank too much and misplaced a socket wrench, he'd blame them.

"Goddamn kids from town're coming down here, nights," he'd say, "fixin' their jalopies with my tools and not putting 'em back."

Or when he had to refill too many propane bottles: "Kids from town're sneaking into these campers, nights, screwin' on the bunks and burnin' up all the gas."

Miller took care of mechanical maintenance—equipment, vehicles, trailers, and, of course, campers' requests—but when the bathhouse toilets got so clogged and littered with paper and downright foul that there was no other solution, he would have to wade into the sewage-soaked mess with a plumber's snake or a wrench and start cranking.

"Je-sus Aitch Kee-rist!" Nick could hear him clear across the parking lot, his curses rising like a ripe breeze out of the vent windows.

"Goddamn kids from town're coming down here, nights, climbing up on the crappers and shittin' off 'em backwards!"

And when Nick told Miller about the garbage truck at Phil Sweeney's, Miller laughed. "Good!" he said, holding his cigar at arm's length. "Let that pain in the ass wake up and smell the garbage. I'm up to my elbows in sewage and it ain't even teatime yet. I got no sympathy for Mr. Sweeney."

Other chores called: Nick made his upriver canoe runs, Charlie patched the roof over the firewood shed. Nick fixed a couple of leaky canoes and set up four tents for a Girl Scout troop. Charlie helped Bear Brown adjust the wheel weights on the John Deere. Nick didn't get back to the garbage truck until late afternoon, and by then Phil Sweeney had complained three times at the office.

Another car sat on Phil's site, a '62 Cadillac with Jersey plates. Nick could see two figures inside Phil's trailer.

"About time," Phil called when Nick approached. "Let somebody else smell that shit for a while."

Muffled laughter came from the trailer. A curtain pulled wider. Nick could make out Phil's Mets cap on one side of the table, but the other head was obscured. Cigarette smoke drifted through the screen.

"Hey, kid—" a man's voice called, then paused while Nick heard a murmuring. "Hey, Nick. Don't let Philly bother you. He's got gen-teel sensibilities."

More laughter rippled out of the trailer. A glass rattled on the tabletop.

"Hey, Nick," the man's voice called again. "Come over here a sec."

Up close to the trailer, Nick could make out the guy's face: dark sideburns, olive skin. A bottle of whiskey and two glasses sat on the table.

"Some of us don't mind the smell of garbage," the guy said. "Me? To me, garbage smells like . . ." He took a deep breath. "Like money."

Phil and the guy cracked up. They sounded a little drunk. Nick smiled and waited for them to settle down.

"I'm in the garbage business, Nick," the guy said. "So the sight of a garbage truck thirty feet from my door don't bother me. It bothers Philly here, though, so it would be good for *your* business if you moved it."

"That's what I'm about to—"

"Before you go, though . . ." The guy rustled for his wallet, and for a second Nick thought he was going to come up with a tip for moving the truck.

"Sal, no—" Phil said as the guy's hand moved toward the window.

But it wasn't a tip. It wasn't money.

It was a photograph.

"You know this guy?" ". . . *dis guy?*"

Pressed up against the screen, the photo was clouded by the mesh. It was a black-and-white snapshot taken on a city street: a man getting into a car. The photo was blurry and slightly off-kilter, as if shot in a hurry. Still, Ted Miles was easy to recognize.

"Sure," Nick said. "Sure—"

"Ah, criminy, Sal," Phil said, and blew cigarette smoke across the table. He reached up and took the photo, and then he dipped into his shirt pocket and came up with two dollar bills. He unclipped the screen and slipped the bills out to Nick.

"Thanks for moving the truck, Nick," Phil said. "Give my thanks to your father."

Weird, Nick thought as he fired up Buff and ground away from Phil's site. Why had the guy shown him a picture of Ted? Why did he *have* a picture of Ted? He patted the two bucks in his shirt pocket. A tip from Phil Sweeney? What the hell, it'd buy a round of beers at the Wild Turkey later.

7

. . . Two, three, four . . .

The counter in Nick's head ticked off the strokes; the paddle flashed and dug with the steady revolution of a machine part.

. . . seven, eight, nine . . .

"Hut!"

Charlie's voice was a rasp, a hissed breath. They made a clean switch, didn't miss a beat. Nick's paddle cut across the bow of the canoe, flung a string of droplets, cut back into the water: two, three, four . . . *Purple haze, all in my brain* . . . One stroke per second now that they were into the strong, steady, cruising portion of their run. One stroke per second, keeping pace with an inner metronome—located, Nick imagined, above his brain stem and pulsing to the guitar of Jimi Hendrix—*Lately things just don't seem the same* . . . Ticking off the strokes as his torso and shoulders, arms and hands, wrists and fingertips executed them . . . five, six, seven . . . leaving his forebrain to concentrate on the exact formation of each stroke as it applied to the patch of river at the bow of the canoe: the soft boil of water over a deep-down boulder, ignore it, the gentle lace of foam below a riff, admire it, the smooth shoulder of rock breaking the surface, avoid it. Avoidance came on stroke nine: a harder push on the right, a slight outward twist of the paddle, and he pried the canoe away from the rock with no loss of momentum. He began the switch, swung the paddle out. The rock, snarling water, passed two inches off the right gunwale.

"Hut!"

They switched. They were canoe racers, Nick and Charlie, and this morning they stroked down the river on a practice run, as they did three mornings a week: got up in predawn darkness no matter what kind of night they'd had or how little sleep, got up and threw the canoe on top of Charlie's VW microbus and drove up to Long Eddy, stretched out a little, then launched the canoe with the river surface reflecting the lightening sky, or more often, obscured by the low-lying fog that would not steam off until they'd made the fifteen-mile run to Delaware Ford.

This morning the fog was patchy. Wisps hung below the deep green spruce and swirled past in the early gray light. The river shone black as polished obsidian, the surface broken only by an occasional kingfisher touching down, a trout rising, and, of course, by the quiet rush of the canoe. Boulders hunched their backs to the paddlers, centuries-old river druids that seemed to whisper: *stay away, stay away*. Nick set a course toward the fastest water, and matched his stroke to that internal counter: four, five, six . . .

Dew dripped from every leaf and twig and blade. When they launched at Long Eddy, Nick and Charlie got soaked portaging to the river. Soaked again getting into the canoe, holding it out in the deeper water so as not to drag its thin cedar hull on the rocks. Now, halfway through the run, they were soaked with their own sweat, and it felt good, like a fine oil that lubricated the machine they had become.... seven, eight, nine ... A paddling machine, rolling their shoulders over and over, bringing the blade down again and again, slashing at the river, guts tight, legs braced, one breath for every stroke.

"Hut!"

Nick was in perfect rhythm with himself, with Charlie, with the boat. He and Charlie had paddled together so much, their strokes were so well matched, they were like two synchronized gears linked by the hull of the canoe. Through the contact points of his knees and feet and buttocks, Nick could feel the taut energy that was Charlie. When their strokes matched exactly, he didn't feel Charlie's stroke, but rather a tension that communicated through the hull to keep his spring wound tight, to keep him at his rapid, repetitive motion.... three, four, five ... He focused on his stroke, on forming each perfect stroke, on cutting a slash. That's all he was doing: cutting a slash with his paddle, slicing the same perfect line in the water, over and over.... six, seven, eight ... Behind him Charlie was doing the same thing, although Charlie was also making slight corrections to their course: drawing and J-stroking to keep them where Nick had the bow pointed. But these things were so natural that they forgot them. They focused only on executing the perfect stroke each time: one stroke per second, sixty strokes per minute, an hour and forty-some, fifty-some minutes—it was too much to calculate, but again it pressed in on Nick as the work of a well-oiled mechanism, and he attuned himself to the machine tension coming through the hull. When they both subsumed this tension as their natural state of being, when their strokes entered the river and exited the river at the same instant, and when the force of their effort was so precisely matched that neither overpowered the other, a fantastic and rare thing would sometimes happen: A wave began to form. When the bow cut across the quiet surface, it parted the water into a curl, a wave on either side. This wave ran under the canoe and eventually broke down under the thrashing hull. But when the canoe was moving forward with greatest efficiency, smoothly and steadily, it rose up on this undisturbed bow wave and rode it. The canoe seemed to plane off like a speedboat, to overcome the resistance of the water, and to glide across the surface almost effortlessly. This was the moment they sought. This was why they cut perfect slashes in the river, why they turned themselves into machines. And as they caught the wave, they tried to maintain it. The only way to maintain it was to not think about it, but to keep paddling those strong, perfect strokes, to keep the boat from rocking, to keep their bodies from shifting even the little bit that would throw them off, and if they could do all these things, and do them without thinking—if they could achieve a Zen-like state where they were doing fully what they dared not think about—they would feel the pure thrill of riding the wave of their truest effort.

It would not last for long. Once they noticed it, they were sure to lose it. On this morning the loss came not as it usually did, gradually, like an instrument going out of tune, but suddenly. When you're the bow paddler in a light racing canoe, and your stern man's stroke is even slightly off, you feel it. When his stroke is out of synch—if his paddle is in the water while yours is in the air—the canoe feels choppy. But when he completely misses a stroke and hisses "Jesus Christ!" as you're snapping off the last stroke before a switch, the canoe lurches past its balance point and starts to go over.

Nick threw a brace and steadied the boat. Charlie had stopped paddling. Nick thought maybe he'd gotten a cramp.

But Charlie stared past him at the riverbank.

"Look!"

Nick noticed two things in quick succession: the Van Voorens' fishing cottage sitting high up off the river in cedar-shingled stateliness, and Eva Van Vooren—a completely naked Eva Van Vooren—stepping from a just-discarded robe toward the edge of a huge boulder at the riverbank.

"Jesus," Nick whispered.

Against the muted, misty palette of the morning, Eva glowed like a cream-colored lily. She faced the river in perfect silhouette. Her hair covered her eye and shoulder.

"She see us?"

"Shhh . . ." Charlie hissed back.

They kept their paddles off the gunwales and floated quietly. Eva swung her arms and flexed her knees, swung and flexed—three, four times—and then dove, drawing a quick feminine arc over the river. Her pale form shone below the water for a moment—a glide and a stroke—and then disappeared. She became a ripple of bubbles, then nothing. The surface settled back to flat.

Nick looked at Charlie: Did we really see that?

But Charlie had his eye on the calm water. Nick followed his gaze, and that's where Eva surfaced. She broached head and shoulders and breasts out of the river, hair slicked back like a seal, and then floated on her back. She gazed up at the sky. She broke into a lanky, practiced backstroke, turned her head, and looked directly at the canoe.

Or rather, Nick thought, she looked directly at Charlie.

He suppressed a self-conscious urge to wave—it would be too goofy—and he fidgeted with his paddle and then Charlie said, "Let's pick it back up." They eased into their cadence . . . one, two, three . . . and Nick focused on the water in front of the canoe, but he couldn't help casting sideways glances at Eva until they had left her slowly wheeling arms in their wake. They paddled downriver toward the next bend. His strokes were choppy; he couldn't concentrate. He kept seeing Eva's thigh muscles as she flexed for her dive, the flattening of her breast as she arced to the water.

When they had passed around the bend and Van Vooren's eddy was well behind, Nick stopped paddling.

"Can you believe that, man?"

Charlie blew air—"Whoa, daddy"—and wiped his forehead with his T-shirt. "A bracing sight, this hour of the morning."

"Any hour, man. Any hour of the day or night." Nick rinsed his hands in the river and splashed water on his face. The sweat from their exertion had washed salt into his eyes.

"Can you believe the luck of our timing?" he asked. "I mean, another minute either way . . ."

"It wasn't luck," Charlie said.

"Whaddya mean? If we'd been a little—"

"The timing wasn't ours. We were going to get that show no matter when we showed up."

"Get outta here. She's going out with Georgie Brewster. She's older than we are. She's—"

"A vibe, man. Just a real strong vibe I've been getting lately."

Charlie always had it easy with girls. He'd come back from his private schools and tell Nick stories about girls and easy sex. He never went with them for very long, and he could never talk to them afterwards, but girls were drawn to Charlie like bugs to a lit window. He hadn't gone with any Delaware Ford girls—they weren't in his league, really, except for the Van Voorens and Julie Busch—but he had hung out with plenty of chicks at the campgrounds, and he'd cruise the off-duty Jewish camp counselors in the bars, and he claimed—*claimed*—to have nailed his fair share.

Nick, on the other hand, was shyer. He had had two girlfriends in high school, Vicki Rykowski and Beatrice Kordt. They had been nice girls looking forward to college or marriage, but both relationships had reached a plateau and gone no higher. In Vicki's case it was a physical plateau. They'd go parking after a dance and when the flesh-to-flesh contact went beyond what was covered by street clothes, she would gently remove his hand from the off-limits body part and continue kissing him. With Beatrice, the plateau had been emotional. She seemed willing to go as far, physically, as Nick wanted to, had even suggested, when they were studying the Greeks in history class, that they practice wrestling at her place after school, before her parents came home from work, and that they do it as "authentically" as possible, with a mischievous glint in her eye. But Nick had not felt much for Beatrice, had been put off by her aggressiveness, in fact, and thought it wise to respect the boundary of their particular plateau.

He had discovered that he was the sort of young man who would do the right thing by a girl, who would talk things over with her and then part ways amicably. He was a good boy. He didn't really like this about himself. He figured he was some sort of pussy. He longed to get laid, but he didn't like Beatrice's cheapness, wished for something more than Charlie's fuck-'em-and-shuck-'em approach. He wanted to meet a girl who really rocked him.

He didn't think it was going to happen in Delaware Ford. So when Charlie offered his opinion about the timing of Eva Van Vooren's dive into their field of vision, Nick was inclined to distrust his own sense of the miraculous.

"Come on, man," Charlie said. "Let's haul ass on down."

They dug in, picked up their stroke. But the edge was off. They couldn't get the right rhythm, couldn't get back to that oneness of mind and muscle and river, couldn't catch another wave. Jimi Hendrix's guitar continued to riff inside Nick's head, but it did so in awkward syncopation to his arms.

They ended the practice run at the campgrounds, put up a final sprint to the first fireplace in the North Area, and then they coasted, panting, wiping sweat.

"Time?" Charlie asked.

Nick checked his watch: 2:05. Not bad, considering their interlude with Eva.

They backpaddled in knee-deep water and Nick got out and steadied the canoe for Charlie. They always used deep-water entries and exits, to keep the hull off the rocks, as they had built this canoe and it was a thing of beauty. They had caught the racing bug the year before, entered a couple of races with a bulky fiberglass Old Town. They paddled strong enough and worked on their strokes, but they'd been outclassed. Guys a little older, paddling chopped-down racing canoes, sucking on Gatorade through tubes taped to their chests—they blew by like Nick and Charlie were dragging an anchor. Some of those racing canoes were fiberglass, so thin you could see the paddlers' legs through the hull. But the canoes that caught Nick and Charlie's eye were the cedar-strip racers. Built of strips of quarter-inch cedar, laminated and coated with a thin layer of glass, these canoes were cut low like rowing shells so the gunwales didn't interfere with the paddle.

They were light; a guy could pick up his canoe with one hand and walk away. They had a plumb bow that cleaved the water like a straight razor. They tracked as true as a surveyor's line. Just provide power and go, man. Jet-propelled splinters, Charlie called them. The paddlers who showed up with cedar-strip canoes had an automatic psychological edge: Their boats looked so fast, you knew you couldn't beat them. And at the start of a race, those canoes jumped out in front and were gone within a couple of bends in the river.

Nick and Charlie lusted after a cedar-strip boat. They were outrageously expensive; almost nobody made them commercially. But Charlie studied them at races, and that winter he sent away for a set of plans. In the spring when the weather warmed up, the boys took the plans down to Grandpa Nick's barn, cleared a big space in the back, and set up some worklights. They had the lumberyard cut some cedar on the bandsaw, and they set up the station molds every twelve inches to form the shape of the hull. They laminated and beveled the stems at either end, set the keel strips, and then began putting the cedar in place. Charlie tacked a thin ribband of cedar to the forms at the gunwale depth, bent it toward the bow and stern stems until it formed a pleasing sheerline. Then he began setting the thin cedar strips by working off this line, stapling them to the forms. Before he glued the edges, he showed Nick how to use a long sanding block to bevel each strip.

"You keep it pressed against the form," he said, "so it maintains a right angle." Charlie ran the foot-long sanding block across the top of the strip. His hands were firm and sure. "It cuts the edge off that strip. When the paper starts running smooth, you know you've got the right bevel."

Nick tried it and was clumsy at first. The sanding block didn't want to glide as smoothly as it had for Charlie. But Charlie put his hands over Nick's, showed him the correct pressure and angle, and soon Nick was cutting the bevels properly.

"Good," Charlie said. "Now the next strip'll fit right, and we'll get a smooth hull."

Nick appreciated Charlie teaching him his skills, and he marveled at his friend's ability with wood. Charlie seemed able to create any shape he could envision, by methodically working the drawknife and plane and rasp. He seemed to enter a focused, inner state that was so different from the rest of his life. Whether he wanted to or not, Charlie usually imitated his father: always putting himself out in front of everybody, chumming it up, demanding center stage. He made people laugh with his jokes. He secured their company with his dope-dealing. He charmed the girls. If he had been a surfer, he'd have been constantly hanging ten off the front of his board.

But building the canoe, he was deep inside himself, inside the wood, running the grain with whatever tool he held, making the tree conform to the shape in his mind. Nick admired this, and he felt privileged to see his friend so engaged. It was a side of Charlie that no one else ever saw.

They stapled and sanded, fitted and glued. They worked toward the keel ribbands. A canoe shape began to appear. As they went, Charlie took a small rasp and smoothed the sawmarks out of the cedar. When the glue was dry, they pulled the staples, filled in the holes, and popped the hull off the forms. Sanded it inside and out. Sanded it again to bring up the grain. They put a thin sheath of fiberglass over the hull, gave it three coats of epoxy, and fitted the gunwales and thwarts and seats. Then they sanded until the glass was clear and the cedar shone through. The sanding was tedious, but Nick would back the MG into the barn and plug in a tape. Sanding went better with the Cream playing "White Room" and "Sunshine of Your Love."

When they had screwed the last brass fitting into place, when the finish coat of paste wax had dried, they stood back and admired their boat. It was beautiful. Rich, gleaming cedar in the yellow light of the barn. Elegant lines, Charlie's tight joinery. They carried it down to the river and couldn't get over how light it was. Got in to paddle and discovered they had a different type of boat under them. Rather than the broad, stable family canoes they were used to—Old Towns, Grummans—they had a twitchy, sensitive racing craft. They wobbled at first, floating away from the bank, laughing nervously. Then they each gave a stroke, and wow! began to feel what they had wrought. The canoe slicked away as if greased. They stroked some more; it slipped easily across the surface of the river. They fell into their stroking pattern, began to get the feel of the canoe. They learned its balance, its tracking, its steering. By the third practice run, the boys were at home in the boat. In their first race, they finished fifth out of the dozen racing canoes—and well ahead of all the standard canoes. At the clambake after the race, the other racing-canoe teams waved them over, congratulated them, asked about their boat, replayed key parts of the race, and retraced with their hands the tricky turns in the river. Nick and Charlie had been admitted into a new society. It felt good.

They raced all over New York State and eastern Pennsylvania, and they would come up against the same teams in different races. They learned the pecking order, earned their place in it. They weren't always the fastest, but they were strong, focused paddlers, and they got their share of respect on the riverbank before and after the races. They picked up a few trophies. The race they most looked forward to, though, was their own Upper Delaware Canoe Regatta. It was held every Labor Day weekend, and it drew paddlers from the Northeast and Canada. Hundreds of paddlers, thousands of spectators along the river, a huge chicken barbecue and clambake at Firemen's Field after the race, plenty of draft beer and sweet corn. It was the biggest event of the year, and Nick and Charlie practiced like demons for it.

Ted had taught them to canoe. When they were twelve, he got them onto the river in the wood-and-canvas Old Town that he and Francis shared. He showed the boys how to portage a canoe, how to use their body momentum to flip it up onto a car rack. He showed them an array of strokes—pry and draw and J-stroke—and even how to motivate a canoe without a paddle. He could stand on the stern seat and rock, get a rhythm going, and bounce the canoe across the river. He could bounce it around in a big circle and bring it back to the landing, even against the current. It was Ted who first got them hooked on canoe racing; he had done it as a young man, and he had rowed sculls in college.

"The advantage of racing in canoes," he said, "is that you can see where you're going."

He taught them to drive for power in the beginning of a race, to get out in front of the hackers and flailers who tore up the water and held each other back. He taught them to focus their minds so their bodies could become machines. He taught them not to look back.

"As soon as you see how close the next boat is, you give away your edge," he said. "No matter where they are, they're always too close. Better not to even know, just focus on your own work. Make every stroke perfect, stroke after stroke, and you'll do the best you can. As soon as you're aware of the guy behind you, you start to fail."

They flipped the canoe up onto their shoulders and waded through the shallows and stepped onto the bank. Nick knew the portage so well—the trail through the woods from the boat landing, past the campgrounds store, and then up the hill to Grandpa's barn—that he could picture the entire passage from under the umbrella of the canoe. The red-shale dust from the road clung to his tennis shoes and formed an oxblood rim of mud. All the campgrounds' byways were unpaved red shale, like most of the back roads in the area, and when Nick saw that red mud form on the rim of his tennies, he always pictured his grandfather's oxblood Massey-Harris orchard tractor, the cinnamon dust coating the yellow wheels, heard its whine like the whistling of a teapot as Grandpa went about his chores: pruning the orchard, tending his sweet corn. Nick and Charlie bent to the incline towards the barn, hung the canoe from a rope sling in the rafters, and wiped it down with a towel.

Nick's muscles ached, his mind felt as still as the matte surface of the river. Yet energy flowed through him like fast water. Throughout the turmoil of what life in America had become—the assassinations of Martin Luther King and Bobby Kennedy the year before, race riots, student protests at Columbia and Harvard and Berkeley, the meaningless taking and losing of Hamburger Hill and the conviction of the Berrigan brothers for destroying draft records—in the midst of his parents' arguing, in the confusion of what to do at the end of summer, canoeing was the one truth that cut through it all. You could go out early in the morning and lock yourself into the river, you could bind yourself to this natural force by your will and your commitment, and it would be just you and muscle and water for two hours. He would come off the river calm, alert, and eager for the day ahead.

He got busy with canoe rentals: six to Long Eddy and four to

Hancock, which he assigned to Artie Ross. A dozen to Hankins, which went to Shag. Artie and Shag had already loaded the racks, and Artie took off in the four-wheel-drive GMC with three cars following him. Shag's people showed up and he herded them into the shuttle van and pulled out. As he did, a green Grand Prix swung in alongside the canoe shed.

The VA had bought the car for Denny Evans when he came back from Nam, equipped it with hand controls. They paid him a monthly benefit, too, so Denny had plenty of time to drive around, wheel his chair into the bars, and then show up at the campgrounds or the fishing access to tell stories about the war. He had been injured not in combat but during a drunken drive back to base after a night on the town. The jeep was full of grunts, Denny had said, all of them out of their minds on Akadama Red and Tiger Piss and opium-laced weed, and the driver was showing them the proper technique for running the roads in Alabama—"Ya'll mashes down on the foot feed and keeps it mashed"—when he slid too close to the edge and flipped into a rice paddy. Three GIs were killed outright. The driver crawled out from under the jeep with a dislocated shoulder. When the MPs finally pulled the jeep off Denny, they didn't expect him to live: his back was broken squarely above the hips, his torso folded into a right angle to his legs. He had lost a lot of blood through an abdominal puncture. "I guess I had enough embalming fluid in me to keep going," he'd shrug.

Denny would joke about his situation, but even though his lips pulled back in a sneer under a thin, boyish mustache, his eyes would be sorrowful. "Nothing works below the waist," he'd say to girls in the bars. "But I've got the tongue of a timber rattler."

Nick felt sorry for Denny, but he dreaded his visits. Denny had two subjects of conversation: Vietnam and sex, usually both at once. Today was no different. Denny idled the Grand Prix next to the canoe shed, reached down to his crotch, and brought up a Budweiser. An eight-thirty-in-the-morning Budweiser.

"Whaddya hear from old Felix?" he asked, jerking his head toward the Gustaves' house at the end of the campgrounds driveway. "Hope he's getting his share of gook nookie."

"Not too many gory details," Nick said. Felix's letters were personal. Felix wrote to him and to Eva, and sometimes he and she compared notes, but he didn't want Denny blatting Felix's personal situation all over the bars. "He's mentioned some boom-boom."

"It ain't the best pussy in the world," Denny said. "But it ain't bad when you come in from the bush."

Nick wished Denny would put the car in reverse and go. He fiddled with his clipboard, scanned the canoe pile, and jotted down some numbers.

"One of my personal favorites is the Star-Spangled Hum Job," Denny said. He grinned and sipped his beer.

What the hell. Dude wasn't leaving until he got off his punchline.

"First she rolls on a red-white-and-blue condom. No shit. Thing's got stars all over the tip." Denny paused to see how Nick was taking it. "It's a regular blowjob up to a point. She's got a little light on and her kids and mamasan and everybody's in the next room—that's how they do it over there, man. It's a family business. Just when you're about to get your jollies she starts humming the national anthem. 'José, can you see—' Vibration about drives you apeshit."

Denny drained his beer and tossed the empty into the backseat, where it clattered against the chrome tubing of his chair.

"You and Charlie get over to the draft board yet?" he asked.

"Not yet," Nick replied.

"Better get on it," Denny advised. "Put you one step closer to all that humming."

8

THEY DROVE OVER to Monticello on their lunch hour. The Selective Service office occupied a dingy room in the county courthouse. From outside the frosted-glass door Nick could hear the tap-tap-tapping of a manual typewriter. Inside, the source of the tapping—a blowsy middle-aged clerk engulfed in cigarette smoke—glanced up and continued pecking away. The room was painted the institutionally bland green of old junior high schools or mental hospitals. An American flag stood in the corner. Richard Nixon frowned down from the wall. Stacks of official-looking forms crowded every horizontal surface. A big, dusty clock ticked away the minutes.

The woman finished her typing, reeled the paper out of the carriage, and sucked at her cigarette. She turned, and without looking at either of them or asking their business, plopped two little yellow pencils on top of a stack of forms.

"Fill out one of these," she said. "Print so's I can read it."

She was heavy and she had the flat, drained demeanor of a bureaucrat who is more comfortable with processes than with people. She lit another cigarette from the still-burning one in the ashtray and went through a side door. Chair springs wheezed.

Charlie made a silly face and Nick snickered and they filled out their forms. It was straightforward stuff, and as they got to the bottom the chair wheezed again and the woman came in and took their forms. As she typed, Nick found himself thinking about Denny Evans and Felix, how their tours in Vietnam began right here, perhaps with this very same clerk. Had she ignored them the same way? Had she hunched over her Royal, pecking onto paper the first few marks—name, date and place of birth, eye and hair color—that would start a trail of similar official documents which would eventually end in those mud-stained letters that arrived in his post-office box? Did she hear in the hollow tapping of her typewriter the echo of small-arms fire and helicopter blades, or was she just another government bureaucrat who wanted to get these long-haired boys out of her office before lunch?

She handed them two small cards.

"Registration Certificates," she said. "You'll get your Notice of Classification in the mail."

"Which one do we burn?" Charlie asked.

She ignored him and turned back to her cigarettes.

Nick imagined Felix dealing with this same woman, grinning at her with that wide-open German face he'd gotten from his father, running his hand through the red Irish hair he'd gotten from his mother, resting his beefy forearms on the counter, twiddling his thumbs. He'd always been polite, Felix. He wouldn't have been a smart aleck to this woman. Old Man Gustave had beaten the smart aleck out of Felix early, and Felix had learned to be tough but polite.

He hadn't been perfect, though. Felix had had his scrapes with the cops. He and his football buddies were caught one Halloween hoisting a railroad handcart to the roof of the station. Another time he was found to be in possession of some rifles and shotguns stolen from a hunting lodge on Tamarack Lake. And there was the widely disputed drag race between Felix and Bobby Earl, in which, after a few beers at the Black Horse, Felix's Impala and Bobby's Plymouth Fury ran within a length of each other from the Skinner's Falls cutoff to Nobody Road, the official finish line, with the spotters granting the win to Felix by a fender, but it was the aftermath that was disputed. Felix had been in the northbound lane as they raced south, so at the finish line the expected protocol was for Bobby Earl to back off and let the winner in. But Bobby wouldn't back off, and of course Felix wouldn't, so they blasted on down the darkened road. The relatively controlled drag race, with football players and greasers alike stationed along the run to flash their headlights in case of oncoming traffic, turned into a wide-open game of chicken.

At the time, nobody other than Felix and Bobby really knew what happened, but this much was a matter of record: Past Skipperene Road, Bobby lost control of the Fury and skidded in a long black slide—the tire marks traced an arc of sixty yards or more—and then slewed off the road into the ditch. Bobby was okay, but the Fury wound up on one side and had to be towed home by Chris Beagle's dad. Bobby always maintained that Felix had bumped him, that when Felix couldn't win outright he had sideswiped him. But there was no damage to the Impala, and Felix always denied anything but a clean victory.

"Bobby Earl's a crybaby chickenshit," Felix told Nick later. "It's always the bullies who lose. They're the weakest inside."

Felix knew bullies. His father, Fritz Gustave, lived a predictable pattern: return from a long-haul trucking run, drink beers and schnapps until his face turned a bad color, and then start pounding on his wife and son. Whenever Nick saw the massive black Mack tractor backed into the Gustaves' yard, he knew the yelling and profanity would soon follow. And then for the next week Mrs. Gustave and Felix would sport bruised eyes and odd lumps. But Felix never complained, never sought sympathy. He might say, by way of explaining a shiner or a split lip, "The old man came home last night," but it never went beyond that. So when Felix signed up with the army, Nick figured it was to get away from home as much as anything else. It had been nearly a year now, and Nick would sometimes stop at the Gustaves' driveway to say hello to Mrs. Gustave and tell her what he'd been hearing from Felix.

That evening Nick and Charlie showed their draft cards to the gang at the fishing access. The guys made the usual grim jokes, and those who had draft cards pulled them out of their wallets. A couple of the girls turned away. The kids of Delaware Ford were used to talking about Vietnam and whether they would go. Whether they should go. They argued with the righteousness and assurance known only to the young and inexperienced.

"We've got no business being there," Darlene Van Vooren might say. "How many Vietnamese fought in our Civil War?"

"What's right is right," Chris Beagle might respond. "We can't let those people live under Communism."

Darlene and Eva were absolutely opposed to the war, and they preached nonviolence with the verbal equivalent of machine-gun fire. Eliot Winklewitz treated the subject with a bored superiority, as if his guitar-playing and poetry-writing kept him above it all. Chris Beagle and Bear Brown said they felt a duty to go, and maybe Chris really did, but Nick knew that Bear just wanted to get his hands on a jeep and an M-16 so he could tell them about it.

"Oh, man," Eva said, drawing herself up off the picnic table and pulling back her hair. Everybody turned to her since she was the oldest in the group and the most experienced. "At Columbia—"

Many of her conversations started with "At Columbia," or "At school . . ."

"—a lot of the freak chicks will only sleep with guys who burn their draft cards."

She held Charlie's eye a second, lingered with a Buddha smile framed by her wild hair, and everyone was quiet until Bear held his BIC out to Charlie and began flicking the flame on and off. Charlie laughed and tucked his card into his wallet.

Eva was known as a radical. She had been through the student strikes at Columbia the previous spring, and word was she hung out with the SDS cats who ran it. She was remembered for her valedictory speech a year ago—about how she and her classmates were graduating into war-zone America, an arena much different from the promises they'd gotten through school. The adults spoke about it for weeks, wrote letters to the editor about her stance on Vietnam. She and Felix had been dating then, and when they broke up toward the end of the summer, some said it was that split that caused Felix to enlist. Others said Eva broke up with him because he wanted to go to war. At any rate, Felix was in Nam fighting and Eva was at Columbia protesting.

And skinny-dipping in the Delaware. Nick kept seeing all her creamy flesh suspended in that moment of air between rock and water. The muscles of her thigh and buttocks, the tan line from her bikini bottom.

Now, between her cocked, blue-jeaned hip and her lingering smile, Eva was sending a strong vibe Charlie's way. This seemed a little odd, because Eva had been seeing Georgie Brewster, the newspaper publisher's son, who had finished up journalism school and come back to work at his father's paper. Georgie was a cheery, if somewhat dull, fellow, all steno pads and flashbulbs, and Nick didn't understand what Eva saw in him. She was used to those bearded cats in berets and peace signs, and before that, cruising around with Felix in his Chevy. Georgie Brewster must have seemed pretty tame.

Nick wasn't the only one to pick up the vibe between Eva and Charlie. Cecie Van Vooren stepped in to drape her arm around her sister's shoulder.

"Don't listen to her, Charlie," Cecie said. "From what I hear, those freak chicks *at Columbia* will sleep with anybody."

Eva twisted under her sister's arm. "Definitely not with GI Joes," she said, in a dig at Cecie and her relationship with Terence Skinner. "Definitely not aiding and abedding the enemy."

"Enemy? Terence?" Cecie said. "Eee-vaa . . . Terence is red, white, and blue."

"Red, white, and blown, maybe, but—"

"Oh, cut the crap." Darlene, the youngest sister, stepped in. "You're both free to fuck whomever you want to. Here"—she held out a twisted-up joint—"suck on this."

"No, thanks," Cecie said, and shoved herself off Eva.

"Yes, please," Eva said, and accepted a flame from Bear's still-flicking BIC.

Everybody twittered over this minor catfight among the Van Vooren girls. Darlene took a long toke and then, instead of passing the joint to Nick, held it up to his lips. He tried to keep his eyes locked on hers, but he couldn't. Her expression held a kind of challenge, a dare. He focused on the smooth perfection of her eyebrows, on the fineness of her fingers. He steadied her hand with his.

"Thanks," he said through tightened lungs, as Darlene passed the joint to Charlie.

"Eva said she saw you guys canoeing this morning."

Nick nodded. He couldn't tell if Darlene knew any more than that. His lip felt warm where she had touched it. She was so cute. Her hair hung long and loose, and when she tucked it behind her ears her silver hoop earrings made her seem older and more sophisticated. But Darlene was what—sixteen? Just.

Ai yi yi, he thought. Too young.

"Yeah," he said. "We practice mornings."

"Building up your muscles?" she teased, and touched his biceps.

He flexed instinctively at her touch. "Practicing for the regatta."

"We spend the night at the camp sometimes," Darlene said. "Eva gets up before Cecie and me. Sometimes Daddy comes up early to fish."

The Van Vooren fishing camp was a milestone on the canoe practice run, as it marked—at least psychologically—the halfway point. Nick had seen Eva's yellow VW parked under the pine trees plenty of times, and occasionally Old Man Van Vooren would be fly-fishing out in the eddy, head and shoulders rising out of the smoky water like some kind of graven image. They'd acknowledge each other with eyes only, Van Vooren knowing that Nick and Charlie were focused on their paddling, and they being respectful of his fishing.

"Hey," Julie Busch said. "You hear about the trouble the rock festival's running into?"

"Bummer," Charlie said. "The bastards down there are taking it to court."

"They're afraid the hippies are gonna take over," Eva said. "Oooh."

"We've come to take your daughters!" Charlie camped it up, grabbed Eva and Cecie by the arms, pretended to drag them away.

"Well," Julie said. "It might be a legitimate concern. All those people. All those drugs."

"Righteous," Charlie said.

"No, I mean really," Julie came back. "What would we do if they wanted to have a rock festival here?"

"Party, baby," Charlie said. "We'd dig the shit out of it, is what we'd do."

"I wouldn't," Julie said. "Forty thousand people a day? A disaster."

Julie faced Charlie off and held her position, but the kids could all hear her father's voice. Harry Busch made up one leg of the triumvirate that ruled Delaware Ford. The Holy Trinity, as the consortium of Busches, Brewsters, and Van Voorens was known, pretty much ran the town. The Busches were the town's capitalists. In the 1800s they had run a sawmill and an acid factory, and had reigned as the town's largest employer. Through the first third of this century the Busches had operated one of the largest bluestone quarries in the area, and most people continued to work for them. When the demand for bluestone died back, Julie's grandfather had diversified into trucking and railroad freight hauling, and in recent years her father had begun converting the family's landholdings into real estate development. The Busches controlled the commerce in Delaware Ford, and along with the Brewsters at the newspaper and the Van Voorens at the bank and the funeral home, they made up the local Establishment.

"Probably not anything you're going to have to worry about, Miss Priss," Charlie said. "Looks like they're shooting the whole thing down. Another victory for the fat cats."

Julie flushed, and Nick felt a familiar pang. It was common to most kids in Delaware Ford: that hollow pang of wanting to get out. No matter how much they loved the town or the river or the valley, or their friends or families, the kids knew, somewhere within them, that community life had not prepared them for the larger world, that their schools were not up to snuff—how could they be, with teachers like Mrs. Gelblein, who picked her nose and fell asleep during math exercises, or Coach Roesser, who positioned himself outside the girls' locker room in hopes of a glimpse inside? They knew that their parents were hopelessly out of touch with the real world, which they believed to be anywhere but their town.

They wanted to get out. "Delaware Ford," they'd say. "A good place to be from."

They would cruise from the fishing access down the short stretch of river road—the railroad tracks above them on the left, the river below them on the right. Not much chance of seeing anything new there. Oh, they might see a deer swimming the river. Once Nick nearly ran over a mink. They kept their eyes out for rarer things: bald eagle, black bear, gray fox. A canoe full of girls. But usually it was just the potholed and patched river road, and they'd swerve at rabbits for some excitement. In town they'd pass the funeral home and the bars, hoping to see a new face on the sidewalk or an interesting car pulling in off Route 97. Then past the old Erie station and along Railroad Avenue, the storefronts all the same, the same reflections in the same windows, the same dust settling on the same parked cars. Across the creek bridge and down to the campgrounds, hoping to spot some campers their age who might want to hang out or party. The town kids weren't allowed past the campgrounds office, so they'd cut a U-turn around the gas pumps and maybe call out to one of their friends working in the canoe shed or firewood bin, and then cruise on down the driveway to reverse the trip.

They wanted to get out. "Why get out of Dodge when you can leave the Ford?" they'd say.

Their buildings were too old-fashioned, their roads too unpaved. The tall, straight hemlocks and spruces that were so symbolic of the region and which the city people so praised, the kids alternately loved and despised—the trees were their own futures rising high and magnificent over the land; they were looming sentinels past which the kids could not escape.

Getting out was on everybody's list that summer. The subject always came up when they met at the fishing access or in the bars or at the bowling alley.

"Cross-country trip, man." Bear Brown and Shag Foley were planning on packing up Bear's van and leaving at the end of the summer. "Sleeping bags, a few cans of beans, plenty of weed—we're gone."

Several of the kids—Nick and Charlie, Julie and Cecie, Marisse and Eliot—were headed for college.

"Can't wait to be in the city . . ."

"When I go off to Cobleskill . . ."

"Gonna hit Buffalo like a big freight train . . ."

Charlie would be going to RIT to study engineering. Nick was enrolled at the State University at Albany. To study what, he hadn't the vaguest idea. When he thought about college, when he thought about the future, it drifted ahead of him in a haze, a dream, an overbright day. He had no plans, no real aspirations. He was enrolled in something called Liberal Arts. He wasn't even sure what it meant. He imagined a stone building, in the sheer, faceless SUNY style, with College of Liberal Arts chiseled over the front steps, and beside the door a brass plaque that read: The Holding Pen for Kids Who Don't Know What They Want to Do.

Except leave. That much he knew. Leave behind his parents' arguments and the smothering family business and the worn lanes of small-town boredom. Drive off into that hazy future and not look back.

"Maybe the fat cats won't win," Darlene said. "I mean, they've had pop festivals at Monterey and Newport. Why not here?"

"Yeah," Eliot Winklewitz said. "Maybe we ought to go down there to Wallkill, protest in support of the concert."

"Get our heads busted for some rock promoters?" Bear Brown replied.

"No, for Arlo and Janis, man. For the right to assemble peacefully and listen to music."

Eliot met with a couple of cheers and a "Right on" or two, but mostly the kids didn't believe it. Even in Delaware Ford, or maybe especially in Delaware Ford, they believed that the fat cats always won.

9

DURING THE THIRD week of June a heavy storm rocked the river valley. Five inches of rain fell overnight and flooded the creeks. Culverts washed out, lightning toppled a hundred-year-old white pine into the Methodist Church, and shopkeepers along Railroad Avenue built sandbag dams to keep the runoff out of their buildings.

The Delaware came up roily and brown. Kit kept a nervous eye on it as she fed the horses that morning. She watched the water level on the barbed-wire fence that ran out into the river. One fencepost, normally at the river's edge, now stood four feet into the swollen and shifting current. The endpost—eight feet beyond it—was three-quarters submerged. Bad sign. The horses never ventured that far, so it was enough to keep them in. But the river's color had begun to turn from the brown tea of high water to the thick coffee of full flood, and that meant the highest water hadn't yet arrived.

The fence would go, most likely, and she didn't have enough barbed wire to restring it. The horses wouldn't stray during the flood, but as soon as the water started to recede you could bet they'd be nosing past the washed-down posts and the tangled wire. Once around the fence, they'd be on their way to the Conklins' hayfields or running down the river road to Damascus. She'd get a call from one of the neighbors, and she could picture Apache or Midnight mowing through a garden, yanking up mouthfuls of lettuce or stomping young tomato plants. She'd have to replace the garden, of course, and that would get expensive with twenty-some hayburners plowing through the countryside.

She hollered to Eva that she was going to Agway.

"And keep those horses away from the river," she called to Stacey.

All the way up the river road, water streamed off the mountainside. Creeks ran brown, springs gushed, and water ran in places where no water usually ran. At Agway, the talk was all of the storm.

"Got pumps running in six different basements," said Roy Elwood, the plumber. He leaned on the counter with a bunch of hose clamps in his oil-stained hands. "Can't even get to all the calls, trees across the roads and viaducts flooded."

"Tracks are washed out up at White House Curve," nodded Dick Skinner from the railroad. "Waitin' on the work train from Port Jervis."

The men ignored Kit as they discussed the storm. Dick Skinner screwed the lid off a beat-up thermos, poured a cup of coffee, then screwed the lid back down and gave it some extra torque.

"We're about out of chain-saw oil," said fat old Vern Lefevre from behind the counter. "I guess there's been some awful tree damage."

"Gonna be more," Dick said, blowing on his cup. "River's coming up. Once it starts undercutting them roots, look out."

The men nodded and studied the floor as they agreed on the severity of the storm, and then Vern looked up.

"Well hello, Kit," he said. "Wet enough for you?"

Vern delivered this like it was the joke of the century, as if he wasn't always trying to grease the way with some idiocy about the weather—*Hot enough for you? Cold enough for you? It ain't the heat it's the humidity*—and the other two grinned like Vern was Milton Berle.

"I need some bobwire and steeples," she said. She always spoke businesslike to the other merchants in town, to cut through the nonsense. "I know where the steeples are, if you can get me two rolls of wire."

"Two rolls for the lady, coming right up," Vern said. He winked at Roy and Dick and shoved his bulk off the counter.

Kit strode down the aisle toward the nails and fasteners, past fifty-pound sacks of cracked corn, past the plumbing supplies and electrical fittings, a little jog around a barrelful of ax handles. She didn't like Vern Lefevre. Always panting like an overweight dog, always making insipid jokes. She had no use for those other two jackasses, either. Hanging around drinking coffee when there was work to be done. She ran her fingers across the square boxes of nails—eight-penny common, six-penny common, six-penny finish—until she found the fence staples and pulled down a 500-count box.

She could see the plumber and the railroader watching her as she came back up the aisle, though they tried to peer from under their cap brims. Vern emerged from the stockroom and heaved the rolls of barbed wire onto the counter. He started flipping through his price book and she set the staples beside the wire.

"So, Kit," Roy Elwood said with his jackass grin, "how's your plumbing holding up?" Dick Skinner grinned along with him and Vern looked up from his book. "All this water backing anything up, I mean?"

She ignored him, kept her face on Vern's stubby finger as he ran down a column of figures.

"Important to keep the plumbing open, you know," Roy went on. "Ain't good to let things clog up."

Tote it up, she thought. Let me out of here.

"You ever need your lines snaked out, Kit, you know who—"

"Roy." She cocked her head over her shoulder. "If you looked like you knew which end of a wrench to turn, I might consider it. Francis does a pretty good job keeping our plumbing in order."

She turned back to the counter. "Ring me up, Vern, and let me get back to work."

Vern scribbled on his pad, nibbled on his pencil eraser, drew a sharp stroke, and wrote the total underneath. He spun the pad around for Kit to see.

"Put it on our tab," she said.

"Sorry, Kit. No can do."

"What do you mean? Campgrounds account."

Vern shook his head.

"I don't get it, Vern. Just put it on the account as usual."

Vern drew himself up, expelled an adenoidal sigh, shook his fleshy jowls. "Can't do it, Kit. You people are on credit hold until you pay your bill. I can take cash or a good check."

Behind her, Kit heard the plumber or the railroader snicker softly. Goddamn. Credit hold?

"I don't understand—"

"You people have to pay your bills like anybody else. Just because—"

"Here." She plucked a twenty-dollar bill out of her jeans jacket. Embarrassment burned her cheeks. She knew the jackasses were laughing at her. Goddamn this business! How the *hell* did it wind up like this?

Vern rang up her purchase and counted her change. His grin came back.

"Tell Francis to pay a little more attention to his checkbook," he said, "and a little less on the plumbing."

Roy and Dick broke into guffaws, and it was all Kit could do to keep from whirling on them. Riffraff. Worthless riffraff.

"You want a hand loading that wire?" Vern asked.

She pulled her leather gloves out of her hip pocket, shouldered the wire. "You think anybody in here's capable of it?" She swept the staples off the counter. Kicked open the front door. *You people!* God, it was embarrassing.

She slammed the wire into the back of the pickup, slammed the driver's door. She swung the truck out of Agway's lane, down under the railroad viaduct, and hooked a left into the campgrounds driveway. She passed Bear Brown on the John Deere pulling a partially collapsed tent trailer. *You people!* A bunch of bedraggled campers huddled under the pavilion, looking wet and miserable. Francis's Scout was not in front of the office, so she drove on into the grounds.

10

NICK CUT THE last slash in the sumac branch—one every six inches—and used the hammer end of the hatchet to pound the stake into the riverbank.

"Let's keep an eye on that," his father said. "We'll want to know whether we have to haul those river-site trailers."

The campgrounds crew had been working long hours. They had

moved people from the low-lying sites to higher ground. They had hauled picnic tables and garbage cans away from the river. They had battened down the rental trailers, so they could tow them on a moment's notice. High water always threatened the campgrounds. When Tamarack Creek flooded, it added a surge to the already swollen river. A low spot on the riverbank in the North Area would allow the first trickle into the property. If the river kept rising, it would stream down the road in the North Area and seek the low ground toward the bennekill. If it rose enough, the river would cut the campgrounds in half.

In this morning's steady rain, Francis had come out to the firewood shed.

"So," he'd said. "How's the river?"

"Haven't checked it in a while," Nick replied.

"Let's go take a look."

They had taken Francis's Scout and eased along the lane into the North Area. The road up there was the worst one in the place, and Nick had already used the John Deere and a log chain to haul two cars out of the mud.

"Road's like soup," Francis had said, shifting the Scout into four-wheel. "Let's set out a stake. Hatchet's under your seat."

Now, with the stake in the riverbank where the water met the earth, they looked out across the river. Tree branches floated by. On the far side, the roof of somebody's spring house bobbed along. A Styrofoam cooler rode high and bright. High water like this always scoured the riverbank.

"A real gully-washer last night," Francis said. He nodded upstream. "Creek's come in."

"It's gone brown," Nick said.

He could see the surge of Tamarack Creek where it entered the Delaware upstream from the campgrounds. He traced the creek in his mind, its wild white water all rushing chocolate and foam, traced it back from the river to the big rollers behind Agway and then the fast chutes along the Tamarack Lake road and the monster rapids at Sawmill Falls, let his mind negotiate the twists and turns of the creek all the way to its source at the lake, and as he did so he felt drawn to it, felt the hydraulic pull of the water through his legs and hips as he sought to keep his balance in a kayak or a banger of a canoe, the ache in his arms to push hard against the raw muscle of the floodwater, the need to lock into a power greater than himself and ride it out.

His family had always been close to the river. His first cautionary tale was of his father's sister Caroline, who would have grown up to be his Aunt Caroline had she not fallen through the ice and drowned when she was nine years old. He had started fishing on the river when he was four, going out with his grandfather in a flat-bottomed wooden skiff. And not much later than that he had helped with Grandpa's eel rack, setting the stones of the weir in the summer and then helping haul the eels in the fall. He'd always liked working on the river with his grandfather, because Grandpa was patient with him and showed him how to do things: set the stones of the eel weir just so, build the base with big rocks and taper the walls with smaller ones, chink in the holes for a tight fit. When they were done, the eighty-yard wings of the weir spread a glassy vee of water across the river, and they would stand back and look at their work with satisfaction.

In these moments, Grandpa might reach down and bring up a river stone and turn it in the sunlight. The stone would be black at first, wet and polished and dripping, with a line of lime-green moss where it had nestled against the riverbottom. Underneath was a coating of earth, musty and clinging, as if the riverbottom had been unwilling to give up its protective scale. Grandpa would wash the stone in the water and then rub its surface, smooth from years of being tumbled and ground and scoured with the fine sediment near the bed of the constantly flowing water, and as the glistening black dried to gray, he taught Nick about the natural history of the river valley, of the geo-logic forces that formed it. He told how the Catskill Mountains and its rivers were formed from a shallow inland sea, how the shales and sandstones deposited during the Lower and Middle Devonian periods had been worn down by centuries of rushing water that sculpted the steep, green hills, how the Catskills came to be veined with brooks and creeks and the big rivers that formed its boundaries: the Hudson, the Susquehanna, and, of course, the Delaware.

"But how do they get so smooth?" Nick had wondered, holding Grandpa's stone, pondering the effect of water running, century after century, without end, over something as sharp as red shale, as hard as bluestone. Sharp edges rounded, round edges softened, stones became smooth as eggs.

Grandpa had taken the stone from Nick and said, "The river is patient. It shapes everything it touches."

The river's abundant fresh water supported vegetation and animals, and at the end of the last ice age, human beings.

"They followed the lower edge of the ice from Asia," Grandpa had said. "They hunted big game—caribou, mastodon. Imagine it, Nick— they killed mastodon with spears."

As the ice retreated and the region warmed, those early humans hunted smaller game and gathered the wild, edible plants. Later, they developed into the great Indian tribes: the Iroquois, the Mohicans, and the Lenni Lenape.

"Also known as Delaware Indians," Grandpa said. "That's what the English called them, but Lenape was the Indian name. It means 'the real people.' They fished and grew crops along the Delaware—all the way south into New Jersey and Pennsylvania and east to Long Island. They called the area they inhabited 'Lenapehoking.'"

Lenapehoking. Nick loved the sound of the word and played it over and over in his mind. Lenapehoking. It sounded like rushing water.

A splashing in the lane, and Nick and Francis turned to see Kit's yellow pickup sloshing through the muck. Nick jumped away as his mother slid to a stop by his father's door. Her open window had let the rain soak the arm of her denim jacket.

"I just came from Agway," she said. "I needed to buy some bobwire. The high water always takes out the fence, and I'll have to string it back up or we'll have horses from here to Skinner's Falls."

She jerked her head toward the bed of the pickup. Two fat rolls of barbed wire nestled in the matted hay scraps.

"Vern Lefevre wouldn't let me charge the bobwire to the campgrounds account." She delivered this like a verdict. "He said, 'You people are on credit hold until you pay your bill.' Credit hold? What's credit hold? I had money with me, so I paid him cash."

Francis looked concerned. His lips tightened.

"Goddammit, Francis, what's going on? 'You people,' he called us. 'You people haven't paid your bill.' Are you paying the bills or aren't you?"

"I paid the Agway bill," Francis said. "Last week. It's paid up."

"Apparently not. 'You people'! You don't know how that feels. So who else was standing around—Dick Skinner and Roy Elwood, couple of deadbeats. Dick Skinner sniggered behind me, and it was all I could do to keep from popping him one. 'You people'!"

She gave Francis a withering look.

"I paid the bill last week, Kit," Francis said. "Something—"

"Agway doesn't think you paid the bill last week. Agway has us on *credit hold*, whatever that means."

"It means no more credit until our account is settled. Something's wrong. I'll talk with Vern."

"Yeah, well, you'd better talk to your business partner."

"Kit, he hasn't even been around. Let me look into it. I'm sure it's—"

"You look into it, Francis. You look into it damn good and hard, because it's bigger than we know, and it's hurting us worse than we can imagine. Now I'm going to go tend to the horses, and you'd better hope I don't run into Ted Miles."

She threw the truck into gear and spun her tires, spraying mud and splattering Francis's Scout. She had to rock it twice, three times, to get underway, and then she was a bouncing, sloshing, yellow capsule of anger rocketing through the woods.

Francis watched her and then turned his gaze back to the river.

"Let's go," he said.

They hadn't always argued, Nick thought as his father jostled the Scout in his mother's wheel ruts. Oh, their marriage might not have been perfect. Certainly it hadn't been exciting, or even what most people would consider romantic. In recent years they had developed a mutual tolerance, and the angry flare-ups hadn't started until the campgrounds came along. But Nick could remember times when they would take him and Lisa Marie—Stacey hadn't been born yet—out to dinner at the E&N Tavern, times when they might go as a family to the Little World's Fair in Grahamsville. He could even remember when he and his sister would be left at Grandma's house for the evening while his parents went out to dinner or a movie. They hadn't done anything like that—time spent to enjoy each other's company—in years.

His parents had what he would call a practical relationship. They might have bonded for romantic reasons in the beginning, but they had since become a team dedicated to ushering their offspring through childhood. Francis had always been the breadwinner. As the county agricultural agent, he had helped countless farmers and gardeners and foresters with their questions on crops and fertilizer and blight. He had been patient and even-tempered, and people appreciated his honest advice.

Kit had taken care of the kids and the house. But where her husband had been mild, she had been mercurial. She had always been tough and fierce, and everyone—not only family but townspeople, too—knew not to cross her. If she felt she was paying too much for tomatoes in the grocery, she would let Norm Kick know. When Howard Streeter came around seeking reelection for town supervisor, she cut through the smiling and handshaking and told him what she thought about the snowplowing last winter. She had no inhibition about marching straight into school to set the principal straight on the new school-bus policy or to reprimand a teacher about a dubious assignment.

But she had a soft side, too. She would surprise the kids with special treats when they got home from school: German chocolate cake and cinnamon buns and peach pie. She'd crochet scarves and hats for the girls, sew gaiters for Nick and Francis. She'd tend Mrs. Gustave's bruises and she'd mother Felix, love him up like a boy instead of dismissing him as the tough kid in the neighborhood. She'd deliver outgrown children's clothes and good winter coats to the poultry workers living in trailers on back roads, and in turn she'd find crocks of Hungarian goulash and clusters of Spanish peppers left on her doorstep.

Kit and Francis had built the family steadily, had never spent money extravagantly. No fancy clothes, no big vacations. Starting the campgrounds was the biggest leap they had taken, and Nick knew they both believed it could succeed by honest effort and hard-earned sweat. He also knew that his father worried about him. Francis did not like Nick's long hair and hippie rags. Francis worried that his son would not be ambitious, would not grow toward the things that inspired happiness: hard work, straightforward dealings, the saving of money. To his mind, youth culture eschewed all that. The kids seemed to be happy hanging around drinking wine or smoking dope all day, and Francis knew that would not lead to a life where mortgages got paid, children were fed and clothed, and a man's position in society was respected.

And Lisa Marie was promising to be even more of a handful. With the direction he and his sister were tending, plus the trouble the campgrounds seemed to be in, Nick couldn't blame his father for worrying. For drinking two scotches before going to bed. With the prospect of everything they'd worked for being washed away like so much horse fence in high water, he couldn't blame his mother for snapping out the way she did.

And yet he didn't feel like shouldering the blame. He was just being a kid. The long hair and patched bellbottoms were matters of style. The dope-smoking and wine-drinking were what kids did. His parents were smart enough to remember what they'd done at his age, were old enough to work out their differences. Were responsible enough to manage their bookkeeping.

Nick didn't think his father had spent a lot of time raising hell as a kid. The old man had been pretty sober even as a young guy. Both his parents had had meager childhoods, had grown up in the Great Depression, and then had faced World War II. There hadn't been room for fooling around, for dithering about what to do in life or for aimless hanging at the fishing access. And they weren't as emotionally open as people his age—at least his father wasn't. In fact, Lisa Marie had informed him last week that Kit was no longer sleeping in the bedroom. She had taken over Nick's old room and would turn in there while Francis was still at his desk.

Nick traced the erosion of his parents' relationship to the moment the campgrounds trickled into their lives. And it wasn't just the pressures of the business. It had something to do with Ted. Before the campgrounds, Ted might come around on weekends, might bring Charlie up for some fishing or canoeing and then come over to the Laurias' for a shared family meal. After dinner, the adults would sit on the porch with beers and watch the kids chase lightning bugs. But that kind of easy camaraderie had changed in the last few years.

What the hell. Nick watched his father navigate the Scout through the slosh of the flooded lane—his hands steady on the shifter and the steering wheel, his face calm and certain as he anticipated the next washout—and he saw the example he needed to follow. Steer a safe course between his parents for the rest of the summer and then drive on off to college. They'd either work out their problems or they wouldn't.

11

THE RAIN TAPERED off. The skies lightened. The river rose, but not enough to flood the campgrounds. The next day, Ted blew in like the tail of the storm. He roared down the driveway, driving his Buick too fast, as usual, raising a spray of mud all the way, and then braked and got out in one fluid motion, so it seemed like the momentum of the car ejected him into the parking lot. He paused, scanned the store and gas pumps and pavilion with a proprietary bearing, and then headed toward the office. When he saw Nick, Ted gave him the highball without breaking stride.

"You and Charlie up for a little canoe testing?" he asked.

"Sure," Nick said. He wanted to tell him about the guy in Phil Sweeney's trailer. "You—"

"We've got some salesmen coming in this afternoon. Gitchee-gumee Canoes," Ted said, and continued on to the office. "You guys give it a good workout."

"Yeah sure, man, but listen—"

"I'll catch up to you later, Nick. Got to talk to Francis."

At that moment the office door opened and Nick's father stepped out. Ted flashed his smile.

"Hey, Francis," he said. "Just telling Nick here we've got a canoe company coming in this afternoon, so he and Charlie can give it a shakedown—"

"What canoe company?" Francis looked startled.

"Gitcheegumee Canoes. I met them at the Sportsmen's Show. They're fairly new, eager to gain market share, and they're offering ..."

Ted rattled on about volume incentives and price breaks, but Nick could see his father processing the whole thing. Francis scanned the parking lot, the canoe shed, and the firewood bin, squinted and took in the whole panorama of the campgrounds winding down on a Sunday afternoon: travel trailers easing away from the dumping station, motor homes pulling out, Buff crawling from site to site for the last of the weekend's garbage. The place had been only half full this weekend due to the rain, and that made the third or fourth weekend like this. A string of washed-out weekends, and Ted wanted to buy more canoes. Francis's lips pressed tight.

"We need to go over the books, Ted," he said. "I've been waiting for you to show up. We need to make some decisions."

Ted let pass the reference to his absence. He and Francis were more than partners. They'd grown up close, even though Ted went to private schools in New Jersey, and Francis to the public school in Delaware Ford. They saw each other on weekends and through the summers. Ted always looked up to Francis, since Francis was older and doing things first: getting a rifle or a car, dating girls, going off to college. This made Ted want to catch up, to do things bigger and better. Once he became old enough to hunt, he lived in the woods and came out with big bucks and turkey gobblers and, by sixteen, a black bear. He bought a secondhand Plymouth convertible and souped it up, polished it up, and tore up the back roads with his prep school buddies. When Francis came home from Cornell, his flat gray Chevrolet looked pretty drab next to Ted's shiny red Plymouth.

There was one thing Ted could never top. Francis had served in World War II, had been a naval officer in the Pacific Fleet during the big sea-battles there—Java Sea, Coral Sea, Midway. His destroyer had been torpedoed off Guadalcanal, but he had dragged several wounded seamen onto a life raft and kept them alive until a rescue ship picked them up days later. The newspaper ran a big story about it, which Ted had clipped and saved. Ted was too young for this war; Korea would be his. He went and saw action, but it wasn't the same.

"We'll go over the books, Francis," Ted said. "But until our canoe supply can meet customer demand, we're losing revenue."

Francis shook his head. "We're not losing money on canoes. We're fully rented every weekend. Wish we could say the same for the campsites."

Ted puffed a little breath. "We're missing an opportunity. We're losing *potential* revenue. We're turning away canoeists every weekend—if we had a bigger fleet, we'd compensate for the empty sites."

"If, if, if," Francis said. "If we had the cash to spend on the canoes, no problem."

"It's just cash flow, Francis. Christ. We've had a rainy spring. Come July and August, we'll be fully populated on the sites, and the cash flow will straighten out. In the meantime—"

"In the meantime, we need to look at the books." Francis turned and headed back into the office.

Ted raised his eyebrows and flashed his smile at Nick, like *what you gonna do with a guy like this?* He said, "Find Charlie and free him up from whatever he's doing. I want you guys to give this boat a good workout."

He made a fist. "A good workout."

The campgrounds did need to expand its canoe fleet, which was a motley assortment of fiberglass Old Towns and Whites, aluminum Grummans and Searses, a dozen polypropylene off-brands. Every boat rented by nine o'clock Saturday morning and Nick had to turn people away. So Ted had sent word to the manufacturers, and one by one the sales reps started showing up. The hordes of tourists who took to the river every weekend were tough on canoes. They banged into each other, they aimed for the biggest rocks, they pounded the hulls with their paddles. They sank canoes deliberately. They tied canoes sloppily onto their roofs, and the canoes would fly off at sixty-five miles an hour. They smashed beer bottles into canoes, built campfires in them, scrawled graffiti on their sides.

Hamburgers, Nick and Charlie called them. Hamburgers from the city, come out to fry in the sun and wreck canoes. All the other liveries had discovered that Grumman canoes stood up best to the hamburgers' abuse, but Ted always had an eye for a deal.

Nick and Charlie loved it when canoe salesmen showed up. The salesmen had ultimate faith in the durability of their boats, and the boys had equal faith in their ability to make hamburgers look like choirboys. Their duty was to dish out more than the hamburgers ever could. If a canoe could stand up to Nick and Charlie, it could stand up. So when the Gitcheegumee guys pulled in with their yellow sixteen-footer, the boys slapped each other five, raised the tenor of their voices, exaggerated their strides. They tested on Tamarack Creek, where a particularly nasty falls would prove in a few minutes whether a canoe was worth its mettle. Nick and Charlie had been running Sawmill Falls every spring since they were big enough to paddle. They nicknamed it Boat Buster Falls, for a series of chutes and ledges and switchbacks where the creek dropped twelve feet in a short distance. Trying to paddle it during spring runoff or after a heavy rain was like being a leaf in a fire hose. You went wherever the water wanted you to go.

While the Gitcheegumee guys were in the office talking with Francis and Ted, Nick and Charlie checked out the canoe. It was a nice-looking boat, they had to give it that. Its bright yellow paint would appeal to the campers more than the dull-metal Grummans. But Charlie pointed out the rivets.

"Look," he said, running his finger down the keel. "They're spaced like every six inches. The rivet heads stick up like dandelion heads waiting for the mower. They'll sheer off on the first rock."

On Grumman canoes, the keel rivets were spaced every quarter inch, and they were filed flush with the keel.

"There's only three ribs," Nick observed. "Grummans have five."

"And the sheet metal's thin."

The suits had come out of the office, and one of them—pudgy, with little mustachios—overhead Charlie's last remark. He rapped the hull with his knuckles.

"That's aircraft-grade aluminum," he said. "Heat-stretched during the manufacturing process so a thinner gauge can be utilized. You get a lighter weight while maximizing durability. And the paint is baked on in industrial ovens, so that . . ."

While this one was reciting the Gitcheegumee brochure, the other one—wiry and clean-cut, like a cross-country runner—pulled a two-by-four from the backseat.

"It'll take a beating, this baby."

He stepped in front of his partner and whacked the canoe on the hull. Gave it a pretty good rap, but Nick noticed he was careful to aim for a rib, something the river rocks rarely had the courtesy to do. Whacked it again.

"They're tough, these Gitchees. We sell a lot of them to summer camps and Scout troops, where they see more rigorous use than in private ownership."

"You guys are gonna love this canoe," the pudgy Gitcheegumee guy said. "We hear you're the official test drivers."

Nick and Charlie said they'd like to try it out. After the recent heavy rains, they'd have a wild ride.

"Whatever you can throw at it," the wiry guy said.

He drove Nick, Charlie, and Francis up along the creek, while the other guy stayed with Ted at the office. To iron out some wrinkles, Ted said.

They put in where the bridge to Tamarack Lake crossed the road. The Gitcheegumee guy pointed out further strong points: "high-displacement flotation bulkheads," "comfort-molded portage yoke," and "self-bailing seats." Self-bailing seats?

The water ran fast and brown from all the rain—a creek in flood stage—and Nick and Charlie dug into it. The canoe floated high and paddled reasonably well. They shot off around the first bend, and Francis and the Gitcheegumee guy drove to the pulloff above the falls. Nick and Charlie tried to get the feel of the canoe.

"Tracks straight," Charlie said. "That big keel."

Nick tried some pry and draw strokes from the bow, tried to horse it around a little.

"Doesn't want to maneuver, though."

"That should come in real handy," Charlie said, "we get into the falls."

The banks got steeper as the creek veered away from the road. The water picked up. They could hear the falls ahead, and Nick got that quickened-blood quiver in his stomach. He dropped into a kneeling position. Charlie did the same.

Approaching Sawmill Falls was dramatic. Before the creek switched back toward the road, the water ran fast and caused a deep rumble from beyond the bend. Then they swept around and the creek seemed to drop away. They faced a forty-foot shale ledge up to the road, and a mist hanging above the dropoff. Their blood pounded and they paddled like crazy to build up speed for maneuverability, and then they were in it.

The last thing Nick saw before they headed down the first drop was his father and the Gitcheegumee guy, two small figures leaning on the guardrail way above.

The first drop was a clean, fast chute with a small standing wave at the bottom, and the canoe handled it okay. Riding high, it took on only a little water. After that, things got hairy. The creek tightened up, switched left and then right. It dropped steeply. The middle ledges were the boat busters, because the volume of water was forced through a narrow chute, and at the far edge of every switchback sat a big rock. And plenty in between. Some of the rocks were ground flat, so the creek would spit the canoe onto them like a stranded fish. Others were jagged wall or gnarly ledge, waiting to rip open a hull.

They had run this falls many times, and they tried hard now. They paddled fast and hugged the inside of the left switchback, but they took on some more water. They tried to horse the Gitcheegumee into the center of the current. The creek cut right and down, like a banked curve, and it slammed them against the ledge. Aluminum grated with an ugly grunt. They sheared off and kept going. The creek dropped into its steepest section, and they paddled hard, running downhill straight at a jumble of boulders with the riotous white water, the rush making them all nerve endings and quick responses and strong as beavers, but not as strong as the flooded creek and not as strong as the steep downhill angle sucking all the water in the boat toward the bow, which drove the nose deeper into the creek and made it harder to horse sideways, and *wham!* when you hit an underwater rock at that speed you know it. The rock hit behind Nick's knees with a terrific impact; the hull crumpled and pinned his feet against the seat, and then the rock screeched hideously down the length of the canoe.

Nick untangled himself from the seat, but the bow wandered off-center and *wham!* they took another shot as a jagged ledge hove in the left gunwale and popped the center thwart. They yawed dangerously and took on a good deal of creek, tried to keep the canoe upright, and fortunately they *wham!* nailed another ledge on the right, which straightened them out, but which also ripped a six-inch hole in front of Charlie's right knee. Heat-stretched aircraft-grade aluminum peeled back like a Bud can.

Ahead, Stay-to-the-Left Rock. That's what they always called it, because if you were to run the falls successfully, it was crucial to stay to the left of this knife-edged black rock that jutted straight out of the center of the creek. If you went to the right of it, you got jammed into the top of the waterfall. You had to stay left to hold the current, which blasted through a narrow chasm in the ledge.

"Left!" Nick hollered to Charlie. "Hard to the left!"

But crippled as they were, and loaded up with water, the canoe was sluggish. Nick couldn't bring the bow around in time, and *wham!* the worst thing that could happen happened: The bow struck the right side of Stay-to-the-Left Rock, and the stern got caught in the current. The canoe swung around, and there they were, headed into the worst chute of the falls—backwards.

They backpaddled like crazy to hit the chute dead center, but they missed. The creek shoved them up onto the last ledge before the drop, and they hung there a moment, Charlie's end sticking out into thin air, and the water in the canoe rushing from Nick's end to his, sending all the weight his way, and the Gitcheegumee's keel couldn't handle the stress. When it broke, Nick saw three things: the keel kinking like a soda straw and the hull crinkling and splitting; the accumulated water in the boat shooting forward and washing Charlie out backwards; and, an absurd vision, the wiry Gitcheegumee guy somehow instantly at the bottom of the falls—he could only have flown down that cliffside—waving his arms and yelling, "Stop! Stop! Please stop!" as if they had the power to do so. This happened in an instant, and Nick was in frenetic motion again as the broken canoe toppled off the ledge and the creek slammed it down through the last drop. Charlie's empty end hit first and disappeared under water. Nick's end flipped on over, and end over end he rode out the rest of the waterfall by clinging to the seat. The self-bailing seat.

A huge standing wave waited at the bottom of the falls. As Nick toppled down he could see Charlie stuck in it—it had a powerful vortex that could suck you in and keep you there—and Charlie was bobbing head up, head down, like a cork. What was left of the canoe bore down on him like a yellow freight train, and Nick managed to lean out and grab Charlie by his ponytail, and the force of all the wreckage blowing by was enough to yank him out of the suction.

And then they floated in the pool below, Charlie leaking a little blood from his forehead. They were surrounded by shards of aluminum. The "high-displacement flotation bulkheads" were about the only parts of the Gitcheegumee that still functioned, and they kept the thing from sinking completely.

"I'd say the Gitcheegumee flunked," Charlie said.

"I'd say we flunked. We should never have hit Stay-to-the-Left Rock that way."

"We wouldn't have," Charlie said, "if this thing handled at all. With that honking big keel, it wouldn't go sideways."

"Jesus!" the Gitcheegumee guy cried from the shore. "Jesus!"

Nick felt sorry for him, and for the first time he wondered if they oughtn't to test-drive canoes in some little puss riffle on the Delaware. They dragged the pieces of the canoe out where the embankment graded off, hauled the yellow mess up to the road. They had some trouble getting it to stay on the roof rack, but with enough rope and duct tape, they got it all attached.

Back at the campgrounds, Ted and the pudgy Gitcheegumee guy waited in the parking lot. Nick thought the other guy would flip out when he saw the canoe, but he maintained his salesman's smile, and Nick saw him wink at his buddy.

Ted shook his head. He was used to the boys coming back from test drives.

"Well," he said. "I see we've got another winner."

"Handles okay in flat water," Charlie said. "Not worth a shit in the rapids."

"Well," Ted said. "It's mostly flat eddies out on the river."

Charlie pointed to the broken keel.

"Rivets stick out like targets," he said. "Be popping 'em like buttons off a fat man's shirt."

"The keel's too deep for the river," Nick said. "Bang along every riffle."

"Aluminum's thin, too," Charlie said. "Nick'll be patching 'em up like an old pair of jeans."

The lean Gitcheegumee guy started to protest, but Ted held up his hand.

"That's too bad, boys," he said, giving one of his winning smiles. "We just bought a hundred of them."

It was a typical Ted move. Get everybody involved like they've got some stake in the matter, and then go do whatever he felt like anyway. It must have driven the old man nuts, Nick thought. If Ted woke up in the morning with the notion that renting pop-up tent campers was a good idea, by that evening there might be a dozen of them lined up across from the office.

When Ted announced that he'd already signed the deal, Francis paused for a long contemplative moment, and Nick recognized the look. It was the look you give when another person has let you down, the same look Nick had gotten when he brought home a lousy report card or a ding on the car. Francis stared at all of them—at the Gitcheegumee guys for bringing this piece of junk onto the property, at Nick and Charlie for wrecking a perfectly functional boat. He saved his longest stare for Ted. He didn't say a word, though; he just plunked at a shard of aluminum on top of the car. The metal vibrated like a Jew's harp. Francis turned and walked away.

Ted clapped the pudgy Gitcheegumee guy on the shoulder and said, "Looks like Francis agrees—I've made yet another brilliant business decision."

The salesman started to yuck it up, but Ted's smile turned hard. He clamped down on the guy's shoulder.

"You better not have fucked me with these tin cans," he said and held the salesman fast.

The Gitcheegumee guys retreated to the car, and the yellow shards of canoe flopped all the way out the driveway.

"I got a great price on those canoes," Ted said. "Even before you guys showed up with Exhibit A. Wait'll you see the deal they give us on the next hundred."

"They're not worth it," Charlie said. "They're not gonna hold up."

"They're expendable," Ted said. "They're a consumable in this business, a write-off. Who cares if you bang through a couple hundred a season? At the price I got, they're profitable after six weekends. With the money we'll make, we can sell them all for scrap in November and buy a new fleet in the spring."

Nick knew his father did not view equipment this way. You didn't buy things in order to watch them fall apart. You bought things—or built things—that would last. Nick decided to steer clear of his father all afternoon. And he'd skip telling Ted about the guy in Phil Sweeney's trailer.

12

IN THE BACK of the truck, Charlie worked with his shirt off. He slung the haybales up and into the loft, where Nick stacked them in the dim, dusty barnlight. Nick wore his long sleeves buttoned at the wrist, his collar at the neck, but the air was so thick with hayseeds and chaff that he itched like someone afflicted with pox.

He would have preferred working out in the sunshine, but Eva had insisted on sketching Charlie. No trail rides were scheduled for this morning, and Eva had been helping Kit and Stacey tidy up the stalls when the big red truck loaded with bales had backed up to the barn. She had traded the pushbroom for her sketchpad, climbed up onto the load, and begun whipping quick strokes across the page as Charlie worked.

"Take off your shirt," she'd said after a few minutes.

Charlie had been only too happy to oblige. He was a natural showoff and he appreciated Eva's attention. Working out in the sunshine, latching onto the undisturbed bales and swinging them through the haymow door, Charlie could get by with a minimum of chafe. He could breathe clean air. He could hold a pose when Eva asked him to. He could bask in Eva's attention and put the resulting energy into his tossing of the bales. These were first-cut bales, green and heavy, but under Eva's scrutiny Charlie kept swinging like a pendulum, working his way down, course by course.

"Hold it a sec," Eva called as Charlie leaned over to grab a bale. "I want to get your lats."

Charlie did have a great build. He wasn't as big and beefy as his father, but he had gotten Ted's musculature on his mother's tighter frame. He would work all day in cutoffs and workboots, and the silver ankh on a thong glimmered against his tan chest. Nick had seen married women—in pairs, sometimes; their husbands gone back to the city for the workweek—call and wave to Charlie from their cars or trailers as he cut lumber for a new tent platform or delivered firewood on Grandpa's little orchard tractor.

Charlie bent over the bale and flexed his latissimi dorsi as Eva requested, and Nick took advantage of the break to lean out of the loft door and clear his lungs. Marvin Gaye's "Heard It Through the Grapevine" came pumping out of the truck cab. The hay was about half unloaded; the pitching would get more difficult. Several of the off-duty horses, curious, had milled up to the pasture fence, and they touched noses with their saddled compatriots on the near side. They looked good, the horses. His mother kept them in fine shape, and now the sun shone off their flanks and their bright saddle blankets winked from under the leather. Nick could hear his mother's boots as she moved from stall to stall, could hear her muffled voice as she spoke to Stacey.

His mother had always been a farm girl. But after she left her father's farm, she would have nothing more to do with cows. For someone whose childhood had revolved around the twice-daily milking, for whom the muck of the barnyard seemed as viscous and miring as quicksand, and to whom the sight of a glass of milk would cause a gag reflex, running a riding stables was a pleasure. The work was gentleman-farmer stuff, the horses not really farm animals. Horses were clean, for one thing. Sure, they needed to be groomed, and their stalls had to be mucked out, but they did not stand around outside the barn door churning the ground to soup. They did not flop down in the mud to ruminate, cover their teats with grit. When horses shit, they did not cut loose with a stench and a splatter that would encrust the pasture with scabs; they passed discreet, perfect turds that steamed on the ground like fresh-baked muffins. Horses were far preferable to dairy cows. They were big pets.

Nick heard his mother's boots stop, then approach the front end of the barn, then stop again.

"Eva?" she called. "You up there bothering those boys?"

"I'm helping them with the hay," Eva called back.

"I'll bet."

The Doors' "Touch Me" came on the radio, and Eva swayed a little to the music. When the phone rang, the clanger outside the loft door made them all jump.

It was his father, Nick could tell by his mother's voice. She spoke matter-of-factly, as she did with anybody who called, but with more familiarity.

Then she exploded.

"He did *what?*

"A thousand pounds of grass seed?

"Well, what would an investor want with a thousand pounds of grass seed from Agway?

"Who is this investor?

"Francis! How do we wind up with an investor we've never even met? Whose name we don't know? Someone who has put money into this business without our knowledge?"

A pause while Francis said something on the other end.

"And now, without our knowledge, money has gone out of the business? And we find that out only when we go to the store and learn we have no credit? That we've paid somebody off in grass seed?"

Eva mouthed "Whoa" to Charlie and folded up her sketchpad and slipped down the side of the truck.

"What's going on, Francis? They don't have grass seed in New Jersey? They've got to get it from us? Something's fishy as hell—"

Charlie grimaced and tossed another bale.

"—I believe you don't know about it. That's the problem. We don't know where our money's going, and that's—

"Fine. So fine. So what about the next time? This isn't the—

"They're unloading the truck. Then I've got a job for them. They'll be over after lunch."

They heard Kit climbing up the truck bed, and Charlie increased the pace of his bale-slinging.

"Francis needs you guys," she said when she surfaced. "But I've got a woodchuck in the lower flats I'd like you to take care of. His hole is at the edge of the trail, and somebody's going to step into it and pitch off their rider, and then we'll have a lawsuit on our hands."

"Okay," Nick said. "We'll be done here in fifteen minutes."

"Take the twenty-two from my office," Kit said. "I'll leave a box of long rifles on the desk. You can take the thirty-eight from the truck if you think you can hit anything with it."

"We'll stick with the twenty-two."

"Okay. But get down there before too long. He comes out when the sun is high, and if you don't get the drop on him, you won't get the chance."

"We'll get the drop on him," Charlie assured her.

13

A THOUSAND POUNDS of grass seed! She dipped the sponge into the bucket of disinfectant, ran it across Midnight's shoulder, and tried to make the idea of a thousand pounds of grass seed fit in her mind.

It wasn't adding up yet. Yes, Ted owed people money. That part she knew. Yes, there was venture capital behind the business, since the Bank of Delaware Ford had chosen not to support the campgrounds in the beginning. Too much risk, Chuck Van Vooren had said. An unproven market. But Kit had always suspected that the Van Voorens and Busches and, no doubt, the Brewsters, too—since they were all in cahoots on what happened or did not happen in town—had had other plans for the Lauria land, some real-estate development that Harry Busch had in mind, or they simply wanted to keep other development down so that the Holy Trinity retained control. *Too much noise*, they'd written in letters to the editor. *This project will bring in a rowdy element.* So Ted and Francis had had to seek financing elsewhere, and Ted had connections.

But she and Francis had always been aware of these arrangements. They had cosigned the notes that came on legal-looking letterhead from companies in Connecticut and Manhattan. She had never signed anything that said they'd pay somebody off in grass seed. She squeezed the sponge on Midnight's withers and wiped the disinfectant across his broad back.

If they owed someone a payment, why not pay in cash? Well, cash was tight. No doubt about it. Ted had bought all those canoes. They'd arrived this week on two tractor trailers, bright yellow and nestled like sardines. He had to get that payment from someplace. Francis watched over the local books with vigilance. He hadn't made the payment. Hadn't even seen an invoice, he said. So where did Ted get the money for a hundred canoes?

From this unnamed investor? And grass seed?

Midnight quivered under her touch. She found a nick in his hide—a fence barb, probably, or maybe he had rolled onto something sharp—and gave it extra attention with the disinfectant.

Ted always had a hidden side, that she knew. Oh, he was charming. He could charm you out of your pants. When Francis first introduced her to him—in '47 or '48—Ted was still a brash young college man. He was cocky. He always seemed to be moving forward quickly, in his car, on his feet, with his conversation. Always moving beyond where you were, taking you with him—acknowledging your current situation or the story you had to tell—but packing that under his arm and using it to take you to wherever he wanted to go. He behaved like a man who knew he could get anything he wanted: a good grade from a professor, a good time with a girl. That smile lit up his face and his eyes hit you with their high beams and pinned you like a deer.

His image came with a flash of light across her mind's eye, for that is how he first appeared to her. Francis had taken her blueberry picking along the riverbank when he stopped and chuckled, "Hey . . ." She followed his squint into a patch of sunlight rippling across the surface and saw a head, a powerful surge swelling a wave before it, the head again.

"Ted Miles," Francis had said, and she had looked closer to see the fellow she'd heard so much about, watched his breast stroke surge again and again before he stood in the shallows and shook himself like a dog and then moved out of the sun towards them, adjusting his trunks and stepping gingerly on the stones. He appeared in backlit silhouette as broad-shouldered and tapering as an elm tree. She noticed the downward musculature of his loins and the taut density of his chest and then Francis cleared his throat and called, "Hey, Johnny Weissmuller, how's the water?"

Ted jumped, startled, and in the instant that he recognized Francis and took her in, focused on her, he smiled and seemed to glow brighter, and then he ran his hands over his chest and legs, frisked the water out of his blond fuzz.

"Water's perfect," he said. "So this must be Kit."

She offered her hand and he took it and said, "Why, Francis, I don't blame you for keeping her to yourself," and she felt the blush rising.

"Where you swimming from?" Francis asked.

"Long Eddy," Ted replied, nodding upriver.

Francis whistled.

"How far is that?" she asked.

"Fifteen miles."

"You swam fifteen miles?" she exclaimed. He shrugged and Francis explained how Ted was a record-holding swimmer at Princeton and how he swam long distances in the river to stay in training. Ted listened with a bemused smile, then summed it up with two words— "Breast stroke"—and broke into a big grin that took in not only her eyes and face but her whole being.

It was this image that came back to her when she thought of him, which was often in the early years of her courtship and marriage, and which caused her no small measure of disturbance. She told herself that she should redirect her thoughts to Francis, the man to whom she was bound and whom she loved as water loves a rock. But still. She couldn't help her thoughts at odd moments: when she was undressing for her bath, say, or later, nursing her young son.

Or when Ted smiled at her, which, too, was often in those early days. There had been late evenings in those years, at first with Francis and Ted and a girlfriend of Ted's, driving from roadhouse to roadhouse in Ted's convertible, rushing forward in the inky, close night and feeling Ted's big-animal warmth from the front seat and her husband's vitality next to her, quieter and yet stronger. Later, after Ted had married Margaret, the two couples had sat on the porch of the Little House—Nicky and Charlie tucked safely into Nicky's single crib upstairs—and they drank highballs and watched the lightning bugs and Ted would tell stories about Korea, having been back only a year. He tried to draw Francis into his war stories but Francis wouldn't say anything, so Ted would go on anyway, gesturing with his hands and hitting her with his smile and keeping her drink refreshed from the bottle and the bowl of ice cubes at his feet, going on about his own plans for a business and how they all had plans, back then, to start raising their families and bring them along and teach their sons to fish and hunt and play ball and have more kids, and then, after they had all laughed and gotten tipsy in their chairs and the men had retreated across the tracks several times to "water down the ties," Ted and Margaret would get up and bid their adieus, and hug and kiss, a friendly sort of well-wishing, but still, she could feel in the way he rubbed her back when they kissed goodnight that Ted was already moving beyond the moment to somewhere he wanted to be, and she had to pull herself back. She was sure that Francis did not rub Margaret's back so when they said goodnight, but she could not help the small purr that rose in her throat as Ted kissed her, and then, parting, the happy calls of farewell as Ted and Margaret stumbled arm in arm up the lane and Margaret's shriek upon stumbling or turning an ankle, and Ted's deep chuckle.

She ran the sponge down Midnight's flank, so lean and sleek. He liked to take the lead position on the trail, leg it out ahead of the others. Like Ted with the thousand pounds of grass seed, someplace out in front of her and Francis.

14

THEY DIDN'T GET the drop on him. They could see the chuck shambling through the pasture grass and then popping up to look around. When the chuck raised up, they stopped.

"Can you hit him from here?" Charlie asked.

"Not with this," Nick replied.

When the chuck returned to feeding, they moved again. When he raised up, they stopped.

This time the chuck stood facing them, his squinty face all attention.

"He's seen us," Charlie whispered.

The chuck stood still for twenty seconds, then shuffled toward his hole. Nick dropped to one knee and took aim.

At his hole, the chuck raised up tall, took one look—too quick to form a target—issued a shrill warning whistle, and dropped from sight.

"We can try waiting him out," Charlie said.

They hid in the tall grass on the riverbank, where they had a clean shot at the hole. But Nick knew it was a waste of time—once the chuck was spooked, he was down for a while.

"So what's Ted up to?" he asked.

"Oh, man." Charlie shook his head. "Who knows?"

"A thousand pounds of grass seed? That's pretty weird."

"Pretty weird, all right." Charlie gazed out over the river. "No wonder your mom's pissed off."

"She's pissed off all right. She's perpetually pissed off." Nick batted at the tall grass. "Is Ted down at Basking Ridge at all?"

"I don't think so. I haven't been there much myself. But I don't think he's in line for the Ward Cleaver All-American Husband Award or anything. He and Margaret have found some way to tolerate each other, I guess."

"What about that guy down at Phil's trailer?" Nick asked. "Why would he have a photo of Ted?"

"Beats me," Charlie said. "Beats the hell out of me."

Nick sensed Charlie didn't want to pursue this. Ted was a sore spot with them all.

"So what's up with you and Eva?" he asked.

"Don't know, man." Charlie turned his face up toward the sun, shut his eyes. "I'm following her lead."

"She still going out with Georgie?"

"Yeah. Still going out with Georgie. Georgie Porgie."

"But Georgie doesn't know about you."

"There's nothing to know. Nothing's happened."

" 'Take off your shirt, big boy,' " Nick mimicked. " 'Dig those lats.' "

"Hey, what the hell. She's studying art."

"She's studying you, man. You see the way she checks you out down at the fishing access?"

"Yeah, maybe. I don't know." Charlie breathed in the river air and sunshine. "Rich chicks, man. They like fucking with your head more than your bod."

Maybe. Maybe that's all Eva was doing, but Nick didn't think so.

"And look who's talking," Charlie said. "Darlene's all over you. Like she can't wait to jump your bones."

"Jeez, I don't know," Nick said. "Darlene's pretty young."

"Old enough to bleed, old enough to breed. You ought to be moving on that."

"Oh man. Old Man Van Vooren's like to nail us with his flyrod some morning."

"Specially if Eva decides to go for another little swim in front of us."

"Jesus." Nick aimed the .22 at a rock in the middle of the river. What the hell. He fired to release some tension, to hear the ricochet. *Braaannng!* Like in the movies.

"Don't do that, man," Charlie said. "What if there's somebody in the woods over there?"

"What're they doing over there?" Nick put up a bullshit defense. "It's private property."

"So don't shoot them for trespassing, okay?"

They heard a banging of aluminum, and a raft of canoes floated into view. Bunch of hamburgers in bathing suits, doing typical hamburger stuff: banging on the gunwales with their paddles, war-whooping, splashing at each other. Five canoes making a general nuisance of themselves, disturbing the peace of the valley. One big hairy-chested guy stood in his canoe and chugged a bottle of beer and then heaved the bottle at the rock Nick had shot. He missed; the bottle splashed and then bobbed up two feet downstream.

Hamburgers disturbing the peace was one thing—it was natural to cut loose a little. But throwing beer bottles into the river was another. Charlie leaned forward in the tall grass.

"Pick it up!" he yelled.

The hairy hamburger turned. He couldn't see them. He spread his arms wide towards the riverbank and belched loudly.

"Pick it up yourself, asshole."

Charlie started to get up, but Nick hissed him down. The canoes drifted about twenty feet from the rock, and the hairy hamburger clowned for his pals, thrusting his chest toward the grasses. The other hamburgers laughed. Someone said, "Yeah—pick it the fuck up yourself, hick."

Nick raised the .22. If the hamburger saw it come up through the grass, he gave no sign. Nick aimed at the downstream face of the rock, so the ricochet would glance down and into the river, and Charlie didn't do a thing to stop him. The .22 cracked, the ricochet *braaannng*ed, and the hairy hamburger hit the deck. In the moment of stunned silence before ten paddles tore into the river, Charlie let them know he still meant it.

"Only good litterbug is a dead litterbug!" he yelled. "Now *pick up that bottle!*"

While the hairy hamburger heaved toward the bottle, Nick couldn't help it—he still had the gun up—the guy came paddling into his sights, and Nick was overcome with revulsion: He drew a bead on the guy. He knew he hadn't chambered another round. He kept his finger outside the trigger guard. But still, as the front iron came up on the guy's fat, churning profile, Nick felt the beginning of something he had never felt before—a distancing, a stepping outside of himself to observe an act taking place, and underneath, a deep, nervous quiver. Charlie grabbed the barrel and forced it down to the grass.

"Are you fucking crazy?"

The hairy hamburger reached the bottle and scooped it into his canoe. He held it up with one hand, a surrender flag, and kept paddling with the other. That deep-down quiver broke through and Nick felt awash, as if every membrane had given way and water flowed through him. He turned loose the .22.

"Maybe," he said. "Maybe I was, for a second."

Charlie cranked out the clip and set the empty rifle on his far side.

"You ever think what it'd be like, killing Viet Cong?" he asked.

Nick nodded. Every time he got a letter from Felix. Whenever Denny Evans pulled in with his useless legs.

"Yeah, well, I have, too," Charlie said. "And not just war-hero daydreams, either. I mean really thinking about what it'd be like to kill another man. You go to these people's country, you're all full of John Wayne movies, you've got some gung-ho son of a bitch wrapping you in the flag, and you've got more firepower in one hand than they've seen in their whole lives. They're planting rice with their feet, they're cutting bamboo with knives. The closest thing they've got to a tank is a water buffalo.

"You ever draw down on somebody?" Charlie went on. "I mean for real? Not screwing around, shooting to miss like you just did, but really draw a bead on a person?"

Downriver, the hamburgers were headed around the bend.

"I have, man," Charlie said. "Last fall, at school. You're not allowed to have guns there, but I had my little Winchester in the back of the closet. I don't know why. To be different from the preppies, I guess. There was a football game one afternoon, and the dorm was empty. I didn't feel like all that rah-rah bullshit. I was thinking about those twerps out there rooting over some stupid game and I was thinking about Felix, how he's only a couple of years older than them and he knows real combat, not just make-believe. He played football but now he's not gonna get up from a hard tackle and walk back to the bench.

"Next thing I knew I had the gun out." Charlie raised the .22 and aimed it at the rock. "And I was screwing around, staying back from the window, leading people as they walked to the game. But then I had to, I don't know . . . up the ante. I raised the window. There was this big maple tree out there, and its leaves had all turned red. It gave me pretty good cover. I started drawing a tighter lead as the targets got fewer. Most everybody was at the game. I looked both directions—nobody. I loaded the clip."

Charlie slipped the clip into the .22.

"Then along the walk came this one old guy. Sixty or so. Sweater and a tweed cap, not hurrying, not rushing. Enjoying a walk on an autumn day. He was somebody's dad or an alum, I don't know. I imagined I was a sniper and this was Charlie Cong. Every ounce of training I ever had, every warning about not pointing the gun at somebody, every word that Ted ever spoke about hunter safety came back to me, but as I brought that shiny bead up on the guy's tweed hat, and saw the red of the maple leaves glinting off it, I began to feel the power, and the . . . the *intimacy*—I was closer to this guy, in this moment, than his wife had ever been, than his mother even. I could take him out."

Charlie set the gun back down in the grass.

"You know how it feels? It feels powerful and it feels vile. And you know that you can choose not to do it."

Charlie paused and gazed across the river.

"I'm choosing not to do it."

"What do you mean?" Nick asked.

"I've been thinking about going for a conscientious objector defer-ment. I'm getting some literature. Got it back at the lodge."

"Oh, man," Nick said. "You don't have to worry about the VC killing you. Butch Deeker and the guys at the Depot'll do it."

"Why have a choice if you don't use it?" Charlie asked. "Where's the freedom? You think your buddy Butch and the other vets made a free choice when they went to Vietnam? Maybe. Maybe not. Maybe they let themselves get sucked along because they didn't have the balls to say, no, I'm not gonna kill some poor bastard on his way to the rice paddy."

"You'll be in school next fall. You'll have a student deferment."

"I'll have a student deferment as long as I'm a student. If I stop being a student, I stop having a student deferment. It seems kind of soft, anyway."

Nick plucked at some grass. Jesus, Charlie.

He wasn't sure he could take such a stand. Once, while he was helping Grandpa with the eel rack, the old man had tried to teach him the importance of doing so. Grandpa had told Nick how the history of the river valley had been changed by men who acted when they needed to. When Daniel Skinner acted on his idea of floating hemlock logs down to Philadelphia for ships' masts, he'd single-handedly started the forest-products business in the Upper Delaware Valley. That industry had changed over the years—into the tannic acid factories during the nineteenth century and the logging and lumbering of the twentieth—but it still employed local families who could trace their livelihoods back to Skinner's decision.

"He seized the moment," Grandpa said, and went on to give examples of others: the Busches with their bluestone quarries, Nick's great-great-grandfather Tegeler carving one of the first farms out of the Pennsylvania woods. "If they hadn't made their stand when they had to, we wouldn't be here today."

Grandpa had taken Nick to the extreme upriver end of the eel weir, where the stones broke the water. He brought up a new stone.

"Watch," he said, and placed the stone at the leading edge of the wing. "See how the water flows on either side? That stone is now making a stand for this entire eel weir. It's changing the current of the Delaware. Not in a big way, but enough to help funnel eels into our rack. We'll owe our dinners next winter to this stone."

His grandfather's face was lined and creased even then.

"When your time comes to seize the moment," Grandpa said, "you'll do as this stone does."

Nick had always believed he could do that, but still. Conscientious objector. It sounded seriously subversive.

Charlie stood up, unloaded the .22 again, and pocketed the clip.

"Screw it, man," he said. "And screw this woodchuck. Let's go see what Francis wants."

15

NICK WASN'T SURPRISED to see vehicles backed up along the campgrounds driveway. But these weren't the usual Airstreams and Winnebagos. Oh, there were motor homes and cars pulling trailers. Pickup campers, too. But strapped to every available surface were extension ladders and long-handled implements, burlap sacks and wooden barrels and steel oil drums. Goats and chickens peeked out of truck racks. In the beds of pickups, dark-eyed kids clambered over rolls of roofing paper.

They were Gypsies. No little band of traveling minstrels and tinkers, this was a full-boat extended family, an entire Gypsy clan. They mobbed the campgrounds office—swarthy, handsome people of all ages, from white-haired old gaffers to virile men and women to swarms and swarms of Gypsy children. Speaking a language that Nick couldn't understand, they filled the store with a wild commotion. The men at the counter argued with Francis over the price of a two-week stay, and the kids stripped the shelves of candy and gum. The women washed their arms and faces at the outside spigot, even though there was a ladies' room inside.

Francis assigned them to the campsites in the field across from the store. He wanted them close at hand.

"This crowd is trouble," he said. "They want to stay two weeks and do roof and driveway jobs in the area. Keep your eye on them."

The Gypsies trundled their vehicles across the field and pitched camp at the base of Cemetery Hill. The cemetery couldn't be seen from below, just Grandpa Nick's barn perched on the hillside. The Gypsies erected screen houses, strung clotheslines between trees. They made a corral out of aluminum extension ladders and herded in their animals: some goats, a sow and her pigs, a bunch of chickens. The kids headed off to town. A Gypsy man took over the pay phone outside the office and stayed on it all afternoon. Periodically he dispatched his assistant, a feral-looking kid about ten years old, over to the camp and then one of the pickups would spin a trail of dust out the driveway.

Nick left the Gypsies to themselves and got busy. Fridays at the campgrounds were the best. The excitement began to build in the afternoon, with the first of the weekend campers. These early arrivals got the choice campsites and special attention: extra picnic tables or garbage barrels, help with hooking up their electric and water. They tipped Nick and Charlie a couple of bucks or beers, and then towards evening more campers arrived and the boys had to skip the personal favors. They filled propane bottles, delivered firewood, pumped holding tanks. It worked up their energy, got them wired. They cruised through the sites and by the time darkness fell they knew where the best tippers were and the available girls, and still new arrivals kept coming so they worked by headlights or lantern light to set up tents and level trailers and get campfires going.

Towards dusk, a red-and-white sheriff's car pulled up to the office. The deputy went inside and consulted with Francis, and then he took his cruiser and made a slow pass by the Gypsies' site.

Miller barreled up in his Rutabaga, the unmuffled exhaust roaring.

"What's all the goddamn excitement?" he asked.

"Sheriff just left," Francis said. "They've received nine complaints from businesses in town, and a slew of phone calls from the people these Gypsies are soliciting for work."

"That's what they're saying over town," Miller said. "In the gin mill it's all the goddamn Gypsies this, the goddamn Gypsies that."

Miller removed his cigar, which had gone out, and sniffed it. He spit into the dust and gestured toward the Gypsy camp.

"Crew like this passes through every few years," he said. "They'll sell you a driveway topping for twenty-five bucks, and it sounds like a great deal till you give the driveway a day to dry out, and it don't, and you give it another day, and it don't. Just sets there sticky and black, ain't no way you're gonna drive the family see-dan onto it. And finally you check around and everybody in the countryside's in the same boat—they got a driveway full of dirty thirty-weight, and the goddamn Gypsies are long gone."

"Miller," Francis said. "We've got to do something."

"Kick 'em the hell out."

"We'll have to refund their deposit if we do that, and it's a darn good chunk of change." Smoke from the Gypsies' cooking fires rose into the trees below Grandpa's barn. Nick thought his father's response was a little off-key. Francis Lauria was not a man to equivocate over a matter of ethics versus money. You could always make money, but once you sold out your ethics, you were broke for good.

"We can use that deposit," Francis said. "If they leave of their own accord, we don't have to refund it."

Miller studied his cigar, as if pondering what the kids from town had been doing to his Rum-Soaked Crooks, nights, to keep them from drawing. He fired another match, sucked and blew, and when he was satisfied that he had created a sufficient cloud around himself and Francis and the boys, he grinned.

"Gypsies are great at taking everybody else's money," he said. "Let's see if we can't reverse the goddamn trend."

He regarded Nick and Charlie. "You guys know anything about Gypsies?"

"Some cute chicks over there," Charlie said.

"You come with me and see 'em up close," Miller said. "Get a little education before you go off to college."

Most of the vehicles in the Gypsy camp bore California plates, occasionally Nevada. Men strummed guitars under canvas awnings and passed jugs of wine back and forth. Women called to each other. Chickens scuttled this way and that. The smell of grilling meat wafted through the air. Nick and Charlie sneaked looks at the Gypsy girls clustered behind the trailers, but they were closely guarded by tough-looking guys their own age.

"Look like they'd cut your throat without blinking," Charlie said.

"Ahh," Miller said. "They're scareder of you than you are of them. Funny bunch, Gypsies. Used to be a lot of 'em jump off the trains, back when. Flighty. Superstitious as hell."

Miller seemed to know where he was going. Toward the middle of the camp, the center of attention was a long Prowler travel trailer. Miller walked up to it, and two men broke from the fireplace. Though they did not appear unfriendly, they clearly blocked Miller's path.

"Help you?" one of them said.

"Evening, gents," Miller said. "You folks settling in okay?"

"Doing fine," the man said. He faced Miller eye to eye.

"Wanted to introduce ourselves to the Queen," Miller said. "Extend a formal greeting of welcome, so to speak."

The two Gypsy men didn't move, but a woman called from the group.

"Come over, gentlemen. Please."

The men let them pass. Nick could feel them close behind. Several other people sat under a tent fly in folding camp chairs: three old men, a couple of younger women wearing a sort of caftan, some children. But the woman who had spoken was a striking figure: She rose from an overstuffed velveteen chair and stood a full six feet tall. She had a square bearing and she wore one of those flowing caftans, too.

"Good evening." She offered her hand, and her grasp was firm but gentle. "Bethesda," it sounded like.

"Evening, Queen Bathasa," Miller said. "Miller McDonald. I'm sort of the ambassador at large here at the campgrounds."

"And your assistants?"

Miller introduced Nick and Charlie, and Queen Bathasa turned her considerable height and gaze upon them. The boys nodded and shuffled behind Miller.

"Just wanted to make sure you folks was getting settled in okay," Miller said. "And to offer my services in case you needed anything."

What was Miller doing? He was supposed to be getting rid of the Gypsies.

"Have you eaten yet?" the Queen asked. "Can I offer you something to drink?"

"I could probably gag down a cold beer," Miller said. "And I've never known these two to turn one down."

One of the men dug three beers out of the cooler, and he held Miller's eye as he passed them over. Just this one, he seemed to be saying.

"Please." The Queen gestured to the chairs the men had vacated.

"Thanks, Queen," Miller said. "Nice and quiet here this time of day."

The Queen murmured her assent. The two caftaned women rose and went into the trailer. The men remained standing.

Miller nodded to the California plates on the Chrysler parked nearby.

"You folks been on the road awhile."

The Queen raised her wineglass. "A working vacation," she said, smiling.

"Ha! No rest for the weary."

While Miller and the Queen bantered, Nick and Charlie took

stock of the camp. They could see the silhouettes of the two younger women inside the trailer. Heads together, whispering. One of the men tended the coals of the cook fire, basted and turned some chickens. Other Gypsies drifted past the campsite. Some of them stopped to murmur with the men.

Miller finished his beer and his goodwill speech.

"You folks enjoy your stay," he said. "You'll find it's nice and quiet here."

He paused to fire up his cigar, and as he was doing so, his eye rested on Cemetery Hill above the Gypsy camp.

"Oh, and if *they*," nodding up the hill, "start making any noise, pay no attention. They'll quiet down by morning."

Everybody turned to the pine-covered knoll of Cemetery Hill.

"And who are they?" the Queen asked.

"Oh, the restless souls under the stones," Miller said. "In the graveyard."

"Graveyard?" the Queen asked.

"Up on the hill there."

"They didn't mention a graveyard in the office."

"Ah, well," Miller said. "It's only been there the last hundred years."

"Spooks?" asked the man who had blocked their way. "You got spooks here?"

A muttering rose behind them. The kids around the fire burst into a quick jabber. The Queen took two quick steps to the edge of the tent fly, stared up the hill.

"Well, they ain't done nothing too bad lately," Miller said.

The men came around to join the Queen. She straightened, regained her composure.

"Surely a man such as yourself, a—what is it? an ambassador at large—doesn't believe in ghosts?"

"Well, all I can tell you is what I hear up there, nights." Miller studied the hillside. "The graveyard is half Catholic and half Protestant. Now, Catholics and Protestants don't lie easy with each other, and you can take it from one who knows. My ex-wife was a goddamn Catholic—no offense—lot of good it ever done her. Anyway, they're not easy with each other up there. On nights they get agitated and slip out of their earthly resting places, the trouble begins sometime after midnight.

"Well," Miller continued, "nothing to worry yourselves about. This is a real nice place." He drew on his cigar. "You see, when they're out walking the earth, nights, they're not much trouble. You get the occasional wild story from teenagers parking up there, or maybe some pipes banging in one of the old houses. But the real ruckus begins when they go to get *back into* their graves. Sometimes a Catholic'll screw up and lay down in a Protestant's bed, and when the Protestant comes home, he starts wailing and goes and climbs into a Catholic's spot, and that Catholic comes home and starts screaming bloody murder, and on down the line. Some of the most ungodly noises you ever heard."

The men shifted toward the hill.

"Some folks say it's just the kids from town, raisin' hell nights. Well, people are gonna believe what they want to believe."

"Of course," the Queen said, but it was too late. A couple of the men had split off and spread the word. Out in the dusk, figures agitated toward the hill and back.

"You'll know they're out and about if you hear young Nick's"— Miller nodded at Nick—"grandfather's dog barking. Only time that dog barks these days is when the sleepless ones start roaming. Dogs have that extra sense. Barks all night, and then in the wee hours the trouble starts."

The Queen maintained her demeanor, but Nick could hear a muttering from the neighboring campsites.

"Well, as I say, you folks enjoy your stay," Miller said. "Office shuts down at ten. Anything comes up before then, give us a holler. After that, you're on your own."

"So?" Francis asked when they got back to the office.

Miller reached behind the counter and plucked off a fresh pack of Rum-Soaked Crooks.

"Won't be a Gypsy on the place tomorrow morning."

Francis gave him an I'll-believe-it-when-I-see-it look.

"So they're scared," Nick said. "How do you know they'll leave?"

"You know how Siegfried won't sleep anyplace but under the

porch," Miller said. "Remember when he got locked into the cellar of the barn?"

Nick remembered. He was the one who got up in the middle of the night and let the old German shepherd out so everybody could get some sleep.

"About time old Siggy got an evening out, wouldn't you say?" Miller herded them toward the Rutabaga. "We'll let it get good and dark first. Now let's go get us a bite to drink."

The Wild Turkey was crowded. A lot of the freaks were there, drinking tequila sunrises and playing the jukebox, and the place rocked to the electric-guitar wail of the Rolling Stones' "Jumpin' Jack Flash." The Earl brothers and some other Pennsylvania stumpjumpers held down the pool table, stomping around and looking serious. The Wild Turkey had the best jukebox on the river, a decent pool table, and a pinball machine. The decor was fish-and-game: mounted buck heads and rainbow trout on the heavily varnished paneling, photos of local fishermen with their catches or hunters with their game, an antique shotgun above the bar, old cane flyrods on the exposed beams. In the middle of the bar, Denny Evans had parked his wheelchair alongside Butch Deeker, and they matched each other boilermaker for boilermaker.

"Getting ready for your shift, Butchie?" Miller kidded the campgrounds' night watchman.

"Goddamn right," Butch said, wiping his lip with the back of his hand. "Any goddamn Gypsy wants to mix it up, he's found the right man."

"Used to be an old Gypsy gal'd jump off the train in Hancock," Miller said. "Went by the name of Black Maria. Well, she'd jump off the way freight on a Friday night, and by Monday morning all the railroaders up there'd be singing, 'Oh, Mar-ia, it hurts me when I pee-a!'"

"Haw! Give Miller and these two girls a beer, Jake," Butch called to Jake Skinner, the bartender. Nick and Charlie hung around long enough to tip glasses with Butch and order roast beef sandwiches from Jake, and then they headed down the bar.

The Van Vooren girls were clustered by the archway to the poolroom, hanging out with Eliot Winklewitz, Julie Busch, Marisse Evans, and Ray Vann. Nick and Charlie eased into the group as the Stones died back and Blue Cheer came on with "Summertime Blues." Pool balls clicked behind them, and the stumpjumpers slapped quarters onto the table. Eva touched glasses with Charlie. Darlene smiled at Nick, and she raised her drink his way.

Cecie got the jump on her sisters.

"You guys are off early. The Gypsy girls aren't keeping you busy?"

"Dinner break," Charlie said. "And no, they're sticking pretty close to their campsite."

"Ha!" Cecie said. "Too bad the rest of them aren't. You wouldn't believe what's been going on. Old Mrs. Elwood had them do her driveway, and now she can't get her car out of the garage."

"Jesus, they ought to come around more often then. Mrs. Elwood can't see past her hood ornament."

Marisse Evans joined in. "Word over at Kick's was they caught some Gypsy kids stealing chickens. Two little eight-year-olds, pitching whole chickens out the back door into a red wagon."

"Daddy almost wouldn't let me come down here tonight," Julie Busch said. "He thought I might be abducted. He said Gypsies are known to abduct young girls into white slavery."

Darlene rolled her eyes. "No such luck," she muttered to Nick. "An alien abduction, maybe. Our only hope is from outer space."

Jake Skinner's wife, Norma, brought out the sandwiches. Norma was known up and down the river for her "roast beast." It was rare and tender and spiced with garlic. Between two pieces of her homemade sourdough rye, with a tomato slice, lettuce, and horseradish mustard, the sandwich was four inches thick. Norma served it with half a garlic dill pickle on the side. Washed down with a cold beer, it was a perfect summer dinner.

Nick stood aside and set his beer on the jukebox so he could tackle the sandwich.

"Jesus," Darlene said. "You listen to these hillbillies, you'd think the Russians just invaded."

"Ain't it awful. People who aren't like us, going wherever they choose?"

"Land of the free, home of the bigot."

Tonight Darlene wore her hair tied back with a braided leather thong. The jukebox's flashing lights cast orange-and-blue shadows along her cheekbones and glinted off her silver hoop earrings. She poked at the ice in her glass with a red cocktail straw.

"What you drinking?" Nick asked and drained his beer.

"Vodka and tonic."

Nick took their empty glasses and stepped to the bar and signaled Jake for two more. Darlene was underage, but that didn't matter in the Wild Turkey. Jake's son served as a sheriff's deputy, so Jake always knew when a raid was scheduled. If anybody underage was drinking, Jake would give them a little warning with their drink and nod toward the side door behind the beer cooler. Later, when the prowl car nosed up to the sidewalk, Jake would honk on a French taxi horn and there would be a hasty exodus out the side door to the alley. By the time the cops got inside, everybody'd be legal.

Darlene stirred her fresh drink and sipped through the cocktail straw. Nick got a kick out of watching her—such a girlie way to drink. She raised her eyes to his and smiled.

"So," she said, "how's the canoe practice going?"

"Good. Fine. Haven't seen anybody up at your place the last few days."

"Everybody's working. Cecie and I got jobs at Romano's. Cecie's waitressing in the dining room—days only. And I'm baby-sitting. They have a baby-sitting service so parents can enjoy themselves."

"How's it going?"

"God. Such a bunch of spoiled brats. They must get every treat in the world on Long Island. Either that, or they learn how to con people early. While their parents are off playing tennis or drinking around the pool, the kids are demanding ice-cream cake and chocolate sodas. Or they don't want to walk to the jungle gym, they have to be carried. Or the sun is too hot, or the kiddie pool is too cold. You know that whine Long Island chicks have? It starts early, believe me."

Nick knew what it was like, dealing with tourists. He figured, though, that the campgrounds got a hardier breed than the gold-bedecked suburbanites up at Romano's Resort. Still, he and Darlene were better off than the kids who worked on farms or for the county and never interacted with anybody new.

"You ever feel like blowing out of here?" Darlene asked.

"Only about every day."

"Tell me about it. You know where I'd like to go? California. Throw some shit in a backpack and hit the road."

"How would you go?" God, he could imagine heading out in the MG with Darlene in the passenger seat. Sunlight shining on her hair.

"Hitch. Ride my thumb. Meet new people. Crash wherever I landed. It'd be great."

"Mmm . . . I don't know," Nick said. "I don't know how safe it is for a chick by herself."

"Oh, please. I might get abducted by Gypsies, you mean?"

"Ha! No. . . . But there's some weird shit out there. You'd be better off going with somebody."

"Oh?" She gave him a teasing smile. "Any suggestions?"

He imagined them blasting across the Great Plains, tunes pumping from the eight-track. Camping at night in his little pup tent. Darlene's beautiful face illuminated by firelight.

The screen door slammed and everybody turned. When they saw who was there, conversation dropped straight off.

Two Gypsy guys, twenty or twenty-one. Dark complexions. One wore a mustache, the other a full beard. Unlike the Delaware Ford kids in T-shirts and cutoffs and bellbottom jeans, these guys wore collared shirts and flared slacks. They were out on the town.

"Hold on to your wallets," Eliot Winklewitz muttered.

"Ooh, hold on to your women," Cecie said, fluttering her hand over her heart.

The Gypsies stood inside the doorway and ordered two beers. Conversation came back up, the pool balls clicked, Blue Cheer turned into Johnny Cash's "Folsom Prison Blues." The Gypsies eyed the bar and the poolroom, and when their beers came they eased through the archway. They nodded at Bobby Earl as they edged around the pool table, but Bobby leaned on his cue and scowled. They nodded at Nick and Charlie and positioned themselves on the other side of the jukebox.

"You work at the camping grounds," the mustached Gypsy said.

Charlie ticked his head like he couldn't hear over the music.

"Where we are staying," the Gypsy said. "You work there."

"Yeah," Charlie said. "We work there."

The Gypsy nodded and took notice of the pool game. Bobby Earl jacked his cue back and forth, back and forth, and then slammed a bank shot so hard that the five ball hit the bumper and flew into the air, banged the far wall, and caused all the stumpjumpers to hoot and holler. Typical rube shooting, Nick thought. Typical Pennsylvania.

Cecie couldn't keep her eye off the Gypsies. Darlene kept casting glances their way. Pretty soon the Gypsies began scanning the tunes on the jukebox, and then they dropped in a couple of quarters. They played "Love Is Blue" and "The Look of Love." Nick pegged them as softies, but he noticed that Cecie had moved around by Charlie, so she was back to back with the bearded Gypsy.

When Otis Redding's "Dock of the Bay" came on, the Gypsies turned to the group of kids and the mustached one raised his hand to chest level for attention.

"Excuse us," he said. "But would anyone care to dance?"

"Huh?" Charlie replied. "Dance?"

The Gypsy laughed. "We were wondering if any of the ladies would like to dance." He nodded toward the jukebox. "To the music."

The Wild Turkey was not a dancing bar. It was a pool-shooting, rowdy-bullshitting, good-rocking bar, and when people wanted to dance they went to the Black Horse at Skinner's Falls or the Nutshell in Lake Huntington. The Gypsies didn't know that, of course. They gazed at the girls with wide-open, expectant eyes.

Charlie snickered and was about to explain protocol when Cecie said, "Sure," and swayed with the music. She and the mustached Gypsy eased out between the jukebox and the pool game and started dancing, and the bearded Gypsy, so as not to be left awkwardly behind, tapped Darlene on the arm, raised his eyebrows, and nodded toward the room. Darlene joined him without a backwards glance.

The Gypsies were good dancers. They had the right fluid moves for Otis Redding's slow rhythm, and they kept their dark eyes on the girls.

The rest of the bar kept its eyes on the Gypsies. Dancing in the Wild Turkey? Sometimes a group of Jewish camp counselors might push aside the tables and kick it up. Even then, the local kids would stand back and watch. This was different: outsiders dancing with two of the prettiest girls in town. Cecie danced with her arms and legs open, as if practicing cheers. Darlene bopped with a girlie bounce that shook her hair.

Though most of the local boys didn't really dig these foreign-looking strangers dancing with their girls, Nick wasn't surprised. The Van Vooren girls were always the first to try new things, to push the edge. Let them dance with the Gypsies. But Bobby Earl and the other pool-shooters—all greasers from across the river—didn't have the tolerance of the Delaware Ford longhairs. Nick could see Bobby's face clouding up as the dancers crowded the pool-table perimeter, could see Bobby's stance widen out, his pumping of the cue clearing more space. Bobby strode around the table, his engineer's boots clumping on the linoleum, his biceps flexing the pack of Marlboros rolled into his T-shirt sleeve. Bobby positioned his shots from the Gypsies' end of the table. He kept his eyes hooded against the cigarette smoke rising from his lip. His buddies along the far wall elbowed each other and grinned.

The Gypsies were smooth. They kept themselves between Bobby and the girls, but they also stayed out of range of Bobby's pumping cue. The song wound down, and in the relative silence afterwards, Bobby slammed a shot and sent the balls clacking like bones. The Gypsies talked to Cecie and Darlene for a moment, and then "Aquarius" came up and they all started dancing again. Bobby's glances toward the Gypsies became more frequent, his shooting more violent and erratic, his boots loud on the floor.

As the Fifth Dimension sang about "sympathy and understanding," Bobby gave an extra-long pump of his pool cue and caught the bearded Gypsy above the kidney. Bobby then stutter-stepped forward as if pushed and let the cue tip drag the cue ball sideways. The ball hit nothing—a table scratch.

The greasers along the wall fell silent. So did everybody else. The dancing stopped. The Gypsy rubbed his back. Bobby turned and pulled the Marlboro from his lips.

"Hey," he said. "You just fucked up my shot."

The Gypsy rubbed his back and returned Bobby's stare.

"You hear me, Twinkletoes?" Bobby drew himself up behind his pool cue. "Game shot here. I'm ready to nail the eight ball, and you crash my stick."

The other Gypsy positioned himself next to his friend, and they both gave impassive faces back to Bobby. The Van Vooren girls—their dancing cut off abruptly—stood behind the Gypsies with their hands on their hips. Bobby's younger brother Tuggy—as squat and solid as a spruce stump—sauntered over from the wall. From inside the barroom, Butch Deeker and Denny Evans paused in mid-drink to watch.

"Cost me the game, Hay Foot," Bobby went on. "Table scratch on the eight ball. All your prancin' around and bangin' into people cost me the table."

The Earls had a reputation for trouble. They were from somewhere up by Cooley Creek where there were no towns, just odd little settlements along lonely roads. They were known as predators and thieves. Word was that Bobby had done time for breaking and entering, and Tuggy robbed summer houses while the owners were away.

The Gypsies faced the Earls. They were used to this, Nick could tell, used to landing in local bars and having some redneck geek try to call them out. The mustached one kept his hand in his pocket, and Nick imagined the switchblade that was surely there.

"You speak English, Hay Foot?" Bobby garnered some guffaws from the hyenas along the wall. "You hablo what I'm saying—"

"Bobby." Jake Skinner stepped through the archway and positioned himself between the Earls and the Gypsies. In his hand was the Persuader, a two-foot section of black locust root, hard as iron, and spiky on the club end where the roots had been trimmed. "Why don't you go back to your game? Take a do-over."

"Do-over? After Clubfoot here just fucked—"

Jake thwacked the Persuader against his palm. "Take a do-over, Bobby."

Just as the Wild Turkey was not a dancing bar, neither was it a fighting bar. The rednecks and the longhairs mingled fairly well. Everybody kidded everybody else, and trouble was rare. When trouble did start, Jake never let it get far. He was not large or imposing, but he was tough when he had to be, and everybody knew that if the Persuader didn't stop the troublemaker, one quick phone call to the sheriff's office would.

Bobby flicked his cigarette against the pool cue and didn't move, but neither did he look back at the Gypsies.

Jake turned to the Gypsies. "Why don't you finish your beers at the bar?" he suggested. "Some of the local boys get a little proprietary about their women."

This brought a shuffling from the Van Voorens.

"Whose women, Jake?" Darlene scoffed. "Who, exactly, owns whom here?"

"Never mind," Jake said. He stepped around behind the jukebox and pulled the plug. "Box is shut down for the night, until you kids learn to behave."

He turned to the Gypsies with a nod toward the barroom, and as they passed Bobby, the mustached one's hand came out of his pocket. He flipped a quarter through the air towards Bobby, and Bobby reacted instinctively: He grabbed for it but his hands were tangled in the pool cue and his cigarette, so he fumbled, dropped the cigarette and cue both, swatted again at the spinning coin on its downward arc, missed, and wound up scrabbling after it on the floor, looking ridiculous.

"For your lost game," the Gypsy said.

The Gypsies left soon after, and the buzz in the barroom picked up again. Bobby retired to a table by the wall, gesticulating to his friends and glowering out the big front windows. Cecie and Darlene, frustrated by having been cut off, clustered among their girlfriends and shut out the male oppressors in the group. The guys took up their beers and commiserated quietly over what geeks the Earls were, and what might have happened had Jake let the scene play out.

The Gypsies weren't the only ones who had left. As everybody settled into a new groove—one without music, since Jake held true to his word and left the jukebox dead and dark—Nick noticed that Charlie and Eva were nowhere to be seen. Slipped out during the excitement, he figured.

What the hell. Darlene was herded up with the other girls, and it didn't look like she'd be breaking away anytime soon. Fucking Gypsies. Fucking Bobby Earl.

Nick finished his beer and walked down the tracks to the campgrounds. This was the best time, after dark on a Friday night, with the summer air cool and close off the river, passing through the campsites teeming with people out to enjoy themselves, their good spirit infectious, spreading through the night like a happy vapor, raising his mood from the tension in the bar. Laughter rose from illuminated tableaux in the woods. Music squeaked from tinny radios. Kids shouted as they followed flashlight beams to the store in search of treats. Tools clanked as trailers were uncoupled from hitches, cars wampled over the rock-strewn roads, and a haze of dust hung in the red glow of taillights.

Nick liked to move through the campgrounds at this time, when the place still rippled with the excitement of the weekend ahead, with the satisfaction of a destination reached and the sense of adventure that comes with settling down for the night in the open air. He liked the camaraderie of a bunch of guys standing around a campfire, hoisting beers and joking. He felt drawn to the glowing, curtained windows of travel trailers, to these warm pockets of domesticity in the wilderness. Mostly, he longed to be one of those young men up in the remote North Area, sitting at a picnic table with a girl, the two of them reading by lantern light, sharing a bottle of wine, and then, touching arm or cheek, moving to the tent and the pleasure of a double sleeping bag.

Darlene, he thought. Camping with Darlene. A little drunk on wine, the lantern reflecting on her hair. The sleeping bag part made him somewhat anxious.

The Gypsies hadn't been anxious. They hadn't been pussies. They had seen what they wanted and gone after it.

He admired them for that. They reminded him of something Felix had said before he shipped out. They had been returning from a morning's fishing in Pennsylvania, and as they crossed the bridge in Callicoon they passed Bobby Earl in Bobby's grill-less Fury. Felix drove across the bridge in silence and then ticked his big red head rearwards.

"Don't take shit from anybody, Nicko," he said. "Especially assholes like that."

Nick nodded and sat higher in his seat. He and Felix had always been decent friends, but with Felix about to ship out he'd been acting like an older brother.

"You remember that race?" Felix asked. "I won it fair and clear, but when Earl wouldn't let me back in, I fought it out with him. It took me nearly another quarter mile to get past him, but I did. Pulled back into the right lane clean. Stupid, really stupid, to run in the oncoming lane like that with no spotters, so I figured I'd teach Bobby a lesson, and I hit the goddamn brakes right in his face. Must have been doing a hundred, hundred and five, and Bobby panicked, locked himself into a skid and wound up in the ditch."

He paused and gave Nick a guilty look.

"So I never hit him," Felix went on. "Never sideswiped him like he said, but I guess you could say my hands weren't entirely clean. I'll tell you what, though. Old Bobby never gave me any more shit after that, and he sure as hell hasn't asked for a rematch."

Nick understood that Felix's story was part brotherly advice, part confession. Felix was washing his hands before he shipped out. If he'd been in the bar tonight, the scene wouldn't have gotten as far as Jake Skinner and the Persuader.

Nick felt a little sorry for the Gypsies for what he had to do next. He walked up the hill to Grandpa's house and called softly to Siegfried. The Gypsies were only doing their thing. But just as they had to be true to their people and their ways, so did he.

Siegfried, suspicious, came reluctantly, but he licked Nick's hand in recognition and wagged his tail. Nick scratched Siggy's ears and smelled his dog smell and let him into the cellar of the barn. Outside the barn, he listened to Siggy whine and scratch at the door. He looked down upon the Gypsy camp and the rest of the sites, watched the place tune down for the night. Radios shut off and lanterns winked out and fires smoldered to embers. Peace seemed to settle over the place. He felt tired. He could feel the stones under his boots and the fatigue in his calves and the tension in his shoulders, but it was good to know that the campers were all tucked away, that his day's work was done.

Around midnight, from his apartment on the far side of his grand-parents' house, Nick heard the first barks. He pictured Siegfried, locked securely in the cellar of the barn, with any number of comfortable straw or burlap napping places, finally realizing he was not spending the night in his own wretched packed-dirt hole under Grandpa's porch. Siggy set up a magnificent barking, which, filtered through the thick floorboards of the barn and resonating within its cavernous interior, sounded like a canine appeal from the grave itself.

Nick woke up groggy. When he got to work, his father and Miller stood outside the office. Across the field, where the Gypsy camp had been, there was only trampled grass, overflowing garbage bags, and cold ashes. And one more thing: On the side of each fireplace was an odd marking, a cross within a circle, with three hashmarks underneath.

"Hex sign," Miller said. "A warning to other Gypsies."

Francis beheld the sign and nodded. "Let's hope it's a warning," he said. "Let's hope it's not a curse."

July 1969

16

TED HAD CONTRACTED a small circus for the Fourth of July weekend. The trucks and trailers arrived earlier in the week, and the circus people began setting up. They ran some rides for the kids, operated cotton candy and popcorn stands. They erected a main tent with bleachers. A clown juggled balls and bowling pins and flaming torches. A sideshow for adults featured a stripper who appeared to be the animal trainer's wife. The trainer worked with the animals in a makeshift paddock: a donkey painted up like a zebra, a patchy camel, an ostrich that could pull a cart, a cigar-smoking chimp, and an elephant. It wasn't a big elephant, as elephants go, but except for Buff the red garbage truck, it was the biggest motile thing on the place.

Nick marveled at the elephant's appetite. The circus people bought hay from the local farmers by the truckload, and the elephant consumed most of it. It stood in the field across from the office, chained by a hind foot, converting hay and feed and the occasional peanut into manure. Piles of manure. Big piles of manure. When it became clear that the circus people weren't going to do anything with the manure, Francis wanted Nick and Charlie to clean it up. But the boys couldn't go near the elephant—the camel wouldn't let them. The camel was mean, and if Nick or Charlie got within ten feet of the elephant, it would rush up with its ears back and spit at them. Charlie took some peanuts over, wanted to see what an elephant's trunk felt like, and the camel eyed him, worked up a good cud, and let fly the smelliest, foulest mouthful of soup *ka-splat!* on Charlie's head. A brown, stinking helmet, all tangled up in Charlie's hair and dripping down his neck. Charlie staggered off to the river to scrub himself down, and he didn't go near the animals again.

A full house for the Fourth of July. Airstreams and Winnebagos slotted into the prime river sites, pop-ups and pickup campers throughout the Meadow and the Upper Field, and tents and hippie vans in the North Area. The circus took up the field across from the office, where the Gypsies had been. Beyond that, all the way out the driveway, campers stuffed themselves into every available patch of earth. The big weekends were always exciting, but the Fourth was probably the most. Firecrackers popped at all hours, bottle rockets zinged into the air. Lots of celebrating. Lots of free beer. Lots of work, too. Lots of canoes to run, lots of firewood to deliver, lots of garbage to pick up. Lots of little problems to solve. The campers from New York always called out *Hey, Mista. Hey, Mista!* Help this guy level his trailer, *Hey, Mista!* Help that lady light her stove. Hook onto a tent platform with the tractor and drag it five feet west for some finicky bastard. Set up a dining fly, change a flat tire. *Hey, Mista!* Dig up a couple more picnic tables.

"Camping out," Miller McDonald said, shaking his head. "Jesus Aitch, I ever get a goddamn vacation, the last thing I'll do is camp out. Get me a hotel room and a bottle of Dickel and a big-tittied bitch, and no goddamn *Hey, Mista!* for me!"

Most of the campers were fun, but there were always a few pains in the neck. This weekend it was the Bert and Jims. Two identical Airstreams on adjoining river sites, parked circle-the-wagons style so the doorways faced each other. Striped awnings over the picnic tables, a full-sized color television blaring away on one of them. Two middle-aged, middle-American couples. Mrs. Bert and Mrs. Jim, coiffed and sagging and smoking cigarettes, sat out at the television set. Bert and Jim, heavy and tanned from working big construction, wore white-sidewall crewcuts and baseball caps with American flags embroidered onto the front. They spent two hours getting their Airstreams set up just so: back-and-forth, back-and-forth to get the right angle.

"Little to the right, Bert. Little to the right!" Jim waggled his beefy fingers at Bert's rearview mirrors.

Up-and-down, up-and-down to get the level.

"Crank her up, Jim. Whoa—back her down a hair." Bert strode along the sleek silver lozenge and eyeballed it for trim.

Then Jim, emerging with a four-foot level: "We're off on the side-to-side, Bert. Get the jacks."

Nick and Miller watched this as they ran errands past the site. Bert and Jim screwed around with jackstands on the corners of their trailers for a while, and finally waved Miller down.

"Hey! Ho!" they called and approached the Rutabaga. "Why'd you make your campsites so slanty? You can't level a trailer on this terrain."

Miller cocked his head, like a dog that has heard a new sound.

"Campsites slanty?" he asked. Cocked his head again. "Imagine. It ain't level! The earth ain't flat!"

"It's the gas refrigerators," Bert said. "They won't run unless they're level."

"And the wives," Jim said. "They can't sleep unless they're level."

Miller cocked his head back toward them. "You got some cold beer in there somewhere?"

"Oho—plenty of that."

"Then sit down and have one, Mista," Miller said. "We'll have you level in jig time."

Miller gassed the Rutabaga and took off with a roar. Up at Grandpa's barn, he had Nick fit the forks to the bucket of the John Deere. Back at the campsite, Nick jumped down and directed as Miller eased the forks under the Airstream's frame. Bert and Jim looked worried.

"Don't crumple the son of a bitch!" Bert shouted.

Miller waved him away, touched the lever lightly, and set the bucket in position. Nick slipped a four-by-four across the forks, and Miller raised the whole side of the trailer, wheels and all.

He yelled at Nick, "Go get three or four goddamn big river rocks! Flat ones!" Nick went over the bank, hauled back the rocks, and slipped them under the wheels.

"One more," Miller said. When the last rock was in place, Miller let the trailer down easy, and *boom*—it was level. He spun the John Deere around, repeated the trick on the other trailer, and then cut the engine. The whole operation had taken less than ten minutes.

"So much for your slanty-earth theory, Columbus," Miller said to Bert. "Now where's that cold beer?"

Bert got a six-pack of Bud from the back of his truck. Jim followed the wives into his trailer and came out with his level.

"I'll be damned," he said. "That trailer's perfectly level."

"So's the other one," Miller said. "You look at the world from some of the angles I do, you get a pretty good appreciation for level."

Bert passed a beer to Miller, and one to Jim, and cracked one open for himself.

"Excuse me, Mista," Miller said. "Nick here's probably a little dry after haulin' them rocks."

Bert turned to Nick. "You old enough to drink, son?"

"Oh, Jesus Aitch Christ," Miller cut in and handed Nick his beer. "Nobody's gonna call the goddamn cops on you."

Miller took another beer and popped it open. Bert and Jim lived on Long Island and worked construction in the city. Bert was a crane operator, Jim drove a cement truck. Took their vacations together every year. In the summer, a week upstate. In the winter, Florida. The country was going to hell. The city had already gone.

"It's all niggers and hippies," Bert said. "No place for decent people."

A lot of urban rednecks wound up at the campgrounds, guys who had earned their way to a travel trailer and paid vacations, a ranch house in the suburbs, maybe college educations for their kids. Maybe not. Maybe their kids would throw in with the niggers and the hippies, and piss away everything that the Berts and Jims of the world had worked for.

Bert and Jim made a big deal about going fishing. They had a bulky aluminum boat strapped to the cap of Bert's pickup, which was rigged out with surf-rod holders on the grille, chrome spotlights on either door, airhorns and running lights on the roof. Big tires, running boards, a whiptail antenna. A real highway trawler. On the front was a bumper sticker that read, "So Many Pedestrians, So Little Time." On the rear, "America, Love It or Leave It." Jim had a midnight-blue

Lincoln Continental. His wife's car, he said. When they went on vacation, they brought the car for the ladies and the truck for fishing gear.

"Got the outboard back there, tackle box, gas, cooler full of beer—the works," Bert said. "All we got to do is unhitch, take off, and go fishing."

And hope somebody comes along to level your trailer, Nick thought. Miller tossed his beer can into the garbage pail and took the last two Buds from the six-pack.

"Well, you bastards have good luck fishing," Miller said. "Clippers is the best bait for this river."

"We're strictly hardware," Bert said, but Miller had already fired up the John Deere, and the rest of Bert's fishing ethic was lost in the din and clatter.

"Strictly a couple of horses' asses," Miller said, handing Nick one of the Buds. "They'll drive us nuts before this week is up."

THE CIRCUS GOT a big turnout; not only the campgrounds crowd, but a lot of local people, too. The circus drew people all day long—the Whirl-a-Gig, the little Ferris wheel for the kids, the clown juggling, rides in the ostrich cart or on the donkeyzebra—but by Friday night everybody started gathering for the big show. The tent blazed with light, its red and white stripes glowed into the night. Music blared from tinny loudspeakers. The cotton candy and hot dog concessions boomed, and people lined up to toss baseballs at lead milk bottles and shoot popguns at bobbing wooden ducks. Strings of colored lightbulbs hung over the crowd, illuminating faces. Nick and Charlie cruised through, nodding at the campers, shooting the shit with people they knew: Chris Beagle and Bear Brown; Harley McDonald, Miller's brother who ran the movie house; Ray Vann and Marisse Evans, out on a date. Butch Deeker with a Genny Cream Ale in each hand, getting prepared for his shift. The Davis brothers, Rick and Ron, dairy farmers from North Branch and their primary canoe competition. The Davises were a rugged pair. Nick had seen Rick stand in front of his barn and toss a haybale up through the haymow door, two stories high.

"You guys getting any paddling in?" Nick asked.

"Aw," Rick said. "Whenever Ronnie's not up in the barn, squeezin' tits."

Rick and Ron were strong paddlers, gut-committed to going flat out for the fifteen miles from Long Eddy to Delaware Ford.

The Van Vooren girls showed up, languid and beautiful, with Darlene and Cecie cutting a path and Eva gliding along behind.

"Hey, Charlie," Cecie teased. "Win me a teddy bear at the shooting gallery?"

"Sure," Charlie said. "If you guarantee GI Joe won't come gunning for me."

"He's working." Cecie twirled a strand of hair in her fingers.

"I'll come along," Eva cut in. "In case you need protection." She took Charlie's left arm and Cecie took his right, and they steered off toward the midway.

Darlene's long hair was still damp from a shower, and she wore a faded chambray shirt tied at the waist.

"Pretty weird scene," she said. "A circus in Delaware Ford."

"Brings 'em out."

"You want to get high?" she asked, flipping at her leather bag. "I can't get through this without a buzz on."

They headed across the driveway to the canoe shed. Nick kept the canoes stacked in big pyramids, ten on the bottom row, nine on the next, and so on, up to a height of eight feet or so, and he could walk up the pile as if climbing a set of bleachers.

"Come on," he said. "To the top of the aluminum pyramid."

"It's a ziggurat, actually," Darlene said. "At least that's what Mr. Zeckhausen would say."

"Zeckhausen doesn't know his ziggurat from his elbow."

At the top of the stack Darlene produced a joint. Across from them, the backlit red and white stripes of the main tent sent a glow against the deepening blue evening, and the strings of lights looked festive. The crowd was far enough away to appear as one roiling mass. Darlene had a charming way of holding the joint while she twisted the ends, as if it was a dainty thing that might come apart if she didn't handle it tenderly. She gave Nick the first toke. He took a shallow hit.

He didn't want to get too blasted, as he was still working and would no doubt pass his father.

"Eva says I smoke too much," Darlene said.

"You probably do," Nick said in a tight voice, holding the smoke and then exhaling. "I've heard Eva does her share, down in the city."

"She gets high to dull the edges," Darlene said. "I get high to grow outward."

She made a swimming motion with her fingers extended. She wore a single silver hoop on her left wrist.

"Eva still have a thing for Felix?"

"Not really. Not romantically. She's way beyond Felix in that department. But it bothers her that he's over there. That he's at such risk."

"She serious about Georgie?"

"Who knows? Georgie's harmless. Friend of the family. Here, take some more."

Nick took another shallow toke. The end was moist from Darlene's lips, and he smiled at this.

"Anything going on," he asked, "between Eva and Charlie?"

"Huh?" Darlene looked puzzled. "Eva? No way. What makes you say that?"

"I don't know. A vibe. Neither one of them's been at the bar this week."

Since the night of the Gypsies, Charlie had made excuses about going out for beers in the evening: had to work on his van, wanted to be in tune for canoe practice the next morning.

"Eva's a free spirit," Darlene said. "She's probably out with Georgie. Or up at the fishing camp. She goes her own way."

"How about Cecie?"

"How about Cecie what?"

"She really like Charlie? Or just messing with his head?"

"Who knows? She needs the attention. Charlie gives it to her."

Nick passed the joint back to Darlene, and their hands touched and she sort of leaned on him, and it felt good to be out on a summer night with this cute girl who apparently liked being with him.

"You get high with Cecie?" he asked.

"Huh. You kidding?" Darlene rubbed her shoulder against his chest. "She thinks it'll kill her brain cells. Both of them. As if her hair spray hasn't done it already."

Nick leaned back on the canoes, let his arm fall behind Darlene. Darlene leaned back, too, adjusted herself against his arm. She smelled of patchouli. "God, these canoes aren't easy on your butt, are they?" she said, and squirmed until she got comfortable.

"You looking forward to leaving in the fall?" she asked.

Nick felt a pang in his gut; the urge to move made his leg jiggle. Yes, he wanted to leave, but thinking about the world beyond Delaware Ford was like watching a black-and-white movie, or a duotone photograph—all grays and gunmetal blues. He imagined himself at school, in the unfamiliar urban landscape of some city—Albany or Troy or Schenectady—with gritty sidewalks and pieces of litter scudding by, knowing no one and wandering among strangers with no more feeling for them than for the parking meters or the hydrants, catching his monochromatic reflection in a shop window and seeing himself as the shopowner would: a confused kid without money or direction, looking at the wares simply because they were there, not because they fit into some larger blueprint of his life.

If he imagined dropping out of school, he saw himself in the same leaden colors as a draftee: doing time in a cause for which he had no moral affiliation, thrown together with other young men who shared nothing except their overriding confusion and a lack of will to resist, passing through the doors they were ordered to, rising at the time they were ordered to, performing private acts communally—shaving, showering, shitting—allowing himself to be herded through feeding and training and then to be transported to Vietnam.

And if after his years in college or in the army—if there *was* an after—what then? You were expected to learn what to do in life. Actually, you were expected to know already: Julie Busch would be a business major at Vassar; Eliot would study creative writing. They'd go on to become corporate managers and college teachers. But what if you didn't know? Worse, what if you didn't find out? Chris Beagle's brother Clifford came back from the Air Force to take his old job in the garage. Everett Davis came back to the family farm. Nick couldn't imagine finally getting out into the world only to return to the camp-grounds as a canoe jockey.

It was confusing. Confusing and scary. He focused on the red glow of the circus tent, and then on its warm wash over Darlene's face. He stopped the jiggling of his leg.

"Part of me wants to leave," he said. "Most of the time I don't think about it."

"I do." She looked directly at him. "You and Charlie and a couple of others are a lot cooler than the guys in my class. I'm dreading the fall. I'll be stoned my whole junior and senior years, until I can get out of here."

He wanted to kiss her, but he didn't want to move too fast and put her off. And she was so young. But here she was with the top buttons of her shirt open and her warm neck against his arm, a mellow buzz and both of them drifting on waves of patchouli.

A familiar *ooogah! ooogah!* cut through his thoughts, and Lucas Bliss's school bus rolled down the driveway, safety lights flashing.

"Hey, it's Lucas," Darlene said. "Cool!"

They both sat up, the moment broken. Darlene tied her leather bag to her belt.

"Let's go on over," Nick said. "Before we both get a sore ziggurass."

"Zig your ass," she said, and elbowed him to his feet.

Lucas and his crew romped out of the bus and put on a roving car-nival act. They were true freaks, with wild hair and beads and crazy clothes, prancing and dancing through the crowd. Lucas wore a Sergeant Pepper satin jacket with epaulets and wild flower-power surfer jams and sandals. He led his entourage through the crowd like a hippie prince, handing little blue flowers to people.

"Hey, Nick," Lucas said. "Great crowd tonight, man!"

Lucas's twin sister Juicy Lucy was busting out of her denim miniskirt and halter top, and looking like Lucy in the Sky with her blue, multi-beveled wire-rims. She let Nick try them on and it was like having dragonfly eyes—he saw eight images of everything. The rest of Lucas's crew—Captain America, who always wore the Stars and Stripes in some odd fashion; Buck Naked, who wore nothing at all up at Lucas's but put on a buckskin loincloth in public; Mongo of the Congo, in a printed dashiki and a conga drum—had attached themselves to Lucas from New Mexico and Nova Scotia and California. In wild Day-Glo jumpsuits and fringed vests and patched bellbottoms, they entertained the crowd by batting out balloons. They sounded a discordant revelry with the flute and conga drum and box guitar, ringing Indian bells and chanting. The women, in skimpy outfits like Lucy's or in long, flowing saris, danced and waved their arms, while the men pranced about them like satyrs and jesters, whistling and turning cartwheels.

"It's a circus," they called, "and we're the freak show!"

Nick and Darlene met up with Charlie and Cecie and Eva. Cecie carried an orange teddy bear and a big swirl of cotton candy. Darlene picked at the candy as they followed Lucas's roving band.

Nick noticed Bert and Jim standing off to the side with Mrs. Bert and Mrs. Jim. They shook their heads at Lucas.

"Look at that garbage," Bert said. "We come out of the city to get away from that garbage. I can't believe we got to put up with that."

"Somebody ought to call the cops on them," Jim said. "Run them all out of here."

Charlie sized Jim up. "For what, man?"

"Public indecency," Jim said. "Contributing to the delinquency of minors. Anything."

"How about for having fun at a public event?" Charlie asked. "Entertaining people who aren't too uptight to laugh? There's probably a law against it."

The girls giggled.

"Bust them for drugs," Bert chipped in. "They're probably all carrying the stuff."

"Probably," Charlie said. "If they've got any sense."

Charlie's expression reminded Nick of Ted: a cocky smirk that said *fuck you and all your rules.* Nick nudged Charlie and the girls along as the ringmaster blew his whistle and cracked his whip. The chimpanzee rode the donkeyzebra, and the clown threw a bucket of confetti at the crowd. The stripper came over from the sideshow and swung on the trapeze. The ringmaster made the animals do tricks. The camel kneeled in front of the ostrich. "May I have this dance, Olive?" the ringmaster asked over the loudspeaker, and the two animals clumped about while the ringmaster threw in wisecracks, "Nice tail feathers," and "What's that cologne you're wearing," which made the crowd laugh.

The top act was the elephant. The ringmaster made it do the typical elephant tricks: lift a barbell with its trunk, balance on a cube, parade around the ring while the trapeze artist did handstands on its back. The elephant's eye was a moist spot in the middle of its leathery hide, and Nick wondered what the elephant thought of all this. If it ever thought of it. Night after night, going through the motions for a dumb master and these braying rubes in the audience. Day after day, chained by the foot to a stake. Could the elephant ponder its fate? Nick imagined that it could. Elephants were intelligent, after all. They had memories and complicated social rituals and even burial grounds. Nick imagined that the elephant got through its act by staying focused on something more pleasant, remembering perhaps a day when it was a young elephant and still with its family. Spraying off in the water hole. Nestling up against its mother's side, warm as a sunny wall.

The clown came out with a bucket. He set the bucket by the elephant's dangling trunk and pretended to sponge down the broad side of the animal. As the clown worked his way around, the elephant found the bucket with its trunk. The clown came back to the bucket to refill his sponge, and finding it dry, shook his finger at the elephant. The elephant blasted the clown with a trunkful of water and sent him rolling across the ring.

Nick saw his grandparents in the front row, two white-haired old folks getting a kick out of the antics. He imagined mastodons lumbering through the river valley.

How was it that elephants and clowns now performed on this field? Where his grandfather used to graze dairy cows? Where he and Charlie and Felix used to play war and stalk rabbits? One thing led to another. You took one step down a path, and then another step, and if you didn't turn around you wound up someplace else. His parents never could have imagined this scene when they were contemplating a campgrounds, that one day they'd have a red-and-white circus tent and an elephant and the whole town laughing its head off. Never could have imagined, when they were picturing snug little campsites with tents and picnic tables, that they would wind up fighting and angry about their decision.

He would not wind up like them. No matter what, no matter how the movie of his future played out, he would not wind up performing tricks for somebody when he wanted to be doing something else. He would stay loose, free to change direction—*Go, man, just go*—whenever he felt himself on the wrong road.

NEXT DAY, BERT and Jim finally managed to go fishing. They made a big fuss at the boat landing. Bert backed the truck to the river while Jim gave hand signals and kept the way clear. Using mainly gravity, they slid the boat off the roof and flopped it into the water. And then out of the pickup bed they trundled the biggest outboard ever seen on the Upper Delaware. The motor head was as big around as Bert himself, and it took both men to walk it down to the boat.

"I'm strictly an Evinrude man," Bert said. "Always gets you to the fish, always gets you back."

He and Jim clamped the motor to the transom and latched the safety chains; the boat's stern settled deeply into the river. They offset this by lugging a huge tackle box to the bow. Nick carried his lures in a plastic case the size of his hand. Charlie could fit his in his shirt pocket. Bert and Jim hauled out a tackle box the size of a suitcase.

"Never can tell what you're gonna need," Jim said. "Spinners, spoons, poppers. Pork rinds, rubber worms, salmon eggs. Jigs, darts, grubtails. What usually works out here?"

Charlie squinted at Jim.

"Personally," he said, "I favor a Rapala rubbed in skunk oil trailing a bit of panty lace. Cast with a sidearm rolling curve. Usually."

Jim nodded.

"Check," he said. "Floating or sinking Rapala?"

Bert and Jim fired up the Evinrude with a roar and a blue cloud.

They took off from the quiet little beach like the Coast Guard defending the three-mile limit. They made a big tour of the eddy, which was only half a mile between the riffles top and bottom, and then they settled into some fishing. They knew enough to float through the eddy and cast along the way, but Nick could see that Bert retrieved his line way too fast, and Jim changed lures every third cast. When they got to the bottom of the eddy, they fired the motor and blasted upriver at full throttle, the bow riding high, the prop sending a big wake into the swimming area and causing waves to break upon the shore. Kids in their plastic floaters bobbed like ducklings; a family of startled mergansers broke cover and took off for a quieter spot.

Around noon Bert and Jim beached their boat and came up to the canoe shed to complain about the fishing.

"Terrible fishing out there," Bert said.

"Never seen such bad fishing," Jim chimed in.

The American flags on their hats nodded in unison.

"Well," Charlie said. "I'd have to agree with you."

Nick managed to sell them a dozen night crawlers and told them to rig for bottom fishing, this being the middle of the day.

"We usually fish hardware," Bert said.

"We've gone through nearly everything in the box," Jim said. "You sure there's fish in this river?"

"There sure used to be," Charlie said. "You run that big-assed motor up and down a few more times and I guarantee we'll be hearing about record catches down around the Water Gap."

"Yeah, well," Jim said. "We'd have better luck taking the Lincoln out and trolling for hippie poontang, you ask me."

Nick and Charlie went about their day, and all afternoon they could hear the high-pitched racket of the motor as Bert and Jim tore up the eddy. Nick got back from a canoe run at three-thirty, and the first thing he heard when he stepped out of the truck was that annoying drone through the trees. Francis stood by the canoe shed with Miller and Charlie.

"Go wave those guys in," Francis said. "People are complaining. They're afraid to go into the water."

"Hell," Miller said. "The way they're driving that boat, I'd be afraid to get within thirty feet of the riverbank."

"Wave them in," Francis said. "Tell them to go over to White Lake or Wallenpaupack."

"Tell 'em to go the hell back to Long Island," Miller said. "Stop in Monticello and buy a goddamn jar of pickled herring."

At the landing, Nick and Charlie watched the boat's big vee-bow churn through the water. Bert and Jim weren't even fishing now, just ramming up and down the eddy. The boys windmilled their arms at the boat's next fly-by of the swimming area, but Bert and Jim waved them off.

"Aerating the water!" Bert yelled from the stern.

Jim raised a beer bottle.

"C'mon in for a swim, girls—" something lost in the motor—"an Evinrude haircut, haw, haw!"

Nick and Charlie watched the pure white arc of the wake curving off upriver as Bert and Jim took a high-speed turn at the top of the eddy, a little too far north, Nick thought, and then they set a heading for the Pennsylvania bank, a little too close, maybe, and then he and Charlie looked at each other as they realized the same thing at the same time. Charlie raised his hand, and Nick said, "You know . . ." and the moment hung in the air long enough for them to picture the Lincoln Continental–sized, glacially deposited, utterly unmovable ledge of bluestone that waited, as it had for centuries, just below the surface, twenty feet off the Pennsylvania bank. The roaring metal boat scribed its full arc across the still water, and then with a single, momentous thunderclap—in which the lower eight inches of Evinrude met the upper eight inches of Middle Devonian shale, the force of which meeting not only killed the motor but ripped it through the transom—the boat stopped dead in the water. Bert and Jim, however, did not. They were propelled, as if catapulted, through the air and into the river, well downstream.

For a moment, everything was still. The boat floated. The men floated. The water lapped at the gaping, open transom. Then the current nudged the boat off the ledge. The motor, hung by its safety chains and no longer supported by the ledge, dropped into the deeper water and dragged the transom down. The river, finding a new, aluminum-clad hole in which to flow, flowed. The stern of the boat went down. The bow of the boat went up, then down. Down some more. This inspired Bert and Jim, in turn, to action. Their two swiveling heads became flailing arms and splashing river as they struck out toward the boat, but of course there was nothing they could do except tread water and watch the bow go down, and down, and down until the only things on the surface were themselves and the suitcase-sized tackle box, which bobbed between them and to which they clung, as if to a life raft, while they kicked themselves to shore.

Chris Beagle came down with his father's wrecker. He parked on the Pennsylvania river road while Nick and Charlie waded out with the hook and cable. Nick stood shin-deep on the bluestone ledge and held the cable, while Charlie swam down and hooked onto the boat. He was under a long time, and then he surfaced and signaled to Chris to start cranking. The cable drew tight and sprung water drops off its greased surface. The motor lowered an octave.

A crescent-shaped swell of water appeared on the river, and then the bow broke the surface. Charlie turned and hollered across the river to Bert and Jim's campsite.

"Big one on the line! Bitin' strictly on hardware!"

THE NEXT DAY was Sunday, last day of the big weekend. The circus pulled out by noon, and the campgrounds crew was left with the elephant shit. And the camel and the donkey and the ostrich shit, but mostly elephant. Piles of it. Miller went at it with the bucket loader on the John Deere, and Nick manned a long-handled shovel, and they loaded it all into Buff. They attracted attention, between the smell and Miller's cursing over the engine. Kids came by to stop and point, wave their hands in front of their noses. Their parents chuckled and took pictures. Miller worked the situation to advantage.

"Dyin' of elephant gas up here, Mista," Miller hollered from time to time. "Nothing a cold beer wouldn't cure!"

Later, as Nick raked the finer particulate onto the bucket: "Get it clean, boy! This is a paying campsite, when half the Serengeti Plain ain't standing around shitting on it!"

The campers brought them beer, and Nick loaded and raked, raked and shoveled. Miller piled elephant shit four feet deep in the back of the dump truck. It was a fragrant pile. And with a steady supply of Genny and Bud that afternoon, Nick and Miller and later Charlie settled into a warm, fuzzy groove. As they were finishing, Nick got called to pick up some canoes down at Skinner's Falls. Miller told Charlie to park Buff in the shade, to keep the smell down.

"I'm going to dunk the bucket loader into the river, wash it off," he said. "We'll drive this load over to the dump later, surprise hell out of Rip Judge."

After Nick got back from his downriver canoe runs, and Miller and Charlie finished up their work, Miller waved them over to Buff.

"Let's go get some goddamn supper," he said. "Then we'll go deliver Rip the first load of genuine elephant shit the Delaware Ford dump has ever got."

Miller drove. He had some trouble finding the gears, but managed to make enough forward progress to get from the campgrounds to the Wild Turkey. Fortunately, traffic was light by that time of day, most of the campers having left.

It wasn't quite light enough, though.

As they turned the corner onto Upper Main, they spotted the car that made them groan in unison. Parked in front of the Wild Turkey, white sidewalls gleaming in the evening light, was Bert and Jim's midnight-blue Lincoln Continental.

"Sons of bitches!" Miller cursed. "Why the hell didn't they pull out with everybody else?"

"Maybe they're sticking around for some more fishing," Charlie said.

"Pains in the ass," Miller said, and parked Buff in front of the Lincoln.

They were drinking cocktails at the far end of the bar. Their

American-flag caps swiveled when the door opened, but Miller grabbed the first stool inside the door. He'd had enough of Bert and Jim.

Jake set up three drafts.

"Evening, boys," Jake said. "'Bout got 'em cleared out down there?"

"Not quite," Miller said.

Jake winked at them. "I hear the fishing's a bit off."

They ordered dinner, and the evening crowd drifted in. Local tradesmen, canoeists, camp counselors, summer people, seasonal help from the hotels—the usual mix—gathered to drink beer and eat roast beast, listen to the jukebox, and get through the evening on a mellow glide. As more people drifted in, they absorbed the space between the campgrounds crew and Bert and Jim. The din grew steadily.

Lisa Marie came in later. "You guys haven't gone to the dump yet?" she asked.

"Working up to it," Miller said. "You got the office closed up?"

"Francis is closing."

Lisa Marie sat next to Charlie. She looked great: long straight hair, denim bellbottoms, sandals.

Jake set them all up with a round of drinks.

"On the fishermen down the way," he nodded.

Nick and Charlie raised their glasses toward Bert and Jim, who took this as an invitation.

"Oh, Jesus," Miller said. "Don't encourage 'em."

Bert and Jim made their way through the crowd. Before they got far, though, the door swung open and two guys off the railroad came in, grinning.

"Who's driving the red Cornbinder?" one of them hollered.

"Er, that'd be these two lads," Miller said.

"Well, what the hell you hauling?" The guy took off his striped railroad hat and waved it. "Pretty potent stuff."

"That, gentlemen, is one hundred percent pure unadulterated elephant shit," Miller said. "I'd say it's the finest in the river valley at this particular moment in time."

"Elephant shit!" they hollered, and then Miller was off and running with the story of the elephant and its prodigious digestive powers, and he had everybody's attention for several minutes. Even Bert and Jim could only stand back and laugh.

"Ought to take some home and put it on the old lady's garden," Miller said. "Grow some elephant-sized tomaters!"

"Maybe you ought to dump it in the river," Bert said. "Grow some elephant-sized fish."

"Oh, Jesus," Miller said. "When the hell you pains in the asses pulling out?"

"Tomorrow," Bert said. "We like to take a boys' night out."

He glanced at Lisa Marie.

"So what do you do in this town for excitement?" Jim asked. He, too, looked at Lisa Marie, who rolled her eyes and sipped her drink. In the store, she got this question several times a day.

Miller unwrapped a fresh cigar.

"Depends on the time of year, Mista," he said.

"How's that?" Jim asked.

"In the summertime, we fish and we fuck," Miller replied. "In the winter, we give up fishing."

Everybody yucked it up, even Bert and Jim, and Nick couldn't help but compare them to Miller. All three men were of the same age, around fifty—the World War II generation. With their crewcuts and the set of their clean-shaven jaws, Bert and Jim were so locked into their righteousness that they couldn't see past it. Miller faced them off, with his sideburns and wry grin, and not only accepted what was happening in the world, he reveled in it. Bert and Jim were order and control; Miller was sheer chaos.

Bert's eye caught on something outside the window.

"Oh, no," he said. "This isn't happening."

Lucas Bliss's school bus rocked to a stop across the street, uttered a raucous *oogah! oogah!* and disgorged his whole crew of crazies. They tumbled out and headed toward the bar as a colorful, careening mob.

"I can't believe this," Bert said.

"Hot damn!" Miller hoisted his beer. "Let the good times roll!"

Lucas's crowd poured in through the screen door, and immediately doubled the population of the Wild Turkey. They pumped quarters into the jukebox, lined quarters up on the pool table, slapped quarters onto the bar. They started singing along to "Good Morning Starshine" and "In the Year 2525." Juicy Lucy came by with a pool cue, braless under her T-shirt, and Bert and Jim couldn't resist taking a good long look over their cocktail glasses.

Lucas made his way up and down the bar, bullshitting with friends, buying rounds. He wore a straw Panama hat and a white tuxedo shirt, and he smoked a hand-rolled cigarette in rainbow-colored paper. When he got to the campgrounds crew, he raised his glass.

"Great circus the other night," he said. "Great party."

"When it wasn't being disrupted," Bert said.

Lucas grinned at him around his cigarette.

"I like your hat, man," Lucas said. "Really dig that flag."

In 1969, the flag was a rallying symbol. Right-wingers affixed it to hard hats and truck bumpers and lunch pails to show their patriotism, and left-wingers turned it upside down on their army jackets and rear windows and backpacks to show their concern for a country in turmoil. On the back door of his bus, Lucas had painted a flag with a white peace sign where the stars should be.

"You got a problem with the American flag?" Bert asked.

"Nope," Lucas said. "It'd just be more appropriate upside down."

Lucas reached up, but Jim grabbed his arm.

"Keep your hands off his hat," Jim said. "We fought for that flag."

"Which is more than you can say," Bert said.

Lucas removed his arm from Jim's grasp and took a drag on his cigarette. He gave them back a gaze as level as theirs.

"You don't know shit, man," Lucas said.

Facing off against Bert and Jim, Lucas looked tougher than they had reckoned. Lucas had done most of a tour in Vietnam, until one day he was caught in a firefight across a rice paddy. His squad was out on point, drawing heavy fire and taking casualties. "I was scared, man," Lucas had told Nick one night in the Depot, while the other vets were down the bar. "Rounds slamming into the mud, and it was just me and my buddy Walton out there. I think everybody else was dead or wounded. The rest of the platoon was too far back to do any good. All of a sudden the firing stopped. It got quiet, but my ears were ringing and there in the mud and the heat I thought about my property back in the world, my pond up in the Beechwoods, how I could almost be lying in my pond and watching the dragonflies light on the water. I could almost smell the pondwater, man, I wanted to be there so bad. And then the firing started up, and Walton took one under the helmet. I felt this little splash on my cheek and at first I was still off in my pond, and I thought I'd gotten splashed with pondwater, but then I looked over and saw the mess and wiped Walton's brain off my cheek, and that's when I decided to leave. I set my weapon down. I crawled like a bastard back to the platoon. Lieutenant said, 'Bliss, where's your weapon?' I said, 'You can have it, Lieutenant. I'm leaving.' He tried to get tough, told me I'd be court-martialed, called me a deserter. 'Fuck you, Lieutenant,' I said. 'I'm leaving.' "

And he did, too. Lucas walked away from the firefight, got the first helicopter out of base camp. In Saigon, they didn't court-martial him, but they did give him a dishonorable discharge, told him his future was ruined now that he couldn't work for a government agency, but all Lucas kept thinking about was his pond and the dragonflies and going skinny-dipping with the girls he always had around. "So hey," he told Nick, "so I'm not gonna have a career in the State Department."

Bert and Jim didn't know any of this, of course, and Lucas let his eyes go glassy and distant, like he was seeing all the way back to the firefight.

"You motherfuckers don't know jack shit or anybody who does," he said, and wandered off to the pool table.

Bert and Jim made a crack about "getting some hippie 'tang" and retreated to their end of the bar. Nick and Charlie and Miller started pounding back the beers and digging the music and shooting pool with the girls in Lucas's entourage. Charlie held the pool table for an hour and then Jake's wife, Norma, got Nick into a discussion about pickled eels and suddenly it was two hours later and their heads were fuzzy, and Miller was saying, "Well, boys, about time to get along to the dump, wouldn't you say?"

Nick thought Miller was kidding, but on the bar sat a six-pack for Rip Judge.

"We still have that elephant shit in the morning," Miller said, "the old man'll plant us in it."

Bert and Jim were still drinking cocktails and muttering together. They had spent the evening giving bad looks to Lucas's crowd while eyeballing the chicks. Bert hollered up the bar.

"Down in Wallkill they're kicking the hippies out. You'd be advised to do the same!"

Miller picked up the six-pack.

"You bastards're sore you wasn't born thirty years later," Miller hollered back, and then to the rest of the crowd, "Boogie down, you longhair sons of bitches!"

Outside, they staggered to the truck. They were in bad shape. Miller diddled with the choke and the clutch while Nick and Charlie broke into the six-pack, and Buff roared to life and Miller cursed and ground the gears and released the clutch and cursed again when Buff didn't move forward. Nick sat in the middle, straddling the dump lever and the handbrake, and between Miller jostling the shifter and Charlie popping open the beers he was only half paying attention, but he did notice Miller trying to release the handbrake only to discover that it was already released and over the subsequent cursing and the roar of the engine as Miller gave it more gas, Nick heard a familiar whine, and managed to focus on the levers between his legs long enough to see the gearshift absolutely in neutral and the dump lever fully engaged. The meaning of the whine became clear as Buff began to shudder, and Nick hollered, "The dump! The dump!" and Miller hollered back, "Trying to go to the goddamn dump, but this son of a bitch ain't moving!" and Nick grabbed for the dump lever but Miller had the clutch out so it wouldn't pull back. "The clutch! The clutch!" Nick yelled, as the bed reached its apex and Buff shuddered one final violent shudder and the load began to slide, and then like a huge red elephant moving its bowels right there on Upper Main, Buff deposited the entire contents of its bed on the shiny blue Lincoln Continental behind it.

"Oh, sweet Jesus," Miller said, and dropped the bed and found first gear and bucked Buff into motion. "Oh, dear God."

They rumbled off, and in the side-view mirror the second-to-last thing Nick saw was a big manure pile with white sidewalls parked in front of the Wild Turkey. The very last thing he saw was Lucas and his zaned-out crowd in the front windows, cheering and giving them a standing ovation.

17

A COUPLE OF days after the Fourth, an aqua Dodge motor home appeared on Phil Sweeney's site. It was huge, sleek, and shiny, and it made Phil's dinged-up Avion look shabby. As Nick collected the garbage in the Meadow, he could see some activity inside, people moving around. And when he had finished with the Meadow sites and Charlie had swung Buff around toward the office, the boys found themselves trundling behind the motor home's aqua rear end. A dealer plate joggled over the rough stone of the lane.

"C'mon, *c'mon*," Charlie said. "These road hogs can't get out of their own way."

The motor home parked in front of the office, and Ted emerged from it.

"What the hell?" Charlie said.

Nick was surprised. He hadn't realized Ted was back, and seeing him pop out of the side of this big, shiny bus took Nick by surprise. And something struck him as weird. He wasn't sure what, just something.

Ted was all smiles as Nick and Charlie jumped off the garbage truck.

"Climb aboard, guys," he said. "Check her out. I'll go get Francis."

The boys oohed and aahed over the wall-to-wall carpet, the shower and chemical toilet, the sound system. They swiveled in the captain's chairs and put their feet on the dash. Dark-tinted windows cut the glare. The new-car smell inspired possibility.

"Some way to travel, man," Charlie said. "Get a couple of chicks and head cross-country. Friggin' paradise."

They were checking out the bunks when Francis climbed in, talking to Ted.

". . . twenty thousand? And you committed to how many?"

"Twelve," Ted said. A pause while calculations were made. "We got a good deal. Volume breaks in lots of six, and you can't put a rental fleet on the road unless you've got a fleet."

"We hadn't agreed on fleet rentals," Francis said. "Trailers on our property are one thing. Motor vehicles on the road are another. Golly, Ted. The liability."

"The offer was only good for twenty-four hours. They had a livery in Florida asking for the whole lot. I had to make a linesman's call."

"Damn it, Ted! You had no right—" And then Francis noticed the boys on the bunks. "You guys go find something worthwhile to do."

He slammed the door behind them, but they could hear the yelling through the sealed fiberglass shell.

Nick and Charlie could do the multiplication too.

"A lot of bread," Nick said. "Where's he going to get that kind of money?"

Charlie pushed some strands of hair away from his forehead and exhaled.

"Who knows, man."

That motion of his, pushing his hair away and looking slightly baffled afterward, was so familiar that Nick saw, for a moment, a younger Charlie, a photo in his mother's album. When the boys were twelve or so, Ted and Francis had taken them on a bluefishing charter out of New Jersey, and afterwards they had lined up on the dock with their catch. As the shutter clicked, Charlie had pushed his hair back. It was shorter then, of course, but the camera had captured that momentary bafflement and blowing of breath.

"Who the hell knows," Charlie said. "Too many zeroes for me."

Ted had seemed so blasé about it. Like it wasn't a matter of money, it was a matter of finding out where to spend it. Nick and Charlie hung around the canoe shed until Francis stormed out of the motor home and over to the office. As Nick sorted paddles in the gear bin, the image of his father chafed at him: Francis striding across the parking lot, his face twisted with anger while the aqua motor home gleamed like a jewel in the sun. Nick pictured the scene earlier on Phil's site, the figures moving inside the motor home. That's what was weird: Ted had shown the thing to Phil before he had shown it to Francis. He had shown this new venture to Phil the bonehead camper before he had shown it to his business partner.

18

WHEN SHE HEARD the vehicle crunching down the driveway, Kit assumed it was someone for a trail ride. The morning riders had left, and she had nothing scheduled until one o'clock. But people dropped in all the time. She looked out and saw the front end of a big aqua motor home. That would mean four, maybe five or six riders. Eva and Stacey were saddling up for the one o'clock, but Stacey could split off the horses for a ride now. Eva could bring in their replacements. Buckskin hadn't seen service in a couple of days, Big Boy's split hoof was healed, and old Smokey was always game.

Two long blasts of the horn made the horses nicker and stomp, and the coach pulled up so close that its gaudy blue nose poked into the runway of the barn. Kit sprang from her desk in the first stall to wave off the driver—*What the hell is wrong with these city people anyway? This barn look like a bus garage?*—but when she peered up at the windshield and beheld a wide smile under a pair of aviator shades, she flushed and a familiar weight dragged her down.

Ted backed the motor home around in a semicircle, opened a door in the fuselage, and padded down the steps.

"Top of the morning to you," he called.

"Good morning." She was always formal with him now, all business. "You spooked my horses."

"Ah!" He flashed his grin. "They'll get over it."

He nodded toward the motor home. "Wanted to show you our newest enterprise."

His soft belly tipped over the edge of his khakis, and he stood with one hand in his pocket. His loafers splayed at right angles and he seemed comfortable. He had always seemed comfortable, she realized, no matter where he was: in his own living room, in yours, on the bank of the river, in a speeding car. No doubt he was comfortable in boardrooms and investors' offices, and that had the effect of making others feel comfortable, too. Comfort led to familiarity and familiarity led to trust. And with Ted, trust led to his advantage.

She knew he was waiting for her to say something nice about his vehicle—something about how plush and deluxe it looked, or even that she liked the color—but since Francis had come home last night with the news about the motor homes she had alternated between an angry simmer and a plunge into despair. The money hadn't come from the campgrounds, Francis had said. The business account couldn't even cover the down payment. No checks had been written. No notes had been signed. Ted was out on his own with this one.

"It looks expensive," she said.

"Expense is relative." He regarded the motor home and then the saddled horses in the paddock. He removed his shades in a smooth motion and then turned his big soft eyes up at her. "You know what's expensive? Expensive is a family of four flying to Florida or Maine and then renting a hotel room for a week and eating all their meals out. With one of these"—he patted the side of the motor home like it was one of her horses—"they can drive their hotel room wherever they want to go, park at the beach or out in the woods or even in the middle of the city, screw the airline schedules and the No Vacancy signs, and they can do it all cheaper."

Right, Kit thought. Now there's a vacation. Pounding down the highway all day, cooking for the family in a cramped galley, washing the dishes in a sink that holds a coffee cup and a butter knife, and then sleeping communally on bunk beds or a folded-down table. A shower that doesn't have enough pressure, hot water that runs out, a toilet that backs up. No thanks.

"Rental agencies in Long Island are making a fortune on these babies," Ted continued. "People are changing the way they take vacations. The roads are going to be jammed with outdoorsy types, and we can help put them there. Forty weeks' rental on these motor homes will pay for them. After that, it's money in the till. How expensive does a quarter million bucks gross sound?"

He slipped his shades back on in a gesture that was supposed to look dramatic, provocative. An exclamation point after his question mark. But she wasn't being punctuated. She'd heard it a hundred times, how, since they hadn't had to buy the property, their startup costs would amortize in five years; how six Coleman pop-up campers would pay for themselves in three months; how a fleet of canoes would be profitable in one season. Well, Ted's benchmark dates came and went, and she and Francis were no better off than they'd been before they took on each new enterprise.

"Who's going to pay the repair bills when these things start breaking down in Florida and Maine?" she asked.

"Depends on whose responsibility it is," Ted said. "Customer inflicts damage, customer pays. Routine wear and tear, we do."

"And when the customer spends two or three days of their vacation broken down alongside the road, who deals with the angry phone calls? Who pays their motel bills while this thing is up on jacks?"

"Kit." Ted shook his head. "You can't run a business on the most negative vision you can conjure up. If those things happen, we deal with them. Ninety-nine percent of the time everything is fine. You don't let the one percent stop the whole show. You don't let it keep you from moving forward."

"It doesn't keep *you* from moving forward. You're not going to be in the office when the phone calls start coming in. You're not left behind with the problems."

"Now, Kit. We've all got our jobs to do . . ." and he was off on how valuable she and Francis were to the overall cause, how because they did their jobs so well he could do his, but she tuned him out. She drifted off, let his words wash over her without sticking, because if there was one thing she'd come to despise, it was when somebody started a conversation saying "Now, Kit." *Now, Kit. I'm going to tell it like it is. Now, Kit, I'm going to set you straight.* All she had to hear were those two syllables and her blood started to race. *Now, Kit—you dumb woman—let me tell you what you should be thinking.*

So while Ted rattled on about team effort and pulling together— "Like horses on a trail ride, all of us in the same direction . . ."—she drifted not only from the wash of the words but from the man's physical presence, so that she began running down a checklist of the things still to do for the one-o'clock ride: finish saddling Frosty and Midnight, check Roxanne's girth strap because she'd blown herself up on the first tightening, make sure Cherokee's bridle wasn't worn through again. She knew Stacey was in the stall with Cherokee right now, and that's where she needed to be, not out here with this wash of condescension breaking over her head, upon her back as she turned away, growing fainter as she approached the barn. What stopped her was that two-syllable reprobation, "Now, Kit," that came not as a jolt but as a kind of plea.

"Now, Kit," he said. "Don't be that way."

She turned. He looked pathetic in front of the blue motor home, his feet splayed, sunglasses in his hands, squinting.

"I want you to see this coach," he said. "I want you to appreciate what we're getting into here. We're all in this together."

"I can see it fine from here," she said. "It looks like a big blue egg."

"Come on over here and really get a look at it," Ted urged. "It's got wall-to-wall carpeting and stereo throughout. You really get a look at it, you'll see why people will want to rent it. It's got a full-size bathtub."

"Well, I hope people will want to rent them now that we own a slew of them. Or you do, or whoever holds the paper." She knocked her boot heel against the barn door. "I wouldn't want to track horse manure on that wall-to-wall."

"Oh, come on, Kit." He waved toward the river valley. "Kick off your boots. Let's go for a little spin. See the world through a different windshield for a few minutes."

"No thank you."

"Take a break. Stacey and Eva can handle the place for ten minutes. Just a little spin up the river—"

"I am not getting in that thing."

"Five minutes up the river road, five minutes back—"

"I'm not getting in that thing with you, so you can save your breath for paying customers. Thank you for showing it to me. I hope you're right about the renters. Now I have work to do."

She turned and walked down the runway. She could feel his eyes on her, feel his disappointment in the big, brown teardrop lenses of his shades. Well, too bad. You reap what you sow.

"Cookie, Cherokee take that bridle all right?" she called to Stacey to let Ted know she was back to business, that his visit was over. "Eva—everybody saddled up for one o'clock?"

She joined Stacey in Cherokee's stall and pretended to fuss with the tack. The nerve. Come over here and show off his latest expense. Rub it in her face like some big shot. And then try to sweet talk her into that rolling bedroom. She tightened Cherokee's bridle and the little horse tossed his head and Stacey reprimanded her: "Mom, I already got it—you're making it too tight," and she heard the motor home start up, the engine race, so she walked back up the runway as the big blue egg rolled out of the driveway.

She went into her office to check the appointment book again and to reach automatically for her cigarettes—even though she knew she wasn't going to have one, just wanted to touch the papery cylinder, to feel it in her fingers and take some comfort from it—and that's when she noticed the cashbox. It wasn't where she always left it. She kept it on the far side of the desk so that anybody going for it would have to reach across her, but that's not where the box sat now, as she calculated the time she'd been down the barn with Stacey—what, three or four minutes? The box sat cockeyed on the desk, dragged over her clipboard, and the lid was popped. She always kept it latched.

All the big bills were gone. He had left a few ones and some loose silver, but the twenties and tens—the earnings of her morning rides and what she needed to make change—were missing. Ninety dollars, she figured quickly, and she pictured his hand, which a few minutes before had waved her toward the motor home, plunging into the cashbox while her back was turned.

No, not plunging like a common thief. Unsnapping the lid like he owned it, reaching in a proprietary way, calmly lifting out what he believed to be his, and flipping shut the lid. Walking away, folding the bills into his pocket. Another revenue stream.

Stacey had earned thirty of those dollars by giving pony rides to kids while Eva took the adults on the five-mile trail. Little Stacey, their Cookie, always so serious with the kids, making sure they had a good grip on the saddle horn, that their stirrups were adjusted right. She took her job so seriously, was always glad to help in the family business. And Eva, an excellent horsewoman, who sat her horse with such elegance and tolerated no nonsense on the trail even when the young husbands flirted with her, always did her job well and then watered the horses afterwards, loosened their cinches while they awaited the next ride. And Kit herself—she had gotten to the barn early, as she did every morning, for the feeding and the mucking of stalls and the spreading of fresh sawdust, those chores that gave her such pleasure, that rooted her day, started her off with something familiar and necessary that got the daily business cycle turning, that would result in actual cash dollars deposited in the bank, would help keep the family solvent. She dealt almost entirely in cash at the stables, and never once had she thought about pocketing a dollar for herself—it was the family business, and circumventing the agreed-on procedure of transaction-deposit-paycheck would have been like stealing from her own husband, her own children.

And that's exactly what Ted had just done, she thought as she beheld the bereft cashbox. Stolen from her and Francis and Stacey.

Her truck was a dozen strides from the barn door, and she didn't bother calling to Stacey or Eva. She spun the tires in the dirt, kicked up a cyclone of dust, slammed the rear shocks against the bed as she took the potholed driveway at fifty. Sprayed gravel as she hit the river road and turned north—the direction he would have taken, she was sure, since the road upriver to Callicoon was paved and he wouldn't have taken his new machine over the raw red shale that led south to Damascus.

On the hard road she punched in the cigarette lighter and then flipped open the glove compartment. She took out her cigarettes, lit one, felt the relief of the smoke in her lungs, exhaled mightily, and then reached back into the glove compartment for the .38. Set it on the seat beside her.

He had taken from Francis and he had taken from her and now he had taken from their twelve-year-old daughter. Taken her pony-ride money, taken the earnings of a young girl who got up every day to do her job, who shouldered her role in helping the family. And who was saving her paychecks—for what? For clothes or Beatles records? For a horse of her own? No—Stacey, with a maturity that could break her mother's heart, was saving for college. She knew she'd need the money someday, because even though the other two kids assumed that Kit and Francis would pay for their educations, Stacey was the practical one. When she had started giving pony rides she announced that she was saving to go to the veterinary school at the University of Pennsylvania. That was that. Kit was always touched by the gravity with which Stacey took her paycheck to the bank, clutched her passbook in her lap, and then studied it on the way home, totting up the column of numbers, announcing the amount she had saved, predicting how much she'd have by the end of the summer, the end of next year, the end of high school.

Kit knew Ted had no compunction about taking from her and Francis, but to do it to her daughter! She tucked the gun under her thigh to keep it from bouncing off the seat, and she steered with one hand and smoked with the other. Past the neighbors' places on the small road—the Holts and the Mackenzies. They'd wonder why she was driving so fast and maybe curse her or maybe assume it was an emergency, and she should see him any second, come around the next curve and see the blue hind end of that ridiculous bloated vehicle. He hadn't had that big a lead on her and he couldn't be driving as fast as she was—could he have gone downriver?—and he surely wasn't making the tires hum angrily against the curves, wasn't making the tail crow-hop over the frost heaves.

She smoked and drove and conjured coming upon him, slamming around him on the narrow road and cutting him off, forcing him over and then stepping out, keeping her right arm down along her leg so he couldn't see, but she made it all the way to the waterfall off the mountainside and to the Shad Shack and then to the Callicoon bridge, and no sign of him. She turned right to cross the bridge—he'd have to have been hauling, but he was known for his heavy foot—and when she was across the river she swung into Callicoon and gunned it down Main Street.

Still no sign of him. That big blue bus would have stuck out like a spaceship in the hamlet of turn-of-the-century Victorian storefronts.

She turned south on Route 97, but her confidence leaked away like cigarette smoke out the window. She should have come upon him by now. She'd been putting the spurs to it. But as she sped down the state highway, she began to lose the vision of pulling him over, of pressing the gun up against his chest and demanding her daughter's money. She flipped her cigarette butt onto the pavement, and by the time she got to Delaware Ford, she knew it was a lost cause.

She didn't even bother going down to the campgrounds. What was she thinking, pulling a gun on him! She turned up the New York river road and swung into the fishing access—mercifully empty this time of day except for a fisherman's boat trailer, the kids from town either working or sleeping it off or otherwise engaged, and she rolled to the top of the boat ramp.

What a fool she was! Taking off like that—poor Cookie and Eva not knowing what it was all about. Speeding along with a drawn pistol! She held the gun and felt its weight in her hand, clicked her thumbnail over the checkered pattern of the grip. Bastard. Son of a bitch bastard.

As always when she thought of him, his image was accompanied by weight. If she let the image go farther, the weight became the physical sensation of his chest pressing against hers, pushing the air out of her lungs, of his whiskey breath and his urgency on a night of too many drinks and not enough restraint, a night early in her marriage when Francis was at an ag seminar in Albany and she was home with little

Nicky. Sitting on the front porch, listening to the robins in the yard and the peepers in the spring across the Erie tracks, she had heard a car door slam over at the Mileses' lodge—a single car door, she had noted, muffled through the trees—and she had hoped both for and against Ted's call. When it came, she jumped. She knew it wasn't Francis; he had already called from his hotel room and they'd had a brief, slightly stilted conversation, neither of them being used to talking long-distance. So she let the phone ring and ring, even though it might wake Nicky. She hoped it would, in fact, so that she would be transformed from an admirer of a summer evening to a floor-pacing mother with her baby son in her arms, wanting the mother to take over from the dreamy young woman who heard love in the robins' late-evening calls, who sat in the dusk with her coffee cup, wondering if she had made the right choice by marrying a thirty-year-old navy man back from the war, by tucking herself away in a slow little farming community even more remote than her childhood home outside of Scranton.

The phone stopped, and a few minutes later Ted had come strolling along the lane. She had seen the amber glint of a bottle, the briefest of reflections on the inside of her mind. A perfect swimmer stepping out of golden-lit water. Saliva thickened in her throat.

"Evening," he said. "Didn't know if you all were home."

"We're home."

He shifted in the gravel of the lane, bearlike, and gestured toward the house.

"No lights," he said.

"Nicky's sleeping."

He chuckled, and though the light was dim, she could see his teeth flash. "Francis sleeping, too? Or just sitting in there in the dark?"

Francis's truck wasn't in the yard. That was clear, so he needn't toy with her. He shifted again and she could see his teeth but not his eyes, and he stepped closer.

"Join me for a drink?" he asked, raising the bottle.

She knew she shouldn't, knew she should decline and make some chitchat and then excuse herself and go inside. But he was dipping the bottle toward the pale rim of her coffee cup and she quickly dashed the dregs onto the lawn and accepted his offering. The first bite of whiskey was sharp, but the second sip wasn't as bad. The third tasted a little sweet.

"Long drive out of New Jersey," Ted said, and breathed deeply the cool mountain air. He kicked off his loafers and curled his bare feet in the grass. His toes were pale as grubs in the dim light, and she wondered what they felt like.

"Long drive," he said again, "but worth it for this view."

He was looking at her as he said it and then he gazed at the silvery sky above the mountain in Pennsylvania and, without meeting her eye, sat on the step below her. She looked down upon his head. Even in the dusk, she could see his crisp haircut. She caught a scent of hair oil, which reminded her of her father coming home from the barbershop on Saturday afternoons, his cheeks flushed from a straight-razor shave and two shots of bourbon in the tavern next door. A mosquito whined in her ear, and she batted it away.

"Margaret couldn't make it," Ted continued. "Allergies." One of Margaret's many reasons not to make the trip to Delaware Ford. Too busy, morning sickness. Prior engagement. Kit knew that Margaret viewed her and Francis as woefully backwoods, and she resented this. So why, if Margaret was so urbane and sophisticated, did her husband give long, smoky looks to farmers' daughters?

He drank from the bottle and gave a long sigh. "What are you doing here, Kit?"

Here? she wondered. On my own front porch, listening to the robins? Lost in my own thoughts?

"What's a woman like you doing stuck away in a burg like this? I always wonder if there's enough for you here."

He knew how to get to her, how to go for the tender spot and press.

"Mostly there's enough," she said.

"Mostly?"

"Mostly."

She drank from her cup and he drank from the bottle, and then he leaned on his elbow so his head was by her knee. She smelled his hair oil again, and something else . . . a kind of man-scent, a smell she had always associated with men: muscle and sweat and a deep earthiness, like the smell of roots or fresh-cut tree bark. This is wrong, she thought. It's wrong to be doing this. But it was as if she were stepping up to the edge of a rushing creek, as if the long looks and the kisses goodbye had been a creek building towards flood, and she knew she shouldn't be drawn toward such a rush, should take it as her cue to turn back, but she couldn't help it: The fascination was there, as if he could look into her and see a low-lying spot that needed filling.

"So what are you missing?" he asked.

The mosquito came back and droned around her head and she swatted again. She couldn't put words to the missing thing, couldn't tell him about her single woman's vision of a neat skirt and stockings with seams running up the backs of her legs, wheeling through chromed city traffic with her hair awhirl, arriving at a desk with her name on it. She couldn't tell him these things, so in answer to his question she knocked back the rest of the whiskey and held out her empty cup.

He turned toward her, and his chin brushed her knee. And when he refilled her cup, took another drink, and then leaned all the way back and rested his cheek against her thigh, she didn't pull away, even though she knew it was wrong to stay with him like this. It was wrong. She caught a quick image of Francis in his room in Albany, reading a paper on hybrid corn yields. But she pushed the vision aside. Yes, this might be wrong, but sometimes—the thought cut through her alcohol-fuddled brain as she felt a lifetime of correct behavior backing up like bile in her throat, as she felt the years of helping her parents on the farm instead of running around with the town kids, of going to secretarial school and learning how to sit like a lady while taking dictation, of waiting until she got married to really be with a man—sometimes wrong could feel utterly right.

And so, when he drew himself up and leaned over her and she smelled his whiskey breath and his earthiness and his need, she had murmured, "No," but she had not pushed him away. And though she gripped his arms as he began to unbutton her blouse, she did nothing to stop his hands. And when he laid her back on the bare porch boards and loomed over her, she knew it was wrong for the flow of her whole life, but that certainty didn't hold for this moment. The night and the whiskey rushed in her ears, and she gave herself over to the flood that had been building between them for two years.

Afterwards, as he put himself together and she simply lay there feeling the night air on her thighs, he had laughed softly.

"Francis should go off to these ag conferences more often," he said.

And so she knew. The mosquito whined in her ear again and she reached up and pinched it shut in her fist and rubbed the crud on her belly. She hadn't mentioned the ag conference. But of course Francis would have said something, of course Ted would have known. It wasn't a chance encounter after all, a fate-driven confluence of moments. It was calculated, as all of his moves were.

How stupid, she thought now, as she etched the checkered pistol grip with her thumbnail. How stupid and silly, to be a dumb farm girl with no more knowledge of the world than to be swept away by a smooth-talking man. How naive, to let a liar and a cheat get you drunk and seduce you. How wrong, she thought as she watched the glinting river pass before the truck's windshield, to let them take from us the things they take.

19

THE VAN VOORENS' fishing camp was a tidy, shingle-sided cottage set up in the woods, half a mile below Hankins on the Pennsylvania side. Nick had been in the place when he was about twelve, tagging along with his grandfather on a sweet-corn-and-eels delivery for a Van Vooren party. He remembered a black-and-white-tiled kitchen floor and a big soapstone sink. The place always had a special aura about it, for the Van Vooren parties were legendary—it was said that the Rockefellers came over from their Lew Beach summer digs, and Mayor John Lindsay up from New York, and once, even, a couple of

Kennedys. Chuck Van Vooren donated heavily to politicians local and distant, so it did not seem unusual that he'd entertain them at his private retreat.

For the boys of Delaware Ford, the fishing camp had an aura of a different kind. It was here, they told each other, that the Van Vooren girls brought their boyfriends to bestow on them unimaginable favors. Not that Nick presumed that he and Charlie were invited under those auspices. Nor was he expecting to meet visiting dignitaries. "A little get-together," Eva had said when she buzzed into the campgrounds. "My parents' friends and some of us kids."

Now, as he pulled in under the pines, his scruffy MG looked out of place behind Old Man Van Vooren's Chrysler Imperial and Harry Busch's big Olds. But Lillian Van Vooren, in a white sunhat with a yellow-and-orange paisley ribbon, welcomed the boys with a raised gin and tonic—"Ah, the rivermen arrive!"—and waved them into the gathering. Her arms were freckled in that fair-skinned way. She wore a white sleeveless miniskirt dress, cinched at the waist with a sash that matched her hatband. Lillian was about forty, but she wore her short skirt as well as her teenage daughters did, and Nick always thought she was the coolest mom in Delaware Ford.

She swept them into the backyard and motioned around by way of introduction. Old Man Van Vooren, stoking the coals, raised an ominous poker in Nick and Charlie's direction and said, "Gentlemen," and Harry Busch Sr. and his wife, sitting in a crescent of Adirondack chairs with Mrs. Brewster, raised their cocktail glasses. Harry Jr. and Georgie Brewster batted a badminton birdie under the trees and didn't look up from their game. Eva and Darlene came over all smiles and hugs.

Cecie called from the glider on the screened porch, where she swung lazily with Terence Skinner, "Hey, you campgrounds boys!"

Nick presented Lillian Van Vooren with a jar of Grandpa's pickled eels.

"It's early yet for sweet corn," he said, "but Grandpa sends you these."

"Oh, thank you, Nick." Lillian slipped between her daughters to give him a hug. She did it so smoothly, Nick could see where the girls got their grace. And their beauty. With her high, aristocratic cheekbones and blond pageboy haircut, Lillian was the most cultivated woman in town.

"Your granddad knows how to get to me," she said. "We used to say a summer party wasn't a party unless we were serving Nick Lauria's corn and eels. How's he doing, anyway?"

"Pretty well. Campgrounds keeps him busy. He's still got a little patch of corn and some apples on the way. Plenty of fishing to do."

Old Man Van Vooren stepped out from behind the smoke of his fireplace.

"Drinks for the campgrounds crew?" he asked. "Beer in the cooler there? Highball?"

The boys helped themselves to a couple of Heinekens, the green bottles waiting like frozen treasure under their crystalline layer of ice. Nick's hand stung coming up out of the ice chest.

Old Man Van Vooren nodded toward the river and asked them about canoe practice: "What's the concept on those paddles you're using?" He had a neat, squarish head with razor-cut white hair and pinned-back ears. He drank straight scotch on the rocks. Held his gaze as level as his glass, and Nick sensed that the man was taking his full measure: that Van Vooren noted how Nick drank his beer, how he managed his words, how he dressed. The First Bank of Delaware Ford was an independent bank, and Chuck Van Vooren held the mortgages of every homeowner and businessman and farmer in town. He hadn't gotten there by misjudging character.

"How's the river look to you guys this year?" he asked.

"Pretty full," Nick said. "All the rain."

"Yes," he agreed, looking thoughtfully down at the meandering water. "That and the releases upstream. Keeping the temperatures cool. Good for the rainbows."

Lillian came down the porch steps with a bowl of potato salad. She set it on the food table, shook the ice out of her depleted drink, and handed the empty glass to her husband.

"Chuck, be a dear and freshen that up for me, will you?" She turned to Nick and Charlie. "Quite a fragrance drifting down the street all this week."

The boys ducked and grinned. They'd heard that Bert and Jim had driven their Lincoln through town and up the river road to blow off the load. Residual dregs still lingered in the gutters and the parking spaces around the Wild Turkey, and nearly all the shop owners had called gibes at the boys this week. Eventually the traffic and rain would take it away.

"Sheriff asked me if I'd left a couple of stiffs in the garage." Lillian laughed and turned toward the porch. "Terence and Cecie, help me with the salads, will you?" She strode across the lawn, shifting under her short skirt.

Under her breath, Darlene said, "Another gin and tonic and she'll be as pickled as one of her stiffs."

Eva tweaked her sister on the arm, blew an air kiss to Charlie, and glided over to the badminton game. She wore a long muslin dress and sandals. The sun picked up the wave in her hair. She called to Georgie and the two of them conferred, the sun glinting off Georgie's glasses, and then he handed his racquet to Harry Jr. and took off down the riverbank with her. The Van Voorens' lawn was perfect for summer parties: nicely trimmed with a bluestone patio and fireplace, picnic tables and Adirondack chairs, and enough open space for badminton or croquet before edging up to the pine woods. A set of stone steps led down to the river, and Nick could hear Eva and Georgie thumping into a wooden boat, the first eager squeal of the oarlocks.

The salad-bearers appeared. Terence carried a big carved salad bowl on his flat palm at shoulder level, waiter-style, cocky. He approached Nick and Charlie with one of those smartass-jock sneers that he'd practiced with his football pals.

"So how're the canoe bangers?" he asked, and Nick knew this was a not-too-subtle put-down, meant for the senior Van Voorens and the Busches and Mrs. Brewster, because everybody knew how the Holy Trinity had tried to stop the campgrounds in the beginning, how George Brewster had written editorials about the noise of aluminum canoes banging in the shallows early on Sunday mornings, and Nick knew Terence was sucking up to them and likely felt some antagonism toward Charlie—one of his jock friends had no doubt tipped him as to Cecie's constant coo-cooing at the fishing access—and Nick saw Lillian shoot Terence a look, which Terence, in his marine-cut, biceps-flexing self-absorption missed, that big quarterback-team-captain-aspiring-lieutenant sneer on his clean-shaven mug, but Charlie didn't skip a beat.

"Banging everything in sight, Terence." He grinned and looked past Terence to Cecie, and Cecie giggled and Lillian chortled into her gin and tonic. Terence stiffened and lowered the salad bowl to the picnic table, his pectorals flexing like the gills of an excited shad. Lillian took his arm and gracefully turned him toward the cottage—"Give me a hand with the baked beans, Terence?"—and shot Charlie a bemused backward glance.

"Take us for a paddle around the eddy, Charlie?" Cecie asked, leaning across Darlene's shoulder, flipping her hair. "Being careful, of course, not to bang the canoe."

Charlie nodded toward the cottage. "Not right at the moment," he said. "Rain check?"

"Promises, promises."

"How's those steaks coming, hon?" Lillian called as she and Terence returned with a big aluminum pot of beans. Old Man Van Vooren held up five fingers, flashed them twice. "Dinner in ten, everybody."

Lillian must have spoken to Terence, because he took a beer and sat down on the grass next to Harry Busch Jr., at the foot of Mrs. Brewster, who asked, "How's your Officer Candidate School, Terence?"

"It's ROTC, ma'am," and he was off on the glories of regimentation and discipline and, glancing at Nick and Charlie, the benefits of personal grooming.

Lillian swirled her drink. "How are your parents, Charlie? I haven't seen your mother in ages, and Ted only now and then."

"That's about as much as I see them," Charlie said. "I guess they're okay."

Harry Busch Sr. perked up from his slouch in the Adirondack chair. "Ted's off putting together deals, I imagine?" Harry Sr. had a deeply creased face even at fifty, and he smoked a trim, leather-wrapped pipe. He held the pipe in one hand and his whiskey and soda in the other.

"Bought a hundred canoes two weeks ago," Charlie said.

When Harry Sr.'s blank face did not register the anticipated enthusiasm, Charlie continued, "And a dozen motor homes this week, at twenty grand a pop."

"Quite the salesman, your father." Harry Sr. passed the whiskey under his nose, orbited it away, and brought the pipe up and took a thoughtful puff.

"Always such a handsome man, that Ted," Lillian said. "Charlie, I know you're handy with wood. Come take a look at my pocket doors in the hallway—they're forever hanging up." She offered him her elbow.

Darlene nudged Nick toward the river. They sat on a big slab of rock that the Van Voorens used as their boat dock. It held an iron pin, an ancient, rusted eye driven into the striations. Out in the eddy, Georgie Brewster rowed the Van Voorens' old skiff, while Eva trailed her hand over the transom. Nick wondered if she'd ever gone skinny-dipping with Georgie. No way. Probably pop Georgie's glasses right off his head.

"Poor Charlie," Darlene said. "He has to brag so about his father."

"He never sees him. Ted shows up once in a blue moon, stays long enough to show us what he's bought, and then splits."

"Ha! We should all have it so lucky."

The sun had begun to set behind the Van Voorens' cottage, so the dock was already in deep shade. Out in the eddy, though, Georgie rowed from shadow into sun, and he squinted as he shipped the oars and spoke to Eva.

Darlene unlaced her leather pouch. "Want to get high?"

"No way," Nick said. Nobody on the lawn could see them directly, but all Lillian or Chuck had to do was walk to the riverbank. "I'll stick with the beer. You get high in front of your parents?"

"Don't worry—they've been drinking all afternoon. *They* won't notice."

Darlene brought out a tight little joint and bent toward the river to light it. She flipped the match into the water; it whirled and drifted on the current. Farther out, the oarlocks sang again, and Georgie began rowing upriver with long, steady sweeps.

"They look like my Grandma's old pictures," Nick said.

"Hmmm?"

"Like those old pictures from the turn of the century, when people used to come up on the train and stay in the boardinghouses and hotels. They'd row around in the eddies in these old wooden skiffs."

"Oh, yeah. My dad's got some of those, too."

"Put Georgie in a vest and bowtie—and a straw hat, they called them *boaters*, for Chrissake—give Eva a high lace collar and a parasol, and we'd be looking at 1905."

Darlene nodded. "Eva could have lived back then. She's so ethereal." She cupped the joint inside her hand. "And I think Georgie did live back then—he's so old!"

Georgie wasn't exactly the coolest guy in the valley, but he wasn't a bad egg, either. "He just never got away," Nick said. Even when he was off to college, Georgie came back to Delaware Ford every weekend, setting type or printing something down at the newspaper. "He never got out from under his old man."

"Well—that's not going to happen to me," Darlene said. "I'm out of here as soon as I graduate. And I'm not sticking around next summer." She nodded up the bank. "Cookouts with the boozers."

"Where will you go?"

"California, I think. As far away as possible. We have cousins in San Francisco. I could hang out in Haight-Ashbury." She looked up at the cliffs on the far side of the river, and her eyes were wide and clear, those of someone who had always expected to see a happy future in the distance. Nick tried to picture her in San Francisco, and the thought of Darlene out there with all those real hippies flickered a flame of jealousy in his heart. In all her protected innocence, Darlene could play at being a hippie here at home, but out in the real world she'd be as vulnerable as the other Delaware Ford kids.

She scanned the airspace above the river and took another cupped toke.

"Maybe we'll see the eagles," she said, exhaling. "They nest up there."

The setting sun etched the cliffs in sharp relief. Nick had seen the nesting pair of bald eagles along this stretch of the river, gliding along the mountaintop or perched in a pine tree. Darlene's patchouli came to him. He should have kissed her the other night at the campgrounds, lounging with her on the canoes. He should do it now. Surprise the hell out of her by kissing her under her parents' noses.

Darlene wiggled her toes in her sandals, pointed to a school of minnows at the base of the rock. She moved her hands in a fish motion and then flipped the roach into the water. The minnows darted. They came back inquisitively, to touch the roach and then dart back. Darlene giggled, a local girl again.

"They usually hunt this time of day. The eagles. Sometimes you see one dive and get a fish. You guys paddle every morning? My dad says he sees you when he's fishing."

"Couple mornings a week. If the night before wasn't too bad."

"We stay up here some nights."

"Must be quiet."

"Too quiet, Tonto. You ought to come up sometime and take me for a moonlight paddle."

He wanted to make a date on the spot, but from up the bank came the clanging of a bell. Out on the river Eva and Georgie turned toward the cottage and waved. Georgie swung the boat around.

"Dinner," Darlene said. "The bell tolls for we."

The adults had settled around the largest of the picnic tables. Charlie and Terence, their differences put aside, flanked Cecie at one of the smaller tables, and the rest of the kids loaded up and joined them. The adults were discussing the war.

"First troops arrived back today," Harry Busch Sr. was saying. "Beginning of the pullout."

"Supposed to be twenty-five thousand back by end of summer," Old Man Van Vooren added.

"Big mistake," Terence piped up from the kids' table. "Now's not the time to cut and run."

Everybody knew that Terence watched a movie of himself in his head, like those replays of football games, where he was the charging leader, and a zigzag drive down the worn turf of the Delaware Ford gridiron would fade to a hazy green and then fade back in to him hauling through a jungle or rice paddy, waving at his squad to follow.

"Big shindig down in D.C.," Harry Sr. continued. "Westmoreland addressing the troops."

"That's where George is right now," Mrs. Brewster said. "Ellie Glyzinski's boy Lester was in that group—what is it? The Second Battalion or something."

"Third Battalion, Second Brigade of the Ninth Division," Harry Sr. said.

"Whatever. Who can keep it all straight? George wanted to interview Lester when he arrived at McChord. Sullivan County Boy Returns Home and all that."

"Beginning of the end, maybe," Chuck Van Vooren said and then he lowered his voice and the other adults glanced down at Eva and some at Nick, and Eva and Nick exchanged a quick look, not obvious enough to catch each other's eye but enough to make sure they knew Felix was in their thoughts. Eva continued peppering her potato salad, and Nick kept digging into his beans. The adults spoke in lowered voices for a while, but it was enough to give Terence an opening. He raised a forkful of steak and said, "Vietnam is only one of the hot spots right now. We've got the Israelis and Egyptians fighting it out, and the Chinese and the Soviets flaring up. You take those idiots wanting to dismantle the ABM system—now's the time we've got to stand tough. Vietnam could still be a flashpoint for Russia." He popped the steak into his mouth and looked to the adults for confirmation. He got a vague nod from Harry Sr.

The first troops were coming home, and Nick's draft card was still fresh in his wallet. It felt weird, as if the card was attached to a long wire that could yank him out of his placid little pond at any time. In a strange way, it also felt good. The draft card was tangible evidence, like the Heineken he drank with the town fathers, of his passage into the adult world. The draft card said he wasn't a kid anymore. He could trade it in for a buzzcut and an M-16. He could burn it, if he dared. Or he could sit back and see what happened.

"Did you see where the FBI caught those chicks who trashed the draft board in the city?" Charlie asked.

"Good," Terence said. "Serve the dumb bitches right."

"Terence!" Cecie exclaimed. "They have a right to express themselves."

"Not by destroying government property," Terence said.

Nick had seen a picture in the newspaper: a pretty young woman, slim with dark hair and a miniskirt, scattered shredded draft records like so much confetti in front of Rockefeller Center. How vulnerable she looked in that little skirt, with nothing to protect her beautiful long legs from the FBI agents in their dark suits and sunglasses. She stood her ground, made her small act of protest, taking the war to the streets in a pair of wobbly platform sandals. In the next picture, agents with twisted faces hauled her off as their compatriots fought with the other protestors. The article said the FBI arrested six women.

"Terence," Eva said. "The government is destroying us. Nearly forty thousand of us so far. What's a few draft records compared to the loss of so much life?"

"It's the price of freedom," Terence said. "It's what you give to—" And then even he, too, seemed to remember Felix, how he had been Eva's boyfriend and Nick's pal, and instead of finishing his sentence, Terence took another forkful of steak, as if he had more to say but was too polite to do so while eating.

After dinner, Eva took Nick's arm and walked him away from the tables and up to the driveway. Nick could see Georgie giving them the eye, and he mentioned this to Eva.

"Oh, let's keep Georgie guessing," she said. "He's usually worried about Charlie."

"Should he be?"

Eva darted a smile. "What do you hear from Felix?"

"Got a letter yesterday."

Eva pulled a folded envelope out of her dress pocket. "Yeah—he mentioned that. How's he sound to you?"

"Okay," Nick said. "All things considered. Sounds like he's getting eaten alive."

"Yeah." Eva laughed and opened the letter. "He mentioned something about mosquitoes and red ants—'*I wear bug juice like English Leather. Slows the little bastards down anyway.*'"

"And the leeches? Did he mention the leeches?"

She shook her head, and Nick stepped over to the MG and clicked open the glove box. Felix's letter sat on top.

"Let's see . . . '*Fucken leeches're worse than the VC, man. Any exposed flesh, they find it. And if they get near your balls, you got a choice: a lit cigarette or a hefty dose of bug juice. Both of 'em burn down there.*'"

"Ooh." Eva grimaced. Occasionally she and Nick would compare notes, read excerpts from Felix's letters, keep each other up on his situation. Nick held back parts that he didn't want Eva to hear, and he knew she didn't read him the personal stuff.

"He says something about the red earth over there," Eva said and scanned down her letter. "'*Red mud, mostly. Makes me feel right at home!*' He always hated getting dust or mud splattered on his Chevy."

"That's for sure. He kept that thing spotless."

"I once accused him of caring more for his car than he did for me," Eva said. "I wish I hadn't said that now."

"Aah—he knew how to take it. He writes here about weird jungle plants like wait-a-minute vines and poisonous snakes called two-step vipers. '*They call 'em that 'cuz that's how many steps you get if they bite you.*'"

"Eee. He didn't mention that to me."

They both skimmed their letters, and Nick could see a fond smile play around Eva's lips, though she didn't read him any more. And he decided not to read her the last paragraph of his letter: *Got dropped into my first LZ yesterday, a bomb crater blown out of the jungle. They told us it was going to be hot, so we hit the ground and ran for cover, expecting to take fire. Got to the treeline okay, and after the chopper took off and the other guys settled down, the only thing I could hear was the pounding of my own blood. Then the jungle, the fuck-you lizards. Then some of the guys cursing. No enemy. Bad intelligence. Today we cleaned up the place and made a proper LZ out of it.*

Eva looked up from her letter. "So I guess he sounds okay, then?"

"Yeah—he sounds okay."

They walked back down to the party, where Georgie and Harry Jr. were lighting citronella torches. Georgie watched them approach, his glasses reflecting the flame of the torch, his round face curious. Charlie glanced up from the picnic table and his beer, and then returned to conversation with Darlene and Cecie.

20

ON THE WILD Turkey's snowy television screen, Neil Armstrong's left foot touched the surface of the moon.

"That's one small step for man," Armstrong said, "one giant leap for mankind."

Nick and the others at the bar raised their beers and cheered.

"And that's one dude who really knows how to get out of town," Darlene said.

Charlie nodded. "Sky pi-lot," he sang into his pool cue. "How high can you fly?"

"Huh," Miller said. "I've woke up to worse-looking landscapes than that without ever leaving town." He knocked back a boilermaker. "At considerable higher altitudes."

They were finishing off a quiet Sunday night. Nick and Darlene and Miller at the bar, Charlie and Eva at the pool table. Drinking a few beers and watching the moon shot. Nick clung to the television with a kind of awe. It was incredible, watching live images being broadcast from the moon. The moon! Incredible to have hit the target in the first place, to rocket the Apollo 11 spacecraft two hundred thousand miles on a trajectory to intersect a moving chunk of rock. Like shooting skeet on a grand scale, NASA had to lead the target and then get in position to launch the lunar module and then—this was the part Nick liked most—fly the little maneuverable vehicle to the surface. The television said Neil Armstrong didn't like the original landing spot so he flew above the moon's surface to a better site four miles away, where he touched down perfectly. So cool—driving a sports car in space!

Maybe he'd be an astronaut. Fly cool machines, catch some good views. Go on television. But you had to be a scientific or military dude, you'd have to cut your hair.

Still, he admired the astronauts. President Kennedy had urged Americans to put a man on the moon by the end of the decade, and some smart people had gone and done it. America wasn't afraid to take on big, bold projects. With enough technology and planning and gumption, Americans could do whatever they set their minds to. Put a man on the moon. Transplant a beating heart. Stop the Communists in a steamy little Asian country.

So Nick and the others raised their glasses to the astronauts. Charlie ran five stripes and buried the cue ball behind the four. Norma shut down the kitchen and came out to sit with Miller. Darlene ordered another vodka and tonic. She watched Charlie execute a bank shot and tap the eight ball into a corner pocket, whipped her drink down, and called, "Nice shot!"

Charlie took Eva's quarter and racked the next game. By now it was no secret: Charlie and Eva were spending time together, even though Eva was still officially dating Georgie Brewster. Georgie, however, didn't seem to have a clue, and since he never showed his face in the bars, there was little chance of him discovering Eva and Charlie. He would take Eva to the movies on Saturday night, and maybe see her once during the week. That left plenty of time for Eva to dally with Charlie.

But tonight Charlie was paying attention to Darlene. He grinned as he held up the cue ball and the eight.

"Give me luck, Darlene. Touch my balls."

Darlene smiled around her straw and glanced at the television.

Eva looked at Nick and then slammed the cue ball into the fresh rack.

Nick and Darlene had grown closer. Since the cookout at her parents' place, they'd gone to the movies twice, seen Barbra Streisand in *Funny Girl* and Paul Newman in *Winning*. They went bowling once, although Darlene didn't really dig it, didn't like hanging out with all the straights in crewcuts and farmer's tans, the women in bouffants and caked eye makeup. Nick didn't like bowling that much either, but he could drink beers while watching Darlene's hiphuggers crease her sweet denim-clad buns as she approached the long expanse of hardwood, and—maybe the coolest thing about the game—he got to wear those funky red-and-green shoes.

They first kissed on a float trip down the river. They took a big truck tube—Beagle's sold old tubes for a dollar; it was up to the kids to make them hold air—and put in at Van Voorens' cottage. They trailed a bottle of Boone's Farm in a mesh bag. It stayed cool and Nick hauled it up whenever they got to shallow water. They splashed and drifted, kicked and teased. Darlene wore a blue cotton bikini, and they touched feet across the tube or kept each other from slipping off. Her breasts beaded up with water and the soaked bikini pretty much showed everything, and Nick was glad he could keep his cutoffs under the tube so she couldn't see what was happening there.

They went swimming off a big rock below Callicoon and then baked on the slab, drying in the sun side by side, elbows and knees and feet touching, and then Darlene made a joke and Nick laughed and they turned their faces toward each other, and they kissed. They were still smiling from the joke, still chuckling in their throats—Nick could feel it in the kiss—but then it got serious and Darlene turned both eager and tentative, wanting to go forward, to kiss him harder, to let go, yet she held herself back and so he did, too, and they kissed long and sweet on the warm rock in the middle of the Delaware.

After that they were tender with each other, quieter. Nick helped her into the tube, and they sat arm in arm and passed the cool wine back and forth. They kissed some more as they floated along, and he tasted wine and river water and his own desire for more—a taste like blood or iron that made him want to keep going until he overcame it. In this way they made slow, drifting progress toward the fishing access, a couple more dates, and now this evening in the bar.

Eva won the pool game and hung up her cue.

"Finish those drinks," she said to Nick and Darlene, "and let's go see if there's a moon."

"Cool," Darlene said.

Charlie bought a bottle of Boone's Farm from Jake. He cranked it open as soon as everybody settled into his bus.

"Where to?" he asked.

"High Rock," Eva said. "It's about as close to the moon as we can get."

High Rock was the local party spot. Across the river from Delaware Ford, it rose in a sheer bluestone cliff from the river. Charlie plugged in a Steppenwolf tape, drove down Route 97 to Cochecton, crossed the bridge into Damascus, and chugged up the Pennsylvania river road. Nick and Darlene made out in the back of the bus with "Magic Carpet Ride" and "Born to Be Wild" pumping their blood. Nick fluttered one eye open to make sure Eva wasn't watching him kiss her little sister, but all he could see was her wild hair backlit by the headlights as she rocked to the music. Once, though, he met Charlie's eye in the rearview mirror, and his friend's look was full of devilment and humor and something else Nick couldn't identify. He shut his eye and shifted his shoulder to block Charlie's view.

Nick was relieved to see no other cars parked on the worn pull-off at the top of the hill. A misty Sunday night, everybody watching the moonshot on television. The weeds were wet on the trail. Trees dripped. Wind whooshed the leaves, and heavy clouds dragged across the mountaintops.

"Not a great night for moon-watching," Eva said, as they stepped out onto the ledge.

The sky was torn and mottled, but across the river Delaware Ford glowed in the valley. The streetlights and houselights defined the town's bone structure: the parallel spines of Railroad Avenue and Upper Main and the eight ribs of residential streets. On the north end of Upper Main, the theater marquee announced *2001: A Space Odyssey*. They could see the barber shop, two real estate offices, the Chuck Wagon, Darnell's Clothing Store, Kick's Superette, the hardware store, the Delaware Inn rising four Victorian stories above everything else, and behind it, in deep shadow, the darkened Opera House. The old stone library, the modern brick bank. The neon beer signs of the Wild Turkey and the Depot and Doc's ("Stop in for a Treatment!") glittered orange and blue and green. A single car rolled down Railroad Avenue and left a red-taillight sheen on the wet street. At the campgrounds on the south end of town, gas lanterns and campfires spotted the riverbank. Up on the spur to Route 97, Beagle's Gulf sign shimmered in the mist.

"There's your moon," Charlie said, nodding at the round orange sign.

"Have to do, I guess," Eva said.

Darlene hugged her arms. "I wish we had a campfire."

Charlie handed the Boone's Farm bottle to Nick. "One campfire, coming up." He headed back down the path.

Nick wondered how Charlie was going to build a fire. All the wood was wet. But the van door slammed and Charlie came back with two canoe paddles and a can of Coleman lantern fuel.

"The old canoe-paddle campfire," Charlie said. "An ancient Lenape Indian tradition, passed down through the generations."

The paddles were the junky rental paddles they gave out at the campgrounds. They weren't worth much, it was true. The blades split, the shafts splintered. Canoeists used them as prybars, cracked them on rocks. Francis ordered them by the dozen; they cost only a couple bucks apiece. Still, it seemed like a waste to burn them up.

"Business expense," Charlie said, and stomped one in half with his work boot.

"You're going to be up the cliff without a paddle, Charlie," Darlene teased.

Charlie patted his shirt pocket. "Better than being up the cliff without a whiff." He pulled out a fat joint and handed it to Darlene.

"Soon as we get a fire going, you can burn this." He stomped the paddle into kindling and then piled it near the edge of the cliff.

"And now, the ancient secret of fluid tinder." He doused the pile with Coleman fuel and motioned toward Darlene. "The lady may have the honor. Come on, baby, light my fire."

Darlene laughed and kneeled down and her hair swung forward as she touched a match to the pile and the fire flared up and both Nick and Charlie reached for her at the same time. Charlie got her first and caught her hair and lifted it back as she stood, so she wasn't aware of the danger that had been averted: She turned to Charlie and smiled, as if they were all alone on the ledge and he was stroking her hair.

Eva caught Nick's eye and sang, in tune to the Doors' song, "Try to set your head on fi-yur!"

Nick rolled up a couple of logs, and Charlie laid a good-sized branch next to the fire to dry out. Darlene sat on one of the logs. Nick squatted next to her, Indian-style, and took a shallow hit off the Boone's Farm bottle. He could see Charlie pretending to fuss with the fire, but he knew what Charlie was doing. Sure enough, when he had finished poking at the flames and adjusting the logs, Charlie sat himself on the other side of Darlene. Eva watched this maneuvering, too, and stayed off a bit. A bemused look flickered about her face, and then she leaned against a stump on the other side of the fire, rummaged in her backpack, and came up with her sketchpad.

Darlene lit the joint and passed it around.

"So what's the latest on the big concert?" she asked. "Anybody hear anything?"

"Oh shit, yes," Charlie said. "With all the news about the moon, it about got drowned out. The paper said it might be coming here."

"Here?" Darlene asked. "What do you mean?"

"They got shut down in Wallkill. Town zoned them out. So they started looking for alternative sites, and they've got two in mind: Newburgh and White Lake."

"White Lake! *White Lake* White Lake?"

"That White Lake. Dude who owns a motel over there's talking about moving the festival up here."

"It's still speculation, then," Eva said, sketching as she spoke.

"Yeah, but what the hell," Charlie went on. "It's been all talk all summer anyway. Why not talk about it coming here?"

"That would be so cool," Darlene said. "White Lake."

"They won't have it here," Eva said. "The local yokels won't stand for it."

"Never can tell," Charlie said. "Slip enough cash to the local yokels and see how accommodating they become."

"But this is so last-minute," Eva said. "The concert's supposed to be what—a month away? How could they pull that together?"

"Who the hell knows?" Charlie said. "I'm telling you what the paper said. There's supposed to be a press conference tomorrow, some kind of announcement."

"Cool," Darlene said.

"You getting my best angle?" Charlie mugged for Eva, swiveling side to side.

Darlene joined in, posing and cocking her head, flipping her hair. She and Charlie put their faces together and leaned toward Eva.

"Couple of knuckleheads," Eva said. "I'm getting Nick, actually."

"The quiet one," Darlene said.

Nick had been quiet since Charlie and Darlene took notice of each other. He always got that way when Charlie started showing off. He figured there was room in the spotlight for one only, and he was happy to let his friend have it. But he was bothered by Charlie's cozying up to Darlene. Why did Charlie have to have *all* the girls?

Darlene turned and offered him the joint in exchange for the wine.

"What're you thinking about, quiet one?" she asked.

He toked at the joint, pointed it up at the sky.

"The moon," he said. "Thinking about Neil Armstrong walking around up there. How strange it must be. Wonder what *he's* thinking?"

"About his air supply?" Darlene asked. "About gravity? If he jumped high enough, maybe he could float away."

"He *has* floated away," Eva said. "I mean, he's out there on that little dead planet. You can't get farther away than that. He must be thinking about his wife, about all of us back here on Earth."

"Right," Nick said. "And we're here with our rock concerts and our war. Life goes on, but one of us is walking on the moon."

"Maybe he's thinking about how to take a leak in a spacesuit," Charlie offered.

Darlene giggled at this, but she leaned over against Nick, and Nick put his arm around her. The wind scudded the clouds across some faint illumination and caused the campfire to ripple horizontally.

Eva whipped a page over her sketchbook and began drawing Charlie.

"I think our mom has a thing for your dad," she said.

"What?" Darlene sat straight up, shrugging off Nick's arm. "Our mother has a thing for whose dad?"

"Charlie's," Eva said. "Haven't you heard her talking about the campgrounds?"

"Everybody talks about the campgrounds," Darlene said.

"She always manages to bring Ted Miles into the conversation, though. *Ted Miles must be doing okay, all those new yellow canoes. Ted Miles has got himself a new motor home.* And he actually had that thing parked in front of the funeral parlor the other day. She was walking around with stars in her eyes."

"Eva! She was not."

"Like hell she wasn't," Eva said. "She carries on no end about Ted Miles."

Charlie smirked and leaned back. "A man's gotta do what a man's gotta do. Sport around in a new motor home, suffer the adulation of good-looking women. You know."

Eva folded her sketchpad and set it on her backpack. She eased around the fire, the breeze billowing her long skirt, and then she stood over Charlie and kneeled so she straddled his hips. She took the bottle of wine from Darlene and tilted it in a long swig.

"How tough is it, big man?" she asked and then covered his face with her hair.

Darlene turned to Nick and they leaned against the log. When they kissed, Darlene took the lead, opening her mouth and nibbling his lip. Nick eased his hand inside her shirt and she stiffened but let him go. Her skin was damp and her muscles tight, and he wondered if she did situps or whether she was just nervous. He opened an eye to get a clue from her face, but she was turned from the fire and shadowed. The wind gusted and the trees swooshed. A volley of drops pelted the fire and hissed. Was there light up on the moon? Moonlight? Could old Neil Armstrong see where he was going? When Nick touched the edge of Darlene's bra she swiveled, and Nick knew to stay on the familiar terrain of her stomach. The wind gusted again and made the fire hiss some more, and Nick wished the clouds would part so he could glimpse the moon.

21

THE FIRST SHIPMENT of Dodge motor homes arrived—three beige and two more aquas. Francis refused to sign anything the factory rep handed him, instead had Lisa Marie type up his own signatory note: *Acknowledge delivery of five (5) Dodge motor homes purchased by Ted Miles. Signed in his absence, verifying delivery only, Francis Lauria.* The factory rep briefed Miller on operating the appliances and the generator, emptying the holding tank, and maintaining the oil and the transmission fluid.

"Ooh, can I trade my Scotty in for one of those?" Celeste Gennaro asked Francis while trying to keep her kids from climbing over the shiny new bumpers and grilles.

"Not going to raise our site rentals now, are you, Francis?" Paulie kidded.

"Wouldn't trade my Aristocrat for one of these pieces of crap if you paid me," declared Ralph Cusack. "Who the hell wants to drive around in a house? Whaddya? I'll drive my Bonneville, sleep in my trailer."

Phil Sweeney shook his head. After Francis returned to the office and the other campers drifted away, Phil sidled up and plucked at Charlie's sleeve.

"Seen your father lately?" he asked.

"Not in the last few minutes, Phil. Why?"

"When you see him, tell him he needs to see me. It's important."

Charlie snickered. "Sure, Phil. I'll tell him. The second I see him. Your name will be the first words off my lips."

"You laugh it up, smart boy. Your father's in deep water on this one. You have no clue."

"He can swim, Phil."

"Not with these guys, he can't. Just have him see me."

Charlie made faces at Phil's retreating back, mimed an ape walk with dangling arms. But after Phil disappeared down the lane, Charlie asked, "What's he mean by that?"

"Beats me," Nick replied. "When was the last time you saw Ted?"

"Week ago, maybe. He took off in his motor home, hasn't shown up since."

Ted's latest disappearance had put Francis into a mood. Lately he'd been testy, his temper on edge. When Nick had seen a For Sale sign in the window of Mr. and Mrs. Haberley's beat-up Mallard camper, he had joked with his father about it. Francis had snapped, "No, I am not interested in buying another trailer, thank you!" When he wasn't holed up in his office with the door shut, Francis left terse directives on the clipboard in the store: "Miller check electrical service on Knoll. Charlie repair tent platform in North Area. Today." And when he did emerge, he seemed preoccupied, vague. Nick watched Francis pause by the driver's door of his Scout and gaze into the woods behind the pavilion for a full minute, then two. Nick finally walked over and asked him what he was seeing. "So," Francis responded, jarred back to the present. "Nothing. Mayapples growing right by the firewood bin. Never saw them there before."

The hubbub around the motor homes died down, and Miller came out of the store with the paper under his arm and a twinkle in his eye.

"Hash pipes in good working order?" he asked. "Stocked up on rolling papers?"

Sure, the boys said. Why?

"The hippie festival's coming to town, that's why. Wallkill kicked 'em out, and now we're taking 'em in. They're talking a hundred and fifty thousand hippies showing up in Bethel next month. Max Yasgur signed a deal with these Woodstock people, and I guess they're having the shindig over to his place."

Charlie grabbed the Middletown *Record* from under Miller's wing.

"Whoa, check it out." He scanned the article and read: "'. . . Miss Costello described the three-day event as a virtual camp-in aimed toward the younger set who bring their own trailers, tents, and sleeping facilities.' Blah, blah, blah. '. . . contracts signed with many national and international stars . . .' The Band, Jeff Beck, Grateful Dead, Janis Joplin, that's cool—and, oh man, Hendrix! Hendrix is coming to this thing!"

Nick couldn't believe it. Jimi Hendrix playing at a neighbor's farm, eight miles from Delaware Ford? It seemed surreal. Nobody famous came to this part of the world. Now Jimi and Janis?

Word spread quickly, and later that afternoon the fishing access was abuzz.

"Just over at Yasgur's, man!" Shag Foley said. "Hendrix at Max Yasgur's, can you dig it?"

"And Arlo Guthrie, the Dead," Cecie Van Vooren said.

"Creedence, the Airplane."

"Joe Cocker. Johnny Winter."

"Ravi Shankhar, the paper said. Wonder if he'll bring the Beatles?"

"Yeah, right," Bear Brown said. "The Beatles."

"The Stones, though. I heard the Stones were coming."

"Right. The Rolling Stones in Bethel. Maybe Max can get Mick to work in the barn between sets."

"Bob Dylan on the manure pile, man. Joan Baez chucking haybales."

A car pulled in, dual exhausts burbling. The Earl brothers, Pennsylvania greasers, in Bobby's jacked-up black Fury. They blatted the exhaust and spun a gravelly doughnut in the parking lot. The Fury was a battered heap, made up to look bad with chrome reverse wheels and big tires, a broad yellow racing stripe down the hood, and STP stickers in the rear windows, but it bore the scars of abuse: the grille still knocked out from the drag race with Felix, the passenger door bashed low where it had clipped a stump. A smelly haze of burned oil hung in its wake. The Earls pulled over by the outhouses, gave one final blat of the exhausts, and shut down.

Unlike other greasers, the Earls didn't stay in their car. They sauntered over, oil-stained jeans and boots, wolfgrins and veiled smirks.

They still wore sideburns and Vaseline, and they looked at the Delaware Ford freaks as curiosities to be mocked. Bobby lit a cigarette and rolled the Marlboro pack into his T-shirt sleeve. Tuggy hitched at his belt buckle and avoided eye contact.

"So what's going on?" Bobby asked.

Not much, the kids murmured. Not much. They didn't open ranks for the Earls as they would for their own. Nods, wary hellos. What did these jack-offs want?

"Not much," Bobby agreed. He stood with his weight on one leg. Smoke leaked from his nostrils.

"Shooting the shit about this concert," Eliot Winklewitz said.

"What con-cert?" Bobby asked.

Oh man, Nick thought. These guys were so out of it. Typical Pennsylvania. Always behind New York. Cross the bridge into PA, and you drove backwards about a decade.

A general bubbling about the concert, but the Earls didn't seem to know any of the groups. It would take Johnny Cash or Merle Haggard to get a rise out of these guys.

Eliot was always intimidated by greasers, and he started sucking up.

"So how's the Fury running, Bob?"

"Not bad," Bobby said, turning to admire his car. "Hundred and ten through White House Curve last night. Still the fastest thing on both sides of the river."

Tuggy nodded his confirmation, made flickering eye contact from behind his brother's shoulder. Bobby aimed his cigarette at the kids' cars.

"Faster'n all these VWs and hippie vans," he said.

None of the kids really gave a shit. The Earls were locked into a different era. The girls turned away; a couple of the guys joined them. Eliot started strumming his guitar.

Bobby, losing his audience, waved toward the cars again.

"Always wanted to have me one of them hippie vans, though," he said. "Anybody want to sell me one?"

Three vans sat in the cluster: Charlie's VW microbus, Bear Brown's beat-up Econoline, and Eliot's psychedelic delivery van.

"How 'bout it, Miles," Bobby sneered. "Sell me that kraut can?"

Charlie gave a little smile. "Think you can afford it, Earl?"

"Ho!" Bobby spun a half-circle in the gravel. "Man thinks I can't afford it. Man thinks I ain't got the scratch."

He reached into his hip pocket and pulled out a folded packet of bills.

"Name your price, Miles. Two hundred bucks says you ain't got the balls to sell me that piece a shit."

"Not for sale, Bob."

Bobby tapped the bills against his thigh.

"Two hundred bucks, Miles. Shit, your daddy gives you that for your weekly allowance."

"Not for sale, dude."

Bobby changed his stance, shifted his weight to his leading leg. Took a long drag from his cigarette.

"Tell me something, Miles." He blew smoke through the dual exhausts of his nose. "Those hippie vans good for getting laid in?"

"That one sure seems to be."

"Then maybe you ought to loan it to your old man."

This got everybody's attention. The girls turned toward the action. The guitar stopped.

"Yeah," Bobby went on. "Loan it to your daddy, Charlie. From what I seen of him and . . ." He paused and let his gaze rove over the kids and then settle on the trio of Van Vooren girls. ". . . a prominent leading *businesslady*, he could put it to good use. How's the shocks in that thing?"

Bobby and Tuggy snorted at each other, but now the intent of their visit was clear. To come over and humiliate somebody, somebody a little better off, somebody a little happier, to take out the frustrations of a life going nowhere at a hundred and ten miles an hour, and see if they couldn't rub somebody else's face in the shit of their own humiliation. Charlie was their perfect choice. He wasn't a true local. To the hillbilly Earls, he was considered rich and educated and therefore something of a pussy.

"The shocks are going fast, Bob," Charlie said. "I don't know who wears 'em out faster, me or my old man. Go through a set every couple of months."

Everybody clustered around. Bobby's insult to Charlie was overt, and the implication to the Van Vooren girls hung in the air. Nick stood shoulder to shoulder with Charlie, and Bear and Shag loomed on the other side. The rest of the crowd fanned out behind.

"One of those occupational hazards," Charlie went on. "How about you, Bob? Still on your original set, I'd reckon."

Snickers rippled out, and Bobby Earl squinted.

"Get my share," he said.

"Yeah, but your right hand doesn't count, Bob."

"You watch your ass, boy. You watch your ass."

Charlie nodded toward Bobby's Fury and then took an exaggerated breath.

"Jeez, Bob," he said. "Those shithouses over there need cleaning out, or you need to find a car wash?"

This brought outright guffaws from the crowd, and when Bobby and Tuggy stepped forward, Nick and Bear and Shag did the same. The kids' long-haired counterparts in San Francisco might be all non-violence and flowers, but the Earls couldn't be sure about the Delaware Ford crew.

Bobby flicked his cigarette at their feet.

"You stick up for your daddy, boy. We see you around. Catch you out on the road."

Charlie gave him a peace sign, and the Earls walked away. Pulled out of the fishing access in a roar and a spray of gravel.

"What a couple of assholes," Shag said.

"Way to go, Charlie," Darlene Van Vooren said.

"Yeah, Charlie," Cecie said. "What's all this about your love bus?"

"Yeah, Charlie," said Eva, striking a pose on the bumper. "Can we go for a ride in the Love Bus?"

Thus was Charlie's microbus given a name, and the vehicle was swarmed with kids pantomiming acts of love.

"Sure, sure, sure," Charlie said. "We can all go for a ride in the Love Bus. We can wear out the shocks in the Love Bus."

Cecie stuck her thumbs in the waistband of her bellbottoms and puffed out her chest.

"Yeah," she said in a hillbilly accent, "but cain we go a hunnert and tin through White House Cu-u-urve?"

"No, we cain't," Charlie said. "Hit's the slowest thang on both sides a this-here river. But let's go for a ride anyway!"

They piled into Charlie's bus and Eliot's delivery van and cranked up the stereos, passed around a bagful of weed, and took a slow, rocking ride up the river road. Eva rode up front with Charlie; Nick settled between Darlene and Cecie in the backseat, and behind them, Marisse Evans and Ray Vann lolled around on the floor. With the late-afternoon sun glinting off the water on the left and the Erie tracks rising on the right, the kids smoked and buzzed on about the Woodstock concert, and who was going where in the fall, and about the astronauts on the moon.

Nobody mentioned Charlie's dad and nobody mentioned the "prominent leading businesslady."

22

NICK'S DAY OFF, and it was pouring rain. He and Darlene had planned a hike and a picnic, but the pounding on the porch roof said that wasn't happening. It drummed him out of bed. He didn't feel like hanging around; he needed to get out of Delaware Ford. Even with the rain, he and Darlene could drive off to someplace else.

He started with breakfast at the luncheonette. A few guys drank coffee at the counter: Arvin Johnson, Kenny Wozniak, Roy Elwood. Miller waved Nick over.

"So what you doing on your day off?" Miller asked. "Get drunk and get laid?"

"No doubt," Nick said.

Maxine, the ageless counter waitress, served Nick a cup of tea, removed a pencil from her dyed-blond beehive, propped a receipt book on the shelf of her bosom, and took his order for bacon and eggs, over easy, with home fries and toast.

"Gonna win the canoe race this year, Nick?" Arvin Johnson asked.

"Gonna try."

"No practice this morning?" Kenny Wozniak asked. "I seen you and young Miles flying past my place the other day. Looked like a log in a flume."

"A log with hair," Arvin said.

"Gonna be a lot of wet hair over in Bethel, all this rain," Roy Elwood said.

"Rainin' like a cow pissin' on a flat rock," Miller agreed.

"It's them messin' around with the moon, is what it is," said Maxine. "They go knockin' around up there with their rocket ships and their big heavy boots, it's going to disturb the water."

"Jesus Aitch Christ, Maxine."

"I say, Miller. It's them messing with the moon. The moon controls all the water on earth, don't you know that?" Maxine regarded Miller like he was the town simpleton, and then turned to put on a fresh pot of coffee. "They're disturbing the balance. They shouldn't be messin' with the moon like that."

"That's prolly what made that Kennedy drive off that bridge," Miller claimed. "Didn't have a load on, didn't have that young dolly settin' on his lap. The astronauts shifted his water. Got him off his balance."

Maxine whirled around.

"Ted Kennedy drowned that young girl on purpose, and don't you tell me he didn't!" She drew a bead on Miller with the coffeepot. "She went to her death carrying his baby. The Kennedys are payin' off the family to keep an autopsy from turning up the truth. You mark my words."

"Lot of wet hair over in Bethel," Roy Elwood tried again.

Maxine glared at Miller, and Miller turned to Roy, who took this as his prompt to continue. "What the hell," Roy said. "Prolly the only time they get a bath."

"Who?"

"All them hippies Max Yasgur's got fixing his place up for the concert. Scurvy-looking bunch, you ask me."

"Jesus Aitch Christ," Miller said, glancing at Roy's unshaven face and fuel-oil-dribbled workshirt. "You're one to talk."

"Max's got to be making out on this deal," Arvin said. "Lost his corn crop, his hay, letting them kids run hogwild over the place."

Miller lit a cigar. "Getting a new suit, I heard."

"A hundred thousand, I heard."

"Two, I heard."

"Rick Davis says he was driving the hay truck past Max's place the other morning, and two of them hippie girls was bathing right in the cow pond. By Jesus, I don't know whether they'd smell better coming or going."

"Not that you'd give two shits what they smelled like, Roy," Maxine said, dropping Nick's bacon and eggs before him. "Diddle an old sow bear out of hibernation, still groggy and senseless, and consider yourself quite the stud."

Everybody had a good laugh at Roy, and Nick plowed into his breakfast. The newspaper lay on the counter, and the front-page headline read, "Construction Proceeds at Festival Site." A sidebar stated, "All Systems Go for Rock Fest."

Bingo! Destination.

THE FUNERAL HOME had a big circular driveway in front for the hearses and flower cars, and a private drive in back for the Van Voorens. The building was so big and sprawling that the family's living quarters felt detached from the business. Painted warm yellow with red shutters and flowerboxes, the funeral home always seemed like one of the happiest places in town.

Darlene met him on the back porch. She stuck her hand out into the drizzle and made a face. "So much for our hike."

"Hey, we can still blow outta here," Nick said, and told her about the festival site. During the past week, more and more hippies had been turning up in Sullivan County, hitching or walking or driving colorful vans to Bethel. They created a buzz of excitement. They revved up the local kids. Everybody wanted in on the action.

"Cool." Darlene ran inside and then came back in a bright green slicker.

They took the twisty creek road to Tamarack Lake, going easy on the wet blacktop. The rain corrugated the surface of the lake, pounded the car's hood. The wipers slapped, slapped, slapped the windshield. The MG's top leaked, and Nick caught a steady drip on his left knee. Darlene laughed and hunched her shoulders. On the shortcut to Fosterdale, a doe stepped into the road in that slippery, awkward footing deer have on pavement. Nick braked. Two fawns followed her across and into the woods.

Before the intersection with Route 17B, another figure stepped in front of them. This one stuck out a thumb. A short, skinny guy with a floppy hat. Army jacket a few sizes too big, bellbottoms. He was dripping wet, and he bobbed his head as Nick pulled over. Darlene hiked herself up on the transmission hump.

"Thanks, man," the guy said. He bobbed his head again and wedged his pack behind the seat. A thin mustache sprouted from his upper lip. "Been passed by six pickup trucks already. Two of them gave me the finger, one dude shook his fist at me, and one swerved and I had to jump into the freakin' ditch."

"Local hospitality," Nick said. "Where you headed?"

"Yasgur's. Working construction for the festival, man."

"Yeah?" Darlene asked. "Doing what?"

"Different scene every day. One day I'm laying water lines—I'm a freakin' plumber. Next day I'm digging fenceposts—I'm a freakin' farmer. Laying and digging, man. Digging and laying. What the hell—twenty bills a day. Keeps me in weed."

He fished around inside his army coat and came out with his stash.

"Looks like you're going to be working in the rain," Nick said.

"What's new, man?" He licked the edge of a rolling paper and stuck it to another. "Been working in the rain ever since we got here. Been telling these dudes to forget about building a stage, man—start building a freakin' ark."

He tapped some weed into the paper and rolled a joint. He licked the last edge of the paper, gave the joint a twist, and then wet each end between his lips.

"Smoke?"

"Sure," Darlene said, and popped in the cigarette lighter.

"You people from around here?"

"Delaware Ford."

"Been there. Good bars." The guy lit the joint and inhaled deeply, passed it to Darlene. "Great countryside. Lots of cows."

Darlene took a hit and asked the guy where he was from.

"Florida. Heard about this Woodstock thing and came north with some people. That Wallkill was a bummer, man. They fucked us over good. Better vibes up here. Better site. Better all the way around."

"Except for those dudes in the pickup trucks."

"Yeah, well. What you gonna do, man—cut your freakin' hair?"

Nick turned onto Hurd Road. For a country lane that normally got a few farm trucks and tractors, it was busy. They passed vans and utility trucks, and then got behind a slow-moving dump truck. Nick tried to pass a couple of times, but finally backed off and took another hit from the joint. The rain lightened; he switched the wipers to low. He felt the pot kick in as they crested the hill and beheld the festival site.

"Wow!" he said. "You guys are doing some work."

Ahead of them spread the hillside. It crawled with tractors and backhoes, bulldozers and dump trucks. At the bottom of the hill a wooden structure was being built, and metal towers were going up around it. Nick had to dodge an electric company cherry picker as it swung its bucket too close to the road.

"Stringing up electric lines," the guy said.

Everywhere, gangs of kids swarmed to their work. Off in a field, a haying crew tossed bales onto a wagon. The last of Max's hay, Nick guessed. Down the hill, another gang bent over a water line. Along the road, some kids wrestled with a chain-link fence.

"Wow," Darlene said. She had a wide grin across her face, and Nick realized he did, too. The pot had it stretched on tight. "Far out."

"Hope I'm not on the fencing crew today, man," the guy said. "Hope I can work on the freakin' stage. Take me down there, okay?"

He pointed to the structure at the bottom of the field. The stage was already covered with workers.

"Looks like you're a little late," Darlene said.

"Yeah, all the dudes at the boardinghouse split early and left me. I'm probably stuck on fencing." He pointed to a construction trailer. "This is good right here. Hey, you people want a job? They're taking about anybody shows up. Twenty bills, man."

"Day off," Nick said.

"Day off," Darlene said. "Thanks for the buzz."

"Thanks for the lift, people. Go in peace."

Nick eased through the workers at the bottom of the hill and made the corner onto West Shore Road, pulled into a dirt track. Off to the left, some longhairs were unloading a truckload of portable outhouses—aqua monuments shining in the rain. Nick pointed out a yellow backhoe grinding up the lane, and his eye caught on a familiar sight at the top of the hill: the psychedelic school bus of Lucas Bliss.

"Look!" he said, and Darlene exclaimed, "Lucas! Cool!"

The rain had lightened to a sprinkle, and Darlene put up the hood of her slicker. Nick dug an old mashed cowboy hat out of the trunk.

The bus sat next to some wooden structures. Juicy Lucy waved to them and hugged Darlene. Lucas's pals—Ralphie the Reefer and Johnny B. Badde—carried lumber awkwardly, and Captain America pounded nails with much more effort than was required. Buck Naked, clad only in a carpenter's apron and sandals, danced around the edges of the work, blessing it all with two handfuls of hay.

Lucas wore a pair of ratty jungle fatigues and a nail apron. He held a board up to one of the structures and appeared to give directions to the half-dozen people around him. Nobody moved. He shook his head and then happened to glance Nick's way.

"Nick!" he said. "Just in time, man!"

"Hey, Lucas. What you building?"

"Vendor stalls. Grab hold of this board, will you, Nick?"

Nick held his end as Lucas directed. It was a cross member that connected two upright two-by-fours. Lucas eyeballed it for level, said, "Close enough," and nailed up his end. He was handy with the hammer, landing long, solid blows that quickly sank the ten-penny nails.

"Vendor stalls?"

"Granola, man. Juice. T-shirts. Hash pipes, whatever." Lucas spiked up Nick's end with a brisk tattoo. "Shit, man. I ran a head shop, I'd be setting up right here. Gonna be head shop heaven in about three weeks."

Nick nodded. That's what he'd been hearing too.

"Hey, Nick, man—you want to give us a hand? We could use some decent help. A lot of these people never seen a hammer before."

Before Nick could make excuses about his day off, Lucas handed him his hammer and nail apron.

"Take this, and you and Darlene finish off this stall. Cross members around the top, shelf across the front, sheet plastic over the roof—check out one of the finished stalls for a pattern. I've got to go help these clowns before they fuck it all up."

Darlene and Nick set at the stall. She held the lumber while he nailed. The uprights were already in place, rising from knee-high cross members. They nailed on another set of cross members at waist level, where a counter would go, Nick figured, and yet another set to frame out the roof. They left one end open for access.

As he picked up the last two-by-four from the lumber pile, Nick spotted something in the grass underneath it. A wild turkey feather, brown mottled with black and flecked with white, pressed flat under the lumber. He scooped it up and presented it to Darlene.

"Oh, how beautiful!" she said. She shook the water off and then brushed the feather across Nick's face. "It's good luck to find a turkey feather. Thanks."

Nick gave her a short gobble. Another one. His grandfather had taught him to imitate all kinds of birds, and he had turkey gobbles down cold.

She laughed and tucked the feather behind her ear.

"Perfect," he said. "Pocahontas."

"Hey, look at that!" she exclaimed. Down by the stage, a crane hoisted a girl through the air to the top of one of the scaffold towers. She looked like a minnow on a hook, but she stepped onto the tower and waved the crane away.

"This festival's gonna be so cool," Darlene said.

"And big," Nick said. "The paper said a hundred and fifty thousand people."

"Coo-ool. An Aquarian Exposition." She gazed dreamily down the hill. "So romantic."

"Besides the bands, they said they'll be showing films and having songfests and artists and stuff."

"Poetry readings."

"Great. Maybe Eliot will read. Maybe we'll get to hear Eliot play his guitar."

"There's a bonus. But maybe some big poets will come. Allen Ginsberg and Whoosie-whatsie Ferlinghetti. Eva likes them."

She looked excited as she gazed down the hill, taking it all in, ready to jump into the next cool thing. Nick could see how this field was going to be a good place to watch a concert, the hill being a natural amphitheater for the stage.

"Your parents going to let you go to this thing?" he asked.

"Oh, screw my parents. Of course my dad said no. My mom's cooler, but Daddy's being a pig. A pig, a prig, and a prick." The rain picked up and Darlene pulled her hood over her head. "Eva's going for sure. They can't stop her. I think Terence has forbidden Cecie to even look at any guy with hair over his ears. But I'm going. Whether I ride with Eva or you or if I have to hitch, I'm going."

Nick pictured the MG loaded up with camping gear and him and Darlene buzzing over here. Since they knew the area, they ought to get a good place to camp. But where would that be, he wondered. The hillside was too sloping, and there were no trees. He envisioned a pup tent in a clearing in the woods, Darlene and him retiring there after a day of listening to Jimi Hendrix playing his guitar and Allen Ginsberg chanting his poetry. A little campfire, some wine. Darlene's excited face in the firelight.

"They must be planning on camping someplace else," he said. "Tough to camp in this field."

"You have stuff?"

"Stuff?"

"Tent, sleeping bag. You know, camping stuff."

"Darlene. I work at a campgrounds. Camping gear I got."

"Okay, duh," she said, passing him the ridge rafter. "Make sure you've got it ready."

That sounded like an invitation, and Nick felt the heady sense of the pot and Darlene's attraction. He finished nailing up the rafter.

"Lucas said something about plastic for the roof."

"Right—I saw it over there."

Nick watched her walk away, and his heart did a little flip. She was waiflike and beautiful, and they were going to the Aquarian Exposition together.

As they stretched the plastic across the framing, the rain came down harder. They got wet, but it was fun. They tacked the plastic up and made a roof, and then Darlene said, "Smoke break."

They passed Darlene's hash pipe back and forth. The rain peppered the plastic, and they could hear the yips and hoots from the others still working outside. Darlene shook off her rain hood. Her hair was wet and matted, and Nick tucked it back. He hoped nobody would come along to crash their party.

She scooched against him. He put his arm around her and she snuggled in.

"Apple?" she asked, and pulled a shiny Red Delicious from under her slicker.

The apple tasted fantastic. They shared it, leaving ovals of golden flesh in the deep ruby skin. When they kissed, Darlene tasted like apple and smoke and salt and rain. The hash kicked in and Nick felt a part of himself slip out and look down from above. This watchman always seemed to appear in moments like this, to separate and float above him, observing his actions with a detached, wry humor.

Darlene set aside the apple core and kissed him again. He felt flushed and heady and warm. She kissed him with a soft urgency and she smelled lightly of patchouli. Her scent floated up from her neck, and as his vision drew back he saw her cornsilk hair spilling over his arm, her tan ankles tucked under her blue-jeaned legs, her sure hand on his back. He felt so good that he wanted to laugh out loud, but then he was back inside the kiss and aware of nothing but the pleasure of her lips and warmth of her flesh and the endless smooth blanket on which they floated.

Until something began soaking his leg. A rivulet of water ran down the hill and he suddenly noticed how hard the rain was pounding the plastic of the roof, how the wind shook the stall.

"Getting kind of wet in here," he said.

"Hoo—" she said, fluttering her slicker. "I'll say."

"Wow. It's really pouring."

He expected to see the fields cleared of people as the rain pounded the site. But everywhere, the squads of workers still bent to their tasks. Nobody seemed to mind the rain. Many celebrated it. One guy down the hill did a rain dance, and near him, a soaking-wet girl had taken off her top and raised her arms to the sky, let the rain wash down her shoulders and breasts and belly.

Then a heavy wind hit. Everybody yelled. Loose plastic blew away, wind-driven rain lashed the hillside, and people turned their backs or sought shelter. Everybody working on the vendor stalls ran to Lucas's bus. There was a press of bodies at the door, a lot of joking and moo-ing, and then they were settling into the seats with wet clothes. Nick shook out his hair; Darlene pulled off her slicker. She wore a denim shirt, and her wet hair stuck to the darker blue patches across her shoulders.

The inside of Lucas's bus was painted with wacky cartoon characters: Wile E. Coyote chasing a joint-smoking Road Runner, Daffy Duck with a Beatles wig and electric guitar, Mickey and Minnie Mouse balling and grinning out at the audience. Mr. Natural, of course, truckin'. Lucas started the bus and plugged "Magical Mystery Tour" into the stereo, everybody broke out food and dope, and it was an instant party. Darlene brushed her hair and then Nick's. Somebody passed them a wineskin and they took a couple of hits and passed it along.

The wind rocked the bus. On the field even the stalwarts had run for cover. The storm showed no sign of slacking, and Lucas blew the horn for attention.

"Okay, people!" he yelled, without turning down the music. "We're just gonna get wet and wetter hanging around here, so we might as well go dry out and get something to eat. Myself, I could eat some pancakes! Anybody up for pancakes?"

"Pancakes!" came the chorus, and the bus rocked from within.

"Cool," Darlene said. "I love pancakes."

Nick would have liked to go along, but he didn't like the looks of the storm. It had now been raining since last night, and with the strength of this downpour, the creeks would rise fast. Big storms usually raised hell at the campgrounds.

Lucas revved the engine and rammed the shifter into gear. He caught Nick's eye in the wide rearview mirror.

"How 'bout it, Nick? Join us for some pancakes, man?"

"I better check in down at the grounds. Drop me at my car at the bottom of the hill, and maybe I'll catch up to you later."

Darlene touched his arm.

"I'm gonna get some pancakes with these guys," she said.

"Sure," he said. "You need a lift home later?"

"I'll catch a ride with Lucy."

Nick drove back to Delaware Ford soaking wet but happily buzzed. His mouth still held the taste of Darlene's kiss; his hands, the feel of her through her clothes. He smiled over at the passenger seat. Then he pictured her on the bus, Buck Naked or Captain America draped over her in the seat. He dodged a puddle. Fuck it. Whatever.

He drove along the slippery creek road. Rain dripped steadily on his knee. Tamarack Creek ran high and brown. When he crossed the bridge at Delaware Ford, the creek was already a good eight inches up the abutment. The fast water brought a pleasurable rush: the urge to paddle, to tuck into the water and work it with a blade and a light boat, riding the force, going wherever it would take him.

A lot of campers had set up along the driveway. He thought maybe a large party had arrived, a Good Sam club maybe, but he began to recognize campers that had been parked along the river. Then he saw Bear Brown driving the John Deere, towing a car *and* a travel trailer, the whole works spattered with red mud.

"Where in Sam Hill have you been?" his father asked before he could get out of the car.

Nick couldn't begin to tell him, so he said, "Day off."

"Day off nothing. The river's not taking a day off. It's coming up faster than I've ever seen it. Already running through the North Area and more rain's predicted. We're pulling people out of the river sites and moving them to higher ground. Go find Charlie and give him a hand—he's picking up picnic tables with Buff."

Nick started to go but Lisa Marie hollered from the store and waved him over.

"Letter from Felix," she said. "Came in today's mail."

He shoved the letter into his back pocket and cut through the woods to the North Area. Miller came splashing down the lane in the four-wheel GMC. He had a collapsed tent trailer hitched to the back.

"Jesus Aitch Christ, kid," he said. "What you been up to? Eyes look like two pissholes in the snow."

"Day off," Nick said, for about the hundredth time.

"Here." Miller passed him a Budweiser. "Cure what ails you."

Miller took off with a splatter and clank, and Nick slogged on. The river was indeed running down the lane that bisected the North Area, and beyond the bank, the main river ran high and seething. It usually took a couple of days of rain to do this, but there must have been some violent storms upriver. Once all the flooded creeks hit the Delaware, the big river came up fast.

He found Charlie shoving a picnic table onto Buff's bed. Eight or ten other tables were already stacked there.

"Just in time, man," Charlie said. "These tables are starting to push back."

"What's with all the water? Place was fine when I left this morning."

"One hell of a storm blew in from upriver. Campers on the lower end are stranded. Bear's pulling them out with the tractor."

They got on either side of a picnic table and flipped it onto Buff's big, scratched bed. Charlie sprang up and shoved the table against the others. Whenever the campgrounds got high water, the river would carry away tables from the low-lying sites. The boys usually launched a jonboat and ran downriver to round them up. They'd find tables washed up on banks, snagged in trees, and stuck on sandbars, and then they'd float them to common access points and collect them with Buff. Of course, they could never get all the tables—or somebody else would beat them to the strays—so now they tried to get them before the river did.

"One more and we've got a load," Charlie said.

They loaded the last table and then rumbled up to Grandpa's barn. Along the way, bedraggled campers stepped off the lane to let them pass. They looked like refugees, with sleeping bags and tents slung over their shoulders, lugging jugs of water and cooking utensils.

"So how was your day off?" Charlie asked.

"Great," Nick said. "I went over to the festival site."

"No shit. What's happening over there?"

Nick told him about the construction crews and helping Lucas. He didn't say anything about Darlene, but he couldn't help thinking of her at Lucas's place. He pictured her at a tableful of people, wedged in between Buck Naked and Captain America, each of them feeding her pancakes.

"Let's go get those tables in the lower sites," he said. "Or we'll be chasing them tomorrow."

All afternoon the rain pounded the campgrounds, all afternoon the river rose. Nick and Charlie got as many tables as they could from the lower end—with Buff they could drive through a foot of flowing water. They helped the rest of the crew haul campers to high ground. They got everybody, except for one travel trailer stranded on the point. The main river flowed beyond the tongue and the flood through the campgrounds ran behind the rear bumper. Francis loaned the family a rental unit, and the crew kept an eye on their trailer, but there wasn't much anybody could do. If the river kept rising it would take the trailer with it.

The flood carried all manner of debris: trees and railroad ties, flipped canoes and swamped boats, abandoned coolers and beach toys, fenceposts and gnarls of barbed wire. Oil drums. Tires. The water roiled chocolate brown, came up and covered Grandpa's eel weir, smoothed out the riffle at the bottom of the campgrounds. Nick set out a stake by the canoe launch. After the water covered it and came three feet up the beach, he set out another, taller one. They worked into the evening, secured or hauled off everything that could float away, made sure the campers were as comfortable as could be under the circumstances, and checked the stake in the headlights. The water rose another seven inches. When it finally held, they figured they had done all they could. They headed to town for something to eat.

Nick was drenched, covered in mud, bone-tired. His visit to the Woodstock site seemed as though it had happened days before rather than hours. Kissing Darlene in the stall was a dream, a dope-inspired hallucination. As he pulled across the tracks, he checked the street for Lucas's school bus and wasn't disappointed when he didn't see it. In the bar they ordered burgers and beers, and when he reached for his wallet he discovered Felix's letter. It was mud-stained from Vietnam, as were many of Felix's letters, and now it was wet from riding all day in soaked jeans. Some of the ink was blurry, but he could read most of it.

Feels good to be alive today, old buddy, even with jungle rot eating up my feet. The creepin' crud is unbelievable. What I wouldn't give just to have my old athlete's foot. I go for days without taking off my boots. Something blurry. Then *really stepped in some shit last night. Had our asses saved by Puff the Magic Dragon. We're in a firefight and taking it pretty heavy. Giving it back, but we can't move. Air support, lieutenant's calling for air support, and we've got the M-60 sweeping the treeline and the M-16s on full rock 'n roll. We're taking return fire the whole time. We're in the shit, and lieutenant's screaming for air support, and pretty soon in comes Puff. An old C-47 stuffed with machine guns and cannon, throbbing in low and slow. Pilot hangs a slow turn over the bad guys, starts streaming red tracer lines into the trees, and it's pure hot dragon breath for a few minutes. Thousands and thousands of rounds, and we're sitting back like it's the Fourth of July in Narrowsburg. After Puff pulled up and lumbered away, it was real quiet over there in the trees. Not a single shot. I think we could have walked across the rice paddy smoking butts and bullshitting, but we called in a dustoff for our wounded and sent a squad out in the morning. Confirmed six enemy dead and lots of blood trails leading away.*

Jesus. Nick couldn't imagine what it must be like for Felix.

"Listen to this, man." He read it to Charlie.

"Whoa, daddy," Charlie said. They drank their beers and regarded Felix's handwriting. Charlie studied his reflection in the barroom mirror, raised a finger and started to elaborate, but then stopped. He had caught Eliot Winklewitz's eye in the mirror. Eliot stood on the far side of the pool table, making a toking motion to his lips.

"Business calls," Charlie said, and swiveled off the barstool.

There was some more blurry ink in the letter, but Nick could make out the last couple of lines: *Hope you're canoeing and catching your share of fish. Give a big squeeze to Eva if you see her. (But not too big!) How far away she seems from this life here.*

Nick let the damp letter close into its folds, and then he aligned it against the edge of the bar. His wet clothes pulled at him. He thought of Felix sleeping in fatigues probably wetter than this, with no chance of getting dry, with rain pounding some little shelter. Or probably he wasn't even in a shelter, just out in the rain hoping not to get ambushed in the night. Out through the bar's front window, the neon beer signs washed red and green and blue on the wet street. Nick wanted a shower and dry sheets. The river would flow by while he slept. It would recede hour by hour, and tomorrow they'd deal with the mess.

23

THE ROAD TO the Acres of Bliss, as Lucas called his place, wound through the Beechwoods, the rolling hillsides of farmland and wood-lots between Callicoon and Jeffersonville. A few miles from the river, these hills were more gentle and rounded than the steep, evergreen-covered ledges in the valley.

Nick and Darlene drove through the country lanes with the top open. Nick had worked long hours the last two days cleaning up after the flood, and Darlene had been hungover from Lucas's pancake din-ner. She claimed to still be a little rocky, so they wanted to get out into the countryside and feel the wind in their hair. It was a beautiful evening with a few streaky pink clouds in the west. They drove among the pastures and stands of pine, and the air smelled pungent and fresh.

They needed to swing by Lucas's place, where Darlene had left her slicker.

"I hope it's still there," she said. She wore a little dress made out of denim bib overalls, and her legs were lovely against the MG's cracked leather bucket seat. She looked concerned, though. She picked at a piece of duct tape on the dashboard.

"Where'd you leave it?" Nick asked.

"I'm not sure, exactly." She picked at the tape. "I was pretty wasted by the time I left."

"You ride home with Lucy?"

"I don't remember. I woke up yesterday afternoon feeling awful. I didn't get out of bed until dinnertime, and even then I couldn't get through the meal. Thank God Daddy had his Kiwanis meeting last night."

The tape covered a big split in the MG's dash, and Nick didn't want her to pick it open, so he took her hand and held it between the seats. He should have gone back there after work and brought her home.

"So are you okay?"

She squeezed his hand. "I'm okay. I drank too much wine. A couple of people brought me home, I guess, because Eva helped me upstairs and gave me some coffee."

Nick felt better knowing that Eva was involved. Still, the thought of an incapacitated Darlene at the hands of all those wacked-out crazies didn't settle in easily.

He turned onto Bliss Road—Lucas's family had owned the land for generations—and climbed the hill to the farmstead. The old barbed-wire fences held ribbons and pinwheels, and Japanese lanterns hung from the occasional telephone pole. Across the fields stood some teepees, a VW bus with a canopy, and an army wall tent flying the American flag. The farmstead itself sat at the end of the lane, a cluster of buildings around a circular drive. Parked here and there were the various vehicles of Lucas's entourage: the wild school bus, vans, pick-ups, a couple of motorcycles, and an old hearse up on blocks. The vehicles were scattered among the buildings: the barn that Lucas had converted to his pad, where he lived with his current girlfriend; a long ex-chickencoop where the crazies lived in an open, communal room; and the usual outbuildings—corn crib, silos, smokehouse, springhouse. Nothing was painted up fancy, but nothing was falling apart, either.

Nick parked in front of the farmhouse. It was a little worn, a little faded, but it still maintained its foursquare geometry. On the front porch sat Lucas's mother, Pearl, sipping a tall glass of lemonade. She raised her hand when he got out.

"Well, hullo there, young Nick!" Pearl greeted him with her usual heartiness. She used to run a tavern in Callicoon, and Nick had been delivering eels to her since he was big enough to ride with Grandpa. Pearl was a large woman, with a wide, open face. She presided over the Acres of Bliss with a firm, matriarchal hand. She made what few rules existed. *No dumping bhong water in the cat bowls. No peeing in the pond while skinny-dipping.* She disbursed loans judiciously and collected debts promptly. She arbitrated domestic disputes among the tangled and shifting cohabitational partnerships in the chickencoop. Everybody on the place loved Pearl. She baked them pies. She floated with them in the pond, her big old boobs buoying her up. "Lucas and them are up at the pond," she said. "Go on up."

"Thanks, Pearl," Nick said. "We're here to retrieve Darlene's jacket."

"Probably down in the chickencoop." She waved. "Hasn't found its way up here."

Through the front door of the chickencoop they could make out a boisterous gathering around a long table. The smell of cooked cabbage and broth wafted through the screen.

"Looks like we're interrupting dinner," Nick said.

"Oh, they don't care," Darlene replied and rapped on the door. "Hel-lo!"

Conversation lulled, heads turned, and a woman's voice called, "Come in, people!"

When Darlene stepped in, another woman said, "It's that chick."

Captain America screeched his chair back. "Hey, Darlene! Daring Darlene! Come and join us."

A couple of the women murmured, and Darlene put her hand out. "Don't want to interrupt your dinner," she said. "I just came to pick up my raincoat. Did I leave it here?"

One woman, carrying an armload of dirty soup bowls, smirked at

Darlene. "Honey, you're lucky that's all you left here," she said, and padded on to the kitchen.

Darlene reddened but then brightened when Captain America retrieved her green slicker from a peg.

"Daring Darlene's rainy-day wear," he announced, and hung it out like a matador's cape. When Darlene reached for it, he swung it away.

"Toro!" he cried, and Buck Naked, wearing only a napkin tied around his neck, sprang up from the table. Holding two soup spoons to his head, he charged the green slicker.

"Woolly Bully!" Captain America shouted, and swirled away. The grubby little kids at the table giggled.

"Come on," Darlene said.

Captain America was an older guy in his late twenties, muscled like he'd seen hard labor—stonemasonry or highway work or maybe a stint in the service. His chin was square and stubbled, and he had eagle-and-flag tattoos on both biceps. He nearly drooled as he grinned at Darlene.

"You come on," he said, shaking the slicker. "Come and get it, Daring Darlene."

She made a grab, but he swirled and tucked the slicker to his far hip. She laughed, nervously. "Come on. Please?"

Captain America did a little shimmy toward her, cackled, swirled the slicker through the air like a magician's cloak, danced a quick two-step, and draped the thing over Darlene's shoulders. With a flourish, he brought his hand up in front of her, and in it he held the turkey feather Nick had given her.

Captain America brushed the feather across her nose.

"Typical nasty weather," he leered.

She giggled and took the feather.

"Enchantée, dude." She held out the feather and twirled. The slicker floated out from her shoulders, and her denim skirt flared. "Au revoir, turkey."

Captain America called, "Ya'll come back now, heah?" and a woman's voice followed them into the yard: "Don't bother."

At the car Darlene looked embarrassed, her face still flushed and her lips pursed in a self-conscious, frozen smile, like she couldn't let it break through all the way with Nick, but she could have if it were just her and Captain America. Again, jealousy flared around Nick's heart. He wanted to give it air and let it flame up—he had given her that feather, damn it; he had taken her to the Woodstock site—but he knew it wasn't cool. You weren't supposed to put restraints on each other, not that the women in the chickencoop had any reservations about showing their claws to Darlene.

Darlene chucked her slicker behind the seat. She stroked the tines of the feather smooth, strapped herself into the bucket, and then leaned over and kissed him.

"I'm glad to have your turkey feather back," she said. "I felt so bad yesterday when I thought I'd lost it."

She began braiding it into her hair, and across the field Pearl made her way to the pond. Pearl walked stiffly, her progress aided by a stout stick. Nick had a sudden vision of her tavern, a younger, nimbler Pearl sweeping round the bar to greet Grandpa on his weekly delivery. Light in her eye, lightness in her step.

The memory made him smile at Darlene, and Darlene smiled back at him. The turkey feather hung from her braid like a talisman.

"Let's cruise," she said.

They did. Nick slipped a red bandanna around his head to keep his hair out of his eyes, and they wound down out of the Beechwoods, through the maze of country roads and farm lanes that seemed to lose everybody but the most attentive locals. The evening had deepened into sunset. They came over a rise to see a pasture drenched in pinkish light, then drove down into a cool purple dell with black-and-white Holsteins, then up over the next crest into a fiery rim of setting sun. The wind whipped Darlene's hair, and she held it back with one hand. They came down into North Branch and then up over the hill to Fremont Center, stopping once so Darlene could pick some wildflowers and cattails, and then down into Hankins and the deep cool air of the river valley, running smooth along Route 97. Nick scanned the cliffs by the high school because they were across the river from the

Van Voorens' cottage, and sure enough—"There!"—he pointed into the air over the river, and Darlene turned in time to catch the stark white head of the bald eagle. "Oh, beautiful!" she cried, and they watched it chop its way downriver, its eye fixed to the patterns on the surface. Darlene settled back into the seat with a happy smile, stopped trying to control her hair, let it fly in the wind, and as they blew down the long hill into Callicoon and across the creek viaduct she turned to get a view of the sunset—deep purple now, streaked with melon— and the fresh smell of creekwater rose to them. Running a straight seventy over the next couple of hills and down to Delaware Ford, Nick looked over and she was so pretty and so full and open to the possibilities of her life that his heart swelled for her, and he felt so lucky to be cruising past his hometown with this lovely girl that he wished somebody he knew—his father or Ted or Felix somehow transported back from Nam—would pull up from a side road and see him blasting past with Darlene, their hair flying, and think well of them.

And then they were past Delaware Ford and over the next hill and blowing into the long flats before Cochecton, and there were deer in the hayfields and the smell of new-mown hay, fragrant and warm, and the deer drew up at their mad rush and Darlene looked back as the deer flickered their flags and returned to feeding and then she turned to him and smiled and touched his hand on the gearshift, as if to say *This is it, right here*, and he didn't know, he was so . . . so *touched* with love for her that he downshifted and accelerated into the long, flat straightaway, wound it up to eighty, ninety, upshifted and watched the tach needle barely break motion as he ran it up to a hundred and held it there, the wind washing them and their faces peeled back in big grins as they were young and freer and faster than they could ever be. He knew that anyone who saw them would think that driving at a hundred miles an hour was a foolhardy thing to do, but they'd never ridden in an open sports car with Darlene Van Vooren on a fragrant summer night, never felt her hand touch theirs on the gearshift.

He backed off then, went through the big curve at Cochecton at reasonable speed, and maintained an even sixty as they moved forward inside the wave of their good feeling. They approached the turnoff for

Skinner's Falls, and Nick knew in an instant where he wanted to take Darlene. He wound down the little spur, across the Erie tracks, past the Black Horse Inn getting tuned up for the evening's honky-tonking, and then putt-putted down the red shale path under the bridge and rolled to a stop near the water. The bridge creaked above them. Bats fluttered across the river's surface. The MG's engine ticked and sent up heat waves. A muffled roar came from downriver.

"Come on," he said. "I want to show you something."

The light faded quickly from the valley floor, but Nick knew his way in the twilight. The river glistened silver and picked up the purple residue from the sky. He took Darlene's hand and she came willingly, agile and light on the rocks.

"Is that a train?" Darlene asked.

"It's the falls. River's still high from the flood."

They picked their way toward the roar. The light faded and the sky turned a deep silver-gray. It reflected off the whorls and pocks in the surface of the river. Nick led Darlene out onto the broad, flat ledges above the falls where it was easier to walk and they could stop to dangle their hands in the river blasting through the crevices. They got out to where the first ledge dropped, and the rush of water was tremendous, just inches from them, tumbling and splashing as it hit the next ledge.

"Wow," Darlene said, and drew near him. She took his arm and stood close as the water roared past. Nick pointed out the series of ledges that stepped down the river level, told her how this rapids was named after the raftsman Daniel Skinner, how the log rafts used to break up in the crashing waves, and how the raftsmen would make their way back upriver by pulling skiffs laden with goods from Philadelphia over the rapids by ropes strung through iron eyes driven deep into the shale— "Like the one on your dock"—how it was a great rapids for canoeing and kayaking, especially in high water. With a kayak you could play the river like a fish on the line. Shoot through a set of rollers, and then spin around and paddle hard and surf upstream across the backwash of a rock, get into the smoother water above. Set a brace with your paddle and ride back through the wave and ferry across the current to the next rock. Wheel around like a gymnast and tuck the nose of your yak into the backcurl and, if you balanced right, take your paddle right out of the water and let the river hold you there, showboating, your nose tucked into the curl, water blasting all around you—a rush.

"Cool," Darlene said. "That sounds like fun."

"You can snorkel here, too," he said. "So many canoes tip in the rapids that you can find all kinds of stuff on the bottom: fully loaded packs, rods and reels, campstoves. I found an Eddie Bauer down shirt last summer and it kept me warm all winter. Charlie found a rain jacket with an ounce of pot in a baggie—completely dry! But you know what you find the most of?"

"What?" Darlene asked.

"Sneakers. Mismatched sneakers. They're everywhere down there. The river takes them off your feet."

"Get out," she said.

"I'm not kidding you. I've had it happen. The water comes through these crevices so fast it can suck your shoes right off your feet."

He removed his sandals and rolled up his jeans and stepped off the ledge. The water raced at knee level, wanting to drag him with it. The bottom felt good under his feet, the familiar round stones conforming to the concave of his instep. He beckoned Darlene in, and she, too, stepped out of her sandals and he held her hand as she got her footing and giggled, scrunched her shoulders, and then relaxed to the flow of the river. She stood beside him in the rushing water and the darkening sky and the splash and roar of the rapids. They drew together and kissed, really kissed, and he was lost for a moment to Darlene and the river and the night, and then they drew back and beheld each other, and they kissed again.

They stepped out of the river and lay down on the smooth shale ledge, still warm from the day. They traced each other's arms and backs and cheekbones. When he caressed her breast lightly under the bib of her overall, though, she tensed up. She kissed him harder, but there was a tension between them. Captain America, that fucker. Darlene seemed to arch away at the same time she got more intense, and finally they had to let go and study each other's faces and listen to the cacophony of the river.

"I'm sorry," she said. "I'm still a little woozy from the other night."

"It's okay," he said. "There's no rush."

She smiled and touched his lip. "You're sweet."

They drove back up 97 and when they got to Delaware Ford, Darlene said, "I'm staying at the fishing camp tonight—can you run me up there?" On up to Kellam's Bridge and down the rocky Pennsylvania river road, going easy so as not to bottom out, and when they approached the glowing Van Vooren cottage they could see Eva's VW and Charlie's van.

"Ooh," Darlene said. "Let's surprise them."

Nick switched off the headlights, killed the motor, and eased the MG under the pines. They pressed the doors closed and she led him around to the back patio, where a rectangle of light spilled onto the bluestone pavers.

In the living room, a lamp on the coffee table shone on a dinner tray and two Heineken bottles. Lights flickered on the stereo console and something jazzy was playing, too low to identify.

"Come on," Darlene whispered.

She led him to the edge of the patio and into the grass, to the next lighted window.

"Mom's old art studio," she whispered. "She doesn't use it anymore, but Eva does."

The window was a little high, and they tried jumping up.

"Give me a boost."

Nick gave her his knee and steadied her as she braced against the wall. She grabbed the windowsill and pulled herself up. Her denim skirt stopped at his chin, and he had the urge to rub his cheek along her thigh.

"Holy shit."

Her voice was more hiss than whisper. She jumped down and landed beside him.

"Get a chair." She pointed toward the patio.

He was careful to set the Adirondack chair quietly under the window. It was steady enough, but he had to stand on the arms to see through a gap in the curtains.

"Holy shit is right," he agreed.

Charlie stood with his back to the window, naked, weight on one leg, arms akimbo. Eva sat on a couch sketching him, a sheet draped over her shoulder. Charlie's ass was bright between his tan back and legs, but that wasn't what took Nick's attention. It was the sketches of Charlie tacked up on the walls of the studio, dozens of them. Charlie looked back at him from every angle: Charlie, shirtless, leaning on a windowsill. Charlie nude, sitting backwards on a chair. Charlie standing with his jeans unbuttoned, arms folded.

"Let me up," Darlene said.

He made way for her in front of him, and they both balanced on the wide arms of the Adirondack chair.

"Wow," Darlene whispered. "Looks like she's found her subject."

Nick watched her face as she flickered back and forth between Charlie and the sketches on the walls. Charlie reclining on the chaise, Charlie with a leg up on the chair, Charlie asleep with his arm thrown back. Nick had seen Charlie unclothed since they were kids—swimming in the river or showering after a race or getting dressed on a camping trip—but those situations were always part of regular life. These pictures made him look so . . . so naked, in every sense. It wasn't just his private parts. Charlie's nakedness was more in his eyes: He seemed to implore the artist, or the viewer, to handle his image with care.

Charlie moved and Darlene took a quick breath. He turned sideways and there was some communication between him and Eva. She motioned to his hand and he pointed to a sketch on the wall. She nodded. He held himself as his image did in the sketch, gently, as if cradling a pair of delicate eggs. In the sketch he looked out with that fragile expression. With her charcoal, Eva had captured a glimpse of Charlie that few people ever saw. It was an expression to which he might give way in the privacy of his own room, an expression that his sometimes baffled, what-in-the-world look might give way to, if he would let it. But the Charlie that Nick knew never went that far, never allowed that side to show. He was always Charlie Miles, son of Ted, in control, on top of the situation. And plenty of sketches showed Charlie that way, smiling broadly. Young manhood in full, muscled glory.

So rapt was Darlene's attention, she seemed to forget Nick. "Oh," she said as she focused on a picture of Charlie with his eyes closed. Maybe it was the fact that he wasn't looking back, or maybe it was that he held himself vigorously, that his arousal conveyed his excitement back to her. Nick was embarrassed for Charlie, as if he and Darlene had intruded on a deeply private act, but Darlene stood transfixed. She scarcely breathed.

Nick wanted to leave. So this was where Charlie had been on his days off, on evenings when he didn't show up in the bars. Stacks of drawings stood on a side table and littered the floor.

"I think I'm gonna split," he said.

Darlene seemed not to hear. She stared, unblinking, unbreathing, at the drawing of Charlie holding himself in his fist.

"Darlene?"

She turned, and then she began to come back into the night. "Mmm?"

"I'm going to run along," he said. "This is too weird."

She took another look into the room and then she came fully out.

"Yeah," she said. "Good idea. I think I'll go with you. I think I'm better off in town tonight."

She asked him to put the top up, and she hugged herself in the bucket seat as if she was cold. They didn't talk much, except to exchange the occasional exhalation or glance or murmured "Wow." When the lights of Delaware Ford came into view, Darlene asked, "Do you think he does everything she asks him to?"

"Sure looks like it."

"I wonder," she said. "I wonder if it's the other way around."

"What do you mean?"

"I wonder if he tells her what to do. If he strikes the pose and has her draw him."

Nick didn't know. He swung the MG into the Van Voorens' driveway, and Darlene allowed him only a little goodnight kiss. In his brief brush with her lips, he could feel that she'd retreated to wherever she had been when she was looking through the window. Something was missing. She wasn't there. She was thinking of those pictures, he knew, of Charlie's nakedness. She'd never seen a man in such a state before. Despite her reputation for rebellion, despite her eagerness to do the next wild thing, Darlene had never had a steady boyfriend. And despite the rumors of skinny-dipping and the fantasies of sex jags at the cottage, he could attest that it wasn't so. For all her big talk and posing, Darlene was an innocent. How else to explain her controlled passion when they made out? How she would go so far and then retreat? She wasn't sure what she was in for, and she wasn't ready to find out.

He drove through town feeling a little sad and kindly towards Darlene, as he might toward a dear cousin or a close friend of his sister's, and he realized that this thing with Darlene would wind up like the others: They'd wind up friends.

And then he felt angry—angry at himself for not being able to take a relationship in another direction, angry at Charlie for being able to do exactly that. He wound out of town, slammed the gears and howled the engine, took a long blast up 97 through Callicoon and Hankins and Long Eddy, and then up over Rattlesnake Mountain with his headlights picking up each bend in the road, the stands of trees at the edge of each curve, the flashing eyes in the brush. He shifted and accelerated, ground and punched, until he had driven the anger out and left it behind like carbon particles blown through the tailpipe. He came back down through Fremont Center and North Branch and Tamarack Lake cooler and calmer. He would not try to make a girl do what she didn't want to. As if driving a twisty road in a sports car, he would go with the natural flow of the blacktop, push to reasonable limits of speed and adhesion, and not beyond.

August 1969

24

"Pull it tight, Eva."

The shiny strand grew taut as Eva increased pressure on the prybar. Kit positioned a staple in front of the barb.

"That's it. Now back me up with that sledge."

Eva leaned the sledgehammer against the backside of the post, kept the pressure on the wire. Kit whacked the staple home.

"Good. Next strand."

The river had finally come down enough that they could restring the fence. One wet summer, Kit thought, as she bent to the second strand of barbed wire. Third time for this job, counting the last two floods and the spring repair after the ice went out. Had to be done, though. The best pasture was the river flats, and she couldn't let the horses in there unless this fence below the barn ran well out into the water.

She enjoyed fixing fence. It felt good to draw a sharp, taut line at your boundary and know where you could and couldn't go. She enjoyed working in close quarters with Eva, who concentrated on her wire-stretching and worked up a little stitch between her eyebrows. Kit liked the pulling together as the sweat began to stick their hair to their faces. She liked the dew sparkling in the midmorning sun, the steam rising from the river. She liked the radio drifting down from the barn, where Stacey mucked out the stalls and spread new straw and, Kit was sure, danced in the runway to the New York rock-and-roll station. She smiled at her daughter's private pleasure, even though the news at the top of the hour had been about those crazy murders in California.

"Here." She pulled an elastic out of her pocket. "Tie your hair back before I nail it to a post."

"Thanks."

Eva fixed her hair and they heard a car up at the barn. A door slammed.

"Nothing scheduled," Kit said. "You expecting anybody?"

"No. Walk-in, maybe."

The radio's volume dropped, and she pictured Stacey talking to whoever it was. And then Stacey was at the top of the bank, calling to her.

"Mom."

She stepped back from the post, rested the hammer on the top strand.

"Somebody here to see you."

Phil Sweeney's baseball cap crested the bank first and then his jittery face. Oh Jesus, she thought. What did this horse's ass want?

He waved a folded newspaper.

"Morning, Kit. Workin' hard or hardly workin'?"

"Phil."

"Looks like you could use a break. Take five, babe."

God damn. A woman needed Phil Sweeney calling her "babe" like she needed a visitation of head lice.

"You come to help us fix fence, Phil? Or waste our time?"

"I don't want to waste your time, Kit. Just want to talk to you about something."

Well, talk then, damn it, she wanted to say as she climbed the bank.

He fluttered the *New York Times* loose and she could see the headline "Actress Is Among 5 Slain At Home in Beverly Hills" and the picture of Sharon Tate.

"Lot of crazy people in the world," he said. He thumped the front page. "This here? This is goddamn crazy."

"I heard it on the radio," she said. "It's crazy, all right."

"This country's going over to the crazies and the sickos, and there's not much we can do about it."

"So you say."

She had never seen Phil with his wife. She imagined some cramped little row house in Newark, the blacks moving in street by street, Phil and his wife wondering where they could go. Nowhere, was the answer, as his wife bent to the stove every evening and Phil escaped to his trailer whenever he could.

"That's not the only item of interest in today's paper," he said.

"Phil, I'm already long on horseshit and short on time."

He flipped to the classifieds.

"You might be interested in this ad, all the same."

"Ad."

" 'Horse farm,' " Phil read. " 'Eighty acres of prime Upper Delaware River property near Delaware Ford, New York. Fully operational riding stables with barn, farmhouse, outbuildings in good condition. Includes twenty-four saddle horses, tack . . .' "

What other farm was so close that sounded so much like hers? Her mind raced up and down the river, and then it came to her and she felt the heat spread up the back of her skull, felt her hair stretch barbed-wire-tight against her head—*God damn!*—but Phil held up his hand and kept reading: " '. . . forty miles of groomed trails. Low Pennsylvania taxes, fifteen hundred feet river frontage. Asking fifty-five thousand dollars.' "

Her hair was going to pop its elastic. She reached out and steadied herself on the fencepost.

"Bastard."

Phil nodded. "He needs the money. Needs it bad."

"Son of a bitch bastard."

"Worse than you know."

She swung the hammer at the fencepost, gouged the claw into the top of it.

"Unfortunately, that won't solve the problem," Phil said. "As a matter of fact, somebody might beat you to that. But the money's still going to be due."

In the steam of her anger and confusion, she saw the note to the farm made out in her and Francis's names—so how could he, how could anybody—but then she saw his scrawl underneath as cosignatory and she heard Francis saying, "It's a formality, for tax purposes," knowing that those words hadn't really been her husband's, that he was repeating what he had believed because of who told him.

"What do you mean, still going to be due?"

"Those motor homes have to be paid for," Phil said. "Ted went to some guys for the down payment, and now they want their money."

"That's his problem."

Phil waggled the paper. "Looks like it's your problem, too."

"Let me see that."

The numbers jumped at her: 80 acres, $55,000. The area code was New Jersey, but the phone number didn't look familiar. She walked over to the barn and checked her address book. It wasn't Ted and Margaret's number in Basking Ridge.

She picked up the phone and dialed.

"Hi, honey—let me speak to Francis, please."

When Francis came on the line, she asked, "Have you seen the *New York Times* today?"

He hadn't.

She read the ad. He was silent, as she knew he would be. She imagined him in his office, sorting this news in his methodical way, her call having interrupted whatever he had been doing—going over the previous day's receipts, figuring out how to pay a supplier—and now he had to get his mind around this new development. It was too big to take in all at once.

"Francis."

She heard him set down the receiver, walk the half-dozen steps to his office door, click it shut, and return.

"So . . ." Francis began.

"*So* nothing," she said. "What are we going to do?"

"No one can sell the farm but us," he said.

"But his name is on the goddamn note! I knew we shouldn't—"

"It doesn't matter that he—"

"I knew we shouldn't have let him sign that. Tax purposes, my foot!"

"Kit. He's the cosignatory. He can't sell the farm on his own."

"You're not looking at this ad, Francis. It's here in black and white. 'Forty miles of groomed trails.' Who the hell did the grooming? Who the hell put the buildings in good condition? Fifty-five thousand dollars on the backs of our labor!"

"He can't sell it."

"You'd better be sure of that." Outside, Phil lurked by the corral fence. "You'd better contact a lawyer."

Silence on Francis's end. She pictured him mulling this, not wanting to take such a step. A lawyer would make it official.

"You hear me, Francis? A lawyer."

"I'll handle it."

"And not one of those Monticello lawyers, either. They'll wind up owning the place."

"I'll handle it, Kit."

25

WHEN FRANCIS CAME over to the canoe shed and asked him to run to town, Nick could see that the old man had something on his mind. He wore that strained look that was his face nowadays, and the blood vessel in his temple pulsed. The *New York Times*, he wanted.

Nick hopped into the MG and threaded through the hippies along the driveway. With the festival only five days away, the campgrounds, the town, the whole county was filling with kids. They came in painted-up cars and school buses, in VWs and down-on-the-springs fifties cruisers, on the backs of motorcycles. They came by thumb. Hitchhikers were everywhere: lots of hair, floppy clothes, knapsacks, and on every face a calm, peaceful expression, as if it didn't really matter whether you stopped or not. They were okay where they were; they'd be okay if they got a ride. And of course, they were all going to one place.

A guy and a girl flagged him down at the end of the driveway. Their bellbottoms were damp to the knees and their hair was matted, but they smiled when he stopped.

"I'm only going to town," Nick said. "Picking up the paper."

"We'll take it, man," the guy said, flopping into the passenger seat. His girlfriend climbed in on top of him. "Any lift we can get."

"Heading over to Yasgur's?"

"Finishing up the stage today or tomorrow. Jessie's painting backdrops."

"Backdrops?"

"For the stage."

"Where you guys from?"

"Missouri, man."

He dropped them at the Tamarack Lake road. They thanked him and the guy said, "Probably move our shit over there tomorrow. They're supposed to open the campgrounds there."

The luncheonette was mobbed with kids buying breakfast and ordering sandwiches to go. Roy Elwood and Kenny Wozniak sat at the counter eyeing all the hair and commotion and cracking stupid jokes.

"Jesus, Nick," Roy said. "You look halfway civilized compared to this crew."

"A regular goddamn Boy Scout," Kenny agreed.

Two kids standing nearby looked at Roy and Kenny and then at Nick, as if deciding whose side he was on. Nick figured his hair made it easy to tell. He bought the *Times* from a frazzled Maxine, and then nearly collided with a familiar bulk at the door.

"Hey, Nick!" Bear Brown said. "What's happening, man?"

"Buying the paper. Some scene."

"No shit. Shag picked up this dude hitching in from Texas, took him all the way over to Bethel? Dude laid an ounce of Jamaican on him."

"Heh. A thank-you and an ounce beats a thank-you every time."

"And Eliot? You hear about Eliot?"

"Tell me he's playing at the concert."

"No, man. He ran out of gas on 17B and left his van out there overnight. When he came back yesterday morning, this couple from California and their baby were living in it. Gave him a hassle. Said it was 'people's property' and they only got out when Eliot gassed it up and started driving away from the festival site."

"Getting pretty wild all over." The paper had said how the county was filling up: The people running Woodstock were desperate to house their workers, not to mention the hundreds of concertgoers arriving early. The motels and hotels were full. The boardinghouses, which had closed their upper floors for a decade, were suddenly back in business. Even some of the derelict resorts were reopening.

"Wildest thing this neck of the woods has ever seen," Bear said.

"You get your tickets yet? Eva's going over to White Lake to pick up a batch. Want her to put you on the list?"

"Shag and me're figuring on sneaking in," Bear said. "Dirt bike and wire cutters—get you anywhere you want to go."

Nick eased back through town, and as he was about to turn into the campgrounds driveway, Phil Sweeney cut him off and barreled down the lane. Phil didn't give any leeway to the strolling hippies; he drove right next to them so they had to step off the road. Nick followed slowly and gave the pedestrians wide berth. He smiled as if in apology.

Outside the store, the regular campers were carrying on about the new visitors.

"Don't these people work?" Phil Sweeney asked, stepping from his car. "Hell, no. Who the hell'd hire 'em?"

"I'm afraid to go into the shower after them," Mabel Cusack said. "Ugh."

"I sleep with my service weapon under my bunk," Ralph Cusack joined in. "After those murders in California, you never know."

Ralph nodded at the paper under Nick's arm. Nick scanned the article: Beautiful movie star eight months pregnant, brutally carved up; her friends shot and stabbed, "pig" written in blood on the door.

To Ralph and Mabel, the prime suspects were playing flutes on the next campsite.

"You can't be too careful," Ralph said, patting his hip. "Always get your copycat crimes after a big one like this."

Nick eased toward his father's office. He noticed Phil watching him, and as he rounded the corner of the store, he saw Phil pluck at Ralph's sleeve.

Fuck off, Phil, he thought.

26

WORD HAD GOTTEN around about the *Times* ad. Francis had been shorter than ever with the crew, and the newspaper had stayed on top of his in-basket the last couple of days. Now, as the big blue motor home came rolling down the driveway, Nick felt he was watching an accident in slow motion.

Ted pulled past the gas pumps and stopped in front of his Buick, which had sat in overflow parking all week. As he stepped into the gravel of the driveway, he flashed his smile at two wet-haired freak chicks coming out of the showers. They ignored him, fat cat in button-down. He raised his hand to Miller rumbling by in the Rutabaga; Miller hit the horn and the accelerator and left Ted waving away the dust.

Francis intercepted his partner on the sidewalk between the store and the office. He thumped the newspaper against his open palm.

"What's this all about?" Nick heard him ask Ted.

Ted grinned. "Good afternoon to you, too, Francis."

Instead of appearing large and masterful, Ted looked merely sloppy. His shirt was uncharacteristically wrinkled and untucked.

"It's nothing, Francis. A feeler."

"A feeler."

"A feeler. A tickle. A test of the market."

"Putting someone else's home up for sale is a *tickle*?"

"Francis, I wasn't— Look, this wasn't a serious thing—"

"Not serious?" Francis exclaimed. "Our farm shows up for sale in the *New York Times* and you think we don't take it seriously?"

Three long-haired kids came out of the store. One of them tapped at a pack of Winstons. They wore blissful smiles, but as they passed between the two older men they felt the tension in the air. One of them shot up a peace sign, said "Peace, dudes," and nodded as if that settled the matter.

"Let's go inside, Francis," Ted suggested.

Nick edged behind the firewood shed and into the woods that backed up to the office. He crept quietly, kept low, and when he got in view of his father's window he hunkered down on all fours and crawled. He could see the top of Ted's head, could see that Ted sat in the chair across the desk from Francis. He crawled to the edge of the building, wild-rose briars snagging his jeans and scratching his feet through his sandals. When he was directly under the window, he tucked up against the logs.

"—didn't mean anything by it," he heard Ted say. "It was a way to test investor interest. We know what the farm is worth as a business unit—it does pretty well. But we won't know its true value unless we test it on the market."

A pause, and then his father said, "If you pulled into the parking lot and found a For Sale sign on the windshield of your Buick, what would *you* think? That we were testing the market? Or that we were trying to *sell your car*?"

"Look, I see how it could be taken the wrong way," Ted said. "But other things are at work here. We need to leverage every asset we have."

A sharp query from Francis.

"To grow, that's why." Ted sounded as if he was talking to a child. "If we don't grow the business, we lose."

A sweat bee buzzed around Nick's hair and he batted at it.

"Look, Francis. Other liveries are already putting as many canoes on the river as we are, and that competition is only going to increase. Campgrounds are popping up. We can either slug it out on those terms or we can diversify. We can get into markets ahead of the small-timers and own them."

The sweat bee began showing interest in Nick's big toe, and he shooed it away.

"—the motor homes, Francis. Expand our reach beyond property lines. Put rental agencies in Long Island and New Jersey and we bring the business to the customer. I'm talking with someone close to Disney in Florida. We put a motor home park in an orange grove down there, and we'll be drawing vacation dollars from all over the country. I'm talking with Mel Stottlemyre of the Yankees. He wants to rent one to take deer hunting in the fall. We'll give it to him and then pump out the publicity. Get the Yankees renting these things for spring training—and, hell, the Mets, too, the way they're going—and we'll have all the publicity we need. 'The Camper of Champions'! I'm talking with Cousin Brucie—he'll mention us on his show. We'll be putting so many asses in driver's seats, Hertz and Avis'll be looking over their shoulders."

A chair scraped.

"This is *not* what we went into business to do, Ted. We didn't start this to run up a debt so big it would crush us. We didn't envision fleets of motor homes running all over the country. We pictured a nice, manageable business on the property. People camping out, enjoying themselves. They pay for their site, they buy some supplies in the store, maybe rent a canoe. We earn enough to be comfortable and make the property pay—"

"Sounds pretty bucolic," Ted laughed. "Peaceful and sleepy and an aw-shucks nice business. That's more your vision than mine. And there's no reason we can't have both visions of the business. We just have to get past the financing of these motor homes."

"We?"

"We."

"I've got no financial interest in the motor homes. I've signed nothing over as collateral."

Nick felt a sharp sting on his toe and he slapped at the bee, rubbed at the pain.

"Ah, Francis," Ted sighed. "There are people out there who will loan you money and not make you sign away your collateral. Not make you sign anything at all."

Nick heard Ted's feet on the floor, identified the squidge of deck shoes on pine boards. They stopped at the window.

"But what they can take from you is more dear than anything you own."

There was a silence, and then Francis spoke.

"Jesus, Ted."

"They could even take your Jesus boots," Ted said.

Nick drew his feet back. The window eased shut, and that was all he heard. He imagined what it must be like for Ted. With the campgrounds up and running, the business was too sleepy for him, too regular and unsurprising. It was a bennekill, and Ted needed a river, something that would carry him along, something more glamorous than the camp-grounds' muddy roads and balky plumbing. Sure, the motor homes would do it for a while. The motor homes would keep Ted in a high-rolling crowd.

An hour later, when Charlie chugged the Love Bus up to the canoe shed, Nick told him about the scene in the office.

"He'll find some way out of it," Charlie said. "He always does."

"I don't know. He sounded pretty serious."

"Hey, he's renting those things to Mel Stottlemyre and Cousin Brucie? They've got plenty of bread."

"Just telling you what I heard."

"Don't sweat it, man. Ted always finds a way to hook onto the gravy train. Whoa, mama—" Charlie paused to admire a beautiful girl on her way to the showers: long, straight blond hair flowing over a loose army jacket.

"Ooh, baby," Charlie said quietly. "Need a hand in that shower? Somebody to wash what you can't reach?"

The funky freak chicks in the campgrounds had Charlie on edge. They walked to the showers wrapped in towels. They went skinny-dipping in the river. Picking up garbage early one morning, Nick had stopped by a campsite with a sagging Coleman tent trailer. Suddenly the door zipped open and a large woman wearing only underpants and a bandanna leaned out. Her pendulous breasts, looking more *National Geographic* than *Playboy*, swung in his direction, and she called, "Don't forget these!" as she handed him a bag of disposable diapers.

And as Miller and Nick had driven through the North Area one afternoon, they came upon a group of bathers. Framed under the boughs of the willows, incongruously bright in the drizzle, the four women waded into the river in various stages of exposure. Like some classical painting, Nick thought. *Bathers on the Delaware, Rainy Day.* One rose torso and breasts out of the water as she washed her hair. Two others waded in the shallows, draped in beach towels. The fourth, heavyset with a wiry mass of hair, turned at the rattle of Miller's Rutabaga and waved him down.

"Yo!" she hollered. "Do youse have the time?"

Miller leaned out the window. "It's uh, it's uh . . ." He couldn't seem to raise his eyes above her thick pubic thatch. "It's uh . . ."

"Four-thirty," Nick said.

"Four-thirty," Miller repeated. "Ma'am."

"Oh, *ma'am!*" the woman exclaimed, and turned to her friends. "We got a real gentleman here, ladies!"

She turned back to Miller and cocked her hip. "Well, can youse gentlemen tell us when this rain is supposed to stop?"

"Not until we get a good six inches," Miller said with a twinkle. "If we're lucky."

She laughed and slapped her butt at him. "Everybody likes to get lucky," she said, and sashayed gracefully into the water.

Now, as Nick watched the blond girl cross the parking lot to the showers, he considered the crowd that milled through the campgrounds. The place was packed. Straights and freaks camped side by side, and many of the sites were double- and triple-loaded. Festivalgoers socked into the overflow areas along the driveway. Grandpa had started letting kids camp in his yard, and Grandma made vats of lemonade and disbursed them to her new lodgers.

"Man," Nick said as a salmon-colored Nash pulled up to the store and disgorged a gang of kids. "This is Tuesday. What's it gonna be like later in the week?"

"Gonna be wild and wilder, man," Charlie said. "Gonna be party time for sure."

A familiar churning in the driveway, and Eva's VW eased up behind the Love Bus. Eva rolled down her window and Darlene leaned across from the passenger seat.

"Looks like the hippie festival's happening right here," she called.

She and Eva had been tie-dyeing and making love beads. Eva handed Charlie a beaded choker, and Darlene gave Nick a blue-and-yellow tie-dyed T-shirt.

"Hey, thanks," Nick said, holding up the shirt.

"Cool," Charlie said.

"Something to wear to the festival," Eva said. "When you heading over?"

"Later in the week, I guess."

"Well, we ought to get it together," Eva said. "Show starts Friday, but we'll want to get there early."

"Definitely," Charlie said.

The crowds of campers churning past gave Nick a bad feeling. "Hey," he said to Darlene. "Aren't you supposed to be at work?"

"I quit. They weren't going to let me off for the festival, so I said screw 'em. Let the Long Islanders mind their own brats."

"Dar's helping me over at the farm today," Eva said. "Campers are packed in there, too. But I already told Kit I'm splitting for the concert. She's cool with it."

"I'm packed," Darlene said. "You guys got your tents and shit?"

Charlie thumped the side of the Love Bus. "Always ready to roll, baby. Ready to rock, ready to roll."

"Ready to replace the shocks?" Darlene teased.

"Hah! If this van ain't rockin', please come knockin'."

Darlene tapped her knuckles on the vent window and gave Charlie a teasing smile. But Nick knew better. She was sending out signals she wasn't ready to back up.

"Just be ready to split," Eva said. "We want to find a good spot."

Nick watched uneasily as the yellow car sloshed out the driveway. Even as it pulled away, two more psychedelic vans loaded with camping gear rolled into the lane.

27

AT THE SOUND of his car door she took a final drag and stubbed her cigarette in the ashtray. Got his plate out of the oven: ham and fried potatoes and snap beans, all shriveled and congealed from sitting for four hours. But she couldn't be angry. She, too, had worked late, making sure that the families camping along the barn lane were settled in okay. Their campfires and lanterns glinting through the kitchen window gave her comfort. She'd provided a place of quiet shelter. With the campgrounds so full of hippies, these people would have had no place to go.

Francis came in through the mudroom, as always, and stopped at the telephone table to drop his briefcase and flip through the mail. When he entered the fluorescent kitchen, he looked worn. Worn and old, she thought. How quickly that had happened.

"So," he said. His usual greeting. Never a courteous "Hello" or a familiar "Hey" or an inquiring "How are you?" Just a noncommittal "So," that monosyllable that broke the silence but offered as little insight into his emotional state as it asked about hers.

"Ham and beans," she said, setting the plate at the head of the table.

He popped a beer at the refrigerator, took a long drink with the door open, and then sat to his meal.

"Cookie's gone to bed," she said. "Long day for her. God knows where Lisa Marie is, or what she's doing."

"She worked in the store till ten," Francis replied. "Didn't stop all day."

"Well, I appreciate her sending me families. The last thing I need is a bunch of hopped-up hippies raising hell all night."

Francis cut his ham, and she wondered if the fluorescent lighting made his eyes so baggy, if it accentuated the shadows and made his skin so gray. Did it have the same effect on her? Did she look as old to him? How had the years piled up so? Well, they had. Piled up like cuttings on a compost heap. Somewhere under there lay the scraps of the person she used to be—but how completely she'd been smothered, and how thorough the transformation. Who was she now, compared to the woman who had moved into this old farmhouse with such high hopes, who had cleaned and scraped and painted until it shone? Who had believed she could make a life by her own hand, where happy, well-tended horses served equally happy, well-tended customers and what money was left after buying oats and hay and liniment and tack and fencing and roof shingles would help them put food on the table, would help pay college tuitions.

And who was that woman—that strong, athletic farm girl who could take on maintaining a herd of horses or restoring a house and barn—compared to what she had been before, the house mother, the domestic during all those years in the Little House raising the family—fifteen, sixteen years, so hard to believe. She had been happy tending her flock, though she hadn't always known it at the time. She had still felt the connection to her younger self, the free and independent spirit set loose from the family farm to work in industry and earn her own way. And what had happened to her, that young woman in silk stockings and the business skirt? She was still down there, deep inside the compost heap, piled over and over with the inevitable accumulations and compromises of a life.

Jesus, she thought as she watched Francis chew his ham, as the shadows under his eyes undulated with the movement of his jaw. Replace these goddamn fluorescent lights.

"Eva said Ted was back," she said. "Saw his motor home over there."

"So . . ."

"Did you talk to him about the ad?"

"Yes. I did."

"And?" She reached for her cigarettes but didn't take one. "Francis, talk to me."

He set down his fork.

"He said he didn't mean anything by it. He said—"

"Didn't mean anything by it! Jesus Christ, Francis—he advertises our home—"

"Kit, I know. I know what happened. You asked what he said and I'm trying to tell you."

He angled his jaw as he probed his teeth with his tongue. A shred of ham.

"He's trying to assess—I think he's trying to figure out his net worth. Or how to make his net worth appear as big as—"

"Our farm isn't part of his *net worth*. It doesn't factor in."

"*Appear*, I said. We know that, a potential investor doesn't. If he makes them think he's worth more than he is, they're likely to give him more money. I guess that's his thinking, anyway."

"So I'm supposed to believe this ad was a ruse to lure investors into the business? Jesus! Which is worse?"

"How the hell do I know what's worse? I don't like it any more than you do. He's doing this on his own. It doesn't involve us."

"Doesn't involve us? Don't kid yourself. We're legally bound to him. He's so far out on the edge of his cliff, one step and he takes us with him."

Francis cut another piece of ham and started to fork it, then stopped.

"Look, Kit. I'm doing everything I can. I'm keeping the campgrounds running, I'm keeping the canoes in the water. I'm there every minute I'm not here. I'm dealing with him whenever he shows up— he's got some plan with the motor homes and Disney, the New York Yankees—"

"Of course. The New York Yankees. President Nixon. God Almighty. Francis, it never stops. We've got to get out of this thing with him. We can get by on the campgrounds and the horses—we don't need all the rest of it."

"How do we extract him from the campgrounds? It's a joint deal. He owns half, as we do."

"Then give him the campgrounds. We can get by on the horses and your pension."

"We've got a ton of debt, plus three college educations coming up. Only the campgrounds generates that kind of cash."

"Two college educations, if Cookie has her way." God, the thought of their youngest daughter paying her own way because they couldn't!

"Three college educations," Francis said, and she felt a surge of love for him for saying that. Couldn't they put all this behind them, switch off the bright kitchen lights, and hold each other's hand on the way upstairs?

"We have to get out," she said. "We have to get our lives back. If we stay bound to him, he will take everything. He will take anything from you."

Francis pushed his plate away. He hadn't finished the ham, had barely touched the potatoes and beans. God, she felt bad for him. Work all day with that craziness and now he couldn't even eat. They had to change.

"He already has, Francis."

She hadn't meant to say it, even that much, but there it was on the table, like a fork or the salt shaker.

"What do you mean by that?" he asked.

"He's taken your parents' farm, which is yours by birthright. He's taken your good name—you have no credit in town anymore. He's taken your dreams. He's taken—"

She stopped herself and found she couldn't continue, couldn't look up at him.

"What else has he taken, Kit?"

She couldn't look up. She couldn't look at him. She could only look at the glint off the cellophane cigarette wrapper and hear the cry of the girl she had been trying to break free, the scream of the young, attractive wife and the devoted mother and the hardworking horse-woman. It rushed up through the pile of years and she did what she had promised herself never to do.

She cried. The scream of her whole life rushed to the surface and came out in a hard, cutting sob. And after the first one, others. They came up from parts of her so deep, so buried, it was as if her living tissue were ripping away and tearing at her throat, at her heart. She knew what he was hearing in them, knew she was telling him as surely as if she were speaking quietly, dispassionately, like a lady.

28

CARS KEPT ARRIVING. By Wednesday Lisa Marie had given up trying to charge site rentals—there was no way to keep track. Every spot that could be camped on was, and every camper was headed to the festival. The crowd bought out the contents of the store twice, and the regular distributor in Monticello couldn't restock. Route 17B was clogged, and every grocery and convenience store within thirty miles was begging for supplies. Francis got the same story from distributors in Liberty and even Middletown, but finally he found someone in Scranton who'd come over, although at a serious surcharge. When he had to mark up the prices accordingly, some campers complained about being ripped off. Mostly, though, they bought what was on the shelves.

With all the people and the soggy earth, Nick kept busy pulling cars out of mudholes and trying to keep the bathrooms clean. The washers and dryers ran day and night. Miller's cursing at broken equipment or clogged sewers rose over the campers' guitars and stereos.

Eva and Darlene cruised through around suppertime.

"Wow," Darlene said. "Some crowd."

"Roads are getting bad," Eva said. "We gotta kick out the jams sometime soon."

"Show starts on Friday, right?" Nick said.

"Yeah, but they say it's mobbed already. Like fifty thousand kids? We gotta head over tomorrow at the latest."

"I'll check it out."

When their shift ended, Bear Brown and Shag Foley took off. True to their word, they buzzed away on Shag's Yamaha with knapsacks tied on front and rear. Nick watched them go and figured the campers would probably bail tomorrow. By late Thursday or Friday, the campgrounds would be cleared out. Then he and the rest of the crew could head over.

But on Thursday, even more people came.

"It's hell out there," they said.

"Took us eight hours to get here from Monticello, man. It's totally screwed up."

"The Quickway's stalled out dead. It's like the world's biggest parking lot."

People now camped in Grandpa's barn and in the creamery. When these spaces filled up, campers set up in the cemetery. One couple strung a tarp from Jesus' cross and sprawled out underneath, playing wooden flutes. Another crew rented canoes, anchored them in the bennekill, and used them as a platform for a floating campsite.

By three o'clock Thursday afternoon, Artie Ross and the Evans brothers were gone.

"They split," Lisa Marie said. "Took off for the festival."

The crew was down to Lisa Marie in the office and Miller, Nick, and Charlie on the grounds. Francis called them in for a powwow.

"Look," he said. "I don't have to tell you how serious this is. We've got people on every square inch we own, and then some. The bathhouse on the Knoll has a broken water pipe, we can't pump the sewer tanks fast enough, we're out of firewood, and we're down to our last shipment of groceries. On top of that, there's rain in the forecast. I don't have to tell you what trouble we're in if that river comes up."

"Might have to rescue those ladies in the North Area," Miller said.

Francis turned to Nick and Charlie.

"I know how you guys have been looking forward to this festival. But we've got an emergency here. It's not under control now, and if we get high water . . ."

He didn't need to finish. Nobody wanted to imagine thick brown water rolling through the campgrounds. Not with this crowd.

"They'll probably clear out tomorrow," Nick said. "I mean, they came to go to the festival."

"Have you seen anybody leaving?" Francis asked.

Nick didn't want to acknowledge what his father was asking of him and Charlie. True, some of the people who had tried to get over to Bethel had come back, bitching about the traffic. On the other hand, the show didn't start till tomorrow. These people would be clearing out. When the music started cranking, they'd split.

"The Anderson party left," Lisa Marie said. "From the Shasta down on the point."

"They did?" Francis asked. "When?"

"About an hour ago. Didn't ask for their deposit back, didn't want a refund."

"Just wanted the hell out," Miller chipped in. "Said the hippies was too goddamn much for 'em."

"Don't rent that trailer," Francis said.

"Why?" Lisa Marie said. "We have people begging for a place to stay."

"That trailer is not available for the duration of the weekend."

Lisa Marie shrugged. Okay. Whatever. Nick saw Eva's yellow Bug weaving through the crowds in the driveway. He went out and met the girls by the gas pumps.

"So what's the plan?" Darlene asked. "Eva's heading over tonight."

Eva leaned across the seat. "Radio says there's already a hundred thousand people there. Better get while the getting's good."

In any direction, all Nick could see were tents and vehicles, campfire smoke and people, people, people. Some of them hung out and partied at their campsites, others milled around the store. Bellbottoms dragging, they seemed in no big hurry to leave.

And he and Charlie were the grounds crew.

And here were the Van Vooren sisters—one who had charmed his best friend this summer, one who had charmed him. Or nearly so. Would have, maybe, if things had gone a little differently. If he weren't a polite local boy. If she hadn't seen those sketches of Charlie. But searching for signals from Darlene was like looking for signs of life on the moon. Hell, after you'd touched down on the surface, walked around a bit, shot a few golf balls, and nobody came out to shake your hand or kick you the hell out, you pretty well knew the score.

He'd given it a shot with Darlene. He wasn't getting the right signals back, and no amount of descrambling the static was going to make them appear. She looked up at him and she was so pretty and her eyes were so clear, he wanted to kiss her right there.

Instead, he touched her arm on the car door. "You'd better head on over."

She nodded. This is what she wanted.

"I'll try to meet you by the vendor's stall we built," he said. "Two o'clock tomorrow."

She squeezed his hand. Eva let out the clutch. They were off to Woodstock, and he was standing in a muddy driveway.

A deep disappointment settled in. He had wanted to go to the festival with Darlene, to hang with her on the hillside, to snuggle in his pup tent. But even more than that, he wanted to go to the festival, period.

"This sucks," Charlie said, as the afternoon dragged into evening. "This bites the big one. Half the kids in the free world are partying their brains out in Bethel, and we're stuck in Delaware Ford."

"Bum-fucking-er," Nick agreed.

They were the bosses' kids. Everybody else got to blow out, and they were pinned to this ground. In front of the store, Francis showed two freaks how to light their camp stove.

"Look at that," Charlie said. "He's got this whole place to run, and he's taking the time with those kids so they'll have hot food."

Francis lit the stove, adjusted the flame, and then had the freaks do it.

"So where's Ted?" Charlie asked. "If we ever needed an extra hand, now's the time."

"Maybe he's stuck in traffic over in Bethel."

"Maybe he's partying his brains out in that motor home."

Nick and Charlie weren't the only ones who noticed Ted missing. The '62 Caddy with Jersey plates had been parked at Phil Sweeney's campsite all day. Nick had seen it pull in before noon. He remembered the guy who had the photo of Ted. Garbageman, he'd said he was.

In the evening the Caddy made a slow tour of the campgrounds, swung up the hill to the barn and Grandpa's house, and then disappeared for a while. Rolled down the driveway and swung to a stop near the pavilion, where Nick and Charlie were patching a canvas from a rental pop-up. Phil Sweeney slammed the passenger door and came over.

"So where'd your old man go?" he asked Charlie.

"Beats me, Phil," Charlie said. "Wasn't my day to watch him."

Phil narrowed his eyes but kept them on Charlie.

"Believe me," Phil said, "it's in his best interest to talk to me. He was around here yesterday, and he's a lot better off talking to me than to Sal over there."

Phil jerked his head toward the Caddy. Nick couldn't see through the tinted window in the waning evening light.

"Believe me," Phil repeated. "It's in his extreme best interest. Yours too."

"Oh, I believe you, Phil," Charlie said. "And as soon as I know where he is, I'll be right down to see you. You can be sure that the first thing—"

"Listen, smartass," Phil said. "You have no idea how fucked your father is. You're too busy being a fucking smartass. But if you've got a brain under that fucking nest, you'll listen up and have your father see me."

"I'm scared, Phil," Charlie said, smirking. "I'm shaking, dude." He held out his hands and shook them as if palsied.

Phil went back to the Caddy. When it pulled away, Charlie muttered, "Fuck you, Phil," and then to Nick, "So who's this Sal?"

Nick reminded him about the encounter at Phil's trailer a couple months back. Stocky guy, dark sideburns. Said he was a garbageman. Had that picture of Ted.

"Wonder what he's doing with a picture of Ted?" Charlie asked.

"Don't know. He was looking for him then, too."

"Seems weird. Same guy who was looking for him earlier."

"Well, there's been plenty of chances to find him. He's been in and out all summer."

"Mostly out. I wonder what Phil's connection is."

"Who knows? If there's a way for Phil to weasel into this business, he'll do it."

They worked until ten, when Butch Deeker showed up for his night watchman's shift. He had a six-pack in one hand and a clublike flashlight in the other.

"Gonna be a long night," Butch said, slapping the flashlight against his thigh. "These goddamn hippies get smart with me, gonna wish they'd stayed right the hell on the goddamn com-mune."

THE WILD TURKEY was full of locals exclaiming about the hippies. Nick and Charlie ordered beers and roast beast. On the television, aerial photographs showed mobs of people overflowing Yasgur's farm and clogging 17B.

"Quite a surprise party old Max throwed for the county," Arvin Johnson maintained from the end of the bar. "We're on the map now, by God."

"By God right," Harley McDonald said.

"I come through Fosterdale this morning with the tow truck," Mort Beagle said. "Sheriff's got us towing vehicles nonstop. Clifford's out there right now. Chris'll spell him around midnight. This morning I got a hippie van on the hook and I come up to the four corners, and there's two of 'em in the road. One of 'em's got his thumb out hitching, the other'n's got his pecker out, pissing up against a telephone post!"

"Howard Streeter says he saw a pair of 'em screwin' in the backseat of a car, pulled off of 17B," Arvin said. "Course Howard couldn't tell which was which, and didn't want to get close enough to find out!"

"Heh," Harley said. "Miller says down at the campgrounds there's bare-assed hippies of all sexes goin' at it right in the bushes, up in old Nick's corn patch, anywhere they can find."

Harley was Miller's brother, younger by two years, and had never been married. Never had a girlfriend, as far as anybody knew.

"You ought to come on down, Harley," Charlie said. "It might be catching."

Harley made a face. "Why ain't you girls over there in Bethel?" he asked. "Like every other longhair in town."

They groaned and shook their heads.

"Don't remind us, man," Charlie said.

"Soon as the crowd at the campgrounds heads over, we're outta here," Nick said.

"Huh," Mort Beagle said. "You better figure on walkin' then. You can't get a vehicle close to the place."

"We'll see about that," Charlie said.

Norma brought their sandwiches and Jake drew them fresh beers, and they were happy that in the Wild Turkey, at least, the larder had not been depleted.

"Darlene split for the festival?" Charlie asked.

Nick nodded. "Rode over with Eva."

"The chicks are listening to Hendrix, and we're stuck in this dive with Harley and the Hep Cats," Charlie said. "This really sucks."

"I'm going to try to meet her tomorrow. Soon as we can get away."

"Good luck, bro. We're gonna have to make a break for it, and screw the campgrounds."

"It'll clear out. Soon as word gets round about the music, they'll all head over."

On the way back to the campgrounds, Charlie kept checking his outside mirror. Nick could see headlights up pretty close.

"Fucker's right up my tailpipe, man," Charlie said.

"Hit the brakes," Nick said. "Give him a grilleful of Love Bus."

But on the creek bridge there was a screech of rubber, the headlights swerved around, and the black Cadillac shot ahead and cut them off. Charlie jerked the bus onto the berm at the end of the bridge.

The passenger door opened and Phil stepped out. The streetlight on the bridge hit the brim of his Mets cap and cast a shadow over his face. Then the driver's door opened. Sal, the garbageman, was not as tall as Phil, but he was thick as an Angus bull. His hair oil glistened in the streetlight. As he approached the bus his face fell into shadow, but one long sideburn ran down his cheek like a scar.

"Shit, man," Nick said. He wanted to make himself small in the passenger seat.

Charlie pulled back the handle and swung the driver's door open, swiveled to get out. Sal lowered his shoulder and met the door with his weight. Charlie slammed back into his seat; his knee rattled the shifter, his elbow made the horn bleat.

"Stay put," Sal said.

"What the fuck?" Charlie asked.

"Wrong question, Charlie. Where the fuck? That's the question."

Charlie rubbed his shoulder.

"Where the fuck, Charlie. As in, where the fuck is your old man?"

"Who are you?"

Sal reached in and stopped Charlie's hand from rubbing his shoulder. Then he tightened on Charlie's hand and yanked. Charlie's head slammed the doorframe. The van shook.

"Charlie, I told you once. Wrong question. The question is where. Where. The *fuck*. Is your old man."

Charlie tried to twist free but Sal bore down and pulled Charlie's arm out to full length.

"You understand the question."

"I don't know," Charlie said.

A pair of headlights came down the Tamarack Lake road and swept them as the car turned and passed on to the campgrounds.

"I don't know where he is."

"Charlie. Your father needs to talk to me."

"I'll tell him," Charlie said.

"When will you tell him."

"I'll tell him when I see him."

"When is that."

"I don't know! Look—I told you—"

Sal yanked once and Charlie shut up. Sal spied the ankh on the thong around Charlie's neck.

"What's this, Charlie—your necklace?" He plucked at it, held it up to the light. "Peace sign? Gift from a girlfriend? Good luck charm?"

Charlie reached up and twisted the ankh out of Sal's fingers.

"Heh—hey, Charlie. I got one of them, too."

Sal pulled at a gold chain under his T-shirt and came up with something. Nick thought it might be a piece of bark or a mushroom, and then recognition came like a lens focusing and he couldn't take his eyes off it. Sal grinned as he tucked the human ear back into his shirt.

"What kind of son are you, Charlie? What kind of son doesn't know where his father is? You know where my father is?"

Charlie faced straight through the windshield.

"You know where my father is, Charlie? In his kitchen in Brooklyn, watching Carson and sucking down a beer. A good son knows where his father is."

Sal grabbed Charlie by the ponytail and jerked his head through the open window.

Nick yelled and tried to jump out of the van, but Phil stepped into the door and braced it.

"Stay out of it, Nick. It's not your fight."

Sal had Charlie's head pulled outside the van, his throat vulnerable in the streetlight.

"So where is he, Charlie?"

"I don't know."

"One last time, Peace Sign."

Sal tightened up on the ponytail, arched Charlie's neck even more.

"He's in your mother's bedroom, eating your old man's lunch."

Nick could hear Tamarack Creek gurgling under the bridge, and a low din that he realized was the campgrounds—a background noise that the town now took for granted. Sal looked at Charlie with something like fondness, and then reached his free hand into his pocket.

Came up with a *zzzick!* and a flash in the streetlight, and after Nick saw the blade at Charlie's throat he understood the sound. He had never heard it before.

"You're as dumb as your old man," Sal said.

He twisted Charlie's head sideways and sawed with the knife. Then he shoved Charlie back into the driver's seat. Charlie looked different.

"Make sure your father gets this, Charlie." Sal handed Charlie his ponytail. "It's my last invitation."

The Caddy's shark-fin taillights pulled off into the dark. Charlie rubbed his neck, and he kept touching the ragged shoots of hair where his ponytail had been.

29

IN THE MORNING, Nick found a wad of paper on the driver's seat of the MG. Charlie's scrawl instructed him to *Give the contents to Ted, man. Deliver Sal's fucking message. I'm splitting for Bethel. Fuck the family and fuck the job before they fuck you. Charlie.*

Nick unfolded the note, and there was Charlie's ponytail. Still bound in its rubber band, it looked like a severed body part. Sal might have done the cutting, but it was Ted who moved the arm. Nick couldn't blame Charlie for splitting.

He drove down to the campgrounds. The same tents and cars as yesterday; the same, really, that would be there tomorrow and the day after that, and next weekend and next summer. Who were these people, and what did they matter to him? They paid their seven bucks a night, they'd be gone in a couple of days. He'd never see them again. Why should he stick around and keep them from drowning themselves? The driveway tilted and Nick had to hit the brakes and shift into neutral. He could keep going. Drive past the gas pumps and the store. The back roads would get him close to the site: Tamarack Lake Road to Fosterdale, a quick dogleg to Kenoza Lake and then up to Jaketown Road. Close enough to ditch the car and by God walk in. Fuck these people. He'd looked forward to this all summer.

He leaned over and slipped Charlie's ponytail into the glove box.

A familiar teapot whine caught him up, and there was Grandpa coming down the hill on his little orchard tractor, three gunny sacks of sweet corn on the back. Eight-thirty in the morning, and he was already about his business. He went from site to site, calling to people to help themselves to the corn, not even charging them. They took what was fair. Three ears, four, half a dozen. A lot of people to feed. They waved their thanks to Grandpa; they called to their neighbors and held up, like trophies, the perfect green corn. Nick watched his grandfather wind on through the sites and he felt the happiness that Grandpa spread in the simplest way possible, by giving away the food of his own hand.

Goddamn, he thought. Eva and Darlene had spent the night at Woodstock, somehow, and today they'd be waking up to music.

His father stepped out of the office, looked around, and, when he saw Nick idling in the MG, waved him over. Nick told him about Charlie leaving. Francis squinted. "Apple doesn't fall far from the branch," he said, and Nick knew what his branch expected of him.

Francis called Miller into the store. He locked the door and put up the Closed sign. The place was bare. The shelves, usually laden with canned goods and emergency gear and camping supplies, showed big empty patches. The rain ponchos were gone, as were the Coleman stoves and lanterns and coolers. Even the freeze-dried trail foods, which nobody ever bought, were down to the last few foil-wrapped bags.

"We're as short-handed as we've ever been," Francis said. "If we're going to get through the next three days, we have to pull together and do it smart. I don't have to tell you that we can't take any more defections to Bethel."

He looked pointedly at Nick.

"We have to deal with the essentials," he went on. "No canoe rentals, no garbage pickup—"

"No garbage pickup?" Lisa Marie said. "We're gonna get a lot of complaints."

"If they want the garbage off their sites, they can bring the bags up here and toss them into Buff. We'll give them replacement bags. But we're too short-staffed to make the usual run."

Okay by Nick. No way could he get through this crowd's garbage single-handedly.

"We need to keep the basic functions going," Francis went on. "Lisa Marie, you handle the store and keep a running list of complaints and problems. I'll update the list every couple of hours."

He flourished the two-page list he had already compiled.

"Miller, you keep the bathrooms and showers working, the sewers clear, and handle any trailer repairs—our rental units first. Check with me and I'll give you the jobs off this list. Nick, you keep the bathrooms clean, garbage picked up around the buildings, and the roads clear. We're soggy already, and if we get more rain, we can't have the evacuation routes blocked."

"Oughta get you a load of firewood in," Miller said. "These hippies want a fire they can sit in front of and smoke their weed, and with all this damp, who the hell wouldn't? I stopped a couple of 'em already from chopping a live sycamore tree. Too goddamn dumb to know green wood from dry."

"I've got an order in to Schwab's for a load of slabwood. Should be in this afternoon."

Nick and Miller left the store. A few people lingered outside. A girl bounced up and down inside her loose denim jacket, a dollar bill in her hand.

"Hope she likes freeze-dried shit on a shingle," Miller said. "That's about all the breakfast she'll get in there."

Miller looked back over his shoulder and said to Nick, "So, who's the old man shackin' up with?"

"What?"

"In the Shasta down on the point," Miller said. "The old man spent the night down there. I figured he must be gettin' a little."

Nick glanced through the window. His father was going over some paperwork with Lisa Marie.

"He spent the night there?"

"Sent me up the creamery yesterday to get a Coleman sleeping bag out of inventory—only one left. This morning I seen him coming out of that Shasta and getting into his Scout. Gotta be bangin' something."

Nick set about his chores. One thing he knew, his father wasn't shacking up with anybody. Slept down there to keep an eye on the place, was all. The trash cans around the building overflowed onto the sidewalk, and he carried the mess away to Buff. Then he got the four-wheel-drive GMC and the cleaning gear and headed for the bath-house on the Knoll. Part of him was pissed—everybody else was at the concert, and he was cleaning bathrooms. Another part of him, though, the part that felt violated and angry from the encounter with Sal, was grateful for a simple task to perform. Pick up some garbage and leave the place a little cleaner. Hose down the bathrooms and keep the campers happy. It seemed fair enough.

Through the morning, a good number of people left. Crowded into vans and packed against station-wagon windows, they pounded out of the driveway. Nick waved; some of them flashed peace signs. His hopes rose. If enough people went to the concert, there was still a chance for him. He tried to picture Darlene waiting for him by the vendor's stall. Then he slapped himself out of it. No way, man. She was out there digging the whole scene, and he wouldn't even enter her fun-seeking little mind.

As he made calls throughout the grounds, he tried to encourage the campers. "Lot of people heading out," he said. Or, "Music starts today, should be good."

A few were packing up, but more of them said, "Man, we're here. Why screw around with the roads and crowds?"

And after lunch, some of the cars that had pulled out in the morning came creeping back in. "A zoo over there, man," said one guy in a Day-Glo-orange van. "We're gonna stay here and party—woo-hoo!"

Nick helped some girls repitch their tent, which had fallen in a soggy pile during the night. He towed a couple of cars out of the mud. It always amazed him how, when getting their cars into a mud-hole, the city drivers' first instinct was to hit the gas. They dug in deep and deeper, and by the time he showed up with the truck and a log chain, they'd be mired to the doorsills. After crawling under his third stuck car of the afternoon and looping the chain around the frame, he was wet and muddy and pretty well convinced that the crowd wasn't going anywhere.

On one of his trips through the Meadow, he noticed that the black Cadillac no longer sat at Phil Sweeney's campsite. Phil's trailer door was open, though, so he swung the truck off the road.

He could see Phil at the dinette table. He didn't bother knocking.

"What the hell, Nick?" Phil asked. "Just barge in? Good way to get shot."

"Fuck you, Phil. What was last night all about?"

A half-eaten sugar doughnut and a cup of coffee sat on the sports pages. The trailer was shabby. Plates and glasses choked the sink, a sleeping bag and a ragged blanket hung off the bunk. The place smelled like onions and damp boots. Phil took a big bite of the doughnut and spoke through the wad.

"You a Mets fan, Nick? You a Mets or a Yankees fan?"

"Neither one, Phil. I could give a shit about baseball."

Phil nodded and chewed. "Trouble with you kids today. You could give a shit about anything. Spit in our faces every chance you get."

"Is that what last night was about? You and Sal wiping off the spit?"

Phil swallowed his doughnut. Drank some coffee, made a face.

"Look, Nick. I like you. You're a good kid, never mind you look like you crawled out of a gutter. Your father's a good man." Phil swirled his coffee cup, tapped it on the tabletop. "The Mileses are another story. Ted's up to his ass in alligators. Thinks if he ignores them they'll go away. They won't."

"So why pick on Charlie?"

"Charlie?" Phil waved his hand. "Charlie's a tool. Course he's a smart-mouthed punk and I don't mind seeing him get smacked around, but these guys don't care about Charlie."

"Who's 'these guys'?"

Phil tapped his cup again.

"Sit down, Nick. Let me tell you something."

"I'm fine. Go ahead and tell me." Sitting across the little Formica tabletop was more intimate than Nick wanted to be with Phil Sweeney. He felt grit under his feet and he noticed how dirty the linoleum was. Jesus, didn't Phil ever clean this place?

"Ted Miles is in trouble. Ted Miles needs to start repaying an investor. But Ted Miles thinks he can bullshit and dodge this investor. He can't. He doesn't—"

"Who's the investor—Sal?"

"Sal's a grunt. A bag man. When he's not doing dirty tricks like last night, he drives a garbage truck for—for the investor."

Phil shoved the rest of the doughnut into his mouth. "The investor is a big guy in certain circles. Big contractor in Jersey. Shopping malls, office buildings. Golf courses. Some state jobs. Trucking business, heavy equipment, garbage hauling.

"A big guy. Very big guy. Got his finger in a lot of pies."

But Nick had snagged on something: heavy equipment. He kept clicking back to that, to a vision of big yellow machines rumbling onto his grandfather's farm and carving out the campgrounds. Big yellow machines with black lettering.

"Iannacone," Nick said.

"I didn't say that, Nick." Phil started to drink some coffee, thought better of it and set the cup down. "Remember, I didn't say who this investor was. Is. But his involvement in this business goes back farther than your father and mother know. He's been behind Ted from the beginning."

That explains a lot, Nick thought, although he wasn't sure what. Once he saw Ted as not driving himself so much as being driven by a more powerful man, once he saw Ted as a kind of toy that Mr. Iannacone, whoever he was, could move with his fingers, a certain understanding came to him. A certainty, a rightness.

"What's your angle in all this, Phil?"

"My angle? What you talking?"

"What's in this for you?"

"Nothing, kid. Nada. I'm just a guy who likes to get out in the country on the weekends. Breathe the fresh air."

Phil held Nick's eye.

"I'm a Mets fan, Nick."

"Right, Phil," Nick said. "But thanks for filling me in. It clears up certain things."

"It doesn't clear up shit. And I didn't tell you nothing." He looked hard at Nick. "We did not have this conversation."

As Nick left, Phil called out the door: "And take that garbage with you. How'm I gonna breathe fresh air with that hanging around?"

Nick scooped up the bag, spun the neck into a knot, and slung it into the truck. He'd bring Phil a new bag later.

BY THE TIME the Schwab brothers arrived with the firewood, Ted had popped into Nick's mind several times. The way he had been so assured when the campgrounds was being built. The thousand pounds of grass seed at Agway—sure, a guy who built golf courses might take a payoff in grass seed. The way Ted had handled the Gitcheegumee salesmen. As Nick chucked wood with the husky Schwabs, he realized two things: Ted *was* in trouble. And his mother had been right all along.

Word got out about the firewood, and the orders came quickly. Wood sold for two bucks a bundle, and a bundle was enough for an evening's fire. Of course, if a rowdy bunch decided to throw it all on for a big bonfire, they'd be back for more. But today, this load was it. As Nick dropped off the firewood, he told people to be judicious in their burning.

On his trips to the firewood bin, he kept seeing a girl under the pavilion, reading at one of the picnic tables. Sometimes she'd be on the bench with the book propped on the tabletop; other times she'd be on the top with her bare feet on the bench, elbows on her knees. She was as limber as a cat. When she drew one leg under the other, the book didn't move a whisker. Nick made several firewood deliveries while she sat there, and their eyes met too often for him not to notice. She was cute—a calm face, wet reddish curls. Her rain poncho sagged back from her shoulders, her bellbottoms were soaked to the knee.

Finally, after locking the firewood bin, he spoke to her.

"What you reading?"

She held up a copy of *Trout Fishing in America*. "Richard Brautigan."

"Cool," Nick said. "I like him, too."

She drew herself up and smiled. She had gray-green eyes. "Have you read *Confederate General from Big Sur?*"

He had. *In Watermelon Sugar,* too.

"Ooh, I love that one," she said. Her open-neck blouse revealed a silver necklace in an Indian pattern. She held the cover up to her face. She had a sweet smile and an open expression. "I'd like to be a Brautigan girl. Think I could be?"

"Sure you could." Even if she weren't so cute, he'd have been a fool to answer any other way. "Not going over to the festival?"

"No ride," she said. "I was taking a shower and my friends split without me."

"Bummer. I had to stay and work."

She riffled the pages of her book; Nick sorted his keys. In that awkward moment when he struggled to find something to say, the right thing, so as not to sound like a dork, he noticed the soft, ripe-peach tone of her cheeks. Her fingers were long and fine. She held the book as if it were an instrument she could use with skill. She riffled the pages unconsciously, over and over, and her fingers seemed to want to stop and linger on familiar passages.

They spoke at once, "Where you from—" "You live around here—" and then they caught themselves and laughed. Nick dropped his keys.

"I'm Joanie," she said, and offered her hand. "From Jersey."

"Nick. From right here."

She seemed to be sizing him up and getting a kick out of doing so. She looked like one of those girls who in school was not among the first rank—the popular, flirty cheerleaders or the brainy class officers—but who was pretty enough to be sure of herself, who knew more than she let on, and who would let others make fools of themselves while she quietly made the right moves: learned her subjects and got decent grades, waitressed after school and bought her own car.

"My girlfriends and I drove up yesterday," she said. "We took the back roads through Pennsylvania."

"Smart. Everything on the New York side is shut down."

"My uncle used to have a place up here. In Callicoon. I sort of knew the way."

She used to canoe past the campgrounds, she said, so she envisioned staying here when she left Jersey. Her eyes laughed like that was some kind of joke.

"The place was full when we got here. The girl in the office said there was no room. So we drove in anyway and crashed on a site with a bunch of dudes from Long Island." She waved toward the North Area. "Then this morning I had to wait forever to get a shower, and when I finally got in I wanted to stand there as long as I could."

Nick liked her face. He imagined her dating different guys—serious nerds and hell-bent rebels—simply because she was curious and open to the world.

"When I got back to the site, everybody had split. I've got the campsite to myself."

She held his eye with her it's-all-a-joke smile, and he nodded like an idiot.

"Well, that's a drag you have to work," she went on. "I mean, you live right here. You going to get to the concert at all?"

"I keep hoping all these people will clear out, that's the only way. Doesn't look like it's going to happen."

"Well, listen," she said. She folded her book and stuffed it into the pocket of her poncho. "As long as we're both stuck here, why don't you come down to my campsite later? Site sixty-one? I've got a ton of food."

She gave him that jokey look again. "And you've got the firewood."

He kept hopping the rest of the afternoon. More firewood runs, more stuck vehicles. Every time he lurched through the North Area in the GMC, he cast an eye on Site 61. A cluster of tents, a lantern on the picnic table. No sign of Joanie, but their conversation had lightened his spirits and made his wet clothes seem trivial.

Francis closed the store at eight o'clock—"Nothing much left to sell," Lisa Marie said—and the campgrounds began to settle down for the night. When Butch showed up with his six-pack and flashlight, Nick went back to his place and showered. Washed off the muck of the day, changed into fresh jeans.

He was nervous as he eased the MG along the ruts in the North Area. What was this Joanie from Jersey all about? This chick who wanted to be a Brautigan girl? A lot of freaks and hippies camped up here, away from the Winnebagos and Airstreams on the more groomed sites. It was the wildest area in the campgrounds—wild in its natural state and wild in the campers' partying and carrying on. Especially this weekend. Pot smoke wafted in the air. A steel drum and flutes played a throbbing background music. Nick pulled into the intersection of the main lane and the little one that branched off to Sites 60 to 65. He could turn around now. He could take the firewood back to the bin, go over to the Wild Turkey, and get a buzz on. He could stick with what he knew, what was comfortable.

Or he could turn right and see what this Joanie was all about.

He let out the clutch and ground through the mud in front of the settlement of orange and blue tents at Site 61. The steel drum was close by—beyond the next thicket—and as he shut off the engine, somebody kicked in with a twelve-string.

Joanie sat inside the screen of an orange wall tent, her wet sandals left outside.

"Hey," he said, nodding toward the music. "Whole lotta shakin' going on."

"They've been at it all afternoon," she said, unzipping the tent door and stepping out. "I'm thinking maybe Santana got lost on the way to the concert."

She had changed from her wet bellbottoms into a purple paisley shift, and she had fluffed her hair with a towel. Her reddish curls framed her face.

Nick opened the trunk and showed her the stash of wood. "I come bearing fire."

"Well, let's light it up," she said, and rubbed her hands together. "Chase some of this damp away."

He stacked the wood by the stone fireplace, then used a hatchet to split off some kindling. He knew she was watching him, so he made careful, precise taps with the hatchet. Made a little teepee, and when that caught, he put on a couple of smaller slabs. Joanie squatted in front of the fire, warming her hands.

"Oooh," she said. "That feels good."

Nick squatted next to her. His back twinged. All that crawling under cars and pitching firewood. The fire took their attention for a few minutes, and he liked that better than having her watch him. He gazed at the fire, poked it nervously with a stick, got the feel of being with her. Sitting next to him in the heat and flickering light, she gave off a scent of shampoo and clean skin. Another scent, too. Pears, strong as a shot of whiskey. Pear blossoms. Some kind of essence or oil. It made him want to move close and find out where it came from. Her paisley shift made a little tent over her knees, and she folded it back to let in the warmth. He kept his eyes on the fire.

When the slabwood caught, he added some of Grandpa's hickory.

"We'll make a good cook fire," he said, "and then later we can stoke up a roaring campfire."

"Sounds good. What do you feel like for dinner? They left us plenty."

"I brought some of my grandpa's sweet corn. It's the best around. Something that goes good with that."

They rummaged through the cooler and came up with a sirloin steak and some carrots and peppers. Nick got a bottle of Boone's Farm from the car, unscrewed the top, and offered her the first drink. She took a healthy pull from the bottle. Not a dainty, prissy sip and not a drunkard's chug, but a good, steady drink that said she wasn't shy about putting it away and could handle it.

"To a good meal," she said.

She cut up the vegetables while he soaked the corn. They talked about the concert, the crowds. She steamed the carrots. He set the steak on the grill. She wanted to see Joan Baez; he, Jimi Hendrix. They lamented the rain. Nick slipped the corn into the coals to roast, and the steel drum hammered away in the background. Different instruments kicked in and dropped out: the flutes, the guitar, congas, a tambourine, a wailing harmonica.

He raised the wine toward the music. "To our own little concert."

She drank after him and smiled over the bottle. She seemed like a happy person, happy and open. He imagined she came from a big family. But she came from Jersey. He always imagined suburban kids or city kids as knowing so much more than he and his friends from the country, that they lived life a little faster, experienced things a little earlier, saw more of the world. She'd be more attuned to a guy like Charlie than to him.

The steak dripped fat into the fire, and the little flares illuminated the roasting peppers. Nick turned the corn so it wouldn't burn, dipped it in water when it got too brown on one side.

"How do you like your steak?" he asked.

"Rare," she said. "Still mooing."

He laughed. Fine. A red-blooded American girl. Her hair fell across her face as she tended the vegetables. Her hands moved with that deft, sure motion he had seen earlier. The downy hairs on her forearm shone in the firelight.

"So where you from in Jersey?" he asked.

"Montclair," she said. "I'm living at home this summer, working in my dad's nursery. Saving up for school. Montclair State."

"A real hometown girl?" he teased.

"Not really. Maybe. I don't know." She tossed her hair back from her face, licked her finger. "It was a nice place to grow up, and the school's a good school. I make good money at the nursery. I like the business and I know a lot about plants. You might as well do what you like and understand."

He flipped the steak. "So you going to study plants?"

"Photography."

She had taken photos for the school paper and the yearbook, and she had sold some of her black-and-white flower prints from the nursery. She always thought it would be cool to be a photojournalist, charge around with a couple of Nikons around her neck and a bagful of lenses, always on the scene of the fire or the wreck or the political rally, bring the events of one corner of the world to the rest of it. But those photos lived only for a day, she said. News photos were like day lilies: They had their moment in the sun and then they were gone. She'd really like to take art photos, to use the camera as a paintbrush and take striking black-and-whites of the plants she knew intimately.

"Fashion photography might be cool too," she mused. "Set up cool shots for ads and hang out with models and rock stars. Make good money, travel."

She set her jaw at an angle while gazing into the fire, and Nick saw how the fire reflected in the Indian necklace at her throat, how the silver nestled into the little hollow there, how it jumped as she began to speak again.

"Taking pictures makes me see the world in a whole new way," she said. "Objects and landscapes and people are just so many angles and planes illuminated by light, and as the light changes, so does the world."

She glanced to see if he was with her on that, and he guessed he must have appeared so, because she went on to say how the light in turn had helped her see people anew, how the outer light played off their inner light, or some such—she sort of lost him there, or he just grew more interested in how her peachy skin glowed in the firelight. And her eyes, how they brightened with the little jokes she made, how she looked into the middle distance of the dusk-shadowed campgrounds, at the dripping trees and the water-laden grasses, and then how she seemed to gaze beyond that as she spoke of her father's greenhouses and about the other kids. Her brother drove a tractor and a delivery truck for the nursery; her sister put together potpourri and cut flowers in the greenhouse. Joanie stocked nursery tables and shaped evergreens and handled the cash register. Her mother had a degree in education and a teaching certificate, but after she started having kids, she wound up working part-time in the greenhouse.

"No way I'm turning out like her," Joanie said. "No way in hell."

Darkness settled in as they moved to the picnic table. Joanie lit a candle lantern that gave them enough light to see the red center of the steak, the shining green peppers. Nick stripped the corn, and fragrant steam rose into the air.

"Hah!" she laughed. "I bet they're not eating like this at the concert."

They dug in. The veggies were sweet, the steak a little tough, the corn perfect. It had that smoky, nutty flavor that corn can get only by roasting in a bed of hardwood coals. Nick placed two more slabs onto the fire.

Joanie shifted toward the fire and crossed her legs into a lotus. Her movement was languid yet controlled, at once unselfconscious and aware. She took another good pull from the wine.

"How about you?" she asked. "What are you into?"

"I like canoeing," he said.

"You're in the right place for that."

He stumbled around a little, told her he liked to fish, he liked to read. But he felt like a doofus. He worried that his local version of cruising the strip would seem hopelessly dull—*Hey, nearly hit a rabbit on the river road.* Or, *Yo! passed a milk truck down by Agway.* He did tell her that they'd all been drinking in the bars since they were big enough to get their noses over the rail, and she got a kick out of that. He told her he'd be going to Albany State in the fall.

"Liberal arts," he said. "Whatever that means."

She laughed as though she understood.

"I guess I'll play it by ear."

"There's plenty of time," she said. "And it'll keep you out of the army."

She wanted to know about his family, so he told her about Lisa Marie working in the office—"The strawberry blonde, right?"—and Stacey who helped his mom over at the horse farm—"Ooh, I love to go riding!"—and how his dad was the county agent before he started the campgrounds, so he knew a lot about plants, too. He told her about his grandpa, who grew not only the best sweet corn but also the best apples and asparagus, and grapes for his own wine, and he told her about his grandma, whose bloodlines went back to the first settlers, and how she could preserve Grandpa's produce so they ate well in the winter.

He told her how there was a lot more to do in the summer when the city people showed up. You could take them canoeing or fishing, and they traipsed through the town looking for antiques and ice cream.

"They keep life interesting."

"Yeah, but how about the other nine months?" she asked.

She looked at him directly; she really wanted to know.

"Well," he said. He thought of Grandpa. "When you live on the river, you get attuned to it. You learn its cycles."

He told her how when the ice goes out in the spring, it scours out the winter debris, and how the floods sweep the riverbanks clean. She seemed to be with him, so he told her how the caddis flies hatch in May and the trout go wild for them. How the riffles are the coolest place to sit in the summer, and how the eels run in the fall. He told her how the great blue herons fish and how the deer migrate during hunting season, how they know to swim across to Pennsylvania when the liquored-up Long Islanders start thrashing about on the New York side, and how the deer swim back across two weeks later when the Pennsylvania woods are crawling with red-jacketed farmers and their hooky-playing sons. And, since she was listening, he told her about the pure peace you can feel sitting in a cedar canoe, drifting with the current and letting it take you where it will.

She followed him with her eyes, and sometimes she let her vision drift off toward the darkness beyond the fire—the steel drum and the congas had quieted down to a lower pulse, and a light sprinkle had begun to sift through the trees—but then she foreshortened her gaze and brought it back within their little glowing space, brought it back to him, and said, simply, "Mmm-hmm," and he said the first thing that came into his mind: How late at night along the river, after all the racket of the day has quieted down—the traffic and the canoes and the campers—and the songbirds at dusk and even the peepers after dark, later, in the deep still of the night, you can hear the hollow call of a great horned owl, or maybe the strangled cry of a screech owl, or, if you were lucky, the howls and yips of coyotes, calling up and down the valley.

The sprinkle turned into drops that hissed in the fire, and without saying a word Joanie reached across the table and took his hand and pulled him up and led him to the tent.

30

THEY DIDN'T HEAR owls or coyotes that night, but they did make love twice and Nick experienced the exquisite novelty of sleeping with a woman for the first time. The dripping of rain on tent canvas leaked through his drowse, and he woke quietly, disoriented at first, but then he aligned to the pear scent of Joanie's neck and to the weight of her head nestled between his biceps and shoulder. God, it felt good! He had to stifle a laugh, it felt so good. He didn't want to wake her, as her shallow, regular breaths tickled his chest, but he tried to sort out all the ways it felt good: her taut, lean body touching his, breast against belly, hip against thigh; that sweet, soft embrace in which she had held him, far more wonderful than anything he had imagined; and perhaps the best feeling of all, the happiness of knowing that a sexy, intelligent girl had found him attractive enough to take into her bed. He listened to the rain drip—just tree-dripping now, the rain had stopped—and to the crickets scraping in the background and to something rustling in the brush behind the tent, a skunk or possum most likely, and to Joanie's shallow breathing, and he allowed himself to slip back under, to drift into a pool of happy dream-fragments.

He woke again to the immediacy of empty space. Her head no longer weighed his arm; he felt only sleeping bag along his length. She split, he thought.

But no, she was merely sitting before the screen door. Her silhouette, etched against the deep blue of the night, gave him a rush of warmth. It felt good to be in the presence of a girl so undressed. He sat up and hugged her from behind.

"Everything okay?" he asked.

"Everything's okay. Everything's beautiful."

"Good."

"I was noticing how beautiful the night is. So quiet. Rain washing everything clean."

He put his face into her hair. Pears and woodsmoke.

"What are you thinking?" she asked.

Nick sighed. "I'm happy to be here."

"So am I," she said, and settled into his arms. She kissed him on the cheek. "I was just thinking how happy I am that my friends left me here."

"But you're missing the concert."

"Today. Tonight. There's always tomorrow."

"Another day here in paradise for me, I guess."

"Yeah? You sure you can't split? Head out for the afternoon?"

He pictured himself walking through the field in Bethel, holding hands with Joanie while Crosby, Stills & Nash sang love songs from the big stage. Somewhere over there right now, Darlene was digging the whole thing. How far away she seemed, how unconnected. A shard of a dream fading from memory. If he hadn't stayed here, he wouldn't have met this girl who leaned into his arms. He could take off in the MG with Joanie, cruise the back roads. Miller would still be here. Grandpa could help out. But the thought of his father's face when he learned that his son had left, the moment of comprehension that would come without a blink or a change of expression, only the flexing of a jaw muscle when he realized that Nick had chosen his own temporary happiness over duty to family, and then the moment when he put it aside, put his son aside, and turned to the next task. That's all Francis would show on the outside, but inside he would know that his son had deserted him when he needed him most.

"I guess I'm stuck here," Nick said.

"I knew you'd say that," she said. "I admire the hell out of you. Not many kids would give up this chance."

"Not many kids would be that sappy, you mean."

She turned into him, slipped her arm around his waist. With her head against his chest, she said, "Tell me a secret. Tell me your most private thought, something you wouldn't tell a girl until you felt comfortable with her."

"I feel comfortable with you."

"So tell me something to make it real. Give me something that you'd give only to someone you trust. Tell me what you fear. Tell me what worries you most."

He didn't know what to say.

"You first."

She rubbed her hand up and down his back, and when she spoke she kept her head against his chest.

"Right now I'm a little worried about getting pregnant," she said. "But only a little. I'm more worried about the fall: What if I don't fit in at college? What if I don't like it or keep up with my classes? I think about it."

"I try not to," he said. "I guess I have the same worries, I just try not to think about them."

"Ah, the old I'll-think-about-it-tomorrow approach," she said and traced a line down his rib cage. "The Scarlett O'Hara approach. I can't do that. I have to confront things immediately. Otherwise they build up and get out of control."

He knew she was right, but he wasn't used to it. His preferred approach was to push back from the table and leave his parents arguing, to blast off down the road until he had purged the raw emotions.

"I guess I worry about going to school," he said. "Mostly about not knowing what it's going to be like. If I don't stick it out I'll get drafted. I've got a buddy in Vietnam right now. I haven't heard from him in a while. I hope he's okay. I guess I worry about him every day."

"Oh, God," she said. "Stick it out in school. Don't get drafted."

"I don't want to, but I don't have much control over it."

"You could go to Canada for a while," she said. "That would be fun. A cabin on a lake. A canoe. You know how to fish. I know how to garden. We could chop wood all summer and stay warm all winter."

"Ha! You saying you'll run off to Canada with a draft dodger? Now that's facing your problems head-on."

She walked her fingers up his belly, plucked at his chest hairs.

"A romantic fantasy," she said. "I'm probably too practical to do that, and I worry about that, too—about being too practical. And then I worry that I'll react against the practicality. I'll overreact and fall in love too early and not finish school. I'll marry some dashing loser and wind up in a slummy apartment with a couple of kids, while all my college friends go on to have good lives."

"Yeah, I've played the same thing out," he said. "I drop out of college, come back here, and get stuck running canoes my whole life. Drinking every night with the other guys who never got out."

He thought of Miller, who had turned his menial work and alcohol dependency into a colorful celebration. He thought of Butch, who seethed with anger at anyone who wasn't living as low as he was. He thought of Ted, who seemed to be the opposite of the small-town drunks. But in his bravado and his desperation, he seemed just as lost.

"I worry about my parents," he said. "I worry that my father's working himself to death. That he and my mother are going to split up over the business. That the business is going to fail and their marriage will, too. I try not to think about it, because there's not much I can do and I'll be gone in the fall, and they're grown-ups and ought to be able to solve their own problems, but still it's in the back of my mind." His conversation with Phil came to him: *goes back farther than your mother and father know.* "Sometimes it surfaces and I can't ignore it anymore."

"Gee, it seems like they've got a good business here."

"There's a lot to it."

"I know," she said. "I know what it's like having a family business. It never leaves you. It's like the biggest family member, the one that controls everybody."

She did know, he thought. She had learned from her family's business. She had learned how to live within it and now she was trying to get out from under it. How easily she had taken his hand at the table, with what assurance she had taken him to bed.

"This is some first date," he said. He hesitated, not wanting to screw up the moment. "I mean, it's not a typical first date for me. Steak dinner, live music—"

"Getting laid in a tent," she finished for him. "You mean you river rats don't do this every Friday night?"

"Not exactly."

"It's not typical for me, either."

"You mean you Jersey girls don't sleep with every guy you meet?"

She straightened. He could see a little glint of the night sky in her eyes.

"Yes, I've had a couple of boyfriends," she said. "Yes, I've had sex with them. I'll tell you about that if we get to know each other better, and I expect you'll do the same for me."

Fair enough, even though he didn't have much to tell.

"But no," she said. "I don't fuck every guy who comes along. No, it's not a typical first date. There was something I noticed when I saw you get out of that firewood truck this afternoon and walk across the road."

"That I was the muddiest, cruddiest-looking guy you'd ever seen?"

"No, that you were the calmest, most solid-looking guy I'd ever seen. Now there is a happy guy, I thought. A guy who's at peace with himself."

"So much for female intuition."

"Well, it's true. Whether you know it yet or believe it yet, it's true."

As she sat before him with her hair in silhouette against the tent screen and the night sky in her eyes, the rain dripping from the trees and closing them into their own little sanctuary, he knew he was happy. He was happy enough just being with her.

"So tonight was unique," she said. "Is. It's about you. About you and me."

He touched her face and then her hair, and she kissed the back of his hand and he pulled her to him and eased her down into the sleeping bag. They made love again and he felt like he was thanking her for recognizing him, for seeing past the mud and the crud and the concern he carried for his family and the disappointment he felt about missing the concert and the fear he harbored about the future and the mystery he knew falling in love to be. He gave her the gratitude of his heart and felt her accept it and give hers back to him. They slept again, and towards morning he awoke feeling happy and light but with a tug of something underneath. His dreams had been of Joanie and of Sal and of paddling in churning white water. The first birds broke the silence of the night: a robin, a wren. When he opened his eyes, Joanie was looking at him.

"I'm going to the festival today," she said. "I want you to know that now, so you won't be hurt or bothered when I'm gone."

"Okay," he said. "How will you get there?"

"Hitch. There's plenty of people going over."

"Will you be coming back?"

"Yes," she said. "I'm not sure when, but yes."

As on the day before, carloads of people headed out for the concert. They left on foot, or started hitching beyond the gas pumps. And carloads of them returned. All morning, a steady vertical drizzle played counterpoint to the tidelike motion of the traffic. The rain came down, the cars pounded through puddles. For all the movement back and forth, the campgrounds' population never seemed to change. The tents still stood in forlorn, soggy defiance. The pop-ups and travel trailers seemed a little more hopeful; they were off the ground and had hard roofs. The motor homes seemed like the happiest deal of all, for their owners could simply drive away. None did.

Nick didn't see Joanie leave, but after a while Site 61 was deserted. He figured she must have hitched out while he was cleaning bathrooms. He pictured her in her rain gear, riding along in somebody's van. Stuck in traffic on 17B. Slogging along the shoulder with everybody else.

What the hell. It beat sitting around in a wet tent. Or hanging under the pavilion with a book.

He checked the river level and set out a stake at the swimming area. The river ran high. Swollen and drifting in random surface patterns, it was the color of beef broth. The water level stood a couple of feet down the bank, but the rain fell steadily. It wouldn't take much to bring the level up to the lip.

Back at the office, he reported the river condition to his father.

"Keep a close eye on it," Francis said. "God forbid we have to start moving these people."

His father's concern was legitimate. If the river started running down the soupy road in the North Area, it would be almost too late. The campgrounds could be cut in half in two hours, and evacuation would be impossible in three.

Francis bent over his clipboard, scratched something off, wrote something in.

"I need to talk to you about something," Nick said.

His father looked up. Whenever Nick prefaced a talk like this, it usually meant bad news. He'd smacked up the car. Had some trouble at school.

"Charlie and I had a run-in with Phil Sweeney and his buddy night before last."

"Yes?"

"Sal, the guy drives that Cadillac? He roughed Charlie up pretty good."

"What do you mean?"

"Cut off his ponytail with a switchblade, for starters." Nick told him the story, and his father took it in silence. Then Nick recounted his conversation in Phil Sweeney's trailer, and Francis grew still. Nothing moved on his face, except for that single jaw muscle, steady as a heartbeat.

"So," was all he said. He looked at Nick a moment longer, processing the news, and Nick could tell his father was in two places at once: here with him, beholding his son who had just delivered much more message than he knew; and somewhere else in his life, flying over the country roads in an open convertible with his best friend, the one who would eventually sell him out.

"So," Francis said again and then tapped his clipboard. "Keep an eye on that river."

A GROUP OF freaks had taken over the beach. With the rain, nobody else was hanging out there, so in the wacky, turn-everything-on-its-head spirit of the times, six or eight longhairs had decided this would be a good time to go sunbathing. They had spread out blankets and towels and were lying about in cutoffs and bikinis. They goofed on each other, pretended to enjoy the nonexistent sun, called for the Coppertone. Two guys played Frisbee. Two others kept their heads under a black umbrella stuck into the sand, while the rest of their bodies soaked up the drizzle. Budweisers rested on their chests. Two girls stood in the river. One wore only a bikini bottom, the other a wet T-shirt that read "Make Love Not War."

Nick eased up in the truck and lowered the window. From under the umbrella, a transistor radio kicked out "Hair."

"Time to turn over, dudes," he said to the rainbathers. "Getting a little too wet on this side."

One guy stuck his head out from under the umbrella. "Thanks, man. We don't want to get too soaked."

The other guy offered a pipe. "Toasted, maybe, but not soaked. You wanna do some hash, man?"

What the hell. A little buzz might help cut the drizzle. He put up his hood, squatted next to them, and passed the pipe around.

The girls had waded deeper into the river. Now only their shoulders and heads were visible above the bruised water.

Nick nodded toward them. "They ought not get out too far," he said. "This current's picking up."

"Ah, man. It's cool. They dig the water."

"So do I, but you see how dark it is? It's beginning to flood, and it brings stuff from upriver. Logs and railroad ties below the surface. Something submerged could really do a number on those two."

They studied Nick like they were trying to comprehend.

"Something else. If the log has branches, or say it's a fencepost with some fence, and you get wrapped up in it? You're going where the river wants you to go."

The guy with the pipe looked disappointed. "Ah, man," he said. "It's just a couple of chicks in the water."

"Yeah, I know. But they should come in to where they have better footing."

The other guy leaned up on one elbow. "Hey, Sweet Buns! Marcia!" The girls looked up. "Cat here says you're too far out!"

The one in the bikini bottom shielded her eyes from the rain. "Thanks!" she called. "We think he's pretty far out, too."

"No," the guy said. "He's the Man, the River Man. He says you gotta come in closer."

"So he can get a good look at you," the other guy called. "Man needs a positive ID on anybody out for a swim."

"Gotta see your tan lines!"

The girls waded in closer, until once again their torsos were out of the water.

"This better?" the one in the T-shirt called.

"Perfect!" Nick called back, and shot them a strike fist. "Call me if you need to be rescued!"

Their smiles brought him back to Joanie, and he thought how these two girls had the potential to give the same pleasure that Joanie had, how any woman could do that, and he felt giddy at the possibilities of the world. How fine it was. He felt washed with gratitude for Joanie for opening him to it.

The sun came out in the afternoon. The river rose one notch on the stake and held there. Steam lifted from the standing puddles and

wet underbrush, and the campers took this time to dry out wet sleeping bags and clothes. Nick helped them string up clotheslines, hoisted
their sodden canvas into the muggy air.

Again he thought of Joanie, how she was doing over at the concert,
who she was hanging out with. Would she meet another guy? Would
she get stoned and curl up with some dude? He recognized these fears
as the normal jealousies of an eighteen-year-old, but he had no power
to stop them. He could only push them aside and try to replace them
with hope of good things for his new friend: that she was listening to
some decent music, that she had enough food. That she would come
back tonight.

But as afternoon turned into evening, no change occurred at Site
61. Nick kept an eye out as he drove down to check the river. Vapor
rose from the tents. All was still. As evening deepened, the conga
drums kicked in from the next site. But no lights appeared on Site 61,
and then the traffic died back. Around ten o'clock he checked the
stake one last time. The river was holding at the same notch. He
turned the place over to Butch Deeker, knocked back a couple of
beers at the Wild Turkey, and went home to bed.

31

THERE WERE HIPPIES in the barn when she opened up Sunday
morning. She knew something was wrong when she saw Big Boy at
his stall door, his ears cocked, a heavy hoof knocking the floor. Usually
he stood deep in the shadows with his head close to Roxanne, his girlfriend in the next stall. Then she heard the low voices, and smelled,
with a shock that sent a ripple through her nerves, cigarette smoke.

She grabbed the .22 from her office and headed up the loft ladder,
keeping the gun above her so it was the first thing they saw when she
emerged.

"Put out that cigarette—now!" She spoke before she could discern them in the dim loft. Some movement, a murmured "Oh man," and they began to assume separate shapes: two boys and a girl, it looked like, all hair and rags and knapsacks.

"Now," she said, backing up in the soft hay and motioning toward the ladder. "Down. Get your stuff and move it."

They did as she ordered, but the girl—young, frizzy-haired, a pimple on her chin—said, "We're not hurting anything."

"And I aim to keep sure of that," Kit said.

The first boy stared at the gun, and she could see that he was afraid. The second boy looked defiant, though, and ignored her completely. He shook his long hair as he dropped through the loft hole. He'd be the one with the girl, the tough one, macho. Though who knew anymore? Maybe they shared the girl, or maybe they were all in it together.

They milled around the front barn door as she landed on the runway. She unclipped the rifle so they could hear it, but they just dragged their bags toward the door. City kids. That ashy paleness of not being outside enough. Italian or Jewish, she'd guess. They looked lost, and she felt bad about kicking them out. Still, the image of a barn on fire and the horses trapped in their stalls was too much. She'd start locking the barn at night until this music festival was over.

Outside, everything dripped from the night before, and the air hung heavy with humidity. Another day like the last few. Thunderstorms later, no doubt. The kids looked like stray cats, with bits of hay stuck in their hair and to their damp clothes. Forlorn, no place to go.

"You on your way to the music festival?" she asked.

"We were there already," the girl said. "We split last night and got lost and wound up here."

The girl was barely older than Lisa Marie. She still had those clear eyes of girlhood, those upturned lips. Crazy matted hair. Not even a jacket, only an oversized denim shirt with embroidery on the collar. And damp, as if she'd walked in the rain and then slept in her clothes. Kit felt a rush of mother-love for her, out on the countryside with all the hippies. These boys didn't look harmful, just young and scraggly. But still.

"You trying to get back home?" she asked.

The boys shuffled in place.

"We don't have to be back for a while," the girl said. "And Johnny doesn't have a back to go back to."

The defiant-looking boy kicked at the ground.

"We thought we'd hitch up to Binghamton," the girl said. "My father lives there."

Broken home. The girl's parents were divorced, and who knew about this Johnny? If he had no home to go back to, maybe he had no parents either.

"Have you kids had anything to eat?" Kit asked.

"They fed us at the festival," the girl said. "Rice and gravy."

"And we had some granola with us," the scared-looking boy offered.

Unbelievable. Go out into the world with your thumb and a baggie of granola, and trust you'll get by. Well, she had to admire it. She and Francis, children of the Great Depression, always made sure they were prepared for anything. Anything they could anticipate. When they went for a drive or to visit someone hours away—back when they used to do that—they made sure they had chicken sandwiches and one thermos of coffee and one of water, and raincoats, and blankets in the trunk. Francis always carried a toolbox and jumper cables and even a spare fan belt. But these kids traveled light, as did everybody who came to this concert, apparently, if you could believe the radio news. Helicopters were bringing in medical supplies and food, since trucks couldn't get through the traffic jam.

"Well, you look like you could use something to eat," she said. "Come up to the house and let's get a real breakfast in you, and then you can hit the road with a full belly."

They all brightened, and the girl thanked her. "We can help."

"Maybe you'd like hot showers," Kit said. "And I could run those clothes through the washer for you."

"Wow, thanks," the girl said. "I knew this was a good place. I could feel the vibe last night."

"Let's keep it that way," Kit said. "The first rule on a farm is no smoking in the barn."

"Okay," the girl said. "No smoking in the barn."

"No smoking in the barn," Kit repeated. The scared-looking boy, who seemed less frightened now, nodded.

"No smoking in the barn," he said, and joined the cadence of their step.

"No smoking in the barn, Johnny," Kit said and passed the defiant boy her own pack of Luckies.

He took the cigarettes and his sullen demeanor broke. He sniffed and agreed: "Okay, man, no smoking in the barn."

To her surprise, they all linked arms: Johnny with the girl, the girl with the other boy, and he—timorously—with her, and together they goose-stepped up to the house, chanting, "No smoking in the barn! No smoking in the barn!"

Stacey eyed them skeptically from the kitchen, but Kit made the introductions—Johnny, Allison, and Daniel, they turned out to be—and ordered her daughter to round up some clothes while she did their laundry. Stacey warmed to the idea of entertaining company, and she showed Allison the "girls' bathroom" that she shared with Lisa Marie and directed Johnny and Daniel to the main bathroom in the hallway.

As Kit sliced potatoes for home fries, she heard the water running upstairs and wondered about these kids. You weren't supposed to do this. They could rob her jewelry box. They could pull a gun on her and Stacey. But they were decent kids. A little lost, was all. Who wasn't, these days? And without parents to go home to—they could use a little help along the way. She thought about Lisa Marie and Stacey, was glad she and Francis were there for them, but then she remembered with a quickening in her stomach that Francis had not been home the last . . . what? Three or four nights? He was minding the crowd at the campgrounds, he said, but what if it was more than that? What if this was the first step toward moving out?

She imagined herself on the farm with the girls, Nick having gone off to Albany, and the three of them tending the horses and the garden. But then a sinking thought: She might not be able to keep the farm. It would be lost in a divorce, or the campgrounds would swallow it up. What would she do then? A little house in town? She couldn't go back to living next to Grandma and Grandpa without Francis. She couldn't return to Scranton, wouldn't want to. This was her life now, and she wouldn't want to give up her friendship with Francis's parents, wouldn't want the kids to be separated from their father. Cookie, especially. She was the closest to him. She could kid and play tricks on him as the other two couldn't, or never had. With Nick it was more man-to-man, and Lisa Marie was distant from everybody these days. But what would it do to Stacey to not have her father around?

And she herself—how would she like it? Sure, she could live without him, could live without any man. But would she want to? Despite the desert that their marriage had become—long empty stretches punctuated by business talk or snapping at each other—she knew that Francis loved her, in his way. He always remembered their anniversary with some small gift. A pair of gardening gloves, a kerchief. He always did what he had to for the family: took the kids to basketball games, taught them to fish and to identify plants. He was not demonstrative about love, but that didn't mean he didn't feel it.

The business had gotten in the way of everything else. She felt certain that Francis would enjoy a walk with her some evenings—a stroll around the backyard under the beech trees, or along the riverbank while the horses grazed. He might like to go apple-picking with her in Grandpa's orchard. Maybe even take a drive through Pennsylvania in the fall. Admire the foliage, have dinner in a roadhouse. But there was no time for any of that.

And now he was sleeping with the business. Sleeping in a miserable little rental trailer like one of these vagabonds from the city. Well, this was an unusual weekend, the worst they'd ever seen. But still, she couldn't believe the business was the entire reason.

He had been distant since her crying scene the other night, since she had as much as told him about her and Ted. He had folded deep into himself as if considering the enormity of it, of the deception, of his disillusion. He had let her cry herself out, had sat and watched what he had never seen before. Oh, he had seen her raging and he had seen her giddy with a new baby and he had seen her melancholy over the deaths of her parents, but he had never seen her cry. He had not shrunk from it, but neither had he tried to console her. He had offered no soothing words, no touch. He had simply sat at the bright-lit table, his hands resting on the cloth where he had pushed back his plate, watching as the years of grief and anger ripped out of her, and then he had gone to bed for the night. He'd left for work in the morning and hadn't been back since.

She felt sorry for him, sorry that he'd had to learn that his wife had deceived him, that his best friend was a fraud—sorry that it all had to come at a time when he was too busy to deal with it. During a slower time he might have taken his canoe and gone to the river for a couple of days, worked it out while feeling the pulse of under-water life through a fishing line. But he had to handle the emergency at the campgrounds, so who knew if he'd even had a chance to think about it? She hoped he had. She hoped he wouldn't come home in a couple of days and everything would be the same: dull and flat and painful. She hoped he would come home with a plan, even if it meant he was moving out or was kicking her out—no, he'd never do that, never impose hardship on her or the kids. Most of all, she hoped that he would understand the real cause of the problem and deal with that.

They could live without the campgrounds. They could live without the farm, for that matter, although she'd prefer to keep the farm. The stables would pay their way, if not hobbled by the campgrounds' debt and Ted's dealings. A peaceful life on the farm—that's all she wanted. She'd tend the horses with Cookie for as long as Cookie was around, and Francis could do whatever he wanted. Garden, plant fruit trees. He'd always dreamed of setting up a cider mill. Well, he could do it. Get shut of the campgrounds and go their own way.

She tossed the potatoes into the hot skillet and turned to the eggs. She heard the water coursing through the pipes. Let this weekend be over, she whispered. Come home, Francis. Come home, husband, adversary. Partner in life.

32

THE SUN CAME out midmorning and the air turned muggy and full of gnats. A few people broke down their camps. These were the straights, the Middle Americans with kids and mortgages, drawn home by their jobs. The freaks played and goofed as usual, using the sunshine as a call to frolic.

Nick pumped gas, helped people with travel trailers empty their holding tanks. He always got a certain feeling around noon on Sundays, when people packed up and began to pull out: a sense of denouement. The final act was winding down, the curtain about to close on the weekend. One by one the players would leave. Their exit was usually accompanied by a sense of relief: the campgrounds crew had gotten through another show, and tomorrow the pace would even out for a few days.

But the big split didn't happen this weekend. A trickle, was all. Those few families who felt compelled to reenter the world pulled out, the fathers armed with maps and a grim determination to get around the traffic disaster to the east. Most people kicked back and decided to give it another day or two. After all, the papers and the television news had been full of the Woodstock Festival all weekend. Everybody knew what a mess it was. People lined up at the pay phones to call in and take Monday off: "It's a horror show up here, Walter, absolute horror show. Nothing's moving." Or: "They've called out the National Guard. The roads are completely shut down. I'll be in Tuesday or Wednesday."

Nick wondered when Joanie would be back and how long she'd stay. This was only Sunday. The music was scheduled to go on into tomorrow, and then there'd be the hassle of getting out. It could go on for a couple more days. She could hang over there for a while, he figured, and that bummed him out because the longer she stayed, the more he would fade, the fainter their little encounter would become.

Engaged in these thoughts as he filled the tank of an aqua Rambler wagon stuffed to the roof rails with camping gear and kids, he took in his domain: the bathrooms outside the store, the trash cans, the dump-

ing station, the canoe shed. But then he saw something familiar and
out of place at the same time: Joanie, standing by the canoes, her hair
tied back in a blue bandanna, one hand on her hip, that reality's-a-joke
smile. She squinted in the sun and gave him a little wave. He went
awash and blurry, but he finished pumping out the fill-up, took the
guy's cash, made change, and all the time he felt Joanie's eyes. No,
more than that. He felt pinned by her complete attention. In those
few too-bright moments when he screwed the gas cap onto the filler
neck and took the wrinkled and damp twenty and peeled off the bills
from his change roll and wished the guy a good trip, his every movement seemed cast in the spotlight of her scrutiny. He felt like a buck
deer, when it senses something and looks up and in one moment
understands the immensity of the hunter and the scope.

". . . best way to get around that crowd?" the guy was saying.

"South on 97 to New Jersey," Nick said automatically. "Steer clear
of 17B."

And then the Rambler was an aqua blur at the edge of his vision
and he was crossing the driveway, stuffing his cash roll into his jeans,
hyper-aware of the length of his stride, of the swelling in his chest.

"Hey," he said.

She stepped forward and kissed him, and he smelled pears and
sweat and damp clothing. "Hey."

She was a little sunburned, her hair frizzed out and her bellbottoms
muddy, but she looked lovely.

"So how are you?" he asked.

"Good," she said. "Really good. Really tired, but it's like I'm on this
high that I can't come down from."

"What'd you take?" There was something different about her eyes.

"It's nothing I took—I didn't really take anything, except an occasional toke—it's the whole scene. The vibes are so good, it's like
another existence. I don't want it to end."

"Cool. Who'd you see?"

"Oh, man. Santana, Canned Heat, Janis. Santana was so good. The
Who—"

"Jesus." It was really happening. All summer Woodstock had been this mythical thing, this grandaddy of all concerts, and for the last few days it had been a big hassle. But here was this girl he could trust, a disheveled messenger from the front, and she had seen firsthand all the bands he had speculated about.

"Sly Stone put on a great show," she continued. "Let's see, Creedence, the Dead. And the Airplane. Grace Slick came on this morning with 'White Rabbit' and it was so cool. She did a few more and then cranked us all up with 'Volunteers of America.' Then everybody started to crash."

"No Hendrix?"

"He's on the lineup for today. So's The Band and Joe Cocker. I forget who else. I'm beat."

"Wow. What time's the music start today?"

"I don't know. Everybody was crashing when I left. There's still more people coming in. They say there's like half a million people there."

She looked at him but she saw beyond. That's what it was about her eyes. She had the thousand-yard stare like the vets back from Nam, as though she could be there by the canoe pile but she could see through the hills and the crowds to Bethel, could stand here and see Grace Slick in her fringed vest and that hillside full of kids.

"I am really, really beat," she said. "But I'm wide awake. I haven't slept since . . . with you in the tent, and . . . well, you know."

"Yeah." He smiled. "You've been up since yesterday morning? That's like thirty hours."

"Yeah. I'm gonna go try to crash, but I wanted to come by and see you first."

"I've been wondering when you'd come."

"Look, it was fun over there, no question. It's a wild thing. The vibes are totally beautiful. It's also a real mess. It's a mudhole, and there's no shelter, and the johns are overflowing, and people are cutting their feet on poptops in the mud, and there's kids on bad trips and they say a couple of ODs, but that's not why I came back."

"So why did you?"

She leaned up and kissed him again. "To be with you. To be with this cool guy I met on my trip to Woodstock. To spend the night with you again.

"I'm going to go sack out for a while. A good long while, I hope. But come down and get me later. Let's have dinner together."

The rain started again as she slipped into the woods in back of the canoe shed, and then it picked up. By two o'clock a steady downpour pounded the roads and trees and river, and people crowded into the store and under the pavilion. More people left. They stuffed their wet gear into their cars and pulled out, unable to face another soggy night. Nick sloshed through the North Area a few times to check on his stake, and each time he passed Site 61 he felt good knowing that Joanie was sleeping inside her tent.

She had come back for him. This knowledge made him so happy he didn't care if it rained all day and night. Let the river rise, let the campers leave, let the music play on in Bethel. Joanie was there, and she was there for him, and that was what stayed in his head and in his heart all the wet afternoon.

Around five o'clock, a massive thunderstorm boomed in. The sky turned dark purple with streaks of chartreuse, lightning forked down behind the mountain in Pennsylvania, and thunder shook the valley. Nick was filling a propane bottle when the storm hit. The wind whipped sheets of rain across the parking lot, and over in the field a wall tent tumbled to the ground. A dozen people were hanging under the pavilion, seeking a dry respite from their campsites, and they huddled in a knot.

Nick worried about Joanie down in her tent, but after half an hour the storm abated. A little while later she came up to the store with a towel and some bath stuff.

"That sure woke me up," she said.

"You get wet?" he asked.

"Hah! Sure did. Tent's as wet inside as out."

"You have dry clothes?" She could borrow something from Lisa Marie; he'd run over to the house right now.

"Yeah, I had some in my bag." She raised an embroidered backpack.

"Good. Go take a shower and get dried out, and then we'll grab some dinner."

"Starving."

They went to the Wild Turkey. Joanie destroyed a big roast beast sandwich, a bowl of potato salad, and a plate of fries. Then she eyed Nick's plate for scraps. They drank cold draft Genesee, and she told him more stories about the concert. She had run into her friends— miraculously, it seemed, since there were so many people. "They're still tight with the Long Island dudes," she said. "They're in deep."

He asked her if she ran into any good dope. She rolled her eyes. "I don't do anything stronger than pot or hash," she said. "Plenty of other stuff going around, including a lot of warnings about bad acid."

He liked that she wasn't embarrassed about being a druggie light-weight, and he got a kick out of her story about this hippie guy who offered her a drink of water, and she thought for sure it was laced with acid so she gave him a prim "No!" and darted away. He loved the way she laughed at herself for this reaction, as if she thought she was being a goody two-shoes but didn't care. She squinted as she laughed— "Hah!"—and showed laugh lines that made her look wise and self-assured. She laughed a laugh that came from the back of her throat, a spontaneous "Hah!" as if she were surprising herself. Nick imagined her laughing out loud frequently, getting a kick out of an encounter at the post office, or remembering some funny incident in the green-house. Over beers and dinner, he laughed easily with her.

So did Jake. The barkeep kept looking down their way from his perch by the television. Every time Joanie yelped out that "Hah!" he'd swivel around with a bemused expression. When he drew their third drafts, he asked, "Ain't you introducing us local boys to your friend, Nick?"

Joanie shook Jake's hand, surprised him with a brotherhood hand-shake so he had to adjust to the whole thumb-swivel thing, and by the time he did, she had pulled the handshake into an Indian-wrestle move that let her flex her biceps at him. Jake grinned good-naturedly and Joanie yipped out another laugh, and he said, "Jesus, honey. Come back after last call for wrestling practice." He must have said something to Norma, because she came out from the kitchen and sipped her nightly Seven-and-Seven and smiled at them over her cocktail straws.

The rain had stopped after the storm washed through, so when they finished at the Wild Turkey, Nick suggested a drive up to High Rock. He bought a cold six-pack from Jake and then swung down to the campgrounds for some dry firewood he had set aside. It was dark by the time they got to High Rock, but the sky seemed to be lifting. They could see the lights of Delaware Ford. To the east, the clouds flickered with a glow that had never been there before.

"Woodstock," he said.

"Wow. Cool," Joanie said. She mused on the flickering sky while he spread an army blanket onto the rock slab. They had the place to themselves. Everybody else was eight miles east, under the lighted clouds. He built a fire. When it was going nicely, he settled back on the blanket with Joanie. They drank some beer, and then they made love, free and good in the firelight and open air.

A car door slammed down by the parking area. Then another. Oh well, he thought. They'd had the place to themselves a good long while. They pulled on their jeans, and he felt fuzzed-out and embarrassed but glad to be with Joanie, who laughed so easily and made love so readily and who made him feel wanted. Made him feel desirable. Made him feel stronger just being with her. It didn't matter who was coming up from the road—he and Joanie would face them together.

Two figures emerged from the woods. It was too dark to recognize them, and they edged to the far end of the ledge, so Nick figured it was no one he knew. He laid a couple more slabs on the fire, and Joanie opened another beer. They could hear the other couple settling in and talking to each other in muffled voices. Nick caught a strain here and there, a familiar timbre. He heard a cork pop. A woman's laugh. He and Joanie drank their beer. In the distance, the lights at Woodstock flickered off the clouds like heat lightning.

"This is so great," Joanie said. "Thanks for bringing me up here."

"Sure beats listening to Hendrix and them," he said. "Fending off LSD-laced water."

"Hah! Fuck you. It does, actually."

He felt a renewed flare of warmth for her, the desire to protect her. He would fight for her against any threat. Through the flames he could keep an eye on the couple across the ledge. They hadn't built a fire, so all he could see was the glow of a cigarette and the occasional glint of a bottle.

God, he was lucky. To be here, on this slab of rock with this girl, pleasantly drunk and just-laid. He couldn't imagine being happier. He gazed across the river at the lights of Delaware Ford, at the spotty campfires and lanterns of the campgrounds. How far away that turmoil seemed, how distant his parents' troubles. Had his parents ever had moments like this? And if they had, why hadn't they kept having them?

Pretty soon the other couple got up. As they appeared out of the dark, Nick recognized the woman's hair—a straight-cut blond page-boy, too sophisticated for Delaware Ford—before he recognized Ted's voice: "Thought I saw a familiar face in the campfire's glow!"

In the dim, ragged light, Ted loomed burly in a big canvas duck-coat. A champagne bottle dangled from his arm.

"Share your fire for a few minutes?" he asked.

Nick was startled to see him, but not nearly so startled as he was to see Lillian Van Vooren in a black windbreaker and tight jeans, holding a champagne glass.

"Hey, Ted," he said. "Sure, have a seat."

He made room on the blanket, scooched Joanie over by him. They sat in a semicircle, and Ted stretched his boots to the fire. He leaned toward Joanie and offered his hand.

"I'm Ted," he said. "Friend of Nick's."

"Hi—Joanie. Friend of Nick's."

Ted laughed. "This is Lillian."

"Hah! Another friend of Nick's?"

"Oh, yes," Lillian said, and raised her champagne glass. "We're all good friends, aren't we, Nick?"

Several looks passed around the fire: Ted at Nick to see how he was taking Lillian being there, Nick at Lillian to see how she was taking him being with another girl, Lillian at Nick to see what he thought of her being with Ted. Joanie noticed all these looks, flitting across faces like so many shadows from the fire, and took a hearty drink of beer.

"Sounds like a cozy bunch," she said.

Ted topped up Lillian's champagne glass and then his own, and nodded out toward the flickering clouds. "Not over at the big concert?"

Nick shook his head and gave a rueful smile.

"Charlie go?"

"Took off Friday."

Ted looked better than he had in a while. His eyes were animated and bright, and maybe it was the firelight, but his face seemed ruddier and healthier than it had all summer. Mostly he had an ease about him that Nick hadn't sensed in a while—the way he stretched out toward the fire, how casually he extended his arm behind Lillian. He gestured with his champagne glass.

"The big party of the summer, and you're missing it," he said.

"Somebody had to stick around."

He couldn't help but get in a dig. His father swamped at the campgrounds, Phil Sweeney's revelations. And here was Ted, swigging champagne with the nicest-looking woman in town.

"It's just me and Miller holding down the grounds," he said. "Dad and Lisa Marie in the store. We're overrun, if you hadn't noticed."

"The whole county's overrun," Lillian said. "If you can't beat 'em, Nick, might as well join 'em." She raised her champagne toward Bethel. What was Lillian doing here? She and Ted? *Always such a handsome man,* she'd said at the cookout. What would Chuck think if he knew? And Darlene?

"Charlie go by himself?" Ted asked.

"Far as I know, yeah. He left me a note."

"Eva and Darlene are over there someplace," Lillian said. "Bless their cute little butts."

Lillian had had a bit to drink. She fumbled with a cigarette, and Ted lit it for her. As long as they were all not saying things, Nick hoped she wouldn't bring up Darlene in front of Joanie. He wanted to be able to tell Joanie about ex-girlfriends himself. And that, for sure, was what Darlene was.

"And how about you, Junie? Janie?" Lillian asked. "Did you—"

"Joanie. Yes I did."

"And was it—"

"It was fine. Lots of good drugs. Lots of naked people." She smiled pointedly at Lillian. "Not sure if I saw Eve and . . . Darla? Any distinguishing features on their cute little butts?"

Lillian gave Joanie a straight-on look, or as straight-on as she could hold for about three seconds, and Nick could see her censoring various comebacks to his impertinent date. Finally, she dismissed Joanie with a column of cigarette smoke and a sip of champagne.

"You guys been keeping up with your practice?" Ted asked, swinging the conversation in a safer direction. "Gonna defend the hometown honor this year?"

"Haven't had a chance the past week or so," Nick said. "Not since we've been dealing with this crowd."

Nick wanted to talk with Ted, get everything out in the open, let him know about Sal and Phil, and Charlie getting roughed up, and he wanted to ask him if all of the Iannacone stuff was true, but this wasn't the time.

"You going to be around tomorrow?" Nick asked.

"Hard to say, Nick. Difficult to predict."

Joanie prodded him with her knee, and he killed the rest of the beer.

"Okay." He stood up and pulled Joanie to her feet. "We gotta split, but I want to give you something. Hang tight."

He walked Joanie down to the car. While he was groping inside the glovebox, she asked, "What's with your friends? They're pretty screwed up."

He found the envelope and headed back up the slippery trail.

"I'll tell you in a second," he said.

Out on the slab, Ted and Lillian were illuminated in the firelight.

"Met your friend Sal the other night," Nick said.

Ted blinked.

"He wanted you to have this."

Ted took Charlie's ponytail as naturally as he would extend his hand to meet another man's in a handshake, but as he grasped it, he recognized what it was and jerked away, nearly threw it into the fire, and spun halfway around as if catching a fast pitch. He opened his hand and studied his son's hair, still bound in its rubber band.

"Thank you, Nick. I can keep this?"

"Sure, I—"

"I'll talk to you tomorrow."

Lillian waved her cigarette at him. "Nice meeting your little friend, Nick."

"You guys keep the blanket," he said.

He and Joanie drove back to Delaware Ford with steam wisps rising off the tar. He gave her the nickel tour of Ted and Charlie, of Lillian and Darlene.

"So what did you give Ted?" she asked.

"Charlie's ponytail. A guy Ted knows liberated it the other night."

"Jesus. What's that all about?"

"I don't know too much," he said. "Neither does Charlie. But he's over at Woodstock with his hair a lot shorter than he'd like."

"Okay," she said. "And Lillian is Eva's mom, and Eva is Charlie's sort-of girlfriend?"

"Well, sort of."

"And Darlene . . . ?"

He shook his head, touched her leg.

"Yesterday's news."

"Okay. Just getting it all straight."

At the campgrounds, Nick headed toward Site 61, but Joanie stopped him—"We're not really gonna sleep in that wet tent, are we?"—and he swung the MG up the hill and past Grandpa's barn.

They were quiet going into his apartment. Nick kept his voice hushed. His grandparents were old-fashioned enough to disapprove of him bringing a girl home, and he didn't want to upset them. He trickled the water as he washed up; Joanie crept around the three rooms and inspected his books, his canoe trophies, his posters of Jimi Hendrix and Raquel Welch and the Beatles. The Endless Summer poster with a sunset and surfboards.

She waited for him in the bedroom. She had found some emergency candles in the kitchen and stuck one into a beer bottle, so the room had a soft warmth. She raised the sheet for him, and he slid in gratefully alongside her.

"Nice little setup you've got," she said.

"Nicer with you here." He imagined the pleasure and peace of going to bed like this every night, to be cradled in Joanie's arms, to run his hand over her smooth skin.

She stopped his hand and held it to her mouth.

"So what do you think about your friend Ted fooling around with someone else's wife?" she asked.

"It's his business. It's more or less the way he's always operated, as far as I can tell."

"But do you approve of it?"

"I don't approve or disapprove of it. It's their business. They're adults. They're free to do as they please."

"Well, I disapprove of it," she said. "I want you to know that. Yeah, they're adults. Yeah, they're free to screw up their lives as they please. But in the process they screw up other people's lives—especially their kids'—and that doesn't come for free."

The seriousness in her tone caught him. She spoke with conviction, even anger.

"You sound like you know what you're talking about," he said.

"I do," she answered. "I do know something about it. My parents went through something last year, and it hasn't healed over yet."

"You want to tell me about it?"

"Not really. Not now. Maybe sometime, if there is a sometime for us."

He held her close, felt her shiver and tighten. Out on 97 a semi whined up the grade. Under the porch, Siegfried shifted in his sleep and clanked his chain.

"Do you want there to be a sometime?" he asked.

"Yes," she said. "I think so. A lot of that depends on how seriously you take the question I asked."

A bug, attracted to the candlelight, hit the screen beside the bed.

"I took your question literally. You were asking about Ted and Lillian. If you're really asking about me, I'll answer about me."

"I'm asking about you."

He thought about his past girlfriends, about respecting Darlene's limits while they were making out, about not pushing her farther than she wanted to go. He thought about Beatrice Kordt and not going farther than *he* wanted to. He thought about Charlie, who would follow his dick any direction it pointed.

"I'm about as loyal as they come, I guess," he said. "I'm not sure that's always been the greatest thing, but that's the way it is. In case you couldn't tell, you're the first girl I've been to bed with."

"I know," she said. "And I'm not asking that I be the last. I just need to know that I can trust you, because I've seen what happens when you can't."

He shifted, ran his hand along her back. The bug on the screen buzzed itself into a fit of frustration.

"I want you to trust me," he said. "That's the truest thing I know."

"Truth is a fact of life," she said. "Honesty is what you do with truth."

"I'm honest."

"I know you are," she said. "I could tell that the moment I laid eyes on you. We need enough time together to trust that."

"Okay," he said. "I'd like to give you that time."

In the distance he heard a low vibration, an alteration in the frequency of the night. It rose to a hum, a drone. Another bug hit the screen. The drone became a rumble, an ominous wave rising. Joanie leaned over him and kissed his neck. He touched her face as the freight's rumble increased, stroked her hair as the rumble became a tangible wave in the room, as the floor and walls began to quiver. She swung over him as the rumble became a roar, as the train rounded the last bend before the house and pounded up the tracks toward the creamery, and the headlight swept through the window and illuminated her rocking above him, all around him, in the roaring, rocking room, and if it was trust that mattered to her, then trust is what he would give her. That, and their own rocking as the train pushed blindly through the night.

33

MONDAY MORNING, AND the campers were clearing out. Finally. The outbound motion and bustle gave Nick a surge of energy, even though he was beat from the whole weekend. He and Joanie had talked until two, and then he had slept lightly. The campers looked tired, too, but wanly happy, as if the last few days had been an ordeal everyone had survived. The regular crew drifted in, Shag and Bear and the Evans brothers. They raved to each other about the concert, kept telling Nick he should have been there.

He was too tired to care. He was glad to see the campers leaving. With each car that pulled out, he felt a little clearer. He wanted to see open spaces in the field instead of a shantytown of wet canvas and hanging clothes. He wanted to walk from the canoe shed to the gas pumps without hearing "Hey, Mista!" He wanted, simply, to be away from the place for a while.

He felt a little blue about Joanie. Her friends were coming back to break camp and pick her up. When he'd left her sleeping in his bed, she'd looked so peaceful that he'd hated to go. He kept an eye on her campsite all morning, and then on one pass in the truck, there she was. She turned from her tent fly and greeted him with a kiss and a long hug. They didn't say anything for a while. Then he helped her unstake her tent and her friends' tent and pack them into a neat pile on the picnic table. There wasn't much to breaking down the camp; it had barely been used.

"When are they coming?" he asked.

"Oh, they'll be along. When I saw them at the concert, they said around noon. They've got to deal with traffic."

"Yeah—the radio says it's still a mess. Cars strung from Bethel to Monticello."

She leaned on the sleeping bags and looked into the trees, moved her face to seek a patch of sunlight. "I'm happy hanging out here," she said. "They'll show up sometime. Don't feel like you have to stick around. I know you've got work, and I've got my Brautigan book."

"When will we see each other again?"

"We've got two more weeks of summer. Then we're off to school."

"I could come down and see you this weekend."

"I've got a family thing this weekend." She shook her head. "It'll be weird."

"Next weekend's the canoe regatta. You want to come up for it?"

"I'd love to, but it's the last weekend before school. I'll be packing and stuff, and so will you, don't forget."

God. He still needed to come to terms with college.

"I really appreciate last night," he said. "I appreciate the whole weekend. By not going to the concert, I met you."

"You lucky devil. We'll be seeing each other, don't worry about that. Albany is not that far from Montclair, and you don't look like you're afraid of a little road trip."

The prospect of weekend runs from Albany to Joanie's arms almost made college seem worthwhile.

She leaned over and kissed him. "You find Charlie and get back into practice, and then go win your canoe race. We'll see each other after the semester starts."

He must have looked happy, or sad, or something, because she kissed him again, longer this time, and then she said, "We'll see a lot of each other, I think."

He walked away from her site, spaced out on weird emotions. He imagined pulling into Montclair, New Jersey, a town he had never seen, with the top down on a golden autumn day, watching Joanie run out of her dorm. And he kept reflecting on her calm, assured tone about them, about the future. How was it that women—certain women, anyway—could contain such wisdom, such certainty, about things as elusive and hard to fathom as emotions? Grasping the meaning of his feelings felt like trying to interpret a roadsign that had just flashed past his window.

The sloshing of Ted's Buick in the puddled lane snapped him to the present. Ted leaned over and opened the passenger's door.

"Hop in, Nick," he said.

Ted drove with his right arm slung over the seatback, his hand inches from Nick's shoulder. He looked like the old Ted—successful, upbeat, even cocky.

"Place is clearing out," he said. "Almost nobody left across from the office."

The Meadow was opening up, too. Empty sites, garbage overflowing the cans, scraps strung on the ground. Bear Brown eased Buff past a lone umbrella tent in the sycamore grove, not far from Celeste Gennaro's compound. A few Winnebagos and Airstreams remained on the river sites, older folks who had planned their vacations without knowing about Woodstock. No cars by Phil Sweeney's trailer. Nick wondered how cocky Ted would be if that black Cadillac pulled into view.

In the North Area, groups of freaks continued to party and hang out as if they had found a home, but clearly, the biggest weekend in memory was over.

"Charlie hasn't gotten back yet?"

"Nope," Nick said.

Ted gunned the Buick up onto the Knoll. A door slammed on the men's side of the bathhouse, and Shag came out carrying a toilet plunger. He waved his hand in front of his nose and headed toward the office.

Ted parked so the car faced the river. He reached into his shirt pocket and brought out Charlie's ponytail. He held the ponytail under his nose, musing, as if over a flower.

He laughed. "Peanuts."

"What?"

"Peanuts. Ever since he was a baby, Charlie's had a smell like salted peanuts. Didn't you ever smell it?"

Nick shook his head.

"Margaret and I always called him Peanuts when he was a kid, after the comic strip."

He laid the ponytail on the dashboard.

"So," he said. "Tell me about Sal."

Nick told Ted about the encounter on the bridge, about Sal working Charlie over and pulling the knife.

Propped in the nearest fireplace was the cardboard bottom of a pizza box. Somebody had drawn a peace sign on it in charcoal and scrawled, "And in the end, the love you take is equal to the love you make."

Nick told Ted what Phil said about Iannacone.

Ted blew out a long breath.

"Yeah, well, it's true. Mostly true."

"Iannacone has money in this business?"

Ted nodded.

"And you've never told my dad and mom?"

"Not directly, no." Ted tapped his hand on the steering wheel. "People hear what they want to hear. Kit probably has an idea."

"So you're saying it's Francis's fault he hasn't seen through the smoke?"

"No, I'm saying you use every advantage you have to get ahead. When you're paddling in the canoe regatta, you know the river better than any other team. You're going to seek the fastest water. You're not going to ignore the best line through a riff just because your competition doesn't know about it."

"But Francis isn't your competition. He's your partner."

"That's right. And believe me, he's better off not knowing about these people. The less he knows, the less advantage they have."

"Well, he knows now."

"Okay," Ted said. "I can manage that one."

"Meaning you can blow more smoke around the facts? That you're willing to let your kid get cut up because of your debts?"

"No, that's not what I mean, Nick. They're not going to hurt Charlie. They're using him as a pressure point. They think—"

"Jesus, man. That's really fucked up." He didn't care what he said to Ted now. "It's a fucked-up way to live."

"Yeah," Ted said. "I guess you could—"

"It fucks up your life, it fucks up Charlie's life, it fucks up my parents—"

"Nick, I know." Ted began flicking the blinker switch up and down. "I don't need the lecture, thanks. And all that's about to change, anyway."

"How so?"

"Lillian Van Vooren," he said. "Lillian is looking very favorably on our business right now. She's about to become our white knight."

"What do you mean?"

"She's always felt guilty that the First Bank of Chuck Van Vooren didn't back us in the beginning. We're running the most successful business in town—"

"Most successful business in town? Most likely to go under, you mean."

"In the eyes of the town, we're doing more business than we can handle. The town benefits. The more people we bring in, the better everybody does. Kick's sells more groceries and suntan lotion and tennis shoes. Beagle's pumps more gas and fixes more flats. Waitresses earn more tips; bartenders draw more beers. Nobody wants to go back to the way it was, nobody wants to see the campgrounds go under."

"And that's where Lillian comes in."

"Right. She wants to help us wipe out our debt. She's going to put up the money to do that, and then some."

"How much is it?"

"It's complicated, but something along the line of half a million."

"She's going to convince Chuck to invest a half a million dollars in the campgrounds?"

"Better than that," Ted said. "She's going to clear the debt herself— she's got a ton of equity in the funeral home—and get Chuck to invest in the motor home business. Which, I think, you've heard the general outlines of."

Unreal, Nick thought. The guy got somebody to cover his ass every time.

"It's like canoe racing, Nick. Keep your eye on the guy ahead of you, not in back."

Ted drove them up to the office, pulled over by the bathrooms.

"I appreciate you holding down the fort this weekend, Nick," he said. "I know it wasn't easy for you and Francis. The place is emptying out and the other guys are back—why don't you take the rest of the day off?"

Ted dipped into his shirt pocket, brought out a wad of bills, and peeled off two twenties.

"For your extra effort this weekend," he said, and stuffed the bills into Nick's hand.

He dragged Nick's blanket from the backseat. Nick imagined him and Lillian Van Vooren on it by the fire, and the scene was so improbable yet so real that he took the blanket by a corner and vowed to wash it before putting it back into his trunk.

"Thanks for the blanket," Ted said. He reached out and shook Nick's hand. "And thanks for being a good friend to Charlie."

As the Buick pulled away, Lisa Marie rushed out of the store. She looked pissed.

"Where's he going?" she demanded. "Is he leaving again? Twenty minutes ago he barged into the store, punched open the cash register, and cleaned it out. We thought he was going over to see Francis or make a deposit or something, but he ripped us off. Now we can't make change or anything."

Under the blanket, the two twenties felt clammy. Nick handed them to his sister.

"Here," he said. "He gave me these. I'm sure they're part of your stash."

"I tell you what," she said. "This isn't the first time. Francis is spittin', man."

The Buick was at the end of the driveway. Ted didn't even touch the brakes when he hit Cemetery Road.

34

NICK CAME UPON the first abandoned car near Fosterdale. A Dodge Charger, slewed into the grader ditch. On 17B were more cars, and groups of people walking toward him. They looked bedraggled and tired. They ought to, he thought. They just spent three days and nights in a wet hayfield. But they looked happy, too. They laughed with each other and seemed to float along the roadside.

He figured the main way in would be blocked, or the troopers would keep him out, so he cut over on Gabriel Road to Tagart and approached the place from the backside. The roads were still clogged with people and cars, everybody trying to find their way out. When he got to the corner of Perry and West Shore, he figured he was close enough. Everybody else was walking faster than he could drive anyway, so when a painted-up school bus heaved from the field onto the road, he swung into the spot. Had to gas it through the muddy ditch, but the MG was light and rode over it.

He stepped out into mud. No big deal—he'd been muddy all weekend. But as he slogged off the field and down the road, he saw that mud was the theme. Even though the road was paved, it was covered in mud from so many people tracking it off the fields. The kids were covered in mud. Not only their feet or shoes, but their bellbottoms and bare legs were caked, their shirts spattered. Flecks of dried mud clung to their hair. As he walked down West Shore, he noticed the kids looking at him, and then he realized he was the cleanest person there. Sure, he was tracking mud along, but he had put on clean jeans that morning, he had spent the night in a bed, had taken a shower. He walked along, self-conscious about his white T-shirt. He felt like ducking into the field and rolling around. His clean white shirt advertised that he was a newcomer, that he hadn't been through this experience with them. He felt like a benchwarmer among players.

Cans and bottles and wrappers were smashed into the road. Shirts were ground flat. More people streamed toward him, then three guys on a motorcycle, slipping and spewing smoke. At the corner of West Shore and Hurd Road, the cops were trying to keep things moving, and there was the field: the stage and the skeletal yellow towers, all those high-peaked structures, and way up on the hill, the vendor stalls that he had helped build. He wondered if Darlene was out there, muddy and bedraggled as everybody else. The field was a mess. The people were clearing off, and what they left behind was a refugee camp, a landscape of rubble: soaked and muddy sleeping bags, twisted and torn tarpaulins, matted plastic sheeting, improvised tents and lean-tos, overturned milk crates, mashed soda cans, abandoned shirts and pants and shoes, scraps of wood, paper, the detritus of retreat. Through it all roamed a few sorry-looking souls, stooping and picking up this and that, carrying stuff to nascent piles.

A voice came at him from the edge of the field: "Man, hey man, hey, hey man."

He recognized the floppy hat and the army jacket first, and then the hitchhiker from Florida was at him with his rap.

"Hey, freakin' Delaware Ford, right? You and the chick?" He made a toking-up gesture with his hand. "How you doin', man? Some freakin' party, hey?"

They did the brotherhood handshake thing, and the guy's eyes were as glassy as a cat's. He was crusted with mud. His army jacket was soaked but drying, and his mustache hadn't grown any. He held up a plastic garbage bag.

"You wanna help clean up the place, man? They're still payin' good bread, or so they say, and hey—" He waved out across the field. "There's plenty of freakin' opportunity."

Nick thanked him and said he was looking for somebody.

"Your old lady, man? Little blond chick?" He looked around. "Haven't seen her, man. Sure you don't want in on this garbage detail? Get in on the ground floor, business is sure to pick up, heh-heh."

"Thanks. It's my day off, and I gotta find somebody."

"Yeah, well," he said as he wandered off, "you get more freakin' days off than anybody I ever met, dude."

Nick traced his way beyond the stage, under a makeshift wooden footbridge and past a fenced-in area that held generators and utility trailers. He figured he'd walk up the field toward the vendor stalls, and from there get a view and maybe spot Charlie. But two hundred yards past the stage, there was the Love Bus, snugged in under some trees. The curtains were all pulled, but one of the side doors was open and strung with clothing, and a shirtless Charlie bent under the hood and dug around inside the engine compartment.

"Lookin' for your stash?" Nick asked.

Charlie backed out from under the hood, a spark plug in his greasy fingers.

"Hey, man," he said. "You finally got away."

"Missed the show, looks like."

Charlie's hair looked weird curling away from his head instead of tied back in the ponytail. He wore a pair of round blue glasses, so Nick couldn't quite see his eyes. Charlie studied the spark plug. Held it up to the sky, squinted. Then he glanced at Nick, looked at the van, wiped his greasy fingers on his chest. Once again Nick felt the whiteness of his clean shirt.

Charlie plucked a worn navy T-shirt off one of the van doors and began cleaning the spark plug.

"Plugs got damp," he said. "Can't get her to turn over."

Nick noticed a white peasant top hanging from the other door.

"Eva around?" he asked.

"Someplace," Charlie said. "She ran into some friends from the city."

He nodded toward an ancient Chrysler touring car parked next to the van. It too had clothing hanging from the doors and spread out on the roof.

"She's with them someplace," he said. "They all went to school together in New York. These people split and started a commune up in Vermont."

Charlie glanced into the van and then bumped the door with his hip, so it swung to. Then he handed Nick the spark plug and the shirt. "You wanna dry that off for me, and I'll get the next one out?"

Nick squatted by the rear bumper while Charlie worked under the hood.

"So how was the weekend at the campgrounds?" Charlie asked.

"Wet, busy. Nuts," Nick said. "How was the concert?"

"Pretty far out," Charlie said, cranking on the spark plug. "Pretty far fucking out."

"That's what I've been hearing."

"Yeah? A lot of people come back over?"

"Regular crew is pretty much back."

"That motherfucker Sal?"

"No Sal. No Phil, today," Nick said. Charlie handed him the next plug and he gave Charlie the dry one. "Ted came around, though."

Charlie started ratcheting in the dry plug. "No shit. The usual? In and gone?"

"Pretty much. He ripped off Lisa Marie in the store and split."

"Huh? What do you mean?"

"That's what Lisa Marie told me, says it wasn't the first time, either."

Charlie kept ratcheting the plug. "You tell him about Sal? You give him my hair?"

"Yeah."

"And?"

"He seemed shocked at first. But then he seemed okay with it."

The wrench stopped in mid-ratchet, and Charlie disengaged himself from the engine. He turned and stared over the top of his blue glasses.

"Okay with it?"

Nick saw Ted sniffing Charlie's ponytail like a flower.

"He says they're not going to hurt you. He says you're just a way to put the squeeze on him."

"You're kidding me." Charlie took off his glasses and set them by the generator belt. "You are motherfucking kidding me."

"Nope." Nick told him about Phil and Iannacone, about Iannacone wanting his money back, about his father staying in the trailer. He pictured Ted and Lillian Van Vooren by the campfire, the champagne bottle between them, and decided to skip that part. He did start to mention Ted and Lillian's bail-out plan for the campgrounds, but Charlie cut him off.

"Fuck him!" Charlie said. "Fuck him. This fucker Sal comes after me with a switchblade and Ted's *okay with it?* It's a *squeeze?* He didn't hear the click of that knife this close to his face, didn't get his neck wrenched out of joint."

"Well, I think he's got a—"

"Fuck him, just fuck him," Charlie said. "That makes my decision all the easier."

"What decision?"

"I'm not going back."

"What do you mean?"

"I'm not going back to the campgrounds. I'm not going back to Delaware Ford. I'm not gonna be a sitting duck for Sal while Ted gets his shit together. In two weeks I'll be off to school, and Sal, or Iannacone, or whoever can find somebody else to hassle."

"Where you going? And what about the canoe race, man?"

"Oh, fuck the canoe race, Nick. It's bullshit anyway, all that competition. Bust your ass to beat the other guy, and for what? A stupid trophy? It's being Ted all over again."

"Charlie—all our practice. The canoe. I mean, yeah, we haven't been out there for a week or so, but we're—"

"Bullshit, bullshit, bullshit, Nick! It's all bullshit, I'm telling you." He waved his arm around at the field and the stage and the people passing by. "You should have been out here this weekend, not toting firewood like a good little do-bee. You should have had the balls to say fuck it. You would've had your eyes opened. You would've seen what happens when people cooperate instead of compete, when they love each other instead of cut each other's throats."

That set Nick back, the vehemence in Charlie's voice. The *good little do-bee*. Charlie put his glasses on and turned to the engine. Nick gazed up the road, at the people passing. Two girls walked toward him, carrying a bundled tarp. Joanie was on her way back to New Jersey.

Charlie tightened the other spark plug. He switched to the opposite side of the engine.

"Look," he said. "I'm sorry. After this weekend—and I mean everything this weekend—there's nothing for me back in Delaware Ford. I'm splitting for a while. I'm sorry about the canoe race."

They dried off the other two spark plugs and replaced them, and Charlie slammed the hood. He jumped and looked to the van, and then he opened the hood again.

"Here," he said. "You hold this open while I see if she cranks."

"Why hold it open? She'll crank either way."

"I want you to tell me how she sounds."

Charlie wore a funny expression, and as he turned toward the driver's side, the van shifted a little and the curtains fluttered. Someone was moving around inside.

"Charlie?" a voice called, and the side door swung open and Darlene Van Vooren stepped out.

"Charlie? You get it fixed?"

Darlene was barefoot and barelegged, and she wore Charlie's chambray shirt. It was the only thing she had on, as far as Nick could tell. The tail brushed across her thighs like a miniskirt and the top few buttons were open. She pulled her hair back and blinked in the light. She had been sleeping.

She saw Nick and blinked again, glanced at Charlie, and put her hand up to shade her eyes.

"Oh—Nick. Hi," she said. "You made it."

"Yeah," he said. Looks like you did too, he wanted to say. She turned to Charlie, as if trying to look cool, as if she wasn't guilty of anything, as if she was all grown up and sophisticated after her weekend out here.

Charlie eased around Nick, wiping his hands on the T-shirt, and stood next to Darlene. She took her hand away from her eyes and slipped it around Charlie's arm. They stood there, a couple.

"Like I said, man," Charlie said. "You should have been out here."

Darlene nodded, as if their being together was somehow Nick's fault, and a look passed across her face, a look that he had seen last night in her mother's face when she was trying to gauge his reaction. It was a look that said she—both of them—could deceive someone and carry it off.

"Remember what you said about Georgie Brewster, Nick?" she asked. "About him not getting out from under his father's shadow? Maybe that's what you need to do."

Nick laughed. It was his purest, most honest reaction. He laughed at Darlene's advice. If she only knew. He laughed again at the sight of Darlene and Charlie playing grown-up, and at the vision of their parents by the fire last night, playing kids. If she only knew the shadow Ted and Lillian cast upon her and Charlie. It seemed so silly and stupid and dishonest that all he could do was laugh out loud. And when he started to laugh, he couldn't stop himself. It felt good, the laughter rolling out of his chest, and he thought what a kick Joanie would get out of this story and he was happy that they had been open with each other, so he could tell her this, and it felt so good to be grateful for someone to be honest with that he laughed some more, thinking how they would sit in her dorm room one day over a bottle of wine and he would tell her the story of Darlene and Charlie blaming him for their being together.

Darlene and Charlie must have thought he'd gone hysterical or something—over the shock of seeing his supposed girlfriend with his best friend, he guessed—and Darlene came over and touched his arm, "Oh, Nick," she said, and this cracked him up again, knowing that he knew what they didn't: that they were making the same mistakes as their parents, or vice versa, and that there would be no way to tell them, that they'd have to learn for themselves.

"Nick, I'm sorry," Darlene said.

"You guys—" He hiccupped, and in one determined effort got it out: "You guys are perfect for each other."

Darlene smiled, as if with him, but Charlie looked skeptical. He knew something was up, but he also knew he couldn't say anything. Darlene was standing there in his shirt. Her wet bellbottoms were hanging from his rearview mirror.

"We're going to Vermont," Charlie said.

"Eva and her friends invited us to hang out at their commune," Darlene said. "So we're gonna go do that for a while."

That ought to make your parents very proud, Nick wanted to say, but he could see Chuck Van Vooren's reaction—how his pinned-back little ears would flatten even more and he'd bare his teeth at the thought of Charlie Miles—and he cracked up again. Half a million bucks, fucked away in Vermont.

Then he caught himself. *Half a million bucks, fucked away in Vermont.* Charlie and Darlene, standing before him in their defiance and unity, didn't have a clue as to what was at stake—Ted's bail-out plan or Lillian's impending white knighthood. He kept seeing Chuck Van Vooren's reddening ears and gritted teeth and vengeful eyes when he got the news that his youngest daughter had run off to a hippie commune with Ted Miles's horny son. If he told Charlie and Darlene, would they listen? He watched Darlene slip her hand around Charlie's arm again, watched Charlie place his hand over hers, and he knew the answer.

And that gesture told him what he needed to do. Seize the moment, Grandpa had advised him. Seize the moment and alter the course of events.

"Great," he said. He felt purged, washed clean, and sure of his decision. "Have a great trip."

A girl had stopped behind the van and struggled to adjust her bundle—a Mexican blanket tied in rope. She was skinny and her face was broken out, and her lank hair was scraggly from the rain. Her granny glasses, flecked with mud, sat unevenly on her nose.

"Give you a hand with that?" Nick asked.

"Oh yeah," she said. "Thanks!"

"Sure thing," he said, hoisting her bundle. "I'm headed down this way anyway."

Her blanket was dirty and so was the rope handle, and it smeared his T-shirt. He walked her all the way out to 17B, where she was going to hitch back to Connecticut. She thanked him and gave him a hug, and then he walked back down Hurd Road. It was slower going back, because he was the only one headed that way. Everybody else was headed out, but he didn't mind. His T-shirt was finally smudged.

35

FRANCIS CAME HOME on Tuesday afternoon. When Kit saw the Scout jouncing down the lane, she felt a schoolgirl quiver that she quickly suppressed. She set aside her gloves and smoothed her hair.

Inside, she found him by the telephone, flipping through the mail.

"So," he said. Noncommittal as usual, no joy in seeing her. No rancor, either. Just "So." How that monosyllabic space-filler annoyed her. It put her on the spot, not him, who had just waltzed in after nearly a week away. He was the one who should be explaining himself, but she was the one who spoke.

"Clearing out over there?"

"Pretty much," he said. "A big mess to clean up."

He seemed distant, distracted. He flipped through the mail without registering the return addresses—the electric company, *Farm Journal*, Cornell Cooperative Extension. Kit would pay anything that needed paying. He set the stack back onto the table.

"You want something to eat?" she asked.

"Just picking up some stuff."

So. It wasn't over, at least not yet. His tread on the wooden steps sounded so familiar, but it only reminded her of his absence. She hadn't heard him in days. It had been only her and Stacey, Lisa Marie briefly, and the big farmhouse had been awfully quiet.

And now, as his dresser drawers slid and his hangers scraped, she wondered how long it would last. A few more days, now that the big weekend was over? Some calm time to think things through? Or had he just had it? Had enough of her, of the business, of Ted? Saw this as a good time to get away?

The bedroom was dim, as it always was on summer afternoons. The shade from the beech trees kept the room dark and cool. He was packing underwear into a Kick's grocery bag. Good sign, she thought. At least it wasn't a suitcase.

"Look, Francis. You don't have to stay in that crummy little trailer."

He held a pair of socks in mid-gesture.

"Yes," he said. "I do."

"You should be here. You should be with us, with—" With *me*, she'd wanted to say. "You should be with your family."

With a swiftness that surprised her, Francis flung his socks across the room. They rattled the lamp on the nightstand.

"I know what I *should* do!" he shouted. "I'm doing what I have to!"

He gave her a look that she couldn't hold.

"I have a mess to clean up," he said.

"We make our own messes. I'm sorry for any that I've caused."

On the river a canoe banged and someone shouted. They could tell it was a shout of pleasure, of fun and surprise, but instinctively they looked out. One of ours, she could tell by the way he turned back to the dresser.

"Oh, Francis, let's clean up this mess once and for all. Get rid of the campgrounds. Sell out our share. We can get by with the horses. You can start your own business. An orchard—"

"He doesn't have the means to buy us out," Francis said. "Even if we wanted to go that route."

He crossed to the nightstand and picked up his socks.

"If not him, somebody else," she said. "Somebody would want it— it's a good business for the right person. Somebody who wants to get out of the city. It's just not right for us."

He stuffed his socks into the bag.

"Phil Sweeney," she said. "He's always wanted the place. Make him an offer."

"Phil Sweeney."

"One thing I could never figure about Phil Sweeney," she said. "He claims to have a construction business in New Jersey. But you can't run a business and spend half the week lazing around a campsite. He's on somebody's payroll."

Another shout from the river, a paddle banging aluminum. Francis cocked his head. Didn't look at the river but gazed into the leafy green outside the screen, riding his thoughts somewhere. He ran his thumb along the top edge of the grocery bag. The light fell upon his cheekbone and illuminated the white corner of his eye, and for a moment they could have been twenty years younger, newly married, pausing to appreciate a robin on a branch before slipping into bed for an afternoon of enjoying each other.

"Phil Sweeney," he said.

The canoe banged again and Francis shifted and the light fell away from his face. He folded the top of the bag, crimped it once, twice, three times in his meticulous way. The distance was back.

"I'm here," she said. "Whenever you're ready."

36

OVER THE NEXT two weeks Nick called Joanie almost every night from the campgrounds office, since it was long distance. She reminded him of the things to do before school started: buy a notebook and typewriter ribbon, copy her address in a safe place. He got his dorm assignment from Albany. He would be rooming with a guy named Israel Markowitz, from Queens.

His mother gave him a hundred dollars and sent him to Honesdale to buy school clothes. He went to Sullum's and bought two pairs of jeans and two chambray shirts. Kit had kicked at his worn work boots and said, "And buy yourself some decent shoes." He knew she had in mind a pair of penny loafers or something by Thom McAn, but when he passed a leather goods shop and spotted a pair of over-the-calf fringed suede boots, he bought them.

He was nervous about going to college, he was worried for his parents. His father was living in the Shasta at the end of the campgrounds, and his mother seemed to be off in her head somewhere. The weekend of the concert had been one thing, but a week later Francis was still taking his meals at the luncheonette and working late in the office. Nick and Lisa Marie speculated and came up empty. He couldn't talk to his father about something so personal, but he could bring it up to his mother, which he did one day as he picked up the garbage at the stables.

"So what's up with you and Dad?" he asked.

She stopped her pushbroom and studied him. "We're going through a little something, I guess. Something about the business."

"You mean about what Phil said?"

"What about what Phil said? The ad in the paper?"

"No, the money that Ted owes. The Iannacone thing." He had assumed his father had filled her in.

"What Iannacone thing?"

"Dad didn't tell you?"

"Nothing about any Iannacone. What are you talking about?"

Jesus, he thought. Could these guys be any less communicative? How could they be in business and not tell each other things? Ted not tell Francis about things that affect him, Francis not tell Kit. They used bits of information, or withheld bits of information, as tools to grind each other down.

He told his mother what Phil had said about Ted and Iannacone; he told her about Charlie getting beaten up and scalped.

"Son of a bitch," she said. "Son of a bitch bastard."

"Hey," he said. "I don't want to upset you, I thought you knew—"

She hit the floor with the broom. "Don't worry—you're not the one upsetting me. I'm permanently upset these days. Thank you for saying something."

He was sorry to have riled her up and he left with more than the weight of the stables' garbage on his load. He felt the old urge to go— *Drive, man, just drive*—to aim Buff away from the river and head into Pennsylvania and then west, leave it all behind. He thought about Charlie and Darlene up in Vermont, he thought about missing the canoe race. He thought, for some reason, about Eva's drawings of Charlie, and when he got to the bridge in Callicoon he turned up the Pennsylvania river road.

What the hell, he thought. Middle of the day. Chuck'll be at the bank, Lillian at work. Eva and Darlene in Vermont. He could handle Cecie if he ran into her.

But he found nobody at the Van Voorens' cottage. He backed the big red truck into the driveway; if anybody showed up, he was looking for stray canoes. The place was easy to get into. By standing on one of the Adirondack chairs he could reach the studio window, and he jimmied it open with his jackknife.

He thought of the Earl brothers, wondered if this was how they broke into summer places. He felt guilty as he landed on the floor and waited for his heart to stop pounding. Nothing else moved in the house.

It didn't take long to find Eva's stash of drawings. He knew she wouldn't have left them lying about, so he went to the most obvious hiding places: the closet, a bureau, a flat file of watercolors with L.V.V.

printed in the corners. He found them behind the couch in a black portfolio, and he felt illicit as he untied the ribbon.

And there was Charlie in all his glory. Jesus, he thought. He'd be embarrassed to know that such pictures of himself even existed; he'd sure take better care to hide them. He flipped through until he found the one he was looking for: Charlie holding himself, the picture that had sent Darlene over the edge a month ago. He removed it from the portfolio, feeling like a thief, a pervert.

What did he want with this picture? He didn't know. He closed the cottage window and replaced the Adirondack chair, tucked the sketch behind the truck seat. He didn't know, but having it felt right.

37

A BATCH OF letters came from Felix. He had been out on patrol for weeks, he wrote, and hadn't been able to mail them. *We're seeing a lot more action. Hitting the shit every night. They know exactly where we are and hit us with mortars or rockets. I'm beginning to think we don't really know what we're doing here. Sometimes I feel like the guy from the city who comes up to Delaware Ford for hunting season and winds up lost in somebody else's woods.*

Nick tried to reconcile images of Felix in Vietnam with those he remembered. A happy-go-lucky Felix behind the wheel of his Chevy, grinning, his arm around Eva's shoulder. His stocky, freckled calves charging an end sweep on the football field. High school yearbook pictures. Walking to school when they were younger, Felix squinting a puffy, discolored eye against the wind. Nick tried to picture Felix huddled in a foxhole as mortar rounds slammed the ground around him, tried to imagine how scared he must be. It was hard to imagine Felix scared—he'd always been able to handle any situation, and he'd learned, finally, not to fear his father but accept the beatings and the anger as a part of life. But when Nick read the letter about Rogers, he began to feel what Felix was going through. *Lost a buddy today. We were out on patrol and Rogers, a quiet guy from Ohio, was walking point. I was fourth man back on this open trail. All of a sudden BOOM! and everybody hits the deck. But there's no fire. It was a mine in the trail and Rogers took most of the blast. It ripped his legs and abdomen open, and Doc tried to pin him together while sergeant called for a medevac. I did what I could, shaded his face, told him he was gonna be okay, held stuff for Doc. Rogers was a bloody mess from the waist down. He kept asking Doc if he still had his balls, and Doc said yes, but I don't think he did. Rogers went into shock and became still, and then the medevac came. We're all pretty quiet tonight. Rogers had a girl-friend back in Ohio, planned to go back to her and work on his uncle's farm.*

In the two letters after that one, Felix began to sound more despairing.

. . . sometimes I wonder what the chances are of making DEROS, Nicko. With all the shit we're in, it's anybody's guess. . . .

. . . They're in the jungle when we come, they're in the jungle when we go. I watch the ground fall away from the chopper door and I think, what difference are we making?

And finally: *I look at what's happening to these people, and I know there is no God.*

He held Felix's letters, rubbed them in his hands, tried to feel in the mudstains and the water blotches what Felix must be going through. All he felt was the paper, though, and for the first time he looked forward to leaving for college.

38

FRIDAY OF LABOR Day weekend, the Love Bus came chugging down the campgrounds driveway. Charlie and Eva and Darlene looked wild and windblown. And different. They'd put some miles on. Seen things the other kids hadn't. Darlene especially. She wore rose-colored Janis Joplin glasses and had done something to frizz her hair. But it was more than that. She looked leaner along the chin.

She had lost some of her baby softness, maybe, and acquired a more adult face. She smiled at Nick, and he had to admit a rush of blood to his head.

Charlie's hair was growing out. Eva looked as cool as ever. She swung out of the back of the van and gave him a big kiss.

"So—how was Vermont?" he asked.

"Cool!" Darlene exclaimed from the passenger seat.

Charlie nodded. "Pretty cool, all right."

"The commune is in an old apple orchard," Darlene said. "And they've got a huge organic garden, and a kite-making business."

"And a handmade-furniture business," Charlie said. "They make some pretty neat stuff out of apple wood."

Eva rapped on the van door. "Better run us over to town, Charlie, so Dar can start assimilating into the straight world."

"You better drop Darlene a good distance from the funeral home," Nick cautioned Charlie, "or you may wind up staying there."

"We know," Darlene said. "We called Cecie from Vermont."

"We're going to talk with them," Charlie said.

"Darlene's folks?" Nick asked. "Oh, man."

"Ah," Charlie said. "Better to let Chuckles blow off his steam now, rather than gunning for me later."

"Listen," Darlene said. "He can blow off all he wants, but if tries any macho bullshit I'm going back to Vermont. I can go to school up there."

Right. Big tough Darlene. Nick couldn't help but notice how much the Love Bus, as it pulled out, looked like all the other hippiemobiles that had been there for Woodstock. It bore two new stickers in the rear window: a Viet Cong flag and a pig in stars and stripes with the caption *Amerika Eats Her Young*. Another on the bumper: *Fighting for Peace Is Like Fucking for Virginity*. In a matter of weeks, Charlie had gone from a long-haired kid to a full-fledged freak.

The mail came in, and with it another letter from Felix. He wrote about fishing with hand grenades and *blowing beaucoup grass*, and then *I dreamed about Eva last night, that we'd been swimming in the river and were dozing on a big rock, and then she started to shake my arm, but I didn't want to wake up because the sun felt good and it was drying me out. But she was smiling and shaking me and then I did wake up and it was my relief, Kreiger, shaking me awake because it was my watch. I'd gone to sleep soaking wet and it was still raining, and I was sure disappointed to leave that dream.*

Oh, man. He'd have to share that one with Eva. Or probably Felix had written her, too. Little did Felix know that his Girl Back Home had been Banging the Socks Off one of his friends.

Nick tucked Felix's letter away and started stacking canoes. Big weekend ahead; they'd see plenty of action. Especially on Sunday, race day. He was nearly done stacking when the Love Bus chugged in behind him.

"Well," Charlie said. "That's over. I need a beer."

"How'd it go? Looks like you're still in one piece."

"Went better than I imagined. Chuck is pissed, no doubt about it. But Lillian came to the rescue. 'Let us girls breathe a little, Chuck,' she said, and that stifled him. He probably hates my guts, but I think I got two points for showing up. Lillian dug it, anyway."

"You need a beer, man," Nick said. "Let's roll."

A couple of the regulars at the Wild Turkey hooted when they came in—"Whew! Look what the wind blew in!" and "Thought you'd runned off with the hippies!"—and they kidded Charlie about his shorter hair. Jake brought them beers.

"Yeah, man," Charlie said. "That washes down the road dust. Jake, I could use a roast beast. All that brown rice and bean sprouts was getting a little old."

Nick ordered a sandwich too, and Charlie told him about the commune, how the people spent their days working the vegetable garden and tending a dairy goat herd, how some of them took it seriously and others goofed around.

"They go from digging each other one day to bitching each other out the next. Like any family, I guess."

"Sounds like Lucas's crew."

"Except Lucas's crew is goofing. Just hanging out at Lucas's. These people in Vermont are trying to make a living at it. Or a lifestyle. It's pretty cool when it works. Sheds a whole new light on Communism.

Commune-ism. Hanging out with those people, you could almost see it working."

Charlie glanced at himself in the barroom mirror, sipped his beer. "They have these family meetings after dinner where they discuss who's on garbage detail this week, who's going to truck the next load of furniture to New York, who hasn't been cleaning up after themselves. They try to divvy it up fairly. It doesn't always work out that way, but they're trying. Most of them anyway. There's some freeloaders."

Nick laughed.

"What's so funny?"

"You're hanging out on a commune, figuring out how to make Communism work, and Nixon is sending guys like us halfway around the world to kill people who want to do the same thing."

"Go figure," Charlie said. "You hear anything from Felix?"

"Not good." He told Charlie about the tone in Felix's letters.

"Jesus," Charlie said. "Poor dumb Felix, getting his ass sucked into that mess."

"Poor dumb Felix?"

"He didn't have to go. He enlisted, remember? What's the point? What's the point in killing Vietnamese people? In getting your own ass shot off for the fat cats in Washington?"

I watch the ground fall away and I wonder what difference we're making.

"I'll tell you something, man," Charlie said. "The last few weeks have turned my head around. There hasn't been a day that I haven't thought about Woodstock. It's like this thing living inside me. The music, the vibes. It's hard to explain. The people caring about each other. It felt so good at the concert, and those people in Vermont are trying to make a whole life out of it."

Norma brought out the sandwiches. She nuzzled her ample bosom up against Charlie and murmured something suggestive about "them hippie girls," and Charlie put his arm around her and said, "Can't hold a candle to you, Norma," and she giggled and swung away.

"Anyway," Charlie said to Nick, "I'll take working on a commune in Vermont over fighting with a Communist in Vietnam any day. I feel bad for Felix, but it was his choice."

They dug into the sandwiches, and then Charlie asked about Ted.

"Haven't seen him," Nick said. "Haven't seen or heard anything."

"Sal?"

"Nada. Place has been quiet."

Charlie fiddled with his fries and bounced his leg on the barstool and sucked back his beer, and then he finally said what he'd been wanting to.

"I want you to know something," he said, glancing at Nick and then down to his plate. "I didn't make the move on Darlene."

Charlie bounced his leg and slid his empty beer glass across the bar. He waited until Jake had filled it and moved back down to the television.

"She came at me, man. I don't know what it was, but when we ran into each other out there—maybe it was seeing a familiar face in that big crowd—she latched onto me and wouldn't let go. I asked her about you a couple of times, and she said not to worry, that you'd understand."

Nick remembered Darlene's face the night they discovered Eva sketching Charlie.

"I knew she was right," Charlie went on. "I knew you'd under-stand, too." He turned and looked Nick in the eye. "You know me better than anybody. You know what would happen in a situation like that. I did it knowing you'd understand, but also knowing it was a lousy way to treat my best friend."

Nick shrugged.

"No, I'm serious," Charlie said. "I want you to know I'm sorry."

"Don't worry about it, man."

"I'm not sorry about the way it worked out. It's pretty good with Darlene. But I'm sorry about what I've put you through."

"Hey, listen. Darlene and I weren't going anywhere. I think she was after you all along."

"Yeah?" Charlie asked. He seemed relieved, and he ran his hand through his hair. He'd been holding this in for a couple of weeks and was surprised to find it going so easily.

"She was biding her time with me," Nick said. "You're the one those girls dig."

"Jesus," Charlie said. "God love 'em. God help 'em."

He raised his beer.

"This has been one strange-assed summer, bro."

Nick touched his glass to Charlie's. He wasn't ready to talk about Joanie. He didn't want to share her, didn't want to hear all Charlie's questions, didn't want to watch him leer.

"So," Charlie said. "Big weekend coming up?"

"Labor Day." Last of the big summer weekends, and then everything would shut down for the year.

"I saw the entry list for the race," Charlie said. "A lot of people showing up."

True enough. The biggest race was the Ten-Mile Amateur Race from Hankins to Delaware Ford. It got a lot of locals plus tourists who rented canoes from the campgrounds and the other liveries.

"Looks like two hundred teams in the ten-miler," Nick said. "Ought to bring in some bread for the fire department."

"Some tougher competition in ours," Charlie said. "A Canadian team, I see."

Nick sipped his beer. The race was still a sore subject.

"They'll be tough to beat," Charlie said. "But we've got the home court advantage."

Nick turned on the barstool.

"Besides," Charlie said with a grin, "those Canucks are overrated."

"Are you saying what I think you're saying?"

"I'm saying let's get out there and paddle our asses off."

"We haven't practiced in weeks."

"So what?" Charlie said. "We've got more time on this river than anybody else in the race. Including your buddies the Davis boys. Including the Canadians."

Nick could see the first bend in the river winding away from the bow of the canoe.

"I say we go for it," Charlie said.

They clinked glasses. They talked canoe strategy for a while, agreed to get up early and do a light workout in the campgrounds eddy, to get their strokes down.

39

EXCITEMENT RAN HIGH on race day. Up and down the river valley, shopowners opened their doors early to offer T-shirts and suntan lotion and field glasses. Spectators set up lawn chairs and picnic blankets on the riverbank. Cars and trucks carried all manner of craft, from sleek racing canoes to battered and lumpy veterans of the rental fleet. The liveries did a bangup business hauling canoes to the Tadpole Race that started in Callicoon and trailerload after trailerload to the Ten-Mile Amateur Race in Hankins. Few rentals appeared in the two races from Long Eddy. Most paddlers in the Fifteen-Mile Standard Race owned their own aluminum or fiberglass canoes. The Fifteen-Mile Competition Cruising Race was dominated by racing and cruising canoes.

By the time Nick and Charlie got to the launch, they had listened to "Purple Haze" and "Fire" and "Foxey Lady" and Hendrix's electric guitar pumped adrenaline into their veins. *I have only one itchin' desire . . .* They were ready to paddle.

Every racer had his own method of psyching up. Some guys did calisthenics on the riverbank; others snapped off push-ups. Some stretched into silent yoga pretzels; others liked to lean on their vehicles and bullshit with each other. While Charlie parked the van by the Sportsmen's Bar, Nick spread a thin coat of Turtle Wax across the bottom of the canoe. He didn't like to talk much before a race. He wanted to stay deep within himself and tuned to the Hendrix riff, wanted to keep the tension pumping his muscles.

The Canadians were already in the water, stroking their fiberglass racer up and down the eddy. They were a rugged-looking team, lean and muscled, with water-bottle tubes taped to their necks. They paddled with a curious but matched stroke, a kind of staccato chop, fast and deep. If Nick and Charlie cut slices out of the river, these guys chopped chunks. Their canoe shot up and down the eddy as if it were on a wire.

"Looks like a race for second place," Charlie said.

Nick heard a crunching of gravel behind him, and pulling into the launch was a dark brown Oldsmobile 98 with a cedar-strip racer on the roof.

"Third," he said.

Al Camp was the best canoe paddler they'd ever seen. He was the New York State Canoe Racing Association champion, he paddled in races throughout the Northeast and Canada, and he built his own racing canoes and paddles. He was not tall, but he was broad through the chest. His arms were thick and long-boned. When he paddled, his arms had the resilience of elastic: they kept rolling over and over and over, the same hard pace mile after mile. Al paddled bow, and he had a couple of steady partners for the stern—young guys who traded off races. "Put the bull in the front," he told Nick at a race on the Tioghnioga River. "That's where you need the power, because the stern's got such greater control."

Al greeted everyone, and then carried his canoe to where Nick was buffing the dried wax off his hull.

"That's it." He nodded at Nick's work. "Make it shed water like a coot."

Al's canoe was stunning. The red cedar glowed through a shiny coat of wax, and the hull bore no scratches. It looked as if it had never seen water before.

"New boat?" Nick asked.

"Yeah," Al said. "Thought I'd push the specs a little."

The bow and stern profiles were lower than on Nick and Charlie's boat, and the bucket seats seemed farther from the ends. The hull cut a knife-edge entry and exit, then began to flare under the seats to a shallow arch amidships. Topsides, the arch curved in tight for exaggerated tumblehome, so that the gunwales were only an inch from the seats. Nick could see the advantage immediately: Al and his partner didn't have to reach to make their paddles clear the boat. With the gunwales curving in alongside their hips, they could slash down close to their bodies and stay balanced and efficient. Plus, the tighter gunwales meant less open area, so they'd take on less water.

"Third," Charlie agreed, as Al walked away to get his numbers.

Several other racing canoes lined the bank: the Davis boys with their white fiberglass Sawyer, a couple of teams Nick recognized from other races. A few new ones. More fiberglass than cedar in this race. In the standard division there was more aluminum than fiberglass, and no wood at all. About a dozen boats in each race.

Vern Lefevre, the racemaster, walked among the canoes with a shotgun over his shoulder and a whistle around his neck. He checked to see that everybody had their numbers—racers had fluorescent green numbers, standards had orange—and that all canoes met specs. When he got to Al Camp's canoe, he eyeballed it, pulled a homemade jig out of his back pocket, and placed it across the gunwales three feet from the bow. The jig snapped into place as if made to fit.

"I'll be damned," Vern said. "I would of swore that was illegal."

Al grinned at the boys, and Vern strolled on down the row.

"In two years, everybody'll be paddling these things," Al said.

Vern sounded a blast on his whistle, and told everyone to line up in the river.

"Racing canoes in the front row, standard canoes one boat length behind them."

The teams jumbled off the bank, like awkward water mantises trying to keep distance between each other. Nick and Charlie tried to get as far out into the river as they could. The Canadians had never come in from their warmup, and had taken the farthest position. Al Camp zipped out next to them. Those were the two best positions, as the fastest water ran to the Pennsylvania bank at the start of the race, and then, after a short rapids, switched back to the New York side. You had to hang right and then cut left. If you didn't jump out to a good start, you'd wind up in the rapids and then get dumped into shallow water, where you'd have to work like hell while everybody else rode the current. Nick tried to get next to Al Camp, but two guys in a sleek red glass racer cut him off, and while he and Charlie jockeyed to straighten out, the Davis boys pulled in, too. So they wound up fifth from Pennsylvania—not great, but not as bad as the seven teams to the left.

The water ran black between the boats, and doilies of foam floated past. The teams backpaddled to stay behind Vern Lefevre's outstretched arm.

"Standard canoes back off the racers," Vern called. "Standard canoes one boat length behind the racers, please!"

Nick kept a steady back pressure on his paddle and feathered it in the water. His stomach was now so tight he thought he'd puke if he didn't start paddling soon. Puke up a damn big rock, right through the hull of the canoe. Two strokes per second at the start, jump out in front. Get trapped in the pack, you're screwed. *Purple haze, all in my brain.* Backpaddle, feather . . . backpaddle, feather . . . Every muscle wanted to explode into forward motion. Vern's instructions ended and the only sounds were the clunk of a paddle against a hull, the clearing of a throat, and then Vern called, "All right, paddlers. On the count!"

They stopped backpaddling and held tight in the water.

"On your marks!"

Nick felt Charlie's paddle come out, felt his legs brace.

"Set!"

Nick's paddle came up. He leaned forward.

BOOM!

The shotgun fired and the paddlers attacked the water, slashing at the river, shoveling bucketfuls behind them, banging this way and that, hitting canoes on both sides while trying not to break paddles—the usual frenzy at the gun. Flying spray and flailing arms and banging boats and wild cursing, it was rabid mayhem for the first sixty seconds, and at Long Eddy this is enough to get you to the first riffle, where, if you haven't separated yourself with some paddling room, you get jumbled with the others and you've got no water to dig into. Nick and Charlie jumped out pretty well but then slid up against the red glass racer, and their bowman, instead of drawing off from the other side, actually braced his paddle on Nick's bow and shoved, sending Nick off his track and allowing them to gain half a length. Charlie dug for all he could and straightened them out, but they banged the red boat again. "Fucking steer your boat!" the sternman yelled at Charlie, and the boys bent heads down and dug some more.

Up ahead, the Canadians streaked away with Al Camp clamped to their stern, and both boats were already through the riffles and heading for the New York side to avoid the waves on the Pennsylvania end.

The Davis boys had gained a length over the red glass boat, and a little room opened up on the left, so Nick hollered to Charlie, "Get us off these morons!" when all of a sudden from that direction came a thrashing, thumping aluminum canoe that had somehow jumped ahead of the racers and was cutting across the whole pack, and it slammed both the red canoe and Nick and Charlie.

"Jesus Christ!" Charlie screamed as the aluminum canoe careened across the river. The blow swung the boys' bow toward the Pennsylvania bank and the red boat the opposite way, so both teams went crosswise into the riff. The red boat tried to correct without backpaddling, but they took too long and washed through the riff broadside. Charlie backpaddled mightily and Nick pried for all he was worth. They got turned around by the end of the riff and dodged the main roller. The red boat wasn't so lucky. It hit the wave three-quarters on, and water rushed over the starboard gunwale. Nick and Charlie dug in and gunned for the New York side, but not before two more racing boats slid past.

The line of boats evened out, bows to sterns, like a necklace of long beads. The boys paddled in seventh place, and now past the jam-up they could settle into a steady fast stroke. . . . two, three, four . . . Slice! Slice! Slice! . . . eight, nine, *hut!* Slice! Slice! They gained steadily on the red boat, which had taken on too much water in that wave. It wobbled on every paddle switch. Nick knew those guys would have to stop and dump their water, and he'd take them there, so he set his sights on the cedar boat in front of them. When he and Charlie took that boat, number 108, they'd be in fifth place.

Purple haze, all in my brain. . . . seven, eight, nine . . . They switched clean and as they came up to the gravel bar by Basket Creek, the red canoe pulled in for a flying dump. Nick and Charlie shot past and the psych of gaining a place pushed them up onto the cedar boat's tail. The fluorescent green sticker with the ink-markered 108 bobbed a few paddlestrokes ahead.

"Take 'em on the right," Charlie said, and Nick aimed for the Pennsylvania bank, where the water ran fastest. He'd never seen this team before, and being new, they didn't realize how far the gravel bar extended. They hit the shallow water and slowed down. Nick and Charlie nailed them a hundred yards downstream of the Basket Creek, and then Nick had his eye on fourth place.

Up ahead, the Canadians and Al Camp had pulled far away, already heading into the bend for Kellam's Bridge. A long reach of open, flat water stretched between them and the Davis boys. The Davises, both wearing white Agway caps, paddled with their heads down and their eyes on the water. They kept a good three lengths ahead of the fourth-place boat, a raw fiberglass racer. Number 110. The hull was so thin, Nick could see the shadows of the sternman's legs shift on every switch. He and Charlie locked onto their six-o'clock position. Every stroke took all the muscle in Nick's arms, shoulders, back, and stomach, with his butt anchored to the bucket and his legs braced. Slice! Slice! Slice!

Racer 110 cut a low profile two lengths ahead. Chopped down in the stern, the aft gunwales rode inches above the water. They paddled hard, this team. Nick knew he and Charlie would have to work to pass them, but he also knew they couldn't shoot their wad too early. He and Charlie knew how to pace themselves, and they settled into that long, steady groove that kept them on 110's tail and, if not obviously gaining, at least not slipping back. Slice! Slice! . . . eight, nine, *hut!*

It's tempting, in those long stretches of monotonous paddling, to look behind to see where you stand. Ted had taught them not to do that. Especially when they were running in the first few places, because behind you are all these boats, all with their sights on you, and some are a lot closer than you imagine. Once you turn and see how close the nearest boat is, and the whole chain of them stretched out upriver, you feel less like the pursuer and more like the pursued. It dulls your edge. You begin to give up ground. If you lose even one place during the drawn-out middle phase of the race, you'll regain it only if the teams ahead of you tire, or take on water, or run aground, but you won't do it on brute force because you'll have given that up to the guy you turned around to see.

So they didn't look back. They focused on their strokes, on cutting their slices. Nick kept the fluorescent green 110 in his field of vision and paddled hard so it wouldn't slip out. . . . four, five, six . . . He focused on the patch of water ahead of the bow, worked to ride the pulling wake of the 110 boat. Slice! Slice! Kellam's Bridge coming up. . . . nine, *hut!* They passed under the bridge and the cluster of spectators cheered them on. This kicked up their pace a notch, and 110 fell deeper into Nick's field of view. Gaining.

Charlie sensed it, too. The intensity of his paddling increased, and the boat began to rock. It always rocked before achieving a wave, so Nick knew they were really moving. Weird things float into your mind during a race, and when Sal's shriveled ear necklace appeared in Nick's, and then Felix's letters, he pushed them away, bent his thoughts to something pleasant—Joanie, driving with her in the MG—and focused on the river in front of him. On the stretch between Kellam's Bridge and Hankins, he and Charlie continued to gain, stroke by stroke, inch by imperceptible inch. They never got up onto a wave, but when the houses north of Hankins started to appear, they had closed the gap to within one length.

Try as he might to stay focused on his paddling, Nick couldn't help it: His thoughts drifted off course. Remembering Ted's don't-look-back admonition set him wondering if Ted really could go through life without looking backwards. Could the man actually get to a point where he put business deals ahead of a lifelong friendship? Didn't he ever think back to times with Francis—deer hunting in the steep woods above the river, working on a car under a droplight on a summer night? Maybe not. Maybe once an event was behind him, it was past, forgotten, all the value used in the moment, and then a new moment presented itself. Like each paddle stroke—Slice! Slice!—he had to keep himself in the moment. He focused on the water in front of him, on the fluorescent green square with the scrawled 110 a few feet away. . . . eight, nine . . .

Hut! Charlie called, and they switched cleanly.

"Pick it up," Nick said. "Hankins."

Hankins Rapids is the biggest single hazard in the Long Eddy race. The river narrows at the beginning of a left-hand bend, the riverbed drops, and Hankins Creek pours in and spews a gravelly mouth into the main river. The confluence creates a beautiful set of standing waves. Two feet high in race water, perfectly made for dumping canoes. They seem to dance and taunt, beckon you in and then grab your gunwale and flip you over. Afterward they seem to laugh at you.

In a racing canoe, you have to run this rapids right to avoid dumping or taking on so much water that you swamp. Even when you know where to go, you don't always hit it. It's best to hang to the left of the waves, although there's very little space and the river wants to push you to the right so unless you're on your guard and lucky besides, you'll get shoved into the chop. A lot of boats swamp there. Flatwater racing canoes are so cut down they can't take much of a wave. And with their knife-edge bows, they cut through the wave rather than ride up, so the wave tends to break over the canoe rather than under. The idea in flatwater racing is to haul ass through the eddies, avoid the rapids as best you can, and if you do take on water, dump it quickly and make up for lost time on the flat.

Nick and Charlie knew Hankins Rapids. They ran it every practice session and knew where to hit it. Even so, they occasionally got pushed out and slapped around by the waves. They sometimes took on water, but they rarely dumped. Coming into Hankins now, a few strokes off the stern of the 110 team, Nick could see the other boat going around the bend too wide. It was following the current.

"Here's where we take them," Charlie said, and they hugged the line of fast water between the gravel bank and the waves.

Up ahead, the Davises were in the soup. They stuck to the left bank pretty well at first, but on their paddle switch they let the current carry them out toward the waves. The first big roller missed them, but they went diagonal and the last couple broke over the gunwales. They took on some good bucketfuls of river.

By then Nick and Charlie were into it, and they started out perfectly. Nick paddled on the right, where the deep, fast water was, and kept the bow snugged just off the gravel. Ahead on their right, the 110 boat got sucked into the waves. It took the first one—a big haystack with a malicious grin of foam—straight over the bow. That settled the boat in deep, and the next couple finished it off. The waves rolled over the lowered hull, and the canoe dropped out from under the paddlers. They went from paddling to flailing and then to swimming, and finally to hauling on the canoe to raise it before the boulders at the end of the rapids.

"Bye bye," Charlie said.

Fourth place. The boys drifted off course while watching the 110 team flounder, and, like the Davises, let the last wave of the rapids wash over the gunwale. They stroked hard to get around the boulders, but Nick felt the extra water sloshing and making them sluggish.

"Flying dump, man," Charlie yelled. "We got to pull in!"

"You sure?"

"Fuckin' A! They're not stopping—look!"

The Davises were stroking away hard, which meant they had decided against dumping their water in favor of bulling it downstream. It's always a tough decision: take the time to stop and lighten your boat, which makes you more efficient, or keep up your pace and hope you can muscle it out. If anybody could muscle it, the Davis boys could—big, tough farmers used to hard work all day. But Nick and Charlie had a rule: If it's over the toes, out it goes.

"It's up to my freakin' ankles back here, man," Charlie yelled. "We got to dump it—now!"

They had practiced the flying dump below Hankins Rapids many times. The river got shallow on the left, and that's where they usually pulled in. But today, ahead on the right, Nick could see a figure sitting on the Van Vooren landing rock.

"Look." He pointed with his paddle. "It's Eva."

"Let's dump it over there."

The water wasn't as shallow over there, and Nick knew he'd be going in to his waist, but as they drew closer to Eva he could see that something was wrong. She looked up. She didn't wave. She studied them for a moment and then looked back to her lap. Nick was too far away to discern much and his eyes stung with sweat, but he got a bad feeling.

"Something's wrong."

"Hit the brakes upstream from her," Charlie said. "There's a sandy bottom."

They steamed in, backpaddled. As Nick swung over the side, Eva looked at him. She wore a long peasant skirt, and the ends of it were soaking in the river. Her face was red from crying.

Charlie hit the water, too, and they used their momentum to flip the boat to their shoulders and dump the water. But Nick kept his eye on Eva, and she held up a piece of paper. He recognized the scrawl on the envelope.

"It's Felix," she said. "He's gone."

"What do you mean, gone?" Nick panted.

"Gone," she said. "Gone. He's dead."

Nick stood there, panting.

"Mrs. Gustave called this morning."

Nick couldn't say anything. He held the canoe and Eva's words dripped over him, but he couldn't grasp their import. He and Charlie had to throw the canoe back into the river and keep going. The Davis boys were hauling ass down the eddy. Eva held a pile of Felix's letters in her lap. Felix was dead.

"How?" Charlie asked.

Eva hunched forward. "Does it matter? Something about a helicopter crash."

"Oh, man," Charlie said.

"That's all I know."

The current was moving, and they had to be in it, moving too. They set the canoe back onto the water, gently, instead of slamming it as they usually would, and they stood there with the stream running through their legs.

"They're shipping his body to Dover, Delaware," Eva said. "And from there to here, I guess."

The Davises were about at the end of the eddy, their two white Agway caps bright against the green bank. Nick heard a thunk upriver. The red glass racer came through the rapids and wobbled to the shallow water on the New York side.

He blew air and shook his head. Felix was dead. The urge to move, to get into the canoe and *Paddle, man, just paddle* welled in him.

Eva held up Felix's letter. Nick thought she was going to cry, but she stopped herself.

"You guys go." She waved the letter.

"Ah, Eva—" Nick wanted to comfort her, but she waved the letter again.

"No—go, you guys! Look, they've dumped their water." She pointed upriver at the red glass racer, at the paddlers getting back in. "Go! Felix would want you to."

He saw Felix's face, his unruly red hair and the hell in his eyes, and he knew she was right. Neither he nor Charlie said *for Felix*, but they climbed into the canoe and set at their stroke. . . . One, two, three . . . They kicked up to cruising speed and struck a strong pattern, and neither of them spoke except for Charlie's hissed *hut!* every tenth stroke.

They never caught the Davis boys, though they did stay ahead of the red glass racer. At the finish line they did not stop at the fishing access with everybody else, did not look up at the cheering crowd, did not break their pattern when Vern Lefevre announced, "And in fourth place another local team, Nick Lauria and Charlie Miles. Congratulations, boys." Without exchanging a word, they kept on paddling, kept up their race stroke, and cut on past the town, past the campgrounds, past Grandpa's eel rack, past the horse farm. They kept up their silent power-stroking past Cochecton, past Cushetunk, past Milanville. It was only at Skinner's Falls, where they were afraid of cracking the thin racing hull on the ledges, that they broke their pace and portaged the canoe around the rapids. Then it was back into the water and their pattern, only not so frenetic now, just smooth and strong. They moved at an efficient speed, stayed focused on the paddling, surfing along on thoughts of Felix.

Below the falls they passed Nobody Road, where Felix had won the drag race with Bobby Earl. They passed under the steel bridge at Narrowsburg, where Felix used to astound the other kids by diving off—not from the railing like everybody else, but from the upper girders, which nobody would do. They passed the mouth of Ten Mile River, and Nick remembered how Felix used to wade into that stream at Cochecton Center or Luxton Lake with his fly rod and a knapsack and fish his way to the Delaware—sometimes he'd be gone two or three days. They passed Masthope and Minisink Ford and slipped under the Roebling Bridge and then on to Lackawaxen, and finally, in the long stretch above Barryville, after they had portaged around Cedar Rapids, they spoke.

"You know what's weird, man?" Charlie asked. "He's going to wind up in Van Vooren's Funeral Home."

Nick nodded. He had thought of that.

"Lillian's going to have to lay him out."

"Worse ways to go, I guess."

"Yeah, but it's going to be weird for her. Weird for Eva, to have him in the house that way."

"It's going to be weird, period."

They drifted, and Nick remembered Felix's last letter—*we were dozing on a big rock, and then she started to shake my arm*—and he hoped that Felix had been able to think of Eva in his last moments, that he'd been able to envision himself on a rock with her or gliding up Route 97 in his convertible.

They paddled again, worked the river to carry them along until they could feel in each other's stroke that they'd gone far enough. Finally, with the late-afternoon sun edging toward the mountain behind Shohola, they pulled over and took out in Barryville. Nick called the campgrounds from the diner's pay phone. Lisa Marie was concerned— "Where have you guys been? Did you hear about Felix?"—but when he assured her that they were okay and that yes, they had heard, she said she'd send Shag or Bear down to pick them up.

His hands crinkled with blisters and his back ached, but Nick was thankful that he could feel this pain. Thankful even that he could feel the pain for Felix. He was glad this summer was over. He wanted to go to school, to meet new people, to visit Joanie. He squatted on the warm rocks and looked downstream, and he saw his life opening up before him, curving around the bend, reflecting the afternoon sun.

September 1969

40

SHE RAN THE currycomb over Stone Dust's withers and felt his hide quiver. Such a magical feeling, like electricity without the shock. Stone Dust was a good horse, dependable with the riders but independent in the herd, and she liked keeping his dappled gray coat smooth and his mane free of burrs. He turned his head towards her. She murmured at his big liquid eye, and he turned back to the trough.

The season was over. Cooler, drier air had moved in and pushed out the humidity. The girls were back in school. Nick was leaving today, in a few minutes. A soft thud on the runway, and the sound struck her in the heart. Nick had stopped by on his way to Albany, and she had sidetracked him into chucking a few haybales down from the loft. "You're not so fancy yet that you can't get a few hayseeds in your cuffs," she'd said, and she smiled at her transparent method of stealing a few last moments with her son.

The radio news announced Ho Chi Minh's death, and she couldn't help but feel hopeful. Maybe now those god-awful Communists would back off, would see the light. They had to be as tired of the war as Americans were. Maybe now it would end. Maybe it would all be over by the time Nick was at risk. He would be okay at college. They had prepared him for it, and this summer of staying in Grandma's apartment would help make the transition. But still, it was a tough time for a kid. He would know no one in Albany, would be rooming with a Jewish boy—who knew what that would be like? His room and board were taken care of, his first semester's tuition paid. Francis had kept that much aside, anyway.

A goddamn shame that you had to hide your savings from your business partner. Another haybale thudded to the floor. Francis was still staying in the trailer, but maybe now that the last big weekend was over things would get back to normal. The horse muscle quivered again under her hand. Normal was living in debt, in a cocoon of anger. Normal was burying a neighbor boy who hadn't yet seen his twentieth birthday.

A diesel exhaust and rattle of truck metal came from the driveway. She set the currycomb on the stall ledge. Out in front of the barn idled a red corrugated stock hauler. What the hell? She skirted Nick's haybales. Somebody lost, maybe.

KILEY'S AUCTION BARN, the lettering on the door read. Couple of deadbeats climbing down. The younger, skinnier one stretching and looking out at the herd, the beer-bellied one coming around the driver's side and giving her a sideways glance.

"Help you?" she inquired.

"Looking for the boss," Beer Belly said.

"You're talking to her."

That got her another sideways glance but stopped his forward motion.

"Here to pick up those horses," he said.

"What horses are those?"

"Ten head," Beer Belly said. Sideways to his buddy, back to her. "You Delaware Ford Stables?"

"I'm Delaware Ford Stables, but I'm not selling any horses."

She heard Nick's boots hit the barn floor—those ridiculous fringed hippie boots he bought. Jesus, a good pair of Dunhams would get him through the winter in decent shape, where that soft suede would get soaked and ruined. Well, a Christmas present, maybe. A couple months of wet feet and he'd be glad to get them. The truckers exchanged glances and she saw the skinny one's eye flick to the barn door and she knew Nick had appeared there.

Beer Belly began to fluster. His face reddened and his rheumy eyes bugged.

"Ten head, lady. That's what my shipping order says."

Jesus. Who sicced these jackasses on her? Her hands twitched but she forced them still.

"I don't care what your shipping order says. You're taking no horses off this farm."

God *damn*. When had he placed the call? And from where? Some office suite in New York? Some motel room in New Jersey? What had he thought as he was doing it? She caught a vision of him on a summer day when they were constructing the campgrounds: directing a backhoe here, a bulldozer there. He was the man in charge. He could give orders and watch them be carried out.

Well, not anymore.

"These are my horses." She gave the driver a hard look. "Not one of them is leaving this farm."

He couldn't hold her stare. He glanced at his buddy, whose own gaze roamed around the ground at his feet and over towards hers, but rose no higher. They were moments from retreating. She had to tough it out, so she kept staring at the driver while she pictured Ted giving orders, Ted plundering her cashbox, Ted looming over her and blotting out the sky, and she repudiated a world populated by men out for their own gain: these two deadbeats wilting in front of her, Ted Miles, Phil Sweeney, whoever it was that Phil worked for—for she was sure of that now, sure that Phil was in on this somehow. She felt Stone Dust's electric quiver ripple through her and again she suppressed the urge to move her hands to action.

Then: a car in the driveway. The car she'd been expecting, his car, the dusty Buick, and everything seemed to settle at once within her, and she could see what was about to happen even before it did: the motion that Ted made getting out of his car, that propelling-forward movement that he had always had as he swung around the driver's door all white button-down and relaxed khakis, and his forward motion caused the fat trucker to careen back toward his cab, like a cue ball hitting a green-and-white numbered ball on a barroom pool table those nights long ago when she and Francis and Ted and a girlfriend would drink in the roadhouses and shoot some pool and laugh into the night air as they drove away, those days long gone now, and then Beer Belly ricocheting off his truck with a paper in his hand and his voice emboldened now that he had some backup: "Says so right here. Ten head to be sold at auction this Saturday night."

But she stood fast, let the driver bounce off her solidity.

"And does it say who initiated the order?"

"Says it's per Ted Miles." The driver grinned and glanced at Ted, who nodded and grinned back, and she knew how to take the stupid, cunning, asshole-buddy grins off their faces. She finally allowed her hands to move. She reached for the door of the pickup, the pent-up tension shaking so hard she could barely press the button of the glove compartment and then the gun was against her palm, the familiar checkered grip providing instant comfort, the snug weight steadying out her shake.

The driver was too stupid to know what a gun in her hand meant, so he grinned some more to show the men how tough he was. She could have shot him on the spot, but the ignorant driver was not her concern. Her concern chimed in as if on cue, "Now, Kit . . ." and she saw him smirking over her in the dusk of a summer evening.

"God damn you," she said and aimed at the shipping order, which the driver whipped out to arm's length. "Hold that good and steady for me, will you, while I sign it."

The gunshot surprised all of them but her, and it drowned out the "Now, Kit . . ." She pictured the path of the bullet, through the paper, the truck door, lodging in the driver's seat or the transmission tunnel.

"Get off my farm."

Now, she thought, through the roar of the truck and the re-raising of the dust. Now, through the clanking of the hauler's corrugated steel and the stamping of Stone Dust in his stall and the other horses in the field with their heads up and their ears cocked toward the commotion. Now, Kit.

"You tried to sell my horses."

His face worked as if he was trying to come up with his defense, but they both knew it was too late for that.

"You tried to sell this farm."

His face worked some more and she wondered if he saw the same things in his mind that she did—if he looked back in this moment confronted as he was with the sum of all his preceding moments, if he looked back and saw himself raising Margaret's veil at the altar as he bent to signify his vow, or if he remembered Charlie in the birthing room—his first glimpse of a life he had created—or if he pictured himself swimming down the channel of the river or her standing on the bank, because if he did he might do the right thing and repent or confess or ask forgiveness, but as she watched his face shifting and his hands making a gesture she thought he would but then his face shifted again, the muscles fell into the same familiar pattern they had assumed so many times and she knew he had thought of nothing she had, and when that noise came from his mouth, up from his throat, "Now, Kit . . ." she couldn't help it, for the weight that pressed on her index finger had been upon her a long time, "Now, Kit . . ." she finally did what she'd wanted to do for years: She pressed back. And in the enormity of the explosion and the deafening silence she felt what she'd wanted to feel for years: a lifting of the weight, a lightness. She felt herself rise above the scene in the driveway, she watched as Ted spun and toppled and kicked, as she herself—in both places at once, firmly on the ground yet rising, lightly, a petal lifted on the breeze—handed the gun to Nick and turned toward the barn.

41

NICK BENT OVER Ted and saw that his eyes were open and that the blood spread from a dark bull's-eye below his collarbone. Nick whipped off his T-shirt and pressed it against the wound, and Ted made a noise like a dog and closed his eyes.

"Ah, Jesus," Nick said as the blood seeped through the shirt to his fingers and he folded the shirt over to apply a fresh spot to the leaking blood and he heard his mother's voice on the phone. ". . . speak to Francis, please."

He pressed the T-shirt gently so as not to squeeze blood from the wound. It was the shirt that Darlene had given him before Woodstock and he saw that he'd never wear it again, blood on the tie-dye. "Oh, man," he said in a small voice as the blood soaked the fresh part of the shirt and his hand came away from Ted's back covered with blood, too, and he knew he had to stop both holes. The bullet had passed through and opened an even bigger hole in back. He draped the T-shirt over Ted's shoulder and tried to cover both sides at once.

"Ted's shot," he heard his mother say.

"Shot, as in on the ground bleeding."

Ted moved his head but didn't open his eyes.

"I did."

Nick felt Ted's weight under his hand as he held the T-shirt, felt the big man's heaviness upon the ground. Ted's eyes were closed, and the right one crinkled against the pain. He breathed in little gasps.

"He tried to sell my horses. He tried to steal my horses."

Was it worth it, he wanted to ask Ted. He felt Ted's short breath against his hand.

"I guess we could do that. Nick's here."

Oh Christ, what must his father be thinking? One more thing on top of everything else—his wife calling to say she'd just shot his part- ner. He imagined the tone in his father's voice, the gravity, the need to get a picture of the situation. The need to act.

"Just as soon let him lay there and bleed."

Ted's right eye relaxed a little and he let out a longer breath.

"Go ahead and call then. Edie Gottschalk's on duty in the emer- gency room."

The hospital. They would haul him to the Callicoon hospital, and the sooner the better. Jesus! His mother a murderer if they didn't.

"Well, let them call the sheriff. I don't care. I'll tell them the truth."

It came to Nick quickly, and it seemed to come to Ted, too, because his eyes fluttered and he looked at Nick with something like understanding: They always called the sheriff on a gunshot wound. The law had to investigate a gunshot wound.

Murder if Ted lost too much blood. If the bullet had severed a main artery and he bled to death. If a lung filled up and he suffocated. Attempted murder if he didn't. Or whatever they called it— manslaughter, whatever. Nick didn't know the legal classifications of such an act, and he didn't care. He only knew that his mother would be in big trouble if Ted told the truth.

"I don't care, Francis—he's not going to harm us anymore—"

Nick took Ted's hand and moved it to the T-shirt. The hand did not feel strong, but neither did it fall away limp. Ted still had use of his muscles.

"Hold that," Nick said.

He wiped his hands on his jeans. All his stuff for school was packed into the MG, crammed into every space he didn't need for driving. In the trunk was a roll of his posters. He'd taken them off his apartment walls and rolled them into a tight tube so they'd travel well. He hoped Israel Markowitz liked Jimi Hendrix.

He wiped his hands again and, using his fingertips, extracted from the center of the roll a single sheet of sketch paper. He was careful not to tear it or stain it, and he kept it turned away from his mother in the barn doorway. He squatted in front of Ted and unfurled the sketch.

"Ted," he said. "Look at this."

Ted's eyes fluttered open and rolled over the drawing and then recognized the subject. They focused and grew strong. He seemed to gain more life and he looked down at the T-shirt and repositioned it and then looked back at the sketch.

"Right," Nick said. "It's Charlie."

Ted kept his eyes on the picture.

"And it's drawn by Eva Van Vooren."

He paused to let Ted understand.

"See, that's her signature in the corner. She's got about a hundred more of these."

Ted stared at the drawing and then closed his eyes.

"Look at me, Ted," Nick said.

When Ted's eyes opened, they held something different. They reflected something not to be trusted, something that could cause him harm.

Fine, Nick thought. Good. If he had become something to be reckoned with, fine.

"What happened here today? Your shoulder? It was a hunting accident."

Ted's eyes were strong on him.

"A hunting accident, you got that? When the sheriff's deputy asks, it was an accident. Otherwise, Chuck Van Vooren gets this picture."

Nick saw something like recognition in Ted's eyes: A game was being played to rules Ted understood. Nick was unsure of the rules even as he made them, but he was positive about the stakes. The pressure of this knowledge made him want to jiggle his leg, but he didn't. Made him want to blink, but he fought it. He stared back at Ted and held in his mind the gravity of his mother's situation and the calm in her voice as she spoke with Francis and the conviction that what he was doing was right. He held the drawing steady.

Ted was the one who looked away. He shifted from Nick's stare to the drawing and then to his hand on his chest, to the blood leaking. He looked at Nick and then shut his eyes.

"A hunting accident," he said. "Nothing's in season."

Nick rolled the drawing and stuck it back in the MG and his mother hung up the phone and they loaded Ted into the back of Kit's pickup, and Nick rode there with him, holding his head and shoulder to keep him from bouncing. The blood seemed to be slowing, but there was so much of it: soaked through Ted's shirt and all over Nick's hands and arms, and his mother's too. It wet his own chest as Ted's weight pressed against him. A bright smear ran the length of the yellow pickup bed.

Kit gunned the truck past the paddock fence and jounced down the driveway. She slowed to turn onto the river road, and her eyes met Nick's in the rearview mirror and they beheld each other, mother and son, accidental murderer and fully intentioned blackmailer. Then she swung onto the potted river road and hit the gas, and Nick held Ted's head steady against his chest. It would be rough going till the bridge, but once they got onto 97 it would be smoother.

42

THE RED-AND-WHITE SHERIFF'S cruiser pulled up to the emergency room after they got Ted unloaded. The deputy was one of the Pick boys from North Branch—Mark or Mike or Mel—Nick could never keep them straight, all of them as pink and chubby and white-lashed as Yorkshire shoats, two in the sheriff's department and one a Monticello cop. Deputy Pick took one look at Nick and Kit, at the blood on them and on the tailgate, and said, "Wait here, Mrs. Lauria." Then he stepped through the cool sliding door into the emergency room.

A few minutes before, Nick had helped Edie Gottschalk and an orderly move Ted from the truck bed onto a gurney. Ted had grimaced, but when he was strapped down and the orderly had started to wheel him in, he had fluttered his eyes and said to Nick, "Goddamn woodchucks. Always popping up there behind the barn."

And so Nick had briefed his mother, and she studied his face as if to figure out who he was, this son of hers, and then she got her cigarettes out of the truck and lit up. She stood by the front fender and smoked, looking off across the parking lot at Route 97.

When Deputy Pick came out he flipped open his notepad and clicked his ballpoint in that way cops have of making a pen sound like a weapon.

"How is he?" Nick asked.

"Who wants to tell me what happened?" Pick said.

Nick couldn't tell what Kit was thinking, and he wanted to blurt out something about an accident, but a certain hardness in her stare kept him quiet.

"Nick was up in the hayloft," she said. "He didn't see it."

The deputy glanced at Nick, then scribbled on his pad.

"So what happened, Mrs. Lauria?"

"I've got this woodchuck out in back of the barn. Eats the pumpkin vines I planted in the manure pile. Keeps digging new holes all over the place, and I'm praying my horses won't step in one."

Thank God, Nick thought, and he eased out a long breath, slowly, so the deputy couldn't hear him. Thank God. Now don't give too many details, and don't get off on what a son of a bitch Ted is.

"I've been meaning to shoot him—the woodchuck—so today I slipped out back to the manure pile. I heard a car pull in, but I couldn't see who it was from back there. Next thing I knew, the woodchuck comes around the corner of the barn and I aim off at him, and—"

"What were you aiming with, Mrs. Lauria?"

"My pistol. My thirty-eight. I keep it—"

"And where is the weapon now, ma'am?"

She started to swing to the truck cab, stopped herself.

"It's over at the farm," she said.

Nick pictured the gun on the passenger bucket of the MG. He had tossed it there after his mother handed it to him.

Deputy Pick scratched on his pad and then said, "Okay, so you were aiming a thirty-eight-caliber handgun at the woodchuck and then what happened?"

"Just as I went to squeeze off, Ted comes around the corner right behind the chuck and spooks it and me both. I fired and hit him."

Scratch scratch. Something wrong there, Nick thought. A wrong note, though the deputy wouldn't know it yet. "Then what, ma'am?"

"Nick came down from the loft and tended to Ted. I called my husband, who called the hospital. We loaded Ted into the truck and brought him over."

"Okay," Pick said. He finished writing. "Anything else?"

"No."

"How about you?" Pick turned to him. "Anything you'd like to tell me?"

Nick couldn't know what Ted had said, and he didn't want to cross anybody up. He could explain the .38 sitting on his bucket seat—*"Jesus, man, it was confusing. I tossed the gun first place I had the chance and tended to Ted"*—but how to explain the blood-clotted dust out in the driveway when the shooting happened at the back corner of the barn?

"Nope," Nick said. "When I heard the shot I came down out of the loft. Ted was on the ground. Mom gave me the gun and called for help. I took care of Ted."

Deputy Pick studied him through his white eyelashes and then said, "Okay. Let's go have a look at that weapon."

He motioned them to the cruiser.

"We can drive," Kit said. "Saves a trip back for the truck."

Pick opened the rear door and shook his head.

"Procedure, ma'am."

"Well, let me move this out of the doorway then."

As Kit went around to the driver's door, Deputy Pick suddenly snapped his head toward Route 97, looked north toward Callicoon. And in the moment before the truck fired up, Nick heard what Pick heard: dual exhausts splitting the air with a crescendo of a third-to-fourth-gear power shift, and then Bobby Earl's black Fury roared into view, moving at fuck-you speed—eighty or eighty-five, at least—and blasted past the hospital. The deputy cursed, slammed the cruiser's rear door, jumped into the driver's seat, and hit the gas and the flashers. He hollered something that could have been "Wait here," or maybe "Meet there," and when he had screeched out of the driveway and headed south in pursuit of Bobby Earl, Nick took it to be the latter and said, "Let's get over to the farm."

His father's Scout sat next to Ted's Buick, and Francis stood over the spot where Ted had fallen.

"Ted's in the emergency room," Nick said. "Sheriff's deputy took the report. He's coming over here to check out Mom's gun. It was a wood-chuck-hunting accident, in case anybody asks. Mom can fill you in."

Through the window of Ted's car, he saw what he was hoping to see: keys dangling from the ignition. "You got a crescent wrench in the Scout?"

"Vise-Grips in the glove compartment," his father said.

As Nick moved toward the Scout, Francis stopped him with his arm. "What are you doing, Nick?"

"Making sure the details match."

Francis appraised him, and his expression was one Nick hadn't seen before. Wonder and disbelief gave way to understanding, as if his father were perceiving a new species of tree in a familiar woods.

Nick got the Vise-Grips and turned to his mother. "Stone Dust is still in his stall, right?"

"Well, yes—"

"Take him out back by the corner of the barn and walk him around and give him a big bucket of water to drink. Dad, would you pull Ted's car forward until I tell you to stop?"

He lay on the ground and his father eased the Buick ahead. Nick hollered, and then he crawled in behind the front tire. The Vise-Grips didn't hold the oil drain plug as well as a socket, but they did the job. When he had a good steady drip going, enough to splatter over the blood, he slid back out.

"Ought to have Beagle's check that oil leak sometime," he said to his father. "But make sure the car sits here overnight."

On his way to the barn, he got the .38 from the MG and left it on his mother's desk. Then he drew a bucket of water from the inside spigot.

Stone Dust had worked the soft earth around the manure pile to a mushy consistency, and Nick splashed the bucket of water around.

"Walk him through there," he said to his mother, and when the ground was pretty well mashed he tethered the horse to the corral fence.

"Okay," he said. "Have to do, I guess. Let Stone Dust drink his fill and maybe he'll oblige us with some more evidence tampering. You want to get a couple of his mates to help, that'll be fine."

He went back inside to wash up at the spigot, and he could hear his father on the telephone: "Okay. Thank you, Edie. I'll be over later."

Nick got a new pair of jeans and a fresh T-shirt from the MG, and he changed in the first stall. His mother's gun sat like an inert object on her desk. It could be a paperweight, he thought. It could be a machine part. It could be a knickknack, an ornate hammer. It could have all kinds of uses, or none at all.

His mother and father came up the runway.

"I spoke with Edie Gottschalk," his father said. "Ted lost a lot of blood, but he's going to be okay, she thinks. The bullet broke his scapula and they have to reattach some ligaments. Edie says to be more careful next time anybody over here tries to shoot a woodchuck."

His mother wore a strange look. Her mouth was not as set. She was softer somehow.

"I don't know how you fixed that with Ted," she said. "But I thank you."

"No sweat," Nick said. His mother looked . . . *chastened*. His father looked concerned. And he had to hit the road.

"Well, I guess I'm off for college."

In the rearview mirror, they stood in front of the barn door, his mother and father. Nick waved, and his father raised his hand. His mother turned to his father and touched his arm. Then Nick was out the driveway and onto the river road.

43

THROUGH HIS ROOMMATE, Izzy, Nick fell in with a group of freaks from the city and began to adjust to the rhythms of campus life: rising early for classes, hitting the streets in the afternoon to get coffee or soup with his new friends, settling into late-night rap sessions in somebody's room. He hung out with Freddie Hecht and Geri Rudolf, who came from the same block in Queens, and Carmen Romero, a beautiful girl from Garden City, and Darrell Crowley, a light-skinned black who wore knit hats and always turned the conversation to the political. They debated whether or not Paul McCartney was dead, and they played "Revolution 9" and "Glass Onion" over and over for clues. Nick dug it all. It was like the gang at the fishing access with a broader perspective.

Every other weekend he drove to New Jersey to see Joanie, or she came up to see him. He loved the feeling on Friday afternoons when his French class let out, the total freedom of a weekend looming ahead, an open road stretching out in front, and a vision of Joanie running toward him across her dormitory's leaf-scattered lawn. He'd cruise down the Thruway with a rising spirit, knowing that she was waiting for him, picturing her neat dorm room with her India-print bedspread and Buddha incense burner, her flower photos and the blue-eyed Paul Newman poster. She'd watch for him out the window, and when he pulled up to the curb, she'd run out and she felt so good in his arms, so alive, and in her hair that now-familiar smell of pears, and they'd practically maul each other on the sidewalk, so that they'd go right up to her room and fall into bed. Later they'd go out for a pizza or to a concert—they saw The Who and Donovan that fall—and sometime over the weekend they'd take a long hike through a nearby nature preserve. They'd buzz into the city to museums or photography shows or to hang out in Greenwich Village and wander through the head shops. Sometimes they stayed in Joanie's room and studied.

They were falling deeper in love, and it felt perfect. The events of the summer began to drop away. Nick still replayed the scenes: Ted going down, his mother handing him the gun, Ted's weight in his arms. But nothing came of it. Nothing legal, that is. Their stories matched well enough that the sheriff's investigation went no farther than Deputy Pick's write-up.

Ted came to Felix's funeral with his arm bound under his dark suit, but he didn't stand near Francis and Kit. Nor did they talk to each other. Well, Nick thought, he probably wouldn't be too chummy with someone who shot a big hole in his shoulder, either. But there was the business. They'd have to deal with that.

After he and Charlie had stood side by side with Felix's coffin between them, after they had carried their friend to the fresh hole on Cemetery Hill and listened to the preacher's eulogy and the quiet weeping of the Van Vooren girls, they had retreated to the Wild Turkey.

"To Felix," Charlie had said as they tipped glasses, and Nick had nodded, "Felix."

They relived some of the stories, admitted the waste of life. But

Nick realized they had been preparing for Felix's death for months, maybe since he had shipped out. He had never once thought about what Felix would do when he came back from Vietnam. He had never imagined him coming back.

He remembered Ted's advice on their birthday, and he repeated it to Charlie: "Stay in school, man."

Charlie's response was so unexpected that Nick had to set his beer onto the bar.

"I'm not in school," Charlie said.

"What do you mean, you're not in school?"

"I'm not in school, man."

"You've been up at Rochester for two weeks."

"Yeah, but not in school." Charlie tapped his beer glass on the counter. "There wasn't any tuition money. I thought it was all taken care of. That's what Ted said whenever I asked. 'It's all taken care of.' It was all spent, is what it was."

"Oh, man," Nick said. "Jesus. What you been doing?"

"Trying to get in. Trying to find a place to live—I'm sleeping in the bus behind a shopping center. Showering at the gym. Talking to the financial aid people, trying to get some money for next semester. Margaret's trying to do something, but I guess she's as bad off as I am. About ready to lose the house, it sounds like."

"You're kidding me. How could this happen?"

"Ted, that's how. He spent it all. Sometimes I wish your mom had a better aim."

They drank in silence for a minute, then Nick asked about the draft.

"They can't draft me if they can't find me," Charlie said. "Right now I've got no address. I'm gonna keep it low-key until I get into school."

"Oh, man." How could things unravel so quickly? It was like your life was this movie unreeling, and all of a sudden something—a bill, an empty bank account, a bullet—could come along and tear the film, and you were left to face what was really behind the screen.

"Listen," Charlie said. "I'd appreciate it if you didn't mention this to anybody. Especially the Van Voorens."

"No sweat," Nick said. "Ted ever say anything about Lillian Van Vooren helping him out?"

"Lillian? No way." Charlie studied him. "No, he didn't. Why?"

"Ah, nothing."

Lillian hadn't come through for Ted. Nick never heard a word about it, but no bail-out money ever turned up. He figured that once Chuck Van Vooren got wind of Charlie taking Darlene off to Vermont, there was no way he'd listen to whatever Lillian had to say. And Lillian might have been stringing Ted along, for that matter. *Rich chicks*, Charlie had said. Maybe they never outgrew fucking with your head.

44

THROUGHOUT THE FALL, Nixon announced troop withdrawals from Vietnam, but that only sparked, rather than stopped, the protests in Washington. Nick and his pals wore black armbands in support of the October 15 moratorium. In November, his roommate Izzy and Darrell Crowley rode a bus to the massive protest at the Washington Monument. They came back with tales of being arrested and bused to jail and their rhetoric stoked more heat than ever, but all Nick could picture was a raw pile of dirt in the Delaware Ford cemetery, now covered with snow.

The campgrounds continued to struggle. Ted wasn't able to repay his debt, and even though the motor homes rented regularly, service and repair bills began to roll in. Taxes came due. Facing a long, slow winter, Francis laid off everybody but Miller. He mothballed the canoe fleet until spring, pickled most of the rental trailers. But there still wasn't enough money to cover everything. Francis considered shutting the place down and hoping for a good summer to pay off the bills, but mortgaging the future was not his way. And Ted had cleared out after the funeral.

So when Phil Sweeney showed up in the office one day and offered to buy the place by assuming the debt and taxes, Francis took him seriously. He sent a certified letter to Ted in Basking Ridge, placed several phone calls to Margaret. He didn't get any argument from Kit, although she didn't pass up the chance to remind him that she "always knew something was fishy as hell with that Phil Sweeney."

Francis had his lawyer send a notice of the pending sale and its terms to Ted and Margaret, and even that didn't get Ted to show. Margaret told Francis on the phone that she hadn't seen him. "I hear Kit tried to kill him," she said. "Too bad she didn't succeed."

Phil Sweeney was the one who finally found him, tracked him down through Iannacone's connections. Ted was living in a construction trailer at the Westchester County Airport, trying to get in on the action of a nearby country club expansion.

"You should of seen the inside of that trailer," Phil told Nick later. "Half-gallon wine bottles scattered everywhere. Man's drinking himself to death."

Ted showed up for the closing, the final business transaction. Kit wrote to Nick that *Ted looked like hell, and his hand shook as he signed the papers. He barely made eye contact with Francis and me, and he left as soon as the deal was done. I'm sorry I shot him, but not about the way things are turning out. It feels like a tremendous burden has been lifted. Still, I can't look at the campgrounds when I drive by on the way to town. It's painful to know that your grandparents' property is gone.*

By November, Phil Sweeney had taken over. Grandma and Grandpa could live in their house for a year, but after that they'd have to pay rent to Phil. When Nick came home for Thanksgiving, he pulled into the campgrounds out of habit. Phil had changed the store: put big hunting posters in the window, started selling guns and ammo. He asked Nick if he'd be interested in a job next summer.

"Maybe," Nick replied, though returning to the campgrounds made him feel like one of those vets who came back from Vietnam to take their old jobs. The My Lai massacre had been in the news all week.

"Well, I'll tell you," Phil said. "Gonna be some changes. Place gonna get whipped into shape. Garbage gonna be picked up a lot quicker, quiet hours gonna be enforced."

Nick had heard that the railroad was hiring an extra gang for next summer. Bear and Shag were already on the waiting list. Trackman's wages were four dollars and forty cents an hour.

"Gonna make a real business out of this place," Phil went on. "I told you I was a Mets fan, Nick."

"What's that supposed to mean?"

"Mets came from behind. Nobody gave them a chance. And look what they did—won the World Series. Where's the big-shot, showboat Yankees now?"

His parents kept the farm. Francis moved back into the house. Kit slept in Nick's old room, but at least they were under one roof again. At Christmas, things seemed a little better. His mother and Stacey got up early to take care of the horses, Lisa Marie wandered around with a copy of *The Prophet*. His father kept a stack of orchard catalogs by his reading chair, as well as books on fruit trees. Mostly, Nick noticed, his parents didn't argue as they used to. They weren't exactly chummy, and they'd never be lovey-dovey, but at least they weren't biting each other's heads off.

Grandma and Grandpa came over for Christmas dinner, and during grace Francis gave thanks for "being together as a family." Nick felt gratitude, though he knew the moment would pass. Lisa Marie would be off to college in a couple of years, and who knew how long Grandma and Grandpa could last as squatters on their own place. If Grandpa couldn't tend his eels and his orchard, if Grandma couldn't grow her tomatoes . . . Nick didn't like to imagine them in a spiritless future.

And his own future still ran in that black-and-gray movie of faceless strangers in vague cityscapes—though now with a few touches of color. Joanie, for sure. She eased into his thoughts with her reddish hair and purple peasant top and scarlet toenails; her peachy flesh and golden-downed arms suffused him with light. He had never believed in the power of numbers, but a glowing 206 hung in his mind: the number he'd drawn in the draft lottery—high enough to keep him out of the army should he drop out of school, which seemed less and less likely.

He headed to Joanie's for New Year's Eve. As he drove south along

Route 97, the mountainsides and pine trees hung heavy with snow. The road was gritty with cinders and rimmed with dirty plowbanks. Under an overcast sky he drove, and on the entire forty-mile stretch between Delaware Ford and Port Jervis he passed only a half-dozen vehicles: a couple of pickups, a milk truck, a railroad crew, and two cars with families visiting relatives. Deep winter in Sullivan County, nothing much doing.

He pulled off the road near Barryville. The river was iced over, except for a black patch of water rushing through a riffle close to shore. He clambered down the snowy bank and studied the water coming at him, ton after endless ton. It had come a long way, and it had a long way to go. A thin sun broke out and reflected off the ice-clad bluestone cliffs, giving him a glimpse of springtime. He could look forward to top-down weather, to long rides with Joanie. He had learned a few things last summer. There would be plenty of time to figure out what to do.

ML

NOV 2004